THE SHADE OF THINGS

A HUMOROUS PARANORMAL WOMEN'S
FICTION

DEBORAH WILDE

te da media inc.
vancouver

Book Cover Design by ebooklaunch.com

Issued in print and electronic formats.

ISBN: 978-1-988681-62-7 (paperback)

ISBN: 978-1-988681-63-4 (epub)

1

"Mazel tov," my ex-husband, Eli Chu, groused ahead of me in the forest, "you just set feminism back two hundred years."

Excited as I was to be working a missing person case with him, I was less enthused about trekking through the foreboding woods in a rural area outside Vancouver. Had this lead taken us to a spot where the air was rich with the scent of pine? Nope. Was there a wave of verdant green stretching out before me? Nope. How about darting birds trilling and singing? Also nope.

"Clearing spiderwebs for me, a spider-hating person, has nothing to do with gender." Grimacing, I squelched through a puddle, mud seeping through the canvas of my sneakers into my poor socks.

Sunlight fought to peek through the canopy, the uneven ground was a dull brown covered in slippery rotting leaves, and the air weighed down on us, muggy and sticky. Sure, our hands slapping against our necks to kill buzzing mosquitos had an up-tempo rhythm, but it was hardly birdsong.

The final indignity was all the damn spiderwebs.

Eli stepped over a rotting log with moss sprouting out of

it like an old man's nose hair and ants parading up and down the nubby bark.

"Stop a sec." I put fist to palm. "Rock paper scissors?"

Eli hadn't bought my argument that since I'd be taking point when we found the vampire, he should deal with the spiders. So it had come down to this: a children's game.

"You're on." He leaned down, his brown eyes glinting. "One, two, three."

My rock trumped his scissors. *Good call, me, knowing how Eli would play this.*

"Huzzah!" I snapped off a short, dead branch and handed it to my ex with a flourish.

He accepted it with a groan. "How did you know I wouldn't throw rock as usual?"

"Because you hate spiders as much as I do. Using my years-long experience with your psychological profile, I surmised you'd expect me to throw paper to cover your rock and thus, go for scissors instead." I tapped my head. "You can't outsmart me, sucker. Now, clear away the eight-legged creepy-crawlies, my good man, and later I'll protect you from the bloodsucker. The undead one." I slapped my neck and wiped a smeared mosquito off my hand. "Unlike these assholes."

Eli banged the makeshift broom against a tangle of branches before pushing them aside for us to duck under. "Stand down, Buffy. You were explicitly warned. Under no circumstances are we to harm Damien."

"Unless it's in self-defense. Then it's still very much on the table." I smiled grimly. As far as I was concerned, that covered an expansive range of circumstances.

"Stick to fact finding."

I followed close behind Eli, positive that spiders were dropping down the back of my shirt. "I'll give you facts. Vamps having blood donors is disgusting. I don't care if they're getting paid, it's not exactly an equal power dynamic. And that's with Ohrists. Ian Carlyle is a Sapien."

Ian was under a vamp's control and the only person with any potential insight into our case, which was why we had to find him.

"Ian isn't a regular Sapien," Eli said. "He also witnessed magic, allowing him to connect with Damien in the first place. How do you know he's not with the vamp of his own free will?"

Sunlight bounced off a large web dotted with fly carcasses and presided over by a fat spider with bristly fibrous hairs covering its legs. Its many eyes tracked us.

I yelped, making swatting motions. "Kill it! It's the size of a dinner plate."

"It's a bread plate at best." Eli carefully brushed the entire web off the trees, tapping the end of the branch against the ground.

The spider scurried into the dirt, almost running over my foot.

"They shouldn't be measured in dinnerware at all!"

Nature was bunk. In the city, I had a fighting chance at survival. Here? Forget about it. Give me a crowded sidewalk any day over this skinny dirt track fraught with knobby tree roots and unappealing animal life.

Assuring myself the little bastard was gone, I returned to the topic at hand. "Ian didn't 'connect' with the vamp. He was enticed and backed into a corner where the only way out was opening a vein. I highly doubt free will was involved," I said bitterly. "Damien has been preying on him for two years." I stabbed a finger in the air. "Unlike with Ohrists, vamps don't pay Sapiens if they use them as food on a regular basis. Hasn't Ian suffered enough?"

Eli shook his head. "I don't know, Mir."

"Are you kidding me?"

"Think about the circumstances leading him to Damien.

Ian comes back from an alleged abduction, disoriented, distraught, and unable to do much more than repeat that he survived the human race."

"And?" I took Eli's hand to help me down a steep slope.

"Bear with me," he replied. "According to the police report back then, what little the investigating officers got out of him made it sound like he'd been abducted by aliens."

When Ian Carlyle disappeared five years ago, his brother swore that Ian vanished into thin air. Literally. The two had been rock climbing on their survivalist camping trip when Ian supposedly disappeared. Police's initial determination was that Ian had fallen, but it was changed to foul play when no body was found. His brother had been charged.

Everyone was stunned when Ian showed up a week later, shell-shocked. The only intelligible thing he said other than his human race line was that it wasn't aliens. Then he lapsed into silence, diagnosed with depression and PTSD.

We skidded down the last bit of the dirt hill and I recovered my footing.

Eli whacked a dead low-hanging branch out of our way. "Everyone wrote Ian off, and over the years, he became more and more distant from his friends and family. He lost his job, turned to drugs and alcohol to cope with whatever happened to him, and ended up living on the fringes of the Downtown Eastside."

I tore a leaf out of my hair and ripped it in half. "I'm still waiting for the compelling argument that being fed off by a vamp is a step up. Or free will."

"Since this wasn't an alien abduction, Ian's vanishing into thin air has a magic explanation. Hell, that's why the deputy chief constable got me involved. At least with a vamp, Ian is with someone who believes him if he shares what happened while he was missing. He isn't dismissed as insane. Plus, Damien won't necessarily kill him."

From the moment that Eli had asked me to come on board

this case, I'd wondered why the Lonestars weren't involved. After all, Deputy Chief Constable Esposito's daughter Ryann was the head magic cop here in Vancouver. And if there was one thing I'd learned about the Lonestars in my tangles with them, it was that they didn't mess around with their prime directive: keep magic hidden from Sapiens at all costs. These abductions seemed like a no-brainer for them to investigate.

I wiped sweat off the back of my neck with my T-shirt collar, praying there was an explanation that didn't make the magic cops complicit. "The vamp might not kill Ian, but he might turn him."

"He'd still be alive," Eli said with a pointed look. "Wasn't that your argument to Topher Sharma's parents?"

I scowled, hating that he used my words against me. "I like you better when you play good cop."

"Well, I am a saint."

"You've been talking to your mom again."

He winked at me. "Between the opioid crisis here in Vancouver," he continued in a more serious tone, "and risk of overdose, Ian could have easily died from doing drugs. You said that vamps don't feed off addicts, and that means Ian had to get clean to provide blood. It's not a great situation, but it's better than he had."

"Fine," I muttered. "That's still not saying much."

It chafed that our mission wasn't to rescue Ian *in addition* to getting information to help with the actual case we were on—finding Teresa Wong, a second-year theater major who'd gone missing two days ago on Monday.

Like Ian, Teresa had a close circle of family and friends, no rampant or reckless credit card spending or unexpected bills, no criminal record, and no enemies. She'd just started her second year of university and, by all accounts, loved her program.

Also, like Ian, Teresa had vanished into thin air. She and her best friend had been thrift store shopping together, and when her friend had turned around to inspect some faux Fiestaware, Teresa had disappeared.

Eli shouldn't have even been on this job since he was a homicide detective, but his superior, Deputy Chief Constable Esposito, had recalled Ian's old case with its "vanishing into thin air" connection and looked up the records. He'd come to the same conclusion that this involved magic and assigned Eli to an off-the-books job.

My ex was one of the rare Sapiens who could see magic and was thus tasked with tracking Ian down and obtaining information to help Teresa.

Eli, in turn, had insisted on hiring me to help him navigate the magic community. Neither of us had been privy to my boss Tatiana's negotiations with the deputy chief, but she'd emerged from her office smirking while the poor man looked like a boxer who'd been KO'd in the first ten seconds instead of lasting the expected ten rounds.

"The other problem is that Ian being clean now may not even matter." Eli snapped a twig underfoot, startling a tawny-brown owl, who flew away. "He wasn't of sound mind after his abduction. He may not remember anything useful or even real, and he's our only shot at finding Teresa. The Missing Persons Unit has nothing to chase down." He kicked a rock, and when his hands unclenched, there was a moment where they shook. "That girl is only a few years older than Sadie."

I placed my hand on his arm, my heart sinking at how tense he was. "If Ian doesn't know how to find Teresa, then we put the screws to Damien when the sun sets and he wakes up." Pep talks weren't easy while traipsing through a forest with nothing to recommend it beyond being a perfect body dump for the mob, but I did my best.

A series of short howls rising and falling raised the hairs on the back of my neck.

Eli and I froze. My heart was hammering so loud that I almost didn't hear him whisper, "Coyotes."

Their cries echoed all around us, a chilling lament interspersed with barks and yips.

I swung my head from side to side, tensed for yellow slits to blink open and a furry body to leap out of the nearby trees and tear into my soft, delicious underbelly. Damn you, carbs, for being so tasty.

Coyote attacks were reported in these parts on a regular basis, so sue me for having a vivid imagination and a healthy dose of paranoia.

I wanted to devote my energy to tracking Ian down but surviving feral beasts had just shot to the top spot, so I threw my magic cloaking over Eli and me. Coyotes—be they real animals or shifters—wouldn't be able to detect us.

We crept toward where the line of trees thinned out. It couldn't have been more than fifty feet away, but I strained so hard to see any sign of marauding animals that by the time we cleared the forest, my face throbbed.

Eli clamped on to my wrist while we crouched in the tall grass, surveying the deserted house in the distance.

The once-elegant gothic manor hulked like a boxer down on his luck. The upper broken window and front door hanging partially off its hinges gave the impression of a bruised eye and a missing tooth while the sagging roof was like a head hunched into its shoulders.

"This can't be where Damien lives," Eli said. "He'd get fried by the sunshine pouring in through all the holes."

"The description of the bloodsucker who lives here matches Damien," I said, hands on my hips.

Eli snorted. "And you trust Tatiana's information on this?"

I squirmed uneasily at the mention of my boss. Not because I doubted her, but because hearing her name reminded me that I wasn't being wholly truthful with her. About a week ago, I'd discovered a bombshell of a secret tying my parents to her.

Not only had I kept Tatiana in the dark, I'd done the same

to Laurent, her sexy wolf shifter nephew with whom I'd hooked up. To be fair, he'd been away in the interior of the province stalking a dybbuk, and it wasn't exactly a conversation to have over the phone, but that wasn't the real reason I'd been reluctant to talk about it with him.

Zev BatKian, Vancouver's head vampire, had recently hired me to find the Ascendant for him. I snorted. If by "hired me" you meant "blackmailed me viciously and without remorse," then sure. The ways he could destroy me and my loved ones were legion. He powered the ward around my house, keeping demons at bay. He was a master vamp whose minions had been forbidden from feeding off my ex-husband and daughter. And any Ohrist enemies would think twice about coming after me or my family while we were under Zev's protection.

The new condition of all this protection was that he'd sworn me to secrecy about both this job and the magic amplifier in general until he decreed otherwise. Telling either Tatiana or Laurent was out of the question—for now—despite my wishes.

Sadly, in the magical world, I had to stick to those boundaries, or I wouldn't be able to take care of the people who were important to me—including Tatiana and Laurent.

Still, I was sick and tired of Zev using me to fulfill some unknown agenda and angry that I was left with no real choice but to accede to his demands.

I sighed. Those were problems for future me.

Eli shredded a couple of long grass stalks. "Ian's last known address was a shelter and the residents there are transient. Yes, the employee I interviewed remembered him going off with someone who matched Damien's description, and when you suggested we look into the vamps and got a connection, I was hopeful. But looking at this dump?" He brushed grass off his hands. "I'm second-guessing that employee's memory. That or we were too quick to ascribe the mystery person Ian went off with to a vampire."

"It's the only lead we have. Damien does have a Sapien donor, so that's another point for this being the right place."

We snuck through the unkempt weed-choked grass to the rotted front steps. Really the house was best viewed at a distance. Like from the moon.

The first tread creaked under my foot, and the house seemed to shiver, exuding a gust of stagnant air. A family of mice peeked their heads up through a jagged hole.

Eli tested his weight on the unvarnished stairs, which were slippery with moss, but when the stairs held, he quickly joined me on the porch, once more taking shelter under my invisibility mesh. He pulled out a penlight. "Can anyone see this light if we're cloaked?"

I shrugged, peering inside. "The floorboards are all twisted, and I'd rather not break an ankle, so let's chance it."

Eli cast the light around the entrance hall.

The interior walls were cold to the touch. The tattered remnants of wallpaper were sun-bleached almost colorless save for dark spores of mold that blossomed like a Rorschach test. Rusted wires hung from the ceiling, but any lighting had been stripped.

For all the general decay, the blackout curtains over the windows were nearly new. I jostled Eli's elbow. "Dead give-away." I gave an exaggerated wink. "Or should I say undead giveaway."

My partner groaned.

The stairs leading to the second floor listed dangerously so we headed downstairs first. The stairwell was narrow and twisty but at least the treads were solid. It led to a damp basement, which was just as deserted as the rest of the house.

Most of the space was taken up by an enormous ballroom, where sheets thrown over furniture cast menacing shadows.

The warped floorboards with inlaid mother-of-pearl beckoned to be waltzed upon, to be spun, dazed and flushed, by an attractive partner across the room.

Leaving footprints in the thick layer of dust, we wandered through pillars still bearing faint traces of gold gilding. Thanks to a series of warped glass doors, which led out to a wild overgrown garden, there was just enough light to make out the ceiling boasting ornate crown molding.

I could almost hear strains of music over the musty air blowing through the broken panes.

Eli tugged on a crystal knob, but the glass door was stuck fast. "We'll have to check out the top floor, but it looks like this place has been deserted for ages."

I shook my head. "Why hang blackout curtains in a deserted house?"

"Or even just hang them in the entrance hall? Did you see a coffin with a sleeping vamp there? Because I sure as hell didn't." Eli was getting testy, but it wasn't directed at me, and I didn't take it personally. He toed at the dust, erasing a footprint. "We're clearly the only ones who've been down here."

I frowned, teasing out a thought. "Oh! That's it. Come on."

Grabbing his sleeve, I tugged him back up the stairs and into the entrance hall. "Look. The floor is dust-free."

Eli frowned. "So?"

"That means it's been walked on. Damien has been here, which explains the blackout curtains. Hopefully Ian is with him."

"Then where are they now?"

"If I'm right?" I led him outside, turning to examine the rotting door barely holding on to the frame.

Eli prodded me impatiently. "If you're right, what?"

After a moment, a front door zoomed out toward us like a 3D stereogram. The solid modern structure clicked into the frame, almost slyly, as if saying *Little old me? I was here all the time.* Even so its reveal didn't give me the rush of watching a stage magician's showy flourish. It was more a quiet delight that I had access to secrets. Like finding an old book in an archive that you needed or digging up a piece of information at just the right time.

Eli gasped.

"They're still here." Grinning, I pushed on the handle running vertically along the right side and swung the door open.

2

WHETHER CREATED BY DEMONS OR OHRISTS, THESE pockets of reality ranged from a tiny lair to a huge territory such as the vampire-controlled Blood Alley. I'd mastered the art of finding and entering them, which was good since the Kefitzat Haderech didn't go to these spaces.

Eli stood there dumbstruck.

Four large diamond-encrusted lights shaped like spiky sea anemones threw a cool glow over the swank interior. The real house may have been a gothic beauty back in the day, but the mansion it had become was pure swagger.

It was also empty save for leering inanimate gargoyle faces carved into a water feature that spanned the entire two-story height of the entranceway. The facing wall was made up of a dozen glass panels projecting abstract digital art that pulsed in time to the bass-heavy Latin music flowing out of unseen speakers.

I poked Eli to get him moving, placing a finger to my lips to remind him to keep quiet while we remained under the cloaking since vamp hearing would pick up even the faintest whisper.

A wrought-iron spiral staircase led to the top floor.

Each of the four bedrooms was equipped with a king-size bed, shag throw rugs, and a mirrored ceiling. Your basic porn set aesthetic.

In the last bedroom two half-dressed vamps were going at it with abandon, their hips rocking in time to the sensuous melody, a rosy flush across their pale skin. Neither matched the descriptions we had of Damien or Ian.

The wanton writhing of their intertwined bodies combined with their low moans was hot, but it was crazy awkward perving on them with my ex-husband. Not because we were remembering former intimate times together, but because I knew exactly who he was thinking of when he adjusted himself, and he was damn certain who I pictured when I licked my lips.

We both blushed when our eyes met, sheepishly backing out the door under the cloaking. Our embarrassment turned to smothered laughter as we ran back down the stairs.

A loud coyote howl sobered us up fast because the animal sounded like it was right outside the house.

I pointed down and then made a twirling motion with my finger.

Eli stared at me uncomprehendingly, so I motioned again, more slowly, but all he did was spread his hands wide with his eyebrows raised in question. "Downstairs or around the perimeter?" he whispered.

I twirled my finger again. "This means wrap it up," I hissed.

He rolled his eyes but made no further protest.

Luckily, the stairs to this basement were much wider than the ones in the dilapidated house because a man built like a brick shithouse stood partway down with his back to us. He was speaking to a slightly shorter man with a hideous wart on the end of his nose. They held brandy snifters and lit cigars, guffawing over some sporting event they'd attended.

"Vamp?" Eli mouthed.

I shrugged because I'd seen Zev drink alcohol and Spike smoked constantly on *Buffy*. Yes, that did count as a valid frame of reference.

The taller dude turned into profile, and I blanched. Even without the stupid gold braided chauffeur's cap he adored, there was no mistaking Zev's human henchman Rodrigo. Or as I fondly called him "the Undertaker."

For about the billionth time tonight, I wished that we could have snuck in using the Kefitzat Haderech, but it didn't go to hidden spaces.

Eli poked my shoulder. "Problem?" he mouthed.

I bit the inside of my cheek, debating my answer. Tatiana likely gave Zev the description we had for the person that Ian had left a homeless shelter with two years ago and learned Damien's identity and whereabouts from the head vamp of Vancouver himself. In which case, Zev was aware we were coming here today.

Even so, why dispatch Rodrigo? Zev and I were on perfectly good terms. He wanted me hale and hearty to find the Ascendant.

Maybe this visit was a coincidence? Vampires had friends. Perhaps Damien was throwing a dinner party.

I gagged, squashing any visual of potential main courses, and flashed Eli a thumbs-up, gesturing that we'd go around the Undertaker. Thankfully he understood and we maneuvered past the duo without incident.

The short corridor was deserted, but the ornate wood ballroom doors were closed. I didn't want to open them only to have someone get curious about how the doors opened themselves. Unfortunately, the doors were well sealed with no crack to send my animated shadow, Delilah, through to scout on the other side.

Since I wasn't sure if Rodrigo's friend was human, I pressed my lips to Eli's ear, barely whispering. "That's Zev's minion. Human." I pointed to the stranger. "No clue."

Eli frowned. Then he managed to convey in gestures to go outside and spy in through the glass doors. I'd forgotten what a good charades player he was.

We crept back up the stairs, careful not to brush against the two guys chatting. Even though it was impossible for any human to detect our presence under the cloaking, I still held my breath until we were safely at the top.

There was no back door in this hidden space, so Eli and I went out the way we'd come in—through the front.

It was night here, of course, with a bright moon hanging cheerfully in a cloud-free sky. The focal point of the front yard was a stone fountain with a devil statue. Water sprouted from his pitchfork, splashing gently back into the basin, and moonbeams reflected off the droplets. It was actually quite lovely.

Other than that, there was nothing remarkable about the front or side grounds, so we followed the sound of music around back, pulling up short at the sight of the yard.

It was magical. Okay, yes, as a hidden space it was literally magic, but the oversize rosebushes and rhododendrons in saturated jewel tones were like something out of Wonderland. A magnolia tree exploded with fat silver flowers, wavy gold sunflowers that looked painted by Van Gogh stood seven feet high, and a hedge maze rustled as if continually changing its layout.

No wait. That last part was only cool in a hypothetical way.

Light spilled out from the open glass doors onto a terrace where dark figures mingled to the beat of Latin-flavored electronica. I couldn't see inside the ballroom yet, but I heard a woman tell her companion that if he liked a bit of spice, he should sample Rex's redheaded twins.

What the hell did that mean? Then the cold realization crept over me.

Were the vamps holding a tasting party of each other's donors?

I clenched my fists and Delilah shot up in the shadows behind me, scythe in hand. Eli and I had to rescue these poor people. They weren't being paid to be passed around like appetizers. Even if they were, did that make it okay? Did they have any real say in the matter?

Eli squeezed my shoulder, shaking his head sharply, and I sighed.

This sucked, but I couldn't let my emotions get the better of me. We were no match for multiple vamps. No matter how abominably they were treating the humans, I couldn't go after them, nor would the Lonestars do anything, since vamp behavior was outside the scope of their jurisdiction.

I wrestled my animated shadow down.

For now.

It would be harder to find Ian unobtrusively in this gathering of the undead, but every second Teresa was missing was a second too long.

Howls from somewhere by the maze kicked us into action.

Avoiding the revelers on the terrace, we crept inside the ballroom and froze, overwhelmed by the stench of blood, the pounding bass, and the astounding sight before us.

There were vamps everywhere, some dressed in all-black goth attire with heavy eyeliner, others in steampunk gowns and tiny hats. Black tie, bowling shirts, tight dresses, flouncy dresses, suits in all colors of the rainbow, and one memorable partygoer in white pants and a shirt made of balloons—every age, shape, and ethnicity was represented.

In contrast, the Ohrists were all clad in identical loose-fitting beige tunics and wide-legged trousers. They looked like they belonged in a cult, but they weren't physically imprisoned.

A DJ wearing fat headphones over one ear nodded along to the records she spun. "Do you want to go higher?" she cried.

The Ohrists and vamps dancing roared their approval, and

the DJ's fangs glinted in the swirling disco lights when she grinned back at them.

Eli let out a whispered "Fuuuuck."

It was impossible to see past the dancers to whatever was happening at the back. We skirted the wall, heading left instead.

A group of vamps played cards around an enormous poker table. The center was piled high with ridiculous amounts of cash, jewels, and one chubby woman with wispy hair who stood there with a sign around her neck reading, "High acidity. Tart and zesty with vanilla notes."

She trash-talked a young vamp while a familiar androgynous bloodsucker laughed uproariously, encouraging her.

I blinked because I'd seen her audition to become a donor for that vampire.

Drops of water hit us from behind and we turned, skittering out of the way of two dripping-wet coyotes carrying six-packs in their mouths. Were these the ones we'd heard earlier?

My pulse spiked, but no one batted an eye at their presence.

They shifted into a young male and female. Unconcerned with their nudity, they both retrieved signs describing their blood (buttery and smooth; chewy black currant undertone) from a chair and dropped them over their heads.

The woman tugged a beer can free then tossed the rest of the six-pack to a group of donors with similar signs. "Told you there was more booze out at the creek."

What the hell was happening here? Where were the poor abused and shackled humans? I planted my hands on my hips.

We inched toward the bar and Eli nudged me, nodding at a dude with bulging muscles creating cocktails for a small but rapt audience.

The bartender flipped two martini shakers in the air,

twirling and catching them behind his back to the spectators' applause. For his finale, he poured the crimson contents into a series of cocktail glasses without spilling a drop.

Donors sat behind the mixologist. Each one had an IV line running from their arm, dripping blood into small brass basins that sat on a high, narrow table. These donors didn't have signs around their necks, instead placards had been placed in front of each basin.

We sidled closer to read them. Grass-fed, all-protein diet, vodka-based (this in front of an Ohrist who listed precariously off his stool with a dopey smile), the undead bartender scooped out shots of blood to concoct his designer drinks.

A red-faced male vamp in a shiny suit pushed to the front of the throng, holding up his half-empty highball and asking for more citrus.

One of the Ohrists eagerly raised their hand. The bartender handed him a bottle of lemon juice and the Ohrist downed an enormous swig to cries of "Chug! Chug! Chug!"

My lips puckered, my stomach lurching and my mouth filling with saliva at the thought of swallowing all that tart liquid.

When he was finished, he wiped off his mouth.

The bartender grabbed the end of the IV line and dripped the donor's blood into the glass of the vamp who'd requested the citrus top-up.

He shot it back then slammed the glass on the bar top. "Zesty!"

The crowd roared in approval, clamoring for their own citrus drinks.

My head reeled, and I grabbed on to Eli's elbow for stability.

He sucked in a sharp breath. "Ian."

Our quarry stood across the room just off the dance floor in a sea of vampires. Ian Carlyle had once been a ruggedly handsome man. Now he just looked haggard, twisting his hands as his eyes darted between the dancers and the two arguing bloodsuckers to his right.

From our vantage point, Eli and I couldn't see the pair who was fighting, and though we could hear a man's and woman's raised voices, the music was too loud to make out their problem.

"I'm going to grab him," Eli whispered.

I nodded, giving the invisibility shield around us a test flex to expand its hiding capacity. This was something I'd been training for, but training was vastly different than doing it in a stressful situation.

We hurried over to our target.

Eli snaked an arm around Ian's waist, hauling him backward under the cloaking with us and clamping a hand over the man's mouth. "Quiet," Eli hissed.

Ian flinched, hunching his shoulders in like a whipped dog.

Eli wasn't holding him tight enough to warrant that extreme reaction.

Checking to make sure no one had noticed our abduction, I found Damien.

He lounged in a throne-like chair, one leg dangling over an armrest that ended in a silver skull with rubies for eyes. He wore heavy skull rings adorned with gems on his middle fingers, his too-tight clothing an explosion of purple velvet and ruffles. The vampire's face was twisted in a sneer as he yelled at his as-yet-unseen female opponent.

We had to tread carefully to extricate ourselves without drawing attention.

Before I could alert Eli—my ex and baby daddy, a respected detective and brawny tough guy—he let out a loud high-pitched yelp and a stream of cursing that I hadn't heard since he stepped on a pile of our daughter's Lego years ago.

It was impressive how fast an entire party could become quiet enough to hear a pin drop. Even the music cut out.

Eli shook out his hand, teeth marks in his red and puffy skin, while Ian tore free of the mesh.

"Celeste!" he cried, like he was falling from a cliff and she was his last lifeline. "Help me!"

Celeste? *Nonononono!* It had to be a different Celeste, right? Not Celeste BatSila, Zev's great-great-great-something-granddaughter whom he'd had turned. Not only was she a total psycho who was jonesing for a taste of me, Delilah had almost killed her at our last encounter.

Celeste didn't appreciate the importance of the word "almost" as much as I did, and in retaliation, she'd locked me up in a dungeon in Blood Alley. Zev had taken his sweet time rescuing me that night.

The crowd shifted to reveal the one vampire I had hoped never to meet again, standing resplendent in a red leather dress and red stilettos, her dark red hair cascading in waves down her back.

Heart hammering, I grabbed Eli with a sweaty hand to haul ass, but the stubborn bastard stood firm.

"We aren't leaving without speaking to Ian."

Yeah, but at the cost of our own lives? Hard pass. Clearly he'd never dealt with a crowd of angry vampires.

Before I could leave the idiot to his fate and save myself so that Sadie still had one living parent, a vamp next to me got jostled and almost bowled me over.

My magic cloaking fell apart, leaving Eli and me in plain sight.

Laughing, Celeste rubbed her hands together. "Just when I thought this night couldn't get any better."

I attempted to back up, but we were penned in by vampires. Nowhere to run. Nowhere to hide.

3

Damien got to his feet. "I'm going to rip your fucking heads off."

Celeste rolled her eyes, but she didn't make a move toward Eli and me.

Still, my life flashed before my eyes, because Damien was more than capable of following through, even if the nasal quality of his voice made it sound like he had a bad head cold.

More than one vamp smirked—though not where Damien could see it. He was like that universally disliked kid in high school whose parents had a great house and were out of town frequently. An asshole, but he'd always have people showing up at his parties.

How far would the vamps go to keep their in-crowd invites? Would they ask "How high?" if Damien said "Jump"? Ask if he'd like a platter for our heads when he threatened to rip them off?

Panicked, I threw double finger guns. "What's shaking?"

Eli automatically reached for his real gun.

Every single vampire busted out their fangs, and the air in the room sharpened to a knife's edge.

The only thing that saved us was the fact that Eli had left

his weapon behind. He slowly and carefully moved his hands in front of him.

Celeste strode toward me with a cruel smirk. "Gather round, friends, because there's a new cocktail flavor on tap." The vamp pointed down at the crown of my head with both her index fingers. "Banim Shovavim! One night only!"

The undead pressed in on us. Cloaking was pointless with this many bodies; we'd never get away. We had to do this the old-fashioned way—and run.

As I reached for Eli's hand, someone cleared their throat, and I was lifted off my feet by an iron band wrapped around my waist.

I looked over my shoulder. "Hi, Undertaker."

After a quick glare, which was practically a kiss on the cheek from him, he hauled me up even higher using his stupidly strong arm that was snaked around my waist. "Do what you came to do and leave," he murmured. "You have more pressing issues to attend to, and Mr. BatKian's patience is wearing thin at your lack of progress."

Swallowing, I nodded, but if Zev was on some deadline, he could be more forthcoming about why the clock was ticking. I wasn't some mindless minion. That said, I had to survive tonight to get him any answers at all, and looking at the cold, pale faces surrounding us, that wasn't going to be easy. "A little help?" I whispered.

The Undertaker raised his voice. "No one touches her. Mr. BatKian's orders."

After a long, tense moment, the vamps stepped back. Well, all except Damien.

"Hand her over," the vampire ordered.

I practically pulled an *Exorcist* head swivel to catch Rodrigo's reaction, and the man did not disappoint.

He raised one eyebrow, conveying exactly how many fucks he gave. "I don't work for you."

You could see the indecision in Damien's eyes. On the one

hand, he could force some of his cronies to attack—I doubted he was the type to launch an assault himself. On the other, Rodrigo was high up in the Zev food chain.

Damien sat back down in his big boy chair with a sneer that only intensified the impression of sinus congestion. "Keep your human plaything."

Some of the violent current seeped out of the air.

Rodrigo set me on my feet. "Hurry up."

I kicked out at Rodrigo, but the asshole put his hand on my forehead, literally keeping me at arm's reach. "You mean I could have avoided creepy forests and coyotes and figuring out this hidden space existed and simply let you just waltz me in under Mr. BatKian's protection to begin with?"

Rodrigo smirked and stepped back, while Damien clamped a possessive hand on Ian's wrist.

The human flinched. The neckline on his shirt was torn exposing bruised skin with two puncture marks standing out in sharp relief.

Vampires didn't need to hurt their victims to feed. In fact, they usually made it as pleasurable as possible. Either Damien wasn't wasting compulsion energy on a mere Sapien or he was a sadist.

Either way, he had to die, but if I simply manifested Delilah with the shadow scythe, Eli and I wouldn't make it out of here alive. Ian might not survive either.

"Release Ian," Eli said imperiously. "I want a word."

While I scrambled for a plan, Celeste nodded her head at a group who closed in on Damien. Interesting. She was a baby vamp, having been turned relatively recently, and yet she commanded minions and presided over the scene like a monarch. Family connections were a beautiful thing.

Aw, man. Was I going to have to get her on my side? Because that would be a huge pain in the ass. Then I mentally slapped myself. I was surrounded by bloodthirsty vampires and yet working with Celeste was the thing that made it complicated?

Damien's green eyes turned obsidian, and he twisted Ian's shirt in his fist. "Tell your little friends to back off."

"Not until you let go of him," Celeste fired back. "You don't treat fine wine like plonk. Besides, I won him." No belching, no farting, I barely recognized her.

Celeste had a lot of digestive issues for a bloodsucker, and most human blood didn't agree with her. Ian must have been her pick to replace her last donor, Raj Jalota.

The good news was that the focus was off us. The bad news was Eli stood there with his arms crossed and his chin jutting up, waiting for the altercation to be resolved so he could speak to Ian, completely unconcerned that we were penned in by the undead.

Our child did not get her stubborn genes from me.

"You didn't win, you backstabbing cunt." Damien ran his fangs against the inside of Ian's wrist. Was this the vamp equivalent of pissing dogs? "You're not getting sweet fuck all, so you can bite me."

The other vampires let out a round of collective "oohs," like a bunch of high schoolers waiting to see how the popular kid reacted to this diss.

Celeste tossed her hair off her shoulder and wrinkled her nose. "I don't dumpster dive to feed."

Ian cried out, blood streaming from a gash in his forearm where Damien's nails dug in.

The mood in the room turned. Fresh blood had spilled in a shiver of sharks, their party-going joviality gone. The Ohrist donors, who'd been doing a great job of being unobtrusive, tightened into small groups, and even Rodrigo, a badass but a fellow human, looked uneasy.

I put both fingers in my mouth, getting only air and saliva on them when I blew out. One day, I'd learn how to make that ear-splitting, crowd-quieting noise, but today was not that day. I nudged Eli. "Whistle."

The piercing sound stopped everyone in their tracks.

Much as I despised vamps keeping blood donors, Celeste was a much better fit for Ian. Poor guy didn't seem to have many options, and if his sense of safety was tied up in being bound to some vamp, better one who seemed to care about the humans at her disposal. Celeste, to her credit, hadn't killed her last donor, even when bribed to do exactly that.

I waved. "Hi there. Remember me? The one you can't touch? I want to talk to Ian."

Damien licked the blood off Ian's forearm, regarding me with heavy eyelids. "Lose Zev's hands-off policy and you can get as cozy with the Sap as you want."

Celeste pulled a sweaty stick of gum from her underboob, dropped the wrapper on the floor, and shoved the gum in her mouth, watching me thoughtfully. Ah, there was the class act I remembered.

Ian, still in Damien's grip, stared at the floor. My heart went out to the man.

"Here's the thing," I said. "The Lonestars won't get involved even though you're being a psychopathic dick to this poor guy."

Damien flushed angrily, Celeste laughed, and Eli motioned for me to wrap it up. Sure, now he was all about that hand signal.

"If you don't allow me and my partner to have a brief chat with him, I'll ask Mr. BatKian to make the request much more slowly and painfully."

Damien flicked his eyes at the Undertaker, who smiled coldly. Good man.

I snapped my fingers. "Don't look at him. Look at me."

Great, Eli's shoulders shook. I swear, if he blew my masterful performance and got us killed, I'd make his afterlife a living hell.

I moved to block my stupid partner, stepping hard on his foot. "I'm going to count to three and you're going to hand Ian over."

"Or what?" Damien said.

"Or I'll kill you myself." I looked around the room. "Does anyone have a problem with that?" I mean, he did threaten to rip my head off.

The Undertaker looked bored, which meant he'd filed my threat to the vamp under self-defense—the only leeway I had to kill him.

Damien jerked his chin at a short vamp. "Diablo?"

"Damien, Diablo. Did you guys use some online vamp name generator?" I rose onto tiptoes. "Is there a Lestat in the house?"

Diablo pinned my arms behind my back. His rationale—that I had to have the use of my hands to unleash my magic on him or that shifting would take time during which I'd be vulnerable—would have been sound, were it not for the tiny issue that I wasn't Ohrist. He must not have realized that Banim Shovavim didn't subscribe to the same rules.

Heh. This was going to be fun.

Eli pinched the bridge of his nose.

There was a loud crack and I flinched, but it was Celeste blowing and popping a bubble.

"This is your last chance to let us peacefully talk to Ian," I said. "Then I'm going to count to three and kill you."

Once you issued mom ultimatums, you had to follow through, no matter what, even if it got you in trouble later. "One…"

Damien muttered something about me being full of shit.

"Two…"

Ian cried out.

Okay, fuck this.

Delilah jumped up behind Damien, scythe in hand. In a single, beautiful strike, she decapitated him.

The vampire blinked twice after his head hit the ground, and then he crumbled into a pile of ash.

Jumping backward, Ian pressed his fist to his mouth in a silent scream, his eyes wide in horror.

Diablo released me like a hot poker. Phew, because I'd laid fifty-fifty odds that he'd murder me.

"Let's go," Eli said.

"Hang on." Shaking out my poor arm, I addressed the crowd, who, bless their hearts, didn't seem to give a damn that I'd just killed one of their kind. Damien must not have been very popular. I sighed. Friendships were so important. "This is where I remind you that I have immunity. Nor do I have a grudge with any of you. Like I said, I just want a word with Ian." I motioned at the man in question, who stood wide-eyed and frozen like a deer in headlights. "Come on."

Celeste wound the gum around her finger before sucking it back into her mouth. "Go with her."

I nodded in thanks.

"You've got five minutes," she said, "then the first round of Banim Shovavim cocktails are on me!"

The vamps roared their approval.

"You cow!" I lunged for her, but Rodrigo hauled me back, wagging his finger like I was some schoolkid in trouble.

Celeste smirked.

As the mature adult I was, I refrained from further comment, but in my head, I jabbed all manner of pointy things into her for maximum stabbyness.

"Mir—" Eli no longer stood beside me.

"What? Seriously?" I snapped my fingers at the two vamps who'd grabbed his arms. My ex was strong, yet he couldn't even budge these two much shorter females. "Hands off."

"BatKian said you couldn't be touched. He's fair game," one of them sneered.

"Guess again," I said. Delilah appeared next to Eli but neither vamp released him. "Step away. He's mine."

"Technically, poppet, you relinquished all claim on him ages ago." Naveen Kumar strode toward me, his weapon resting on his shoulder almost like an afterthought. "But if that situation's changed, do let me know."

"You have no jurisdiction here," the androgynous vampire said, taking the seat that Damien had vacated.

"You're harboring a demon," Nav said. "Hand her over and I'll be on my way."

The androgynous vampire gave a "yeah, right" laugh and tore the stupid skull decorations off the ends of the armrests, tossing them over their shoulder.

"We always have to do this the hard way." Nav struck the floor with his spear.

Carpe Demon operatives poured into the ballroom.

That's when all hell broke loose.

4

THE BALLROOM WAS ELECTRIC WITH OHRIST MAGIC, snarling shifters, and fast-moving vamps. Apparently the Carpe Demon gang had a way to protect themselves from compulsions because they didn't just lie down and invite the undead to feast on tasty veins.

I ran for my ex, covering my head from the plaster dust raining down. Delilah was already hacking at the vamp holding Eli's left arm with the shadow scythe. Two more swipes and the vamp disintegrated. That shadow of mine followed psychic orders like a dream.

Nav stabbed the other vamp who'd seized Eli right through the heart with his staff made of light. "You chose Miri to play *Buffy* with?"

"No offense," I added, mocking Nav's posh British accent.

"Oh, I meant the offense." He winked.

Now free, Eli rose onto tiptoe, scanning the room, presumably for Ian. "It was work, not play."

"Hey." I tossed my hair. "Working with me is as fun as play and you both know it."

"Fuck! He's gone. You, come with me," Eli commanded

29

Rodrigo, pushing into the crowd without a look back to see if he had been obeyed.

Nav's eyes gleamed at the hard-assed Detective Chu voice combined with his alpha prowl forward.

Ew! Was that what I'd looked like when Eli had used that voice on me in the bedroom? *Not the thing to focus on, Miriam.* I glanced at the Undertaker.

Rodrigo was not known for being meek. He answered to Zev, the head vamp of Vancouver. He wasn't going to let some random nonmagical cop tell him what to do. He'd probably destroy Eli, not—

He strolled docilely after my ex.

My mouth fell open.

Nav made a run-along motion at me.

Grr. Men! I stomped off.

"Yo!" Leaping over a random severed hand, I pointed at Nav's goth colleague, Clea, who grappled with Celeste. "You owe me a huge apology for locking me in a room last time we met."

Clea threw me a flat stare and then walloped the vamp in the jaw with her superstrength.

Celeste hit the ground like a stone.

"If only you were still locked up," Clea said.

"That wasn't half as growly as usual. Awww, I'm growing on you. That's apology enough." I held up my hand for a high five.

Tough as Clea looked with her metal barbell piercing in one eyebrow, a ring through her septum, and studs in the Cupid's bow dip of her full purple lips, I'd swear she smiled, even though she left me hanging. Okay, one of the studs in her cheek where her dimples would be sort of quivered, but I knew what it was.

Since Celeste remained down, Clea spun away to fight another foe. None of the operatives were out of commission yet, and I prayed it stayed that way.

A donor flew past me, bowling over some of his tunic-clad friends. One of them stood up but was yanked back down, narrowly missing being impaled by a series of spikes made of bone. The group crawled toward the glass doors, headed for the other donors who'd bolted outside at the first signs of trouble.

The female operative who'd fired the projectiles at a vampire ran a hand over her forearm, releasing another volley of bone weapons, which whistled through the air.

I ran after Eli using bobbing and weaving skills honed as a chubby kid forced to play dodgeball. Like that child long ago, I was a mass of bruises by the time I caught up to him.

He'd made it to the ballroom doors unscathed thanks to Rodrigo's hulking presence at his back.

"You could have protected me too," I said.

"I could have," the Undertaker agreed.

I'd have roasted him with the beautiful retort I'm sure would have come to mind, but the ground rumbled, low at first, then with the intensity of a hungry bear. It was followed by a jolting lurch that shook the whole house.

Glass tinkled, stereo equipment fell over, and bodies smacked together like tumbling dominos. Not my favorite comparison, but the visual was what it was.

I ended up plastered against Rodrigo like a barnacle on a rock. He kept his footing, plucking me off him and dropping me a few feet away.

There was a collective gasp, and I spun around to face the middle of the ballroom.

Purple flames shot up in a whirlwind, but nothing else caught fire. Not even the gangly demon in its center, shedding her vampire glamour like a second skin. She'd been masquerading as the guest wanting the citrus drink, which made sense given her real skin was as puckered and yellow as a lemon. Well, all except the blackened bits around the immediate area where Nav had stabbed her with his light staff.

31

Once over their initial shock, the vampires looked mostly indifferent to her presence.

The demon stepped free of the flames, swaying her corrugated hips sinuously, and tossed straggly, slimy strands of hair off her shoulder like an A-list celebrity on the red carpet.

Nav flicked a strand of platinum blond hair out of his face, his eyes glinting in challenge.

Next to me, Eli gave a low hum, the corners of his mouth flicking up. Spare me.

Lemon Demon ran a hand over her body, tiny pustules springing to life under her touch, and while I gagged, I couldn't look away.

The entire room, including Eli, Rodrigo, and me, stumbled toward the demon, unable to resist her allure, grotesque as she was.

Nav stamped his staff twice against the floor, and every operative touched their hand to their ear. A second later a high-pitched whine rang out. The operatives remained unaffected, but the rest of us, including the vamps and the demon, yowled in pain, stuck in place.

You'd think my friendship with Nav would buy me a warning. If not me, then my baby daddy, who he wanted to get it on with.

Eli gritted his teeth, sweat glistening on his brow, and shot me a look of helpless frustration.

Had my ears not started bleeding, I would have smirked. Eli hated feeling compromised on a mission. And being frozen in place like this? Nav's plans would be set back a smidge for sure.

The operatives formed a barricade around the still-paralyzed vamps as Clea and Nav charged the demon.

Wait, did that mean Celeste was still out cold, or had Clea just moved on to a different part of the mission?

The noise drilled into me but despite my best efforts, I

couldn't move, not even to rise onto tiptoe and locate Celeste.

Not finding the vamp through my shadow's green vision, I sent Delilah careening up the stairs, but it turns out we had a limited range of contact because any farther and my magic fell dormant.

The horrific noise dropped away, and now mobile, the vampires stampeded. The undead and the Carpe Demon crews came together like a savage horde.

While the coast was clear, Eli and I edged out the door. Before I could race upstairs seeking our quarry, Rodrigo blocked my way. "Present yourself at Blood Alley tomorrow." He named a time. "You'll be expected to have something concrete to deliver."

Eli called out to me from the top of the stairs, and Rodrigo turned away, the threat delivered.

I was so lost to my anxiety of how I'd pull a miracle out of my ass by tomorrow as we searched the house for Ian that I barely registered when we found him cowering in a bedroom closet, knife in hand.

He jabbed the blade at us. "I'm not coming with you."

Eli held his hands up placatingly. "We just want to talk."

"Did my family hire you to find me? I won't be locked up in a loony bin. I'd rather be stuck with a vamp like Damien." He lashed out again with the knife. "Where's Celeste?"

I pressed my lips together. Ian's bad choices were his own, but boy, did my mom side want to lecture him.

Eli placed himself firmly in the man's line of view. "A girl has gone missing."

"Yeah, well," Ian muttered, "shit happens."

Eli tensed, his expression grim. Suddenly he sucked in a breath and exploded into motion. He grabbed Ian by the shoulder and bashed his arm repeatedly against the closet door until the knife clattered to the ground.

I kicked it away.

Eli hauled the man out and slammed him up against the wall. "Shit won't just happen, it'll rain down unless you talk."

Even I got a flutter in my belly at his commanding tone, but Ian flinched again like he expected the beating.

"Eli, stop."

"Five years ago," Eli said. "Who took you?"

Ian's arms shot up in defense, the fight in his hazel eyes dimmed. His hands trembled, then he clenched them into fists at his sides. "Aliens," he sneered.

Eli shoved his arm across the man's neck and leaned his weight into it. Ian went red, scrabbling at my ex, but he was no match.

I grabbed Eli's shoulder. "He's been hurt by vamps. Don't make it worse."

My ex dipped his gaze down to the bruised skin and he released Ian, who gulped down air. "Who took you?" he repeated gently, his head tilted, and his eyebrows raised.

Ian half twisted away, his shoulders up at his ears, but when Eli continued to remain silent, waiting for the answer, Ian's brow furrowed. Almost like he didn't understand Eli's genuine concern.

"I don't know." A forlorn expression crossed Ian's face. "I don't, man."

I stepped closer. "A young woman shopping with her friend vanished into thin air like you did. Can you tell us anything to help find her?"

Ian went white as a sheet. He tried to back away, but as he was against the wall, he hyperventilated instead.

Sighing, Eli gently led him to the bed. "Sit with your head between your knees and breathe."

I took the spot on Ian's other side. "I don't know what your abductors did to you, but you can help save this girl and bring them down."

"Leave him alone," Celeste snapped.

Clea had the vampire in a headlock out in the hallway.

The slender operative of Asian heritage wasn't expending any energy to keep Celeste subdued. How strong was this Ohrist? Not a strand of her dyed-black bob was amiss, nor did any scratch mar the skin under her tank top, her left arm and collarbone covered in intricate tattoos.

I decided then and there that I wanted to be her. "Aww. You brought me a present."

"I'm following orders," Clea said through a tight jaw.

Celeste gasped out Ian's name, unable to say more because the Ohrist had tightened her chokehold.

Eli picked up the discarded knife and held it to Ian's throat. "Okay, vamp. If you're that invested in his well-being, make him talk."

Celeste's eyes darted to the knife and her quivering food source, then in a blur of movement, she punched Clea's gut.

Clea grunted, losing her hold long enough for the vampire to dart free.

Celeste got two steps closer to her blood donor before Clea grabbed the back of her shirt with one hand and wrenched the vamp's head sideways with her other.

Celeste screeched and made a gurgled choking sound. "You made me swallow my gum."

I must have been gazing at Clea with hearts in my eyes because Eli elbowed me and hissed, "Focus."

I snapped back to attention, leaning closer to Ian. "Every vamp in that ballroom knows you chose Celeste," I said. "Help us or Clea will kill Celeste and we'll drop you in their midst for the taking." I crossed my arms with a cold smile. "You say you'd rather be with someone like Damien than locked up, but get real. How long do you think you'd last with one of that crowd?"

Clea raised an eyebrow as if impressed, and I resisted the urge to preen. "I don't take orders from you," she said flatly.

Give me a break already. I jabbed a finger at her. "You

35

need to get over your issues with me. I'm not some mercenary, I am a very good person."

Clea gave me her classic deadpan stare.

I pasted a smile on my face and moderated my tone. "Clea, would you please let Celeste go? A Sapien is missing and we're running out of time."

"I like his style better," Clea said, jerking her chin at Eli. But she released the vampire.

I took the win.

"We both know you're going to walk out of here unharmed," I told Celeste. "Whether Ian goes with you depends on you."

Celeste shoved me off the bed and sat down. "Answer their questions and we can go."

I stood up rubbing my ass. Damn, I hated her.

Ian was slumped over, his elbows braced on his thighs. "No one would hear me out when I tried to talk about... I've spent years trying to forget." He rubbed his hand across his right pec.

"Teresa Wong has been missing over forty-eight hours," Eli said. "You were gone a week. Is that our timeframe to safely find her?"

Lost in some memory, Ian didn't answer, still rubbing his pec.

"Did Damien hurt you?" I touched my own pec. "Do you need a healer?"

Ian blinked back to awareness and shook his head.

Frowning, Clea walked over to him and carefully lifted his shirt, revealing an ugly gash across his torso.

Ian grabbed the fabric and yanked it down, his gaze on the floor.

Eli pursed his lips. "Raised scar tissue. Older wound."

"Tracker," Clea said in her monotone. "Some vamps implant them in donors, but this one was removed." Her frown deepened. "By some ham-fisted butcher."

"Not Damien's style." Celeste wagged her head from side to side. "Not mine either. The butcher part fits Damien, but he wouldn't bother with a tracker. Too convinced of his own prowess."

"So, this predates the vamps," Eli said to me.

I shrugged. "Yeah, well, still plenty of reasons to celebrate Damien's death."

Celeste snorted, jabbing a finger at me. "If you think I'm going to thank you for killing him, guess again."

I pressed a hand against my heart. "You're welcome."

"Your abductors did this, didn't they?" Eli said.

Ian screwed up his face. "Don't make me remember."

Celeste patted his back, shooting us a terrifying glower, but Eli held his ground. The cojones on my baby daddy were impressive.

"Why did they need to track you? Were they worried you'd escape?" Eli said. "Where were you?" The more frustrated he got, the sharper his voice became.

Ian shrank away from him, practically curled into Celeste.

"No one is going to hurt you," Clea said. She shot Eli a warning glance and he backed up.

I crouched down in front of Ian. "Where were you taken when you vanished?"

"A city," he said in a faraway voice.

Eli perked up at that, pulling out his phone and opening a browser. "That helps. Were there any recognizable landmarks? Did you hear people speaking a particular language? What about any memorable signs?" He turned too quickly into Ian's personal space and the other man flinched.

"Slow your roll," Celeste said. "And give him some space."

Eli backed off.

"Vamps and shifters," Ian said. A shudder racked his body.

"Hey, you're doing great. This is all useful stuff for us," I said, with the same soft smile I'd given Sadie when she'd been brave enough to go back to sleep in her own bed after a nightmare. "Was that the first time you'd seen beings like that?"

Eli looked thoughtful when Ian nodded. "They broke your perception filter." Eli rubbed his arm, memories of his own violent introduction to the world of magic no doubt coming to mind. "How? Did one of the supernatural creatures hurt you?"

Ian pressed his palms into his eyes. "It all hurt," he whispered. "I survived."

"You did," Eli said. "Now we want to make sure Teresa does."

Ian clenched his fists so hard that his knuckles turned white. "Can you survive the human race?"

Had revisiting his trauma led him into existential musings on life and death? "That's a glass half empty, half full debate, depending on how you see life," I said. "If we live a long time, have we survived or does death negate any longevity?"

"Oh my gawd, you people are dense," Celeste said. "The human race isn't some philosophical bullshit. You're being literal, aren't you, Ian?"

"Sapiens are being abducted and forced to run an actual race?" I exchanged a horrified glance with Eli, though on some level, it didn't surprise me. When Laurent and I went to the Wise Brothers for information, we'd ended up unwilling contestants in a *Jeopardy!*-style game show where they'd outed some of our most humiliating memories. With those two, there'd been a quid pro quo of sorts with the flow of information.

Was there anything in it for the Sapiens?

I jabbed a finger at Celeste. "Did you know about this?"

She rolled her eyes. "No. I'm just not a total moron."

"This game is employing vamps, but you've never heard of it. As if."

"Yeah, because I guarantee they aren't approaching my

grandfather's vampires. Not all masters run as tight a ship as he does." She gave a crisp nod. "They don't all have Blood Alley to fatten their coffers either."

Ian rocked back and forth. "I survived." He chanted it like a mantra.

The vampire's stomach grumbled. "Are we done? I'm hungry."

"Shut up," Clea said mildly.

My stomach growled as well, and I pulled out a granola bar, trying to unwrap it quietly and hoping Ian snapped out of it enough so we could continue questioning him.

When he remained lost in the past, Eli pointed to the vampire. "If that missing girl is being forced to play some sick game, there's no time to waste. Get him to talk or else."

Celeste sighed. "Time to snap out of it, big boy."

Her fangs descended and Eli tensed, but I placed a hand on his arm since Clea didn't look concerned about the vampire's actions.

I broke off a piece of my bar, but before I could pop it in my mouth, Eli snatched it away and ate it. I elbowed him. "Next time bring your own snacks."

Celeste wrapped an arm around Ian's shoulder, leaning him against her with a surprising amount of gentleness. She took his hand, her eyes locked on his until he gave a small nod, and then sank her fangs into the veins at his wrist.

I'd seen vamps turn feeding into a carnal act and I'd seen it done violently. This was, dare I say, tender.

"That's not what I expected," Eli said to me in a low voice.

"Me neither." I didn't want to like Celeste for any reason.

Clea tilted her head like she was listening to something and headed for the door.

"Where are you going?" I said, hurriedly swallowing. A fed Celeste was probably not a murderous Celeste, but I didn't want to test that hypothesis when I was exhausted.

"I'm not your babysitter," Clea tossed out over her shoulder.

Ian's breathing slowed, his eyes glazing, and the tension seeped out of his body.

"No, you're the UPS of the undead." I jerked my chin at Celeste, who hummed under her breath as she fed. "We didn't order that. Take your package with you."

"Can't," Clea said. "We're pulling out."

"Phrasing, darling." Nav walked into the room as the operative exited.

"You'd know," she said.

"Presumptuous."

It was heartwarming to see that I wasn't the only one Clea ignored.

Eli narrowed his eyes at Nav, a tiny frown wrinkling between his brows. "We've got this."

Poor Detective Chu did not like having his authority usurped. I ate the rest of the granola bar, my toes tapping.

"Oh, I know," Nav said. "I just came to say goodbye."

Eli held up a hand. "Stick around for a moment. You might be able to contribute."

Nav saluted him. "Aye, aye, chief."

Eli's lips quirked, but he quickly pressed them into a line.

Celeste pulled her fangs free and licked Ian's skin to seal the puncture wound.

"Could you—" I wiped my mouth.

She made a big show of using her tongue to get every last drop of blood.

Gross. Sighing, I rubbed my stomach, my snack now sitting in my gut like a lump.

"Ian." Eli snapped his fingers. "How many players were there?"

"Twelve." The donor had calmed down in a stoned way so there was a pause between question and answer.

"Did you talk to any of them? Were they all from here?"

Ian shook his head. "They took us from everywhere."

"Where is this game played?" Eli said.

"Not real." Ian swayed and Celeste caught him.

"The game?" Eli shot me a questioning look.

"Is it a hidden space?" I said. "Ian?"

He sank his hands into his hair but nodded.

I stroked my chin. If they abducted people from all over, there had to be multiple ways into this space. Ian had been taken while rock climbing, so that wasn't a viable way in for us. "Where were you released?"

"Vancouver," Ian said.

"Be more specific." Eli moderated his tone so he didn't upset Ian further, but his fists were clenched behind his back.

Ian had totally spaced out.

"If you fucked him up too badly for answers..." Eli went nose to nose with Celeste. He was a Sapien with no physical or magic weapon, but his absolute disregard of that fact made him terrifying. It also made him an idiot and a hypocrite for bitching at me about my lack of self-preservation.

Celeste schooled her features back into her usual disdain. "Whatever." The vampire flicked her finger against Ian's cheek a few times, until he came out of his daze somewhat.

"I don't remember where I ended up."

"Nav?" I said. "Does any of this sound familiar?"

"No." Any trace of flirtation was gone. He was in full Carpe Demon mode. "If demons were behind something like this, I'd have caught wind of it."

"Ohrists and/or vamps are running it then," I said.

"Sounds fun." Celeste prodded Ian. "Is there a buy-in?"

Ian shuddered again, a stark look on his face.

"Was it an actual race where the first person to the end wins?" Eli said. "Were the vampires and shifters after you? Were you supposed to kill them?" His shoulders stiffened. "Kill each other?"

"We had one week to cross this city," Ian said dully.

"Reach the end point and survive as the sole player until time ran out."

I clenched my jaw, my expression grim. On top of the shifters and vamps, the players were pitted against each other.

"Did you get the sense that there was some agenda behind the game?" I said. "Were people betting on you? Was there a prize of some sort or were you put through this for no reason except the fact that you were still alive?"

Ian threaded his fingers together. "I don't know why they did this, but when we first got there, they told us about crossing the city and holding out until the end. I didn't learn about the prize until the final trial." There was a long pause. "Immortality."

He gazed off for a couple of seconds before shaking his head, dissipating his dazed look. A muscle ticked in his jaw and his eyes sparked. It was the first sign of anger he'd displayed. "They lied and now I'm stuck in this hellish limbo." He banged his fist against his thigh twice. "I want to die, but I'm too much of a fucking coward to just end it."

5

WE COULDN'T GET ANYTHING ELSE OUT OF IAN, AND
Nav had to wrap up his own mission, so Eli and I headed
home to review the case.

The first thing we did when we returned to his black
Dodge Charger was call Sadie. We'd been truthful with her
about where we were going and why because our therapist
had stressed the importance of honesty if our family was to
remain strong. It would be far worse for our daughter to learn
we'd kept this a secret and have her be scared that we were
lying every time we left to get groceries.

Jude had come over to my place to keep her company, and
I'd heard the relief in both their voices when we checked in.

Ian remained with Celeste. With her dietary needs, she'd
treat him well, and I liked how she'd protected him when
he'd grown agitated at our questioning. Much as I was loath
to admit it, she really was a step up from the trauma he'd
faced running the Human Race.

Speaking of which, what was with that bogus prize? The
only way Sapiens could achieve immortality was if they were
turned by vamps. Except the winners weren't, hence Ian will-

ingly becoming a blood donor—caught between hoping he'd live forever and praying he'd die.

Much like how I longed to tell Tatiana what I'd learned and hoped she'd never find out.

Traffic was light on the highway back to town. Dusk had fallen and the streetlamps had snapped on, their light washing over Eli's somber expression like a succession of crescent moons.

"Why offer a prize that was easy enough to deliver and then not bother to? The players are Sapiens, the only humans that vamps are allowed to turn." Frowning, I flicked the heat onto its lowest setting. "Why promise it at all given the circumstances? These people weren't invited and incentivized to play this game. They were abducted and forced to save themselves. Was it just a cruel mind fuck?"

"I don't know." Positioning his hands in a perfect 9-3 driving hold, Eli drummed his thumbs against the center of the steering wheel. "We need to get into that game, save whoever is still alive, and find out everything we can about who's behind this. Shut it down for good provided we can find the portal in. Nav didn't have a clue about that."

"I'll ask Tatiana." Stretching out my legs, I rotated my ankles, ignoring Eli's grimaces at the cracking sounds they made. "And I'll pay Ryann a visit."

"Esposito told me not to bother his daughter. That this was a VPD matter."

I glanced over at Eli. "You don't find that weird?"

"Obviously, but I can't disobey a direct order."

"Yeah, well, he never said squat to me. If she knows anything about this, I'll get her to share." My ankles now loose, I arched my back to stretch it out best I could while wearing a seat belt. "Assume these game masters always kidnap twelve people..."

Game masters reminded me of raven shifters. Would Poe have any insights into this? They might, but I'd rather cozy up to the Wise Brothers before ever playing another game with Poe. Hiram and Ephraim dealt in facts. Engaging with raven shifters brought things into being that wouldn't have existed otherwise. Thanks to a previous encounter, before I'd learned of the consequences of tangling with them, there was now some "new player" on the game board of my life. I had yet to find out who—or what—it was.

"You going to finish that thought?" Eli said.

For a moment, I seriously considered telling him, but what good would that do other than burden him with my troubles? Jude knew because she'd told me exactly why raven shifter games were dangerous. Eli didn't have any useful knowledge about them, and I'd only upset him at a time when he needed to be focused on finding Teresa.

"I got distracted making mental lists of who could help." A semitruck rumbled past, and I instinctively shifted sideways, like that would save me if the thing tipped over on top of us. "What if there's some significance to the number of people they abduct?" I pulled out my phone, searching symbolic meanings. "Twelve labors of Hercules. Twelve tribes of Israel. Twelve on a jury." I turned off the screen. "Twelve has meaning in a ton of cultures, in science, and in numeral systems."

"We're either looking for a needle in a haystack of possibility," Eli said, "or it means nothing at all."

"My favorite either-or scenario," I said dryly.

"I can dig into the databases for any missing persons that fit the parameters of the case, but if people are kidnapped from all over the world, it'll be impossible to assemble a list," Eli said. "And it'll take time we don't have."

Without the copy of Teresa's meagre file that the Missing Persons Unit had compiled in front of us, we ran out of steam, so I closed my eyes for the rest of the drive. I managed to push all thoughts of this case aside, but my mind drifted back to the Ascendant.

Tatiana spent three years looking for the magic amplifier and was finally on her way to deliver it to her client when she'd been involved in a horrific car crash that left her paralyzed. The artifact was stolen and Tatiana's professional reputation was destroyed as thoroughly as her ability to walk. She'd fought to regain both.

My take-no-prisoners employer, of course, had never mentioned any of this to me. I'd put part of it together, with Zev filling in the rest when I discovered that my mom and dad had been the ones to cause the crash. But just because the Ascendant had vanished didn't mean interest in it had decreased. No, there were still plenty of people who could put the pieces together as I had, and one of them had already tried to contact me and force me to find it. Zev had promised he'd protect me from anyone else, as long as I found the magic amplifier for him first.

Obviously, I couldn't ask Tatiana to do the same, and honestly? Part of me didn't trust her to have my back on this.

In the end, it came down to two simple facts: Zev was capable of ruthless violence, and I'd do anything to keep myself and my loved ones safe.

I braced my elbow on the passenger windowsill, my head propped up in my hand. My parents didn't tell me anything about what they were doing or why. Did they fail to comprehend how dangerous their last job was?

I was left in the dark, and then I was orphaned.

Keeping secrets that touched the lives of people you were in a relationship with, be it romantic, familial, or friendship, was selfish and wrong. It truly was a betrayal, simple as that.

It gnawed at my soul that I was doing the same thing to Tatiana and Laurent, but forced or not, I'd promised Zev to keep mum, and I wasn't going to test the limits of Zev's mercy.

Laurent would never break a confidentiality, especially not to Zev, but everyone in the magic community took promises very seriously. If I broke this one, and even got away with it as far as BatKian finding out, I was convinced there would be karmic retribution that was just as bad. I wasn't willing to test that and find out.

That said, I was searching for a loophole.

I blew on the glass and drew a circle in the condensation. That secret was one thing, but I was even keeping the raven shifter's game a secret from Eli. Did it affect him or was it something I'd just brought on myself?

I spent the remainder of the drive watching the circle fade and trying to think this through, but coming up blank, I was happy to arrive home.

Jude and Sadie sat outside on the chairs on my half of our front porch surrounded by my extra-large baking sheets cooling on the railings.

I helped myself to a lemon cookie and perched on the arm of Sadie's chair, resting against her side. "Three different flavors? I warranted maximum anxiety, huh? You loooove me."

"Mock me and I take them with me," Jude said. Her Southern accent always reminded me of magnolias and honey, and hearing her felt like coming home after a long absence.

Eli beeped the fob at his car as he came up the front walk. "Is there peanut butter?" he said hopefully.

Jude pointed at one of the trays. "Right there, sug."

He took a cookie with a blissful sigh, then kissed the top of Sadie's head, before squeezing Jude's shoulder affectionately. "You'd have made a great sister-wife."

"Bless your heart," Jude drawled, and they both laughed.

"Let me shower and then I'll come over with Teresa's file." Eli unlocked his door and headed inside.

A neighbor's car drove slowly to the corner, its red turn signal blinking in the darkness.

"You think you can find her?" Sadie said.

"I hope so."

"Good." My daughter bounded up. "I'm going to call Caleb." She hugged Jude. "Night, Aunt Jude."

"Good night, pumpkin."

Jude waited until the door had closed behind Sadie and helped herself to a chocolate chip cookie. "Is finding this girl going to cause your child and me more stress?"

"Depends." I slid into Sadie's vacated chair, resettling the cushion at my back. "Do you consider infiltrating a *Running Man*–style game to save the missing woman and any other Sapiens who've survived from vamps and shifters stressful?"

Jude swallowed her mouthful and fixed me with a flat stare. "Little bit, yeah."

"Fair." I leaned over and grabbed my own chocolatey goodness off the still-warm tray. "We probably need a few therapy sessions on this topic."

"You're not kidding, are you?"

"I wish." I filled her in on what we'd learned, but Jude had never heard even a rumor of such a game existing.

"You could ask Zev," she said.

"I could."

I wouldn't. If Zev had bothered to send Rodrigo to that party just for my sake, then he wasn't playing around. Further delays on the Ascendant would not be tolerated.

Eli stepped out of his place in his favorite Canucks shirt and sweatpants, with his feet stuffed into flip-flops, and Teresa's file under his arm. He locked up his side, grabbed another peanut butter cookie, and then, with a considering look, took the entire tray and went inside my house.

"Leave the door open," I called.

Jude gathered up her purse. "Don't let him eat them all."

"Thank you." I hugged her.

She tugged on one of her red curls. "I have gray strands now thanks to you. You owe me a very nice meal at a restaurant of my choosing."

"Noted."

"Is Laurent back yet?"

I shot her a dark look. "No. Stop asking. Go work out your stress with that mechanic you've been seeing."

"Oh, I plan to." She heaved a dramatic sigh. "Sometimes I wish we had a connection beyond the physical, and then he eats me out for half an hour and I realize his mouth is already serving the greater good."

I almost choked on my cookie. "Thirty minutes? Bullshit."

She threw me a smug grin and headed down the front stairs, waggling her fingers goodbye over her shoulder. "I'm going for forty tonight."

"Big talk, lady."

Laughing, she got into her car.

Still reeling, I watched her drive off. Half an hour? On that one thing? No way.

At least Jude and I had gotten back to feeling like us again. Her kidnapping had done a number on our friendship, but after avoidance, denial, a fight, and a lot of talking, we were good again. I smiled because I'd be lost without my best friend.

Eli poked his head out the door. "What's keeping... Uh-oh. What did you and Jude discuss now?"

I picked up a decorative pillow and fanned myself with it. "Half-hour oral sex."

Eli scrunched up his face. "I mean, that's a bit long, but some guys take a while to get there. Props to the woman's stamina."

I spun a finger in the air. "Reconfigure what you're thinking."

He pressed a hand to his heart, staggering outside and hitting the railing. "No way. Is that some tantric thing?" He lowered his voice and grabbed the pillow from me, holding it like a shield. "Was I supposed to have gone that long?"

Laughing, I snagged it away from him and dropped it back

49

on one of the chairs. "I couldn't have gone that long." Could I? Laurent was always game to try new things out.

Eli pushed me inside. "Whatever you're thinking, don't share."

I grabbed the remaining two baking trays. "I absolutely wasn't going to."

We went into the kitchen, where Jude won all the good karma in the universe for not only baking but cleaning up after herself. I put the cookies into containers, making a small care package when Eli threw me puppy dog eyes.

He reviewed the file aloud, but it wasn't until he was going through the profile that the Missing Persons Unit had compiled on Teresa Wong that he straightened up with an excited gleam in his eyes. "Shit. I think I've figured out how they choose their victims."

I leaned across the table to see what he was pointing at. "Parkour? Well, Ian was a rock climber. But really? A love of outdoor activities across two people feels less like a thread and more like a coincidence."

Eli licked his fingertip and turned the page of Teresa's file. "Sure, but you're not looking at the bigger picture. Parkour makes any terrain scalable, same as rock climbing, but Ian was also a survivalist. He could build a fire, sharpen a stone into a blade. Wilderness shit."

"Riiight. Wilderness shit. Did Teresa have other useful skills?"

"No, unless she had a dramatic monologue to bore an enemy to death with."

"Mock theater degrees at your peril, man. If our kid heard you? Yikes."

"Teresa only had the one skill set then." His hands tightened on the file. "Wait. What's the first thing you do in a video game?"

"If it's me? Die quickly. I'm the puzzle person, you're the multiplayer guy."

"You pick an avatar. A player character with a *specific* skill set like speed, strength, agility, intelligence, endurance. Teresa only needs one ability because these Sapiens are being chosen as avatars."

"That's a fair assumption," I said. "It answers my question about why they aren't taking people at the fringes of society whose absence wouldn't be reported immediately or noticed at all."

"They want strong players with a shot at winning."

I doodled on a pad, thinking aloud. "It implies that these Sapiens were scouted by their abductors beforehand. Ian said the players came from all over the world. That's an impossible amount of people to whittle through to find suitable candidates."

"True, but don't forget, the people behind these games are double-dipping. Both Ian and Teresa came from Vancouver. That implies a set number of cities they're drawing from." Eli scribbled a note, then threw the pen down and rubbed a hand over his bald head. "We don't have time to find the way into the race by narrowing any connections between the players, and Nav couldn't help us." He drummed his fingers on the table. "You're going to see Tatiana and Ryann… What about the vamps? Who else could you pump for information?"

I imagined bargaining with Yoshi over info again, or worse, the ravens, and shivered. "I've got no one unless it's a last resort."

He gave me a tight nod. I could deal with his unhappiness so long as it came with the acceptance that if I said it was too dangerous, he had to abide by that. It's why he'd brought me on, after all.

"I'll go see Tatiana bright and early tomorrow morning." Yawning, I stood up.

Eli shot to his feet. "You're just going to let this girl spend another night trapped in this game, fighting for her life against God only knows what?"

"I," I said, "am not leaving Sadie again."

Eli nodded, tension leaving him. "Right. Sorry. Stay with the kid. I've got to remember the seventy-two-hour rule isn't necessarily relevant here."

The first seventy-two hours of any missing person case were the most critical. After that, investigators had a harder time preserving evidence and following up on leads because people's memories faded. Generating as many tips and as much awareness as possible with the general public also slowed down after that timeframe.

"Night, Mir." Eli left by the back door, his shoulders falling back into a slump. He'd come back from work on a few memorable occasions when a missing person wasn't found fast enough and the original case became a homicide for his unit to handle.

Even if three days hadn't passed, between her abduction, the reveal of magic, and fighting off vampires and shifters, Teresa might already be dead.

6

AFTER SADIE TORE OUT OF THE HOUSE ON Thursday morning, having left at the last possible second to get to school on time, I went through the rest of the documents in the box of James Learsdon's papers that Zev had delivered to my home after he hired me. Given they belonged to a dead man who'd begged me to save him, it had taken me a day or two to build up my courage to go through them. It's not like I thought he'd haunt me for it, but the more I got to know him as a person, the worse I felt about my failure to keep him alive.

James was an archeology professor who'd followed whispers about the magic amplifier for years. It had eventually led him to learn about my parents and through them he found me. He was dead now at Zev's hands, part of a business transaction with a vampire called Dagmar, whom James had stiffed. I suspected that BatKian had willingly taken this blood on his hands in exchange for access to James's things.

I wasn't an idiot. Zev didn't intend to gift the Ascendant to Tatiana to help her find closure or ease the pain of the past. He wanted it for himself. This was now the second time I'd chosen to retrieve a magic artifact for the vampire without knowing what it did. I didn't trust Zev any more than I had when we'd first met, and I'd lucked out that the previous item ended up being something that Zev didn't intend to use for dark purposes.

I couldn't guarantee that now.

In exchange for the first artifact, the Torquemada Gloves, Zev created a ward to keep supernatural baddies off my property. The gloves were part of the greatest tragedy of the vampire's life and not evil at all.

This second job had come about because Learsdon admitted during an interrogation session that the hunt for the Ascendant had begun again. That search already had a body count that included my parents and a Lonestar complicit in covering up their deaths. I shivered recalling the snap of McMurtry's neck right before he was about to tell me who had hired him and the demon parasite that had inhabited the man for decades before slithering out of his corpse to disappear in the wind.

Had the unseen killer left me alone because I wasn't a threat to them or because the parasite posed a greater danger to them?

What about the next time I crossed paths with them—if there was one? What about my family? Even if this assassin wasn't hunting for the Ascendant now, any new players would be equally dangerous.

I couldn't say no to finding the amplifier in exchange for Zev's protection, but I lay awake a lot of nights wrestling with my choices.

Sighing, I squinted at a paragraph in one of the files. I'd spent the past week going through all of James's papers. Not only was his handwriting almost indecipherable, his notes were sparse. The sole lead I'd found was the name of the Banim Shovavim who'd allegedly hired Tatiana to find the Ascendant: Arlo Garcia.

James had invested a lot of time and money trying to find

Arlo, but the man had lived a very private life and there'd been no trace of him for years. However, there wasn't any record of a death certificate either.

I'd given that information to Zev a couple days ago, but upon hearing that, he'd snapped a marble statue in two like a pencil, at which point I'd fled. I dropped the remaining pages back in their box and rubbed the back of my neck, aware of the blade hanging over it.

All right, time for a trusty list. Arlo Garcia was either dead with no body found, in hiding, or missing.

He'd been wealthy so tracking him down if he'd gone into hiding could take years, plus James had already tried. If he'd been kidnapped and returned, wouldn't James have found some mention of it? Arlo's death seemed more and more likely, especially since he'd been a few years older than Tatiana when he hired her.

What had happened to him and was it relevant to my search? Maybe not, but he was all I had. Swigging down the last of my now-cold caffeine, I drew a cube in red pen on a napkin. Think outside the box.

Hmm. Ian was taken to a hidden space. What if the same thing had happened to Arlo? Not the game, since Arlo wasn't a Sapien, but there were plenty of reasons why someone rich and powerful enough to hire Tatiana would go missing. Especially since the Ascendant was a magnet for trouble.

I sat up, quickly flipping through my notes. The only two relevant to my current line of thinking were that Arlo Garcia had owned an import/export business, which sounded super shady, and he was Banim Shovavim. My parents, Arlo, this was a popular artifact with that crowd.

Sucking on the end of the pen, I circled back to the idea of a hidden space. What if Arlo hadn't vanished, he'd doomed himself to wander the Kefitzat Haderech forever tormented? I accidentally jostled the file and lunged to catch a couple papers before they fell. Heartless as it was to wish for his

55

eternal damnation, there was only one way to test my hypothesis.

I stepped into the shadows, coming out a heartbeat later in the Kefitzat Haderech.

The only time during any of my visits that the reception cave had changed was when Pyotr had been temporarily reassigned to Customer Service and forced to fill out reports of my ineptitude. He'd been replaced by the least charming golem ever, and since then, the first thing I did was ascertain that my favorite morose gargoyle was around to greet me.

He wasn't seated at the fold-out table. The laptop loaded with action movies that I'd bought him lay closed next to the old television set and *Pong* game console. Careful not to whack a shin on a grayish-black stalagmite, I checked all around the large stone slab piled high with single socks.

"Pyotr?" The vents in the rock ceiling depositing socks onto the pile was in working order, and the place stank of fabric softener.

"Am here," said a gloomy Russian-accented voice.

I headed into a far dark corner, almost tripping over the gargoyle sitting on the ground. In his usual brown plaid shirt and brown pants, I'd mistaken him for a shadow. "Ow!" I swore under my breath, shaking out my poor toes. "What are you doing?"

"Gardening." He held up a small pot containing a scraggly fern in his oversize stone hands.

There was a lot to unpack with this image. I rubbed a hand over my chin and compressed all my questions into one. "Why?"

"Am on devices too much. Sign says need other hobbies." He glared balefully at the wall, but his scowl softened into a fond smile for the fern. Near as I could make out, Pyotr's boss was a neon sign, while the CEO of the KH was a ghostly skeleton face made of smoke.

Was the idea that a sign was concerned with screen time

weird? Not particularly. My circle of friends included a couple of gargoyles, a golem, and people with magic, and I was hooking up with a werewolf. Weird was a distant signpost in the rearview mirror of my life.

I crouched down and prodded the dry soil. "You need to water it and plants need light."

"Am not stupid." He lumbered to his feet, carrying the fern over to his table. In this somewhat brighter light, the fern wasn't just scraggly, it was deep into Charlie Brown Christmas tree territory. One good shake and that poor thing would lose all its fronds.

"I'm sorry," I said sincerely, following him. "Then why did you have it back there in the dark?"

"To make night." He tenderly patted the plant and carefully placed it on the table. "I sing lullaby to help it sleep."

Awww. I impulsively hugged the gargoyle.

"Take sock and go," he said, squirming free.

"I have a favor to ask."

His bulbous lips turned down even more, his bulging eyes gazing mournfully at me. "No more demotions." He bent down to retrieve a small, dented watering can and poured a thin stream into the pot.

"You won't get in trouble." Hopefully. "Do you have a list of all the Banim Shovavim currently suffering eternal damnation? Names, locations inside the KH, that type of thing?"

Pyotr tested the soil with his finger. "Like Marauder's Map?"

I blinked. "How do you know *Harry Potter*?"

He added more water. "Other Banim Shovavim gives me gifts now."

"Who?"

Pyotr's face lit up. "I have two friends. Wait." He caressed the fern, repositioning the pot in different places on his table. "Three."

I was the first one to ever give the gargoyle gifts, and now after all the centuries of Pyotr's service, someone else happened to jump on that bandwagon? I didn't like it. "Who is this person?" I unclenched my fists. "Have they asked you to do anything in exchange for these presents? Because they should be given freely."

"Malorie is very nice." Was he collecting people with M names?

"All right," I relented. "What about a list?"

He jerked the planter hard enough that a bit of dirt spilled onto the table and scowled at me. "Requisitions require forms."

I clasped my hands together in begging formation. "Please? It's very important."

He rubbed the stone callus he still had from his time in Customer Service. "In triplicate."

"I will bring you any movie or food you want. Just find out if he's here. Arlo Gar—"

Pyotr slapped his hand over my mouth, his eyes wide. "Must Not Be Named."

I wrestled his hand off me. "Is this a thing with all damned Banim Shovavim or just—"

He made a slashing motion across his throat.

"Or just this dude?" I finished lamely. Pyotr was truly terrified.

Suddenly the neon sign lit up, flickering wildly, and a black tar-like substance oozed from the rock walls.

I shrieked and jumped onto Pyotr's chair. "What the hell is happening? That's not normal! It's not, is it, because—" I shrieked at another glob oozing free.

Pyotr was currently crouched under his table, like those school drills with children attempting to survive nuclear attacks using furniture as shelter. "He heard you," came the gargoyle's haunted whisper. "Bad. Bad. Bad."

"The sign? When did the sign get this much power?" I screeched from the chair. The ooze was making its way onto the floor and heading toward us. "Why isn't Smoky Ghost Face shutting this down?"

"No. Not sign boss. *Him*." He backed out from under the table on all fours.

Why did Arl— Why was he powerful enough to eavesdrop and splooge evil goo and most importantly scare the shit out of Pyotr and Neon Sign while Smoky remained MIA?

Jumping puddles of ooze, Pyotr ran to the stone slab and flung socks at me. "Go! Go! Don't keep waiting."

My pulse spiked in the face of the gargoyle's hysteria.

The narrow green exit appeared across the cave, and I sprinted out, adrenaline giving me an extra burst of speed, and the door crashed shut behind me.

I careened down the dimly lit path, almost running through Smoky Ghost Face, who sprang up out of nowhere, and pulled up short, my heart thundering even faster.

Its eyeless sockets seemed to bore into me.

"Protect me," I pleaded.

The skeleton face's grim expression softened for a fraction of a second, then in a whirlwind of motion, the smoke vanished and the rock face in front of me slid away.

I wiped my sweaty palms on my dress and stepped through.

This place was nothing like the rest of the Kefitzat Haderech. I stood in a room that reeked of wet compost, blinking dizzily against the walls, ceiling, and floor that were painted in jagged black and white stripes.

The space was the size of a soccer field—and the stripes were moving.

Black slowly seeped from the dark stripes into the white ones. As the viscous liquid drained from one side to the other, light glinted off what I'd taken to be the glossy finish but was actually a translucent membrane enclosing the room like shrink-wrap.

Or like the skin of the tormented Banim Shovavim female that I'd once met here.

The pile of socks I held hit the ground.

Out in the middle of the floor was a tangle of black and white—light so bright it hurt to look at it contrasted against an all-encompassing darkness. It was like staring into the heart of the sun and an endless void at the same time.

Blood trickled out of one nostril, and I jerked my gaze away, spinning around for the exit.

It was gone.

As was my magic.

I bit back a scream, attempting to get my trembling under control.

"You enquired after me?" The disembodied voice was that of a soft-spoken old man.

The tangle in the center flared both brighter and darker, and the floor tilted, sliding me forward in invitation.

I'd been in a lot of dangerous situations since I reclaimed my magic. I'd fended off vampires, broken demon illusions, and would soon have to tell an insanely powerful woman that my parents were responsible for the worst moment of her life.

Never had I experienced fear like a knife twisting in my gut and slicing upward with one barbaric thrust.

I dug my heels in, fighting to remain in place, but a primal part of me yearned to stand before that abomination, an urge as violent as a raging hurricane that would batter me until there was nothing left.

Was my fear because of this insanity stretching out before me or because of my desire to get closer? The terror was a weapon, and I wasn't sure which of us wielded it.

Blood continued to drip from my nose, so I pinched my nostrils together, walking with my head thrown back.

The stripes had completely flipped colors by the time I got within twenty feet of the thing in the center of the floor. I stepped back into some invisible safe zone where it no longer felt like my brain was dripping the same black ooze that had come out of the cave walls earlier.

Thanks to my nosebleed, I'd been looking up this entire time, and I had to steel myself to lower my eyes. I managed to look at the tangle for only half a second at best, but that was enough to see the ruined outline of an elderly man made only of burbling black and white, like a plume of water in a fountain.

"What happened to you?"

"I tried to fly with the angels." Arlo's voice turned dreamy.

I frowned. "Do you mean Senoi, Sansenoi, and Sammaneglof?"

Those were the three angels who'd set the damnation of our kind in motion when they couldn't outright murder this batch of Lilith's progeny. Even the KH had a trap laid within it, constructed by the angels, one that I'd been lucky and wise enough to escape. The thought of actually meeting these divine beings? Yikes.

"How did you find them?" I said, my voice strange.

"You don't find angels," Arlo said. "They find you. I showed them the cracks in the seams. They made me the cracks in the seams." He let out a laugh. A single "ha" that went on and on, twisting and turning like an ancient melody.

I was horrified.

I was transfixed.

The laughter cut out to a shocking silence.

Creepy as that was, it had nothing to do with my visit. "What does the Ascendant do?"

Arlo never got the magic amplifier because the device was stolen when Tatiana was on her way to deliver it to him, but he must have known what it was capable of.

Giant eyes snapped open on the ceiling and I jumped, my hand on my heart. They were swirls upon swirls upon swirls.

I screwed my lids shut tight, terrified I'd fall into his madness.

"You seek it?" he said.

"Yes."

"Foolish girl." A velvet touch stroked over the top of my head, and I shuddered. "Leave the monsters in the dark," he said.

I snapped my eyes open, tamping down my irritation. "Banim Shovavim aren't monsters. That's angel prejudice, not truth."

Before I could press him again about the Ascendant, the ground rippled, and a low moan swam around me.

The air became moist, the moan raspy, as if Arlo struggled for breath.

A door opened in the wall, and Pyotr beckoned at me almost desperately with a neon yellow sock.

Two hands made of that mix of light and dark that was Arlo gripped my shoulders so hard that I hissed. "Leave!"

I jerked free and bent my knees, arms thrown wide, surfing the quaking ground. I wasn't retreating without an answer to the most important question. "What happened to the Ascendant after it was stolen from Tatiana? Where could it be?"

"Miriam!" In the doorway, Pyotr jumped up and down like a little kid who had to pee.

Spurts of black and white exploded around me like blood in a Tarantino film.

I held my ground for a moment longer, but an answer was pointless if I died obtaining it. Hunched over, with my hands protecting my head, I lurched my way to Pyotr and safety.

Just before I stepped across the threshold, a whisper skittered across my skin like dried leaves. "'The fault, dear Brutus, is not in our stars, but in ourselves, that we are underlings.'"

I jerked back around, but Pyotr hauled me out and

slammed the door. Something hit it from the other side hard enough to almost punch through before the door disappeared. The gargoyle slid onto the rocky ground, blotting his forehead with the neon yellow sock.

I rested my trembling hand against the restored rock face. Stars wrapped in Shakespeare's *Julius Caesar*, a play about betrayal. Ignoring the alarm bells in my head, I scrounged up half-buried lectures from my English lit degree. Cassius is convincing Brutus to join the assassination plot by saying that it's not fate or destiny but a weakness of character— people perceiving themselves as underlings—that keeps them from action.

How was this the answer to the Ascendant's location?

"*He*"—Pyotr paused until I nodded that I understood he meant Arlo—"will be like that for all eternity."

"For what? Hubris?" Flying with angels. Delusions of grandeur. I shook my head. "Are there others like him?"

"No. More would be...bad for Kefitzat Haderech." Pyotr pressed the damp sock into my hand and unsteadily got to his feet.

With that he patted my head and lumbered off, leaving me to wonder if Arlo's last words referred to the Ascendant or something much worse.

7

ZEV HAD BEEN EXTREMELY CLEAR THAT I WAS NOT to discuss this with anyone, so I couldn't ask Tatiana where she'd originally found the Ascendant. What about the person she'd stolen it from? Could they have enlisted my parents to get it back from her and were once more in possession of it? Possibly, but I had no idea how to find that individual.

My best course of action was to take Arlo's final statement as a clue to the Ascendant's whereabouts—albeit a cryptic one because seriously, what other kind was there in my life—and solve it.

Since I had another forty-five minutes until my meeting with Zev, I decided to touch base with Ryann about our missing person case. I spent the drive to the Park riffing off the quote in hopes that it sparked something.

It was a beautiful September day and I flipped into autopilot, amassing and dismissing a lot of ideas. Brutus killed Caesar because of a commitment to the well-being of Rome. Was there something about the Ascendant that aligned it with causes? Big-picture beliefs that its owners worked toward?

I rolled down my window to let in fresh air because traffic

was gridlocked and I was stifling in the standstill. Finally, I was able to veer onto the exit for Stanley Park, and I zipped under the small stone bridge, coming out in the hidden space of the Park.

Slowing down along the narrow dirt road, I inhaled warm fresh air, rich with notes of earth, cedar, and old growth forest, which always reminded me of Laurent. I filled my lungs, savoring it.

Sun caressed my skin, and birds lazily swooped between cedars with fat knobby trunks, hemlocks laden with flat glossy needles, and cottonwood trees in glowing shades of gold. I shaded my eyes, basking in the beauty for a moment longer. Magic could be awful, but it was equally awe-inducing.

Eli would have preferred I first speak with Tatiana about the game. As a fixer to the magic community, my boss might have heard rumors, but she wasn't part of the Human Race herself. If she had, she'd know about the kidnappings and never have allowed me to investigate this case.

As the head Lonestar, however, Ryann had to have concrete intel since this game was a threat to the prime directive.

The trees pressed in more closely once I turned onto the bumpy road leading to the small parking lot, their canopy barring all but the most tenacious beams of sunlight. If the pristine forest wasn't enough to hammer home the magic of this territory, then Lonestar HQ did the trick.

A treehouse complex built on brown metal struts shaped like trunks, their headquarters branched off to support buildings fronted with wooden shingles, while foliage peeked out of every crack and cranny. Angled solar panels on the roof drew sunlight, and the windows were tinted to reflect the sky.

I strode through the archway carved into a huge hollow tree, trailing my fingers along the spongy deep green moss on the bark and tiny red and purple flowers growing twined around the staircase railing. My first time here, my sense of wonder had been drowned by a tight knot of fear because I'd been hauled in to "chat" about a murder case that one particular Lonestar was convinced I'd committed.

I'd cleared my name and proven myself enough times that coming here now only filled me with whimsy.

Pulling open the front door, I was hit with the scent of pine from the Douglas fir growing up through the lobby. I strode past the glossy framed portraits of previous chapter heads, stopping by reception to request a meeting with Ryann.

None of the magic cops wore uniforms or had any designation, other than Ryann's leader status. An officer in a smart sheath dress and strappy heels escorted me along a series of covered walkways, descending deeper and deeper into the building. She bore the familiar Lonestar tattoo of a six-pointed gold star on her wrist, which resembled a spur rather than a Star of David.

She tapped out texts with French manicured nails. I'd looked like her when I worked as a law librarian—well groomed, wrinkle free, but with feet that constantly hurt.

"Shapewear sucks, huh?" I smiled at her.

She glanced up from her screen. "Amen to that. I hate it but with this outfit?" She shook her head. "I'd look like a sausage otherwise. I just love the dress so much."

"You look great."

"Thank you." She rapped on a door with the word "Morgue" stenciled on it.

I swallowed down my nausea. Arlo and a morgue on the same day? Oh no, universe, I really couldn't.

"I can wait—" The door swung open, and my stomach heaved in anticipation, but I didn't smell bleach. Or worse. "Hey, Ryann."

"Miri!" Big blue eyes blinked at me, then she grinned.

She'd shaved her head down to a half inch of stubble dyed blue and purple. I would look like a deformed Easter egg, but she rocked the do. She bobbed a curtsy, swaying out her tie-dyed skirt. "Come in."

"Love the hair." Odd. I expected more resistance to this visit.

The female officer said bye and went on her way.

I took a deep breath and locked down professional Miri mode, following Ryann into the dead person zone.

"Hi, Gerald." I'd met the coroner in the wrinkled scrubs on a previous case involving a dybbuk. Which apparently was also the case here, given the red streaks on the waxy skin of the male corpse on the metal table.

"Do I not get a greeting, Mitzi?"

My heart lodged in my throat, I slowly turned to Laurent, who was slumped in a chair in the corner, dancing a coin between his fingers.

The pink T-shirt pulled tight across his pecs featured an image of Boo from *Monsters, Inc.*, a nod to the kitten he'd taken in with the same name. He would be the kind of guy who'd wear a T-shirt with a kids' character on it to a morgue, and yet, when he unfurled a lazy smile at me, a fleet of butterflies launched in my stomach, along with thoughts that were adult-only.

"Hi," I said breathlessly, biting my lip and wishing it was his, drawn closer as though by a magnetic pull.

Amusement sparked in his eyes, and in one fell swoop, the butterflies dropped in my gut like a lead weight. Our conversation about what my parents had done might be the end of that look and his carefully guarded smiles, but I owed him the truth. I had to tell him.

Damn Zev. I toyed with the strap of my purse. Could I swear Laurent to secrecy? I sighed. No, it wasn't fair to burden him with that knowledge and not let him speak to his aunt about it. Plus, I'd still be breaking my oath to the vampire, which was a no go with all the nasties that would come out to play if he didn't keep them in check. Fuck. I required a loophole, stat.

It was bad enough my parents had done this to Tatiana; she'd been a stranger to them. I wasn't a killer, but I was still a shitty human being if I didn't give her this information. With so many unanswered questions around the event that had derailed her life, how could she have truly moved on?

I wouldn't have been able to.

Laurent flipped the coin to his other hand. "Did Sadie get her shoes?" he said conversationally.

"Shoes?"

"The last time I saw you, you raced out because of a shoe emergency." His words were playful, but his smile was sharp enough to slice.

It took me a second to place the excuse I'd given after learning about my parents' role in Tatiana's car crash. Laurent wasn't an idiot. He knew I'd lied, but was that as far as it went, or had he put all the pieces together?

I shifted my weight to my other foot, studying him carefully, but I couldn't discern if he was upset because he knew the truth or because I'd ghosted him. "Yeah, the shoes. She's all stocked up. Let's catch up later, okay, because I've got a bit of a situation."

Laurent tossed the coin up and caught it, staring at it as if it provided an answer to an unasked question. His fingers closed over the coin. "Another shoe emergency?"

"Ha." My fake laugh caught in my throat. "No." Unable to take the weight of his gaze any longer, I motioned at Ryann. "Could I speak to you privately?"

She nodded. "Gerald, see if the poison was endemic to this Ohrist or if it was applied topically before Laurent engaged with him."

I grabbed his arm. *"You were poisoned?!"*

"Had a bit of a situation." A predatory current thrummed

through the smile that didn't reach Laurent's eyes and I stepped back. Did he think I'd blown him off?

"Did you see a healer?"

Laurent grunted something vaguely affirmative and returned his attention to Gerald.

Men. I followed Ryann into the hallway.

"What's up?" She leaned against the bamboo walkway railing, threading her fingers into a row of fringe on her tie-dyed skirt.

"I've been hired to help Eli find Teresa Wong."

"Who's Teresa Wong?" Her guileless expression didn't change, but her fingers tightened momentarily in the fringe.

"Ryann." I looked at her sternly.

She shook her head slowly. "I have no idea what you're talking about."

I frowned. "Your dad—"

"Is with the Vancouver Police Department and is completely autonomous from the Lonestars," she said firmly. "I'm sorry if a Sapien citizen has gone missing, but it's out of my jurisdiction. I can't help you." She clapped a hand on my shoulder. "Now I have to get back in there."

She spun with a whirl of color into the morgue.

I narrowed my eyes. Her brush-off was too pointed. I scanned the hallway for cameras, and while I couldn't see any, it never hurt to be paranoid.

I pulled out my phone and sent a text. *You wanted me on this case, didn't you? If you're planning on using Eli and me to suss out another suspected corrupt Lonestar, I'll make your life a living hell.*

Ryann: *I wouldn't do that.*

Me: *incredulous emoji face*

Ryann: *That's not what's happening.*

Three more dots appeared and then disappeared. I tapped my foot impatiently until another message popped up.

Ryann: *These games have been running for decades. Lonestars around the world conferred back when it first hit our radar and decided*

69

it wasn't a threat to the prime directive because no one would believe these Sapiens. It was deemed that population's problem.

Me: *Lovely. Let the ones who don't know a problem exists deal with it. How do we find a portal into this game city?*

Ryann: *No idea. Sorry. What little information we have points to there being more than one person behind these games. A powerful Consortium operating from the shadows. Be careful.*

There were no further dots. Freaking fabulous. I gave her points for caring enough to covertly arrange for Eli and me to investigate this, while being smart enough to keep her hands clean, but this problem had been on the Lonestars' radar for some time now. Their decision to make it the Sapiens' problem smacked of political agenda and cowardice. Now it was mine to fix with no more of a jumping-off point than "Hey, there's a shadowy organization, don't die."

I debated three responses before letting Ryann have the last word. Getting bitchy with her wouldn't change anything.

Glancing back at the door, I tightened my hold on my phone not wanting to leave Laurent while there was this weird vibe between us, but Blood Alley beckoned, and only a fool kept Zev BatKian waiting.

The master vampire received me in his office. There was no hiding the faint smudges of purple under his eyes on his pale marble skin, though he was otherwise impeccably groomed, the picture of power and control.

A fat stack of receipts sat on his desk, the top one bearing a red question mark. BatKian punched numbers into his accounting calculator, comparing the tally to the slip of paper. "Well?"

It was bizarre to see him doing something so mundane as bookkeeping. I figured his role was to menace and destroy priceless works of art with the occasional piece of furniture to mix things up.

I perched on the edge of the chair across his desk, my purse in my lap. "I found the Banim Shovavim who hired Tatiana."

The calculator fell silent, but only for a moment. "And?"

He wasn't usually this clipped.

"He's being tormented in the Kefitzat Haderech by the angels." When Zev's eyes flashed like this was useless to him, I hurriedly continued. "But I think he gave me a clue to the Ascendant's location."

Zev always held himself stiffly, so it wasn't until his shoulders sagged a fraction of an inch to normal rigid lines that I realized how tense he was. "Tell me everything he said from the beginning. *Exactly* as he said it."

I started with how Arlo had shown the angels the cracks in the seams to how they'd made him the cracks in the seams, and through to his admonishment to "leave the monsters in the dark" when I claimed to be seeking the Ascendant.

There was a burst of clattering keys, and Zev swore softly before ripping off a long strip of the adding machine tape. Why had angel prejudice about Banim Shovavim flustered him?

"Where is it now?" he said.

"He gave me a quote, and I think it's the key to the location. 'The fault, dear Brutus, is not in our stars, but in ourselves, that we are underlings.'"

The torn-off strip of paper curled in on itself, and I looked away politely from one of the very large sum totals. But seriously, how loaded was he?

"Shakespeare." Zev frowned. "I've heard it before in context of a place."

"You have?" I gripped my purse in anticipation. "Where?"

"I'll look into it further."

"Maybe if you tell me what's going on, I can help—"

"There is nothing 'going on' as you put it." There was a faint growl under his polite words, and I backed off. He took a breath and moderated his tone. "You have done well. Continue to amass any information you can."

And didn't that feel like a brush-off? My suspicion that he had more intel on this device than he'd let on crystalized into a hard certainty that he knew precisely what it did and it wasn't just a random amplification of magic. What, exactly, did he want it for?

My brooding was cut short by Eli texting to ask if I'd spoken to Tatiana. He'd gotten Deputy Chief Constable Esposito's green light to go into the game. Right. My other job.

"I may not be around for a few days," I said, giving him a bare synopsis of the Human Race.

Zev didn't show any flicker of recognition about the game, nor did he seem at all interested. "As I said, I'll look into the quote."

I raised an eyebrow.

No word of warning about testing his patience by making something else my priority? Was he going after the amplifier without me? This artifact had caused such misery in my life that I wasn't sure I wanted anything to do with it, and yet, I felt entitled to answers.

However, I couldn't hang around snooping after Zev.

Summarily dismissed, I headed back to my car, texting Tatiana's address to Eli with the message to meet me there. Ryann had been a bust, Nav didn't know anything about the Human Race, and Zev either didn't know or didn't care.

Tatiana was our last hope to find Teresa. I shook my head. Negative thinking wouldn't get me anywhere.

Visualize a goal: *I crashed the Human Race and all I got was this crummy T-shirt.* Much better.

8

EMMETT, DRESSED IN A SKY-BLUE BALL GOWN WITH cream piping, let me in to Tatiana's mansion. He clutched the fabric of one shoulder because his back was too broad to do up the zipper.

"Did I miss a party?" I said.

"Marjorie was teaching me to waltz, and Tatiana said I could choose appropriate attire from her costume closet." He jutted his chin up as if daring me to comment.

Tatiana's assistant Marjorie had a reciprocated crush on Emmett. They were incredibly sweet in their fumbling way.

"You look very fetching."

He tossed his head back. "I know. Eli's up in the studio."

Ooh, the artist's inner sanctum. I rubbed my hands in glee, bouncing up the final flight of stairs in time to the Tony Bennett music playing.

I let out a soft "ooh" at my first glimpse of the workspace, which took up the entire top floor.

An antique desk was placed to maximize the light from the row of huge picture windows. Corkboards hung on two of the walls, crowded with scribbled notes, magazine clippings, color swatches, and invites to dozens of art openings, some faded with age. A jungle's worth of plants crawled over one wall, infusing the room with both an earthy scent and a tinge of orange, while a tiny water feature on a low table cascaded a small, soothing stream that was recycled up a length of bamboo and back into the basin.

Paint drips led from the front office area to the studio proper, which was the explosion of art and supplies that I expected. Canvases stacked six deep were all turned to the wall. Brushes spilled out of tiny cubbies in a custom-made wall rack, while paints and other supplies crowded the stainless-steel counter to the sink and were stuffed haphazardly in repurposed wardrobes that were works of art themselves.

With the windows open, I didn't smell the turpentine I expected, just a faint trace of linseed oil.

Tatiana perched on a high stool, her frail frame dwarfed by an enormous blank canvas set up on an easel next to her. She wore the old-timey oversized painter's smock that I'd seen her in before paired with bright green leggings that matched the polish on her bare feet.

She held a magnifying glass up to one eye, examining the side of Eli's bald head.

He shot me a pleading look, receiving a sharp swat on his back from the elderly artist. "Don't move," she said.

I stepped forward to rescue him, but Emmett hauled me back with a finger to his lips.

Tatiana tilted Eli's head in all different directions, her enormous eye behind the magnifying glass blinking owlishly.

Frowning, she hopped lithely off the stool and exchanged the magnifying glass for a digital camera. She snapped about seventeen pictures of his left ear then squinted at the screen on the back. "Feh. This is completely unusable. I had high hopes for your cranium, Eli. I'm very disappointed."

"Uh, sorry?" he said, getting away from her as quickly as possible.

"Miri's here," Emmett announced, tidying the brushes in the wall rack.

I threw Tatiana a small wave, but her returning smile made me feel three feet tall.

Tatiana pulled tubes of paint out of one of the wardrobes and tossed them onto the table behind her. "What do you need, kindeleh?"

Eli and I squished onto a vintage lounge sofa, and I told Tatiana about the Human Race, while toying with a decorative tassel on one of the small, fussy cushions.

"They abduct Sapiens globally," I said, "so they have the ability to access it from anywhere, but unless we find a portal in, we're screwed. How do you find a hidden space if you have no clue where an entrance is?"

She turned the easel around, positioning its back to us. "You could take Route 666."

"You mean Route 66?" Eli said.

Tatiana smiled sweetly. "You heard me."

The knot I'd just made in the fringe was as hard as the one in my stomach. "Do we have to fiddle against the devil at some crossroads?"

"Like I'd send you somewhere requiring musical ability," she said.

Emmett laughed and I shot him the finger.

"You didn't discount a devil," Eli said.

"Don't be melodramatic," Tatiana said. "Although...no one knows how Route 666 works to get you where you want to go, just that it does." The artist uncapped the first tube, squirting paint onto a palette. "I suspect dark magic."

Was it more disturbing that she'd dropped that bombshell in a completely conversational tone of voice or that other than my stomachache growing worse, I accepted that fact and carried on, instead of running and screaming like a sane person would?

"You're so screwed." Emmett blew some dust off the end of a brush.

Eli folded his arms. "What's the catch of using this route?"

Tatiana added two more blobs of color onto the thin board. "It has a ninety-nine percent fatality rate among riders. But desperate times."

"Not that desperate," I protested.

"How do the one percent survive?" Eli said.

"Extreme wealth." She dipped her blunt palette knife in the bright orange, then at our deafening silence, peered around the canvas. "Oh. You mean the passengers."

Eli shot me an "is she for real?" look.

"People who own villas think differently," I said. "Assuming you have a foolproof way for us to use this route, what do we travel in? A car? The back of a dragon?" I snapped my fingers. "Do we get comfy on a unicorn's horn?"

"You've got a weird idea of comfort, toots." Emmett pulled a bottled green smoothie out of a bar fridge that was buried under a jumble of charcoal pencils and dog-eared notebooks.

"I was being sarcastic," I said, my jaw tight.

"It's a train car. Pod." Tatiana scraped her knife against the palette. "It's safe, but the trouble is boarding it. There are things that live in the gap between the platform and the rails that snatch hopeful commuters down."

"Get real," Eli said. "Even with magic strength it couldn't pull me through a gap. My limbs would break off."

"Thank you for that charming visual," I said.

Tatiana grabbed the smoothie and took a long slurp of green sludge. "I never said you would be whole when they did it." She held up the bottle in cheers.

Ew. I shuddered. "What if I cloak us? Odds are the monsters won't see us or hear our heartbeats."

"Oh no." Eli shook his head. "Do you remember Vegas?"

"For the five hundredth time, I was drunk. The odds *are* in our favor on this."

"Even if you're correct," Tatiana said, "if you're cloaked, the pod won't stop. It has to see you." She shoved the half-empty bottle back at Emmett.

"Good luck." The golem flashed me a thumbs-up.

"That's why you're going with them," she said.

"Wait—what?!" He shook his head, capping the bottle and putting it on the table. "No way, lady."

"You've been kvetching all week about how bored you are. It'll do you good to get out."

Eli eyed the golem speculatively.

"Stop looking at me like that!" Emmett covered his crotch and chest with his hands. "I'm not bait, asshole."

"You don't have a heartbeat, tattele," Tatiana said. "The Morph won't register you."

"Oh good," I said faintly. "The monsters have a name."

"An arch supervillain one," Eli muttered in a disgusted voice. "Is that a collective moniker or singular?"

Tatiana shrugged.

Emmett stomped his foot, causing the ball gown to fall off one broad red shoulder. "No heartbeat. That's all I ever hear. Doesn't anyone want me for my mind?"

I glared at a conspicuously silent Tatiana and Eli. "I want you to come because you're a good partner to have in a tough situation."

"I don't know. It sounds like we'll be MacGyvering it," Emmett said, sounding torn between dismay and admiration.

"He's right," I said. "You want us to trust a plan modeled on a TV character's love of duct tape, paper clips, and gum."

"Never underestimate duct tape," Tatiana said. "Besides, many world-changing ideas seemed whack-a-doodle when first proposed. Edison was mocked for the light bulb, the Wright brothers' flight was dismissed as an interesting scientific toy, and the first man to use an umbrella in England in the 1700s had trash and insults thrown at him."

"Yeah?" Emmett said. "What'd you call him?"

Tatiana flicked paint at the golem. "As for you, Miriam, have a little faith."

"I'd rather have a less lethal mode of transport," I said. "Nav didn't mention Route 666 as a possibility, so had he not heard of it?" I shook my head. "I doubt that given the demonic name. That means he thought it was a dead—"

"Phrasing," Eli murmured.

"Futile endeavor," I amended. "If getting on board could be achieved with a golem and my cloaking, Nav would have said as much."

Death had gone from a quiet lurker at the fringes of my awareness to that annoying roommate who never left, even when it was clear you were watching TV with your boyfriend and their presence was unwanted. Okay, yes, I was still touchy about Caroline, but this was about us safely getting to the Human Race.

Tatiana swished her brush against the canvas. "Most people who use it don't have my insider knowledge of its perils and that includes Naveen. Between your cloaking and Emmett's lack of a heartbeat, your odds of success are significantly higher. It'll still be tricky, but I'm not sending you on a suicide mission. I wouldn't do that."

No, she wouldn't. Now was the time to tell her about my parents' role in her accident. That part wouldn't violate my oath to Zev. I opened my mouth as a shaft of light fell upon the elderly artist.

She was humming under her breath, a small smile teasing up her lips as she painted.

I slumped back against the cushions.

"Mir." Eli nudged me. "What do you think?"

I stared at him blankly.

"Route 666?"

"Oh." I scratched my chin. "Despite Tatiana's confidence in our chances, taking this route means risking both of our kid's parents."

Eli acknowledged that but pointed out that it was the fastest way in, our options were limited, and the clock was ticking. He deemed it an acceptable risk given our combined experience, my magic, and the heat he'd be packing.

Emmett remained doubtful, but when Tatiana said we didn't have a hope of succeeding without him, he reluctantly agreed.

Before I cast my vote, I attempted to access the game using the KH, on the slim chance that it wasn't in a hidden space. Not only did I get a stern glower from the neon sign face, I also felt like I'd slammed into the outside of a massive bouncy castle, so that was out.

"Okay," I said, once more in Tatiana's studio. "We'll go in your way."

Once my boss gave us the entrance to access Route 666, we arranged for Emmett to come over with Jude later.

Tatiana stopped me for a moment before I left. "I don't like to talk about my upbringing much because part of me still feels disloyal for running away from my parents and their religious beliefs. That said?" She handed me a folder bulging with envelopes. "These are the letters I wrote my mother over the years from Paris."

They'd been returned unopened.

"I wasn't going to include them in my memoirs, but even though I didn't lose my parents in the same way you did, it still impacted me for the rest of my life." She picked up the top envelope, her lips pressed into a firm line, then dropped the letter. "Anyway, if you think there's something that helps sell my memoirs better, you can use it." She grabbed her paintbrush and attacked the canvas with renewed energy, her spine ramrod straight.

I pressed the folder to my chest as if it could soak up the

loss and regret I felt for her—for us? "Thank you," I said softly.

She paused and gave me the faintest nod.

Eli popped back into the studio. "Let's get going. We've only got three days left in this game to save Teresa."

I gave one last look at Tatiana's frail figure dwarfed by that enormous canvas, yet standing strong as always, a stubborn tilt to her chin, then headed home.

I kept Sadie with me while I dumped a change of clothes into a backpack along with some pouches of water and nonperishable food stolen out of the earthquake kit.

Eli was bringing a first aid kit and we were leaving our phones at home in case they could be tracked.

At the last minute, I tossed in a roll of duct tape. My cousin Goldie agreed with Tatiana on its versatility, using it for everything from making shoe soles less slippery to getting rid of warts.

It didn't take long to get the small pack ready, then Sadie and I curled up against my headboard, our legs stretched out on the mattress.

She lay her head on my shoulder and I stroked her hair.

"Are you sure you'll be okay?" I said. Sadie had been part of the decision about Eli and I working together, but she hadn't signed up for anything like what this mission had turned into.

"No, but yes. I want you to go find her." She wrapped her arms around my biceps, just like when she'd been little and hadn't wanted me to leave.

I swallowed a lump in my throat.

Eli joined us soon after. He stretched out on his back along the foot of the bed and Sadie plopped her feet on his belly. We didn't speak but we were all connected.

Were we really going to bid our child farewell and hie off on this dangerous undercover mission? I reassured myself that Eli and I were both smart, weapon-bearing, and incentivized to get home safely to Sadie. We'd find Teresa, and all of us would make it out alive. That wasn't hubris talking, it was confidence.

I bet Arlo Garcia had thought the same thing about the angels.

Jude and Emmett arrived on time, which was far too early for me. Eli and I put on our hiking boots and hefted the packs, while Jude rested her small suitcase against the wall.

Emmett wore the black sweats he now favored for covert missions and a pair of runners that Tatiana must have bought him. He carried a black garbage bag and the black cane topped with a silver dragon that Nav had gifted the golem when he'd temporarily been missing a leg.

Eli blinked at him. "Are those clothes mine?"

"Actually," Sadie said, "they're mine. You gave them to me."

Emmett gave himself a once-over. "They look better on me."

Jude bundled me in a fierce hug. "You can't die."

"I love you too."

"Not that." She pushed me away and tilted up her chin to reveal two thick black hairs. "Anything happens to me and it's on you to take care of these buggers."

I gave a watery laugh and she winked.

While Eli bid Jude goodbye, I took Sadie's hands. She seemed so young in her pale pink sweatpants and a T-shirt with a sparkly donut on it, her long dark hair in braids.

"I love you more than anything," I said.

"I love you more than you love me."

"That's impossible and ridiculous and impossible and ridiculous," I said loftily.

Sadie grinned at our old schtick. "Here." She dug in her

pocket and pulled out her favorite pair of purple amethyst earrings. Goldie had sent them to her for her sixteenth birthday, saying that amethyst brought good luck. She handed one to me and one to her dad. "Bring them back safe and sound."

Eli closed his fist around his. "We will."

I put mine in one of my ears. "Promise."

Sadie nodded, then she pushed me out the open door, exactly like she did on the first day of preschool. "Go."

And just like at preschool, I didn't let myself look back.

9

THE ENTRANCE TO ROUTE 666 WAS LOCATED INSIDE an underground tunnel for a still-active train line outside Vancouver. We went from walking single file, holding on to each other's shoulders in the near dark, to stepping through to the hidden space: a small wooden platform bathed in bright sunlight. There was a foot-high drop to the rail line, which stretched out endlessly in either direction.

"Doesn't look like much." Emmett broke free of the cloaking I'd laid over the three of us and peered over the edge of the platform, poking his cane into the gravel around the train line.

I hauled him away from the edge. No point taunting the Morph before we had to, not that any monsters were visible. Maybe there was just one and it was busy elsewhere? I sighed. A woman could dream.

Emmett pointed the cane at a distant shimmery black speck. "What's that?"

The rail hummed, glowing, and the speck resolved into an egg-shaped obsidian pod without wheels, yet it made the classic *chuga chuga* sound.

A whistle screeched through the silence and smoke

belched from this odd train. It got close enough so I could make out glowing crimson markings like barbed wire wrapped around the pod.

Even though the pod was still in the distance, the track glowed so brightly that the air above it rippled, and I had to squint to protect my eyes from the heat and the gravel flying through the air.

A hand with the same coloring and markings as the pod wormed its way out of the ground. There wasn't any arm, just a disembodied hand about the size of André the Giant's, with bony fingers, swollen knuckles, and ragged nails.

I jumped back, visions of Thing from the Addams Family dancing in my head. Correction, Thing was a lovely, cleanly severed hand. This was Thing's horror movie cousin, ending in a sawed off, stumpy mass of scars.

"Fuuuuck." Emmett's eyes widened, and brandishing his cane, he clutched his garbage bag to his chest. He was going to put someone's eye out with that dragon head.

Willing the pod to speed up didn't make it so. It seemed as frustratingly far off as ever.

I searched for the way back out but there was no exit. We'd have to fight it out.

A second hand shot up, raining gravel onto the ground. It landed like a jumping spider next to its twin, and all ten fingers drummed against the edge of the platform.

Shadows swirled up my body, manifesting into my scythe. Great. Whatever this was had a demonic origin.

Eli and I crammed more tightly together under the invisibility mesh, standing next to Emmett.

Come on, you stupid pod. I touched Sadie's earring that I wore for luck.

Eli placed his hand on the gun in his holster.

The pod had about a hundred feet to the platform, but it wasn't slowing down.

The hands clattered closer in an upbeat skipping motion,

and with my heart knocking against my ribs, I white-knuckled my weapon, waiting for the perfect moment to reveal myself and take the Morph out.

Next to me, Eli unholstered his firearm, silently sliding it free.

Breathe, Miriam. It can't penetrate my magic and see us.

How was there still a good fifty feet until the pod reached us? Was it moving in some demonic molasses-slow time?

A dry finger scraped across the skin between my jeans and hiking boot.

Yelping, I lost control of the cloaking, which fell apart, and jumped sideways. All of us were now visible but if we spread out, it would be harder for the Morph to grab the whole team.

If it had only two hands, that was. I readjusted my grip, really wishing I could unthink the possibility of more hands buried in the gravel, waiting to spring free.

The right hand skittered forward, and Eli shot the boards in front of it, right as I slammed my scythe into the wood.

Both hands retreated to the edge of the platform, but I sensed it waiting.

I wiped my sweaty hands off on my jeans, keeping my weapon manifested.

Another twenty feet to the pod's arrival. The wind picked up, whipping my hair into my face. Whirlwinds of dirt and gravel made it even harder to see, the platform rattling with the force of the pod's approach.

Its *chuga* sound made my teeth rattle.

I braced myself—

All sound cut out, the air cleared, and the pod hovered in front of us. A door opened upward.

The good news? The small transport was empty and well-lit.

The bad news? We had to step over the hands to board.

"All right, kids. I got this." Emmett reached into his bag

and dropped his voice to a whisper. "It wants a body part to grab, so we'll give it one. When I say go, haul ass."

Emmett pulled out a clay leg and slammed it down between the hands. They seized it with grabby fingers whereupon the golem flung the leg sideways. "Go!"

I never jumped so far or so high in my life. I stuck the landing and scrambled to the side so Eli wouldn't get hurt by my scythe.

The platform shook causing Emmett to stumble to his knees, and an eerie moan pierced me from head to toe. The extra clay leg turned to mist, which hung in the air for a second before being sucked down through the gap.

"Hurry!" I reached out for the golem but snatched my arm inside the pod as the hands whipped back toward us and grabbed Emmett's ankles.

The golem jabbed at the Morph's hands with his cane, successfully dislodging the left one, which disappeared. "Help!" He beat at the monster's right hand.

Eli lowered his gun, shaking his head. "I'll hit Emmett."

"Incoming!" I jammed the point of the scythe into the meaty part of the hand like I was shish-kebabbing it.

The Morph let out a piercing howl and rocked the pod almost onto its side, while the hand flew into the air, along with my scythe. I made the weapon vanish, and the hand splatted to the platform.

Emmett leapt into the pod, landing on Eli, who grunted. Luckily, he'd holstered his gun so no one was injured.

The pod righted itself and the door disappeared, the three of us slumping on the floor in a heap.

"Destination." A voice growled over the furious pounding from outside where the Morph's fists were denting the exterior.

I shrieked, ducking away from a battery of punches that crumpled part of the wall where I'd been sitting.

"The Human Race!" Emmett yelled.

The Morph struck the pod again and a seam splintered.

One bony finger wormed its way inside.

Eli slammed the barrel of his gun against it, while I screamed for the pod to move, and Emmett banged his cane against the walls.

A second finger curled inside the tear.

Time hung suspended for a moment, and then the hand blew off the pod.

Eli crouched underneath the hole, his gun aimed at it. "We're moving," he said.

I didn't feel any motion but took his word for it and, spent, claimed one of the benches. "Where did the leg come from and why did you think to bring it?" I curled my knees into my chest.

"It was Tatiana's idea." Emmett sank heavily onto the bench across from me.

"What?" I exchanged a confused look with Eli. "The whole reason she sent you was because your lack of a heartbeat was supposed to get us on safely. If she didn't think that would happen, why not give us the leg and spare you the journey?"

The golem tossed the wrinkled and torn garbage bag on the floor. "You're forgetting Tatiana's motto, toots. Expect the worst, plan for the worst. I was the solution only if the Morph didn't detect you under the cloaking. If it did, then we needed a body part that wasn't ours to distract it. And even if all went to plan, I had to be visible while you stayed hidden so the pod would stop, which meant I had to come. Lucky me," he groused.

Eli rubbed his temples.

"I guess," I said.

The sky glimpsed through the small hole in the pod changed to a toxic waste palette best suited to movies about the apocalypse, with an accompanying soundtrack of wails.

Duct tape to the rescue. I sealed that puppy right up. Even

so, we covered our mouths and noses, not like that was any real protection.

I was strung tight, those ghastly moans an unholy melody set to the percussion of the pod chugging along the track. Never had I been so happy not to have a window.

When silence finally reigned, I lowered my arm from my face. "We survived the first gatekeeper together."

"Team Feldman-Chu for the win." Eli nodded at Emmett. "You got a last name?"

"Nah. I'm a one-name golem. Like Cher. Or Beyoncé."

"Well, we're a team and we'll have each other's backs no matter what," I insisted, just as the pod came to a gentle stop, and the door unlatched with a soft hiss.

Eli cautiously poked his head out. "I think we're clear. There's no gap."

The pod was flush with the platform, and though I was nervous when I clambered out, we exited without an ambush.

The pod sealed back up, the transport continued on its way, and I let out a breath. We were safe.

Eli nodded at the red door floating at the back of the platform. "Who wants to do the honors?"

Emmett and I exchanged nervous glances. The last time we'd been on a mission together and someone had charged blindly through a door, they'd ended up flambéed.

We played rock paper scissors to see who'd go first through the freaky door with no wall or structure attached. Even if it actually led to our destination, what kind of welcoming committee would we face?

I hadn't been paying attention and wasn't surprised to find that I'd lost. Great, I loved to be the first through creepy doors. I cracked it open, but with my eyes adjusted for the bright light out here, I couldn't make out anything except a vast darkness. Sending Delilah through with her green vision didn't help me see any better, but she didn't trigger a motion sensor or booby trap.

88

I squared my shoulders and took a deep breath. "Showtime."

Once inside, the door behind us vanished with an ominous clang, but I comforted myself with the fact that the pitch black had eased into a depressing gloom.

Eli was already inching forward, taking point, his gun aimed.

"Aw, maaaan." Emmett covered and uncovered his eyes, but it didn't change the fact that we stood in a graveyard, riddled with cracked tombstones and freshly overturned graves.

I clamped my lips shut tight, trying not to gag at the bloated female corpse with bloody foam leaking from her mouth and nose. Covering my nose with my arm did nothing against the stench of rotting meat with notes of a sickening sweetness like cheap perfume. I grabbed a small bottle of hand sanitizer from an outside pocket of my backpack and practically huffed the antiseptic odor, wishing I didn't know that dead person particles had gone up my nose and that's why I'd smelled her.

The woman was close to my age. She'd made it only a few feet beyond the large bright block letters painted on the ground like a starting line. *Can you survive the Human Race?* It read like a taunt.

The deceased wasn't Teresa Wong, but it was a hollow win. She was still a human who'd remain forever lost to her loved ones.

The full ramifications of Ian being the sole survivor of his game hit me with a wave of nausea. It was one thing to talk about a game where people died and quite another to find their grisly remains. Plus, there was no respect for the dead. These people didn't even get the decency of a proper burial.

Congealed blood from the woman's slashed throat stained the dirt, her flesh bruised. Her lean runner's frame and muscular biceps were evidence of her athleticism. Maybe

89

she'd been a triathlete, burning off energy from her corporate job? She'd been kidnapped in her work clothes, a now-shredded cream skirt and jacket with the number three pinned to one sleeve.

One of her stilettos was broken, lying on its side at the start of a blood trail that disappeared into the distance. How much had her inappropriate wardrobe contributed to her immediate demise? If she'd been taken while jogging, would she still be alive?

Hoping she'd managed to inflict some awful injury on the monster that had done this to her, I gently pried a tear on her bloody silk shirt open, feeling for an implanted tracker. Sure enough, something dime-sized and hard was lodged under the skin in the same place that Ian's had been before his was removed.

Shadows slithered over me as I imagined myself one of the players, my breath sounding too loud in a tight, dark hiding hole, praying I was safe for the moment, and ignorant of the fact that hiding was an impossibility.

Magic flared off my body like black fireworks.

Gritting my teeth, I forced it down. This woman had met a pointless, indignant end with no one to mourn her. I closed her lids, saying the first few lines of the Jewish Mourner's Kaddish.

Yitgadal v'yitkadash sh'mei raba b'alma di v'ra chir'utei; v'yam-lich malchutei b'hayeichon u-v'yomeichon, uv'hayei d'chol beit yisrael, ba-agala u-vi-z'man kariv, v'imru amen.

"Mir?" Eli beckoned me over.

Moonlight filtered through spiny branches of naked spindly trees that dotted the cemetery, illuminating glowing ground fog. If there was a ceiling to this false reality, it wasn't visible.

Light slanted down on a wrought-iron fence with spiky finials, but it was too far off to see between the gaps to what lay beyond. Behind me was the wall that had contained the entrance, and to either side, all fell away to impenetrable night.

The lighting was a cue to the players. Head for the fence.

Other than the "Welcome" on the ground there was no evident signage. This was a race, a competition. Ian had said they were given instructions, but I didn't see any speakers for announcements.

I joined my team, avoiding the one other fallen abductee who'd been player eleven.

Eli had holstered his gun, surveying the cemetery with a frown, while the golem poked his cane into one of two piles of ash, looking faintly nauseated.

"I hate vamps," Emmett said.

"You think that all these graves contained vampires?" Eli toed at some overturned dirt. "Because that's a hell of a greeting committee."

Emmett wandered off.

"Don't go far," I said.

"Just looking at the grave markers." The golem bent over to read one.

"Ian said there were also shifters. I don't know if they were here in the graveyard." I scrubbed my hands over my face like could I wash my sorrow and disgust away, leaving only cold logic. "Some of this must have been for show. Think about it. Twelve Sapiens in shock from their kidnapping blink into a cemetery and have their perception filters ripped away with an onslaught of vampires and shifters?" I shook my head. "They'd have been sitting ducks. We'd have a pile of corpses, not just the two."

"Their production design is crap." Emmett returned. "The tombstones don't say anything. They look like they have writing, but it's just an abstract design. And why start a race in a cemetery? Talk about a bummer."

"He's got a point," Eli said. "This entire game world is designed, which means everything has a purpose."

"Maybe the purpose of the graveyard was specifically to break the players' perception filter." I glanced over my shoulder at the woman by the start line. "Could be why there aren't more dead. Just pick off a few to scare the others," I said bitterly.

"That makes sense in terms of the purpose," Eli said. "However, if the people behind this game took the human race to literally mean humanity and our journey, then I'd expect a graveyard to be the last stop."

"Ian said the race took place in a city," I said. "Could they have switched up the design since he played?"

Eli frowned. "Wouldn't that require a lot of magic?"

"Big-time, but probably still less than the cost of setting up this place initially," I said. "First things first, let's get out of here and look around." I adjusted the straps on my small backpack.

Eli gave one last searching glance around, his gaze resting briefly on each of the deceased Sapiens. He pulled a tiny notebook and golf pencil from his pocket and jotted down the numbers of the fallen players. "Two down, ten to find," he said grimly and headed off.

Emmett trailed behind us, whacking everything within cane reach: gravestones, dirt, patchy grass, and trees.

"Why leave the bodies?" I matched my strides to Eli's longer ones. "It can't be that they're short-staffed and only clean up between games."

He sidestepped some rubble. "It's a good psychological deterrent if anyone thinks to hide out here. A way to clear the rest of the players out and keep them moving. We weren't greeted by anyone or anything."

"We don't have trackers and we're not expected," I said.

"True." Eli tensed at a sudden cracking sound, but it was just Emmett stepping on a twig. "In a lot of video games, if you go back to an area you've already played, there's nothing there. That could be baked into the design of this place and

92

explain why there's no sound here. Did you notice? There's nothing, no birds, no mice. They might not waste magic to fully enhance an environment when no one's there."

"They'd have to create animal life in the first place. There weren't flies or maggots on the body I examined either." Grateful as I was for that, it was still chilling and sad having these people decay in this soundless fake world. "Conserving magic makes sense, but why not just find some deserted island out of cell range? Why bother with a hidden space at all?"

"Lots of reasons," Eli said. "Chief among them, weather and time of day." He gestured to the night sky. "Not too hot, not too cold, good vampire conditions. I'm sure those elements are all controllable here. Then there's the risk of discovery. If Ian is right and there is a city up ahead, it had to have been built. More threat of exposure if it's being done in the open, even on a supposedly deserted island. If I were the game designers, I wouldn't want to gamble on the place showing up on Google Earth."

He fell silent after that, and other than Emmett, who kept banging the stupid cane, there was only our breathing and footfalls.

In the end, that near silence was what saved us. I'd never have heard the faint whisper of wind and rustling from a nearby grave otherwise since it all happened so fast. But something alerted me. Maybe it was just a sound or a shift in the light. Maybe it was just luck. Or maybe it really was magic, guarding me when my back was turned.

10

THE VAMPIRE DIDN'T STAND A CHANCE. DELILAH swung the scythe in a cleanly decapitating arc, and the undead woman's head flew past me, a half-smoked cigarette hanging from her lips before she exploded in a puff of ash.

Emmett blinked once, then twice at the dusty pile. "Nope," he said cheerily and pulled out a hip flask.

"Don't you dare." I slid into Delilah's night vision view, sending my shadow scouting in a wide circle. "You know better than to drink when it could send you into a prophecy state."

"But—"

Eli clapped the golem on the shoulder. "You need your wits about you, bud, because we're depending on your fighting abilities."

Emmett puffed up and stuffed the flask back in the pocket. "You can count on me."

Eli winked at me over his shoulder, and I smothered a smile because we'd fallen into an old parenting dynamic where I pointed out the danger and Eli appealed to their sense of pride. My ex squatted down by the grave, running a hand along the ground. "You think that vampire was spying on us?"

"Given the cigarette?" I wrinkled my nose. "She probably heard us while she was on her smoke break."

"Right," Eli said. "Probably came to hang out somewhere quiet between shifts. It's an important reminder for all of us that this may feel like a video game, but the dangers aren't relegated to scripted coding. We need to watch out for off-duty villains."

Delilah floated back to my side, curling around me until she was a nonsentient shadow once more. No point wasting energy this early on, especially when we had no idea how long it would take to make our way through the entire game.

We reached the fence without further incident, and Emmett pushed the creaky gate open.

My heart sunk. A painfully long suspension bridge hung over a chasm whose bottom was obscured by swirling mists. We couldn't go back, and we couldn't see past the wall of fog on the other end of the bridge to determine what new danger we'd be walking into.

I moaned, which turned to a whimper when Emmett ran gleefully onto the bridge and jumped up and down, making it sway and buckle. I buried my face in Eli's shirt. "You're going to have to carry me."

"Nope. Not doing that ever again," he said. "You can hold the rope railing and keep your eyes closed. I'll guide you."

"Then make the Energizer Bunny there quit it."

Emmett skipped back and forth along one stretch, whooping.

Rope and wooden slats attached to posts at either end were exciting in jungle adventure movies, but this was a magic space. There was no need for a bridge at all unless the Powers That Be *wanted* us to die on it. My logic was impeccable.

Eli whistled to get the golem's attention and motioned him over. "Miriam is terrified of these bridges."

Mr. Milk of Human Kindness burst out laughing, prodding me with his cane. "Is the wittle baby scared of a bwidge?"

I snatched the damn cane away. "If you don't want to play a very painful round of 'Where did Miriam shove this?' you'll zip it."

"That's not even a real game," the golem grumbled and grabbed it back.

"Take her pack." Eli helped the golem put it on, then led me onto the bridge.

It wobbled underfoot, and I sucked in a breath, tightly closing my eyes.

"Nails," Eli said in a terse voice.

I loosened my grip on him, increasing it proportionately on the rope, and let Eli escort me across.

"Take larger steps," Emmett said. "I'm growing old here."

I barely heard him over the thumping of my heart. My mouth was dry, my palms sweaty.

We inched along, my hands aching from rope burn, when suddenly the bridge bounced.

"Emmett," I snapped, my lids still screwed tightly shut. "Pull that shit one more time and you're going over the side."

There was a pause. Emmett cleared his throat. "Uh, toots, I don't know how to break it to you, but that wasn't me."

A loud, hoarse rumble like a saw rasping through wood shattered the unnatural silence.

I flinched and ducked like it had been gunfire, my eyes snapping open.

A leopard stalked toward us from the far end of the bridge, its pale blue eyes glinting. Had I seen it on a nature documentary, I'd have proclaimed its fluid prowl magnificent. Now I clenched my bladder as tightly as the rope.

The animal roared again, the sound shivering up my spine

a fraction of a second ahead of the goosebumps I got when it cracked its powerful jaws.

Eli pulled his gun and fired twice. He hit the beast in the shoulder but missed its foreleg. Crimson blossomed against the rosette-patterned fur, but the animal barely stumbled, intent on getting to us.

Falling had dropped to second place on my list of fears so I manifested my scythe and let go of the rope. I'd like to say that I ran at the leopard, weapon aloft like a knight of yore, but I shuffled forward, hacking at the shifter. "Shoo!"

A low growl rent the air, a blood- and mud-splattered wolf stalking us from behind. His steel-gray claws extended from massive paws, tapping against the boards like a clock counting down seconds. He was easily two hundred pounds, and his filthy fur bristled over rippled muscles. The beast flared his nostrils and swung his large, blunt muzzle. He curled his lips to bare incisors sharp enough to slice through his prey like butter.

A tiny sigh escaped me; I was rooted to the spot in wonder.

Emmett cowered behind his hands. "Why am I such a tasty little succulent? I'm too young to die."

Three things happened in rapid succession: the leopard broke into a run, Eli fired his gun at it again, and the wolf roared in fury, shaking the wooden slats.

"Cloak us!" Eli cried.

I was too stunned to disobey. As the mesh locked down around our trio, a furry torso flew overhead.

The wolf bowled right into the leopard, the two locked in a vicious grapple as the bridge swayed.

I stifled a scream. I couldn't draw attention to us, but this bridge wasn't built to handle this much weight. If we fell...

Emmett's flask flew out of his pocket and he lunged for it, but it sailed over the side into the void. The golem whimpered.

97

Eli dropped into shooter stance, his legs planted firmly on the bouncing slats.

"Don't fire! The wolf could have easily gotten the jump on us but he didn't. He's defending us." In my urgency to stop Eli, I rushed my words, the sentences coming out in a fast, sharp burst. "It's Laurent."

The beast assaulted the leopard in a flurry of bites, but the feline sank its fangs into its attacker's neck, using its claws to drive the wolf off the bridge.

"That's not possible." Eli narrowed his eyes. "No, that wolf is simply taking out his own enemy."

"I know when it's him." Releasing the rope, I dropped our cloaking and stepped closer to the fight, but Emmett hauled me backward.

"Are you crazy, exposing us like that?" Emmett hissed.

The wolf's back paws slipped off the edge of the bridge, and Eli raised his weapon because he now had a clear line of sight to the leopard, but if he hit that animal, Laurent would be knocked over the side.

I smacked Eli's elbow away, the bullet going wide and the sound startling the two animals.

The wolf sank his teeth into the leopard's flank, using the weight of the other animal to drag himself back onto the bridge, but the feline swiped along the wolf's torso and got free.

It leapt up as if to attack from above, but the wolf reared onto his hind legs, six feet of lethal predator, and tore into the feline's underbelly. Blood cascaded over the dirty white fur.

"Fuck me," Emmett exhaled.

Eli lined up another shot.

"Stop it!" I cried, wrenching Eli's arm down. "You'll hit him."

The wolf shook the leopard then slammed the animal to the bridge with such force that it broke three slats.

The bridge rolled like a tsunami and we all grabbed the rope.

The leopard tumbled down into the void with a weak cry, but the wolf was safe. His flanks heaved, flecks of blood and saliva dotting his snout.

Emmett scooted behind Eli, while I took a few cautious steps toward the panting beast, my hands up.

Eli hissed at me to get back, but I kept my steady pace forward, my eyes locked on his familiar emerald ones, which now burned with rage.

"Laurent," I said.

He growled, then spun away, racing to the far end of the bridge.

A gunshot rent the air and I screamed, flinching in anticipation of the wolf's body crumpling.

He leapt off the bridge and disappeared into the fog on the far side.

I spun around, my chest heaving.

Eli lowered the gun, which had been pointed at the sky.

"Even if it's Laurent," Emmett said, "how is he here unless he's part of the game?"

"He's not," I snapped, headed in the direction that the wolf shifter had gone.

"Mir." When I didn't stop, Eli pushed in front of me, his gun once more holstered. "Emmett's got a point. How would Laurent have known about this game or gotten here if he wasn't a part of it?"

"Tatiana," I said. "She's recruited him before."

"Then how did he survive the Morph without a golem?" Emmett demanded. "The wolf is suspicious. I've always said—"

"Shut. Up." I held up a hand. "It was Laurent and he's not part of this. Not like you think."

"I'll concede that you're right about his identity," Eli said.

"How big of you."

99

"Then why did he run off?" Eli readjusted his pack on his shoulders. "I know you want to give him the benefit of the doubt, but will you please keep an open mind that you might be biased where he's concerned?"

"It's not bias. It's experience. He's got our backs."

Between the shock of Laurent's appearance, the fight, and my team's suspicions, I'd forgotten to be frightened about the suspension bridge, so good thing the universe decided to remind me.

The damned thing sharply dropped a foot. I fell half into the hole made by the leopard, scrambling back on my ass.

Emmett stepped on my leg in his race to jump the gap and run to safety.

"Ow!" I yelled.

Eli helped me up as the bridge slackened under our feet.

"Hurry!" the golem cried. "The ropes are loosening."

Holding hands tightly, Eli and I hauled butt. The bridge was sinking lower and lower; another couple unwinds of the rope and it would dangle free.

Eli grabbed me and flung me hard. I tumbled through the air, landing on my back on the grassy bank next to the backpack that Emmett had carried for me, the wind knocked out of me.

Emmett was on his belly, hanging over the edge.

I crawled on all fours to peer over the side and gasped.

The golem's cane was extended, and Eli clutched the end with the bridge hanging slackly a good three feet beneath his feet.

I dropped down beside Emmett, stretching my arm out as far as I could. "Give me your other hand."

Eli looked up at me, fear clouding his brown eyes. "I can't swing up that high." His hand slid downward off the cane and he slammed his other on top of it.

The golem grunted, straining to keep hold of the silver dragon's head on his end of the cane.

"Okay," I said with a steadiness I didn't feel. "Just hang on." I grabbed the cane under Emmett's double-handed grip, and the two of us pulled as hard as we could.

The rope broke with a loud snap. The bridge crashed against the side we'd come from and shattered.

I yelped. We were going to lose him.

Eli's pack weighed him down and sweat rolled into his eyes.

My heart hammered inside my chest, but he gritted his teeth as inch by inch we pulled him up, and the three of us collapsed on the grass, safe.

For now.

11

AFTER CAREFULLY CHECKING OURSELVES FOR injury, Eli and I topped up with water and power bars before tackling the fog that led to the next part of the game. The mood between the three of us had shifted. While there was no more joking around, a bond had solidified.

I touched the amethyst earring, sending Sadie thanks for the good luck.

Until we found Laurent, however, our team wouldn't be complete. I didn't know how he'd survived the Morph, but it also wouldn't surprise me if he'd found a different way in. My only question was why he hadn't stuck around? Even if he was mad about our presence here, that was nothing new. He was always annoyed with me when I was in danger. Besides, if Tatiana had sent him, then he was aware this wasn't exactly a walk in the park.

There'd been that moment when we'd seen each other at Lonestar HQ when it had seemed like he knew about my parents' role in Tatiana's car crash. Was his anger now confirmation of that?

"Ready to go?" Eli swung his pack on.

"Yeah." I tightened the straps of my own backpack,

adjusting them from Emmett's larger frame. "I'll cloak us through the fog."

"You sure you're up to it?" Eli said.

"I'll expend less energy on that than confronting something that jumps out to kill us."

"Good point," Emmett said.

Once we were hidden, I released Delilah before it would be too dark to do so in the fog, because her green night vision made it possible for me to navigate.

I stumbled over the uneven terrain, my body aching.

The fog had a sickly-sweet smell like it came from a fog machine, which was entirely possible. Why waste magic when technology accomplished the same thing? We were in there only a couple of minutes tops before the fog glowed. Dimly at first, then brighter as the mist grew thinner.

"This is even creepier than the graveyard," Emmett said when we cleared the fog. "It's not a city either."

All the houses on this cul-de-sac were identical, about the size of a double-wide trailer with an attached carport and a large picture window along the front wall. They alternated between pale yellow, pale blue, and white, each with a stubby palm tree on the front left corner of the lot.

"It looks like the retirement community in Florida that my cousin Goldie lives in," I said.

Multiple streetlights buzzed, but as with the cemetery, there were no mosquitos or birds.

"We've gone from death to retirement." Eli headed for the only house with lights visible through filmy curtains. "Let's see if anyone's in there. If so, we push through our fatigue and get as far away as possible."

It was comical how we crept inside, clearing each room like TV cops, because we were still cloaked and Emmett kept trying to lead, knocking Eli into walls.

Eli finally pushed him to the back of our line, and we

finished our sweep, which admittedly didn't take long. There was no furniture and no personal items.

No, what we found was much more interesting.

I dropped my cloaking in the kitchen beside the large table containing two small daypacks numbered three and eleven—the deceased players we'd found at the cemetery.

The vinyl blue packs contained water, protein bars, a switchblade, a box of matches, and slender lengths of rope. I dumped my canvas bag on the table, motioning for Eli's as well, then distributed the new items between us.

"These game people are smart," Emmett said. Off our incredulous looks, he expounded. "They're total psychos too, but think about it. You guys were talking before about how if this race was the journey humans take, then it should have started with birth, not death. But birth isn't something people remember, so it's hard for it to be scary. Death is. It might be part of how they broke the perception filter."

Eli flicked a light switch, but it didn't move, and the lights didn't turn off. "That's a good theory. Psychologically, running this backward makes a twisted kind of sense. They've survived death and crossed the metaphoric bridge back to the land of the living."

"Where they're rewarded with food, shelter, and a weapon." I nodded. "They're given hope. Good job, buddy."

Emmett preened and tapped his head. "I'm more than a pretty face."

"Let's set up camp in one of the darker homes on this street," Eli said.

"It'll make it harder for Laurent to find us," I said sullenly.

"Good." Emmett shrugged at my hard stare.

Eli shouldered his pack. "If Laurent was sent to protect us, then why wasn't he waiting for us here? This place is a beacon that we'd be drawn to."

"I don't know," I said tightly, "but I'm sure he has his reasons. Maybe he's undercover. You just don't like him because he insulted your precious hockey when you two first met."

Eli opened his mouth, then shut it, and shook his head. "Let's just find somewhere to rest."

I was too tired to fight. With all the new weight, my pack was bulging, adding further strain to my back, and I was minutes away from collapsing.

We let Emmett play one potato, two potato with the houses on the street to choose our destination. His final selection landed on the white house on the corner.

Thank goodness. There were two things on my to-do list: use the first aid kit and sleep. Yawning so loudly my jaw cracked, I followed Eli to the front door.

He depressed the handle, which stuck, though there was a click. The same thing happened on the second try. Frowning, Eli jiggled it. "Third time's the—" The latch clicked. "Chaaarrrr—"

Emmett bowled us over, sending us flying toward the carport.

The house exploded, the blast wave flinging us onto the next lawn.

A black cloud shot up from the decimated home as debris rained down.

My ears were ringing and my eyes stung, but somehow, I got to my feet and ran after Eli and Emmett.

We fled the cul-de-sac onto a straight road that seemed to traverse the complex.

The ground rumbled and my pulse spiked. I braced myself for another explosion, but the road shifted, reforming into a new cul-de-sac, its dead end directly in front of us.

I threw down my pack and bent over with my hands on my thighs. This new dead end had sapped my momentary adrenaline rush and every ounce of energy. I'd faced death a few times since I'd reclaimed my magic but not repeatedly in a short period of time. "I don't care if I die. I need to sleep."

There was no longer a road leading out of here, and we couldn't untangle this maze unless we mentally and physically restored our bodies so we could keep going.

Emmett pulled a nail from the back of his shoulder with a curse. "Seconding the sleep."

Eli wiped soot from his eyes. "We've got to keep moving. I agree we need to rest, but…" He sighed at our pleading looks. "Let's case the homes here as best we can for a safe one."

I shuffled along behind him.

Eli walked the perimeter of a yellow home, then jogged up the stairs, examined the handle, and felt along the door frame. "How did you know the house back there was rigged?"

"Haven't you ever watched an action movie, dude?" Emmett said. "If the car doesn't start right away, if it clicks? Leave it and get the hell out."

"I can't decide if I'm more upset that your action movie trivia saved us or that I didn't think of it myself." He lay a hand against the door as if reading it for bad intentions.

"Totally the second," the golem said, swaggering. "So much for your wolf hero, toots."

"Don't be a dick." I tugged him along with me over to the next lawn. "He saved us once."

"No." Eli jumped down the stairs, having decided against the yellow house. "He acted in a way that happened to align with our best interests. That doesn't make him trustworthy. Even if he is undercover, which I don't buy, that doesn't mean he's here on our behalf."

I trudged up the front walk. "Then trust me enough to believe that I'm not an idiot. He's always had my back. He's one of the good guys."

There was a cheery honk behind us. I turned, blinking at the incongruous sight of Laurent driving an old golf cart with room for four.

Eli was as delighted with this reveal as when his dentist

had come back with X-rays showing he needed two root canals, but I waved, my smile smug. "Told you he was here to help us."

Eli and Emmett shared a skeptical look.

Laurent pulled up alongside us and glanced over his shoulder at the smoldering remains of the home. "Could you make more noise? There's a demon two dimensions over who didn't hear you."

How much of our conversation had he been privy to with his wolf hearing? His expression gave away nothing.

I scanned the shifter for injury, from the crown of his head, along his black Henley and dark jeans, down to his motorcycle boots, but he seemed unharmed.

"Shotgun!" The golem got one leg into the front passenger side, next to the small day pack tossed there, and emitted a weak laugh at the shifter's fierce glower.

Laurent jabbed the golem in the chest. "Back. Seat."

"You're not supposed to play favorites," Emmett said, grumpily getting into the back. "It's not good for morale."

"Heeeey, Huff 'n' Puff." I fired finger guns at Laurent as I clambered in next to him. "Sweet ride. Where'd you get it?"

Eli rolled his eyes as he climbed in next to the golem.

"I took it from one of the workers. They use them to get around." Laurent hit the gas pedal and off we puttered.

"How'd you figure that out?" Emmett said. "Insider knowledge?"

Laurent's jaw tightened. "Yeah. I got it from inside his brain before I tore his head off."

"Touchy," Emmett muttered.

I craned around, checking for vamps, shifters, or more exploding houses. "Does this thing go any faster?"

The road rumbled and buckled.

"No." Laurent jerked the wheel, bumping us over the curb onto a lawn.

"What are you doing?" I held on to one of the poles supporting the hard canopy.

The street shifted to snap into place with the stretch of straight road once more ahead of us.

"If we stick to the main streets, we'll be stuck here forever." Laurent steered us between two homes and onto another cul-de-sac. "The trick is to keep sight of that road but not directly travel on it."

Eli leaned forward, his notebook and pencil in hand. "Have you seen any contestants?"

"Alive?" Laurent shook his head.

"Was it a young woman of Chinese heritage?"

"No. A man, likely of Middle Eastern descent."

Eli relaxed. Teresa could still be alive. "Did you see a race number on him?"

"Six, I think."

Eli's pencil scritched as he jotted down notes.

"What got him?" I said.

Laurent gripped the wheel more tightly. "Another player."

"Why do you think that?" Eli said.

"There were fibers on the man's throat. Vamps and shifters wouldn't strangle someone, and if they did, they wouldn't need a rope."

"There can only be one winner," I said. "Though you'd think they'd wait longer to start offing each other. It would make more sense to work together and then..." I shook my head, unable to voice the awful thought, imagining being terrified and bonding with these other people to survive, only to know that at some point they'd be gunning for you.

Tatiana's face flashed in my mind, but I swiftly shook it off.

"That's so shitty," Emmett said.

"Yeah." Laurent paused. "Guess these people weren't a team."

"Guess not." I pressed my hand against my chest, trying

to slow my heartbeat. He didn't necessarily mean the two of us.

"How *are* you here?" Eli said.

"Tatiana." Laurent didn't elaborate.

"I, for one, am glad you made it safely and we're all together," I said firmly.

Eli gave a vague murmur of assent. Really vague.

"Can you survive the Human Race?" The pleasant female voice asked the question over an unseen speaker system, cutting off any response Laurent might have made.

Goosebumps puckered my arms. "Do they know we're here?"

Laurent shook his head. "It's to freak out the players."

"More insider information?" Emmett said.

"Yeah."

We reached the last cul-de-sac and the straight road to our left disappeared into another wall of fog.

Laurent pulled into the carport of a blue house and cut the engine, but he headed for the yellow home next door.

I followed, slinging my pack over one shoulder, excited to finally rest. *I'd blow someone for a hot shower.*

"Throwing people off our scent?" Eli said. "Clever."

"We're dealing with vampires and shifters," Laurent said grimly. "There is no throwing them off our scent unless we all stay cloaked the entire time. I'm just putting the cart back where I found it."

"Did you find the worker inside that other place?" I said.

Laurent's lips quirked up for the first time since he'd arrived. "Yes." He grabbed the latch, which stuck, then heaved his shoulder into the door as Eli, Emmett, and I ran the other way.

Obviously, I should have saved him, but I'd been reduced to fear, adrenaline, and self-preservation. It was every person for themselves.

Laurent turned, the door open and the house intact, and peered at the three of us. "Are you coming in?"

"How did you know it wasn't rigged to explode?" Emmett asked suspiciously as we trooped up to the door.

"I didn't," Laurent replied mildly.

"I hate you," Emmett said.

The look Eli shot me made it clear he wasn't too fond of the wolf shifter either.

Once inside, we spread out on the floor. Enough light filtered in through the thin curtain to make do, which was good because there weren't any lamps or overhead light fixtures.

I pulled off my shoes with a heartfelt sigh. My feet stank but since everyone else's did as well, I wasn't self-conscious about it. I carefully peeled off my socks, hissing at the raw blisters on three toes and the backs of my heels.

Eli tossed me the small first aid kit from his pack.

Finding the Polysporin, I liberally doused the blisters before bandaging them. I wriggled my toes in relief and helped myself to a couple of painkillers, which I washed down with some tepid water. I followed it up with a strip of beef jerky, savoring the vaguely cow-flavored shoe leather like it was filet mignon in a butter herb sauce.

By the time I felt human enough to take stock of the room and see how the others were doing, Laurent was nowhere to be seen.

"Where'd he go?"

Emmett shrugged but Eli pointed to the kitchen.

Laurent wasn't there either, but the back door was ajar. He lay on the grass, bathed in fake moonlight, staring up at the night sky. It shouldn't have been beautiful and yet it caressed him in a silvery radiance. People kissed by sunshine had an easily visible allure. But those touched by moonlight were the ones you had to brave the shadows to view at their most brilliant.

I folded myself cross-legged onto the cool grass, pulling out blades. "Thank you for saving us from the leopard shifter. Were you badly hurt?"

He shrugged and I sighed in disappointment at his automatic brush-off. "Right," I said. "You're fine."

"Actually," he said quietly. He rolled one shoulder back. "I pulled some muscles down my right side. Shifting helped heal it but I'm still stiff."

I kept my amazement from my expression. "Is there anything I can do to help?"

"No, but thanks." He studied me for a moment. "I didn't know about this game until Tatiana told me."

I frowned. "I didn't think you had."

"No. You wouldn't." He said it in a voice that was half pensive, half wondrous.

The silence stretched out, growing awkward. We'd slipped off our familiar conversation path into unknown territory, but if I could only find my words, I'd make my way back. Several times I opened and closed my mouth, but instead of speaking, my lawn shredding got more intense. The pile of loose grass in front of me grew.

Having successfully created a bald patch of dirt, I brushed off my hands. "How much did Tatiana tell you about the case?" There. Back on common ground.

"Find Teresa Wong, save anyone left alive, track and stop the organizers."

"Should we compare findings so far?"

It was like a switch had been thrown in the face of my simple question, flipping us from an uncomfortable silence to a dangerous one.

Laurent propped himself on his elbow, lying on his side and facing me. His eyes glinted. "Should I go first?"

I ran a finger through my grass pile, scattering it and feeling like there was a one hundred percent pass or fail rate attached to my answer.

Zev was adamant no one learn about the Ascendant. I didn't care if he withdrew his protection against whomever else tried to use *me* to find the magic amplifier if I blabbed, but the vampire had an all-access pass to my home. To my daughter.

And honestly? Right now I wasn't certain Laurent would keep the secret even if I asked him to.

I looked away. "Why don't I start?"

Laurent snorted and flopped onto his back once more.

I curled my hands into fists, wanting so badly to touch him and reestablish our connection. Instead, I closed my eyes against the memory of him being inside me, his admission—much as he could voice—of what I meant to him.

I cleared my throat and summed up Eli's hypothesis that the Sapiens were chosen for their abilities much like video game avatars, then explained how starting in the graveyard was a means to break the perception filter. Having survived death, the players were given hope as they crossed the bridge to life where they were rewarded with food and supplies.

Even in the most extreme reality show competition, rewards were expected after passing crazy tests, but here, even something as simple as food was suspect. Everything had strings and a hidden agenda, and not even as pure an emotion as hope was exempt.

"They start the race literally facing their own deaths." Laurent folded his hands behind his head. "Those who survive the cemetery end up here. They're given a survival pack, but they need to find their way out." He nodded. "Yeah. I buy that."

Footsteps sounded behind us, but Laurent didn't tense up, so I didn't either.

"Just me," Eli said, forgetting that Laurent would have scented him already. He joined us on the lawn, his legs splayed out. "What else did your interrogation turn up?"

Laurent sat up. "Are you disapproving of my tactics, Detective Chu?"

"Nope. You have my full support to do whatever it takes to get the most information in the least amount of time."

"I'm delighted you approve," Laurent said wryly. "Well, this game occurs once a year."

"Giving them time to scout for the appropriate Sapiens," Eli said. "Go on."

"All nonplayers are either vampires or shifters. They remain in-game the entire week, following the abductees."

"I was right then," Eli said. "It's like a video game where once you've cleared a level and you go back, it's essentially empty. That's why we haven't really seen anyone. I bet they assign people to patrol, looking for players who are trying to hide or not going fast enough."

"I agree," Laurent said. "That's how I found the shifter in the first place. He was stationed in this section, but this isn't like a first-person shooter game where players are constantly attacked. Sapiens couldn't survive a continual onslaught so the organizers pick their moments."

"They vary the types of trials they face." I leaned back on my elbows. "Like this section with the shifting roads. Not knowing what to expect keeps them on edge."

"Don't forget the booby traps." Eli scribbled notes in his book.

"Those feel secondary." I smothered a yawn, forcing myself to stay awake long enough to finish this conversation. "Not every house here is rigged. Odds are—"

"We talked about you and odds." Eli grinned at me.

Laurent frowned then smoothed out his expression, pulling up blades of grass like I had.

"Say I'm a player," I said. "I survive the cemetery, grab a pack, and keep going, thereby avoiding the exploding house. I have to contend with the street rearranging itself otherwise

I'm lost." I gnawed on my thumbnail. "Lost in a retirement community. Makes me think of dementia."

"It's fight or flight," Laurent said thoughtfully. "The tests could be stage-of-life dependent, but why put people through this? Why break the perception filter at all? For kicks?"

"Money? A secret game would attract high rollers wanting to bet on it," I said. "Couple that with thrill of watching the hunt."

"People are sick." Laurent swiped his hand through the lawn detritus he'd created. "What do the players get if they win?"

Eli shook a pebble out of his boot and winged it against the house. "Fuck all."

"They're promised immortality," I said, "which is why I assumed vamps were involved, but the one survivor we spoke to hadn't been turned."

"We don't know if every game is offered the same prize. Another reason to find the Sapiens in this one." Eli stood and offered me his hand. "We need to get some sleep and then push hard."

Laurent didn't move.

"Are you coming?" I said, accepting the help to get up.

"Go rest. I'll keep watch." Laurent's expression softened slightly when I stayed put. "Go sleep, Miriam. You'll need it for whatever's coming."

Uncertain whether he was speaking about the game or some reckoning between us, I almost sat down again and blurted out that I was sorry for keeping secrets and I'd tell him everything as soon as I could.

Laurent pushed to his feet, his gaze on me, almost like he was willing me to speak, but it was just wishful thinking because when I took a deep breath, he'd already loped off to do a perimeter check.

I stood there until he disappeared, wondering if there had indeed been a test, and whether I'd passed or failed.

12

ACCORDING TO MY OLD ANALOG WATCH, WE'D BEEN up until 4AM Vancouver time before falling asleep. We crashed for a whopping six hours, before we were woken up by that same ethereal female voice asking if we could survive the Human Race.

My head felt fuzzy and stuffed with cotton, my limbs were heavy, and worst of all? There was no caffeine to guzzle thus psyching myself into feeling awake. No, wait. The worst was having to squat outside behind a bush to pee.

It was now Friday morning; the game would end Sunday. It couldn't come soon enough, and yet it didn't feel like enough time to save whoever was left.

Eli was pissed off that we hadn't yet found a single living player, snapping at all of us to hurry and hit the road. Emmett was as grumpy as a toddler who hadn't had a long enough nap, and my feet were still swollen and throbbing when I stuffed them back into my boots. We were a delightful bunch.

Only Laurent, now shifted to wolf form, seemed rested, which was ironic given he hadn't slept at all. Emmett had been given his small pack, which the golem hung by its straps off his cane, carrying it all like a hobo's bundle.

We walked in single file under the perpetual night sky with Eli in the front and Laurent bringing up the rear. The road out of the retirement complex was a steep switchback, darkness pressing in from either side. Had I not been with Huff 'n' Puff, it would have been terrifying.

I kept my eyes on the ground, so tired that I didn't trust my feet to work without visual confirmation, aware of Laurent prowling behind me. I missed him prodding me in the back with his heavy muzzle like he usually did and our weird human/wolf conversations, but the things we had to discuss required us both in human form.

There was, however, another topic I wanted to talk through with someone, so I quickened my pace, moving ahead of Emmett, who was singing loudly off-key to himself, and falling into step with Eli.

"We're on another connecting section," I said, gesturing around us. "Like the bridge and fog earlier. I'm sensing a trend."

"Another good place for an ambush," Eli retorted. He was twitchy, his hand on his gun.

"Laurent's got wolf smell and hearing," I said. "Nothing will get the jump on us."

Eli dropped his hand to his side.

"Something's bothering me," I said, low enough that Emmett wouldn't hear us over his mangling of Aerosmith's "Dream On."

"Only one thing?" Eli shook his head. "You're doing better than I am."

"Between her art career and being a fixer for the magic community, Tatiana rubs elbows with some pretty powerful people—Sapiens and Ohrists—but she'd never heard of this game?"

"You think she lied?"

I shook my head. "Tatiana wouldn't have let you go poking into it if she was involved in any way." I felt so guilty over keeping the secret of the Ascendant and the true nature of her car accident from her that I couldn't come out and directly voice what I was thinking.

"Ah, but if she wanted information about the game that she could use to her advantage?"

I sighed. "Yeah. That's what I've been wondering. Three ways that Tatiana could profit somehow from the details of the game. Go."

"Blackmailing people for their involvement, getting to bet on the game herself." He pursed his lips, thinking. "We've assumed that people are betting on this game, which means this Consortium is making bank. What if Tatiana wants to join that secret club?"

"She does love her filthy lucre. The third reason seems more likely than the second. As for blackmail?" I resettled the weight of my pack. "That only works with the threat of exposure. The Lonestars have written it off as a Sapien problem, not that Tatiana would get into bed with the magic cops. She also wouldn't go running to the Sapiens, even if she was believed, because she'd be violating the prime directive."

"Either we're back to joining the Consortium or she doesn't have a hidden agenda," Eli said. "She just subcontracted you for a hefty fee."

It was the option I'd wanted to hear, that Tatiana didn't always have an ulterior motive, but I was glad to have someone else who I trusted agree with me.

"I wonder if Tatiana suspects there's more going on here than moneymaking." I twirled a finger around. "You and I agree it would take a lot of magic to create it. This place covers more physical territory than Blood Alley, and we haven't even seen it all yet. There's a specificity to all this that we're missing. I feel like I'm looking at a puzzle through a window hazy with condensation. If I could just get a clear look at it, I'd understand what I'm seeing."

Eli kicked a rock out of his way. "One step at a time."

We walked for so long that my blisters got blisters and my shoulders burned from the pack. After zigzagging around another corner, we were confronted with the glow of office towers in a downtown core about a half mile away.

Emmett and Laurent caught up with Eli and me, the four of us in a line.

"Lions and tigers and bears, oh my," Emmett said.

I slugged him. "Are you trying to get us eaten?"

"Come on." The golem spread his hands wide. "It's like Dorothy and her friends seeing the Emerald City in the distance. There's even four of us." He pointed at himself. "I'm Dorothy, Eli's the Tin Man, and you're the Scarecrow."

"I'm not sure which of us got the better end of that," Eli said.

"That makes you…" The golem turned to Laurent with a look of unholy glee. "The Cowardly Lion."

The wolf growled at him.

I clamped my lips together willing myself not to laugh.

"You're the only one with fur," Emmett said. "Don't hate me. Hate empirical truth." He patted Laurent on the head and strode off, whistling jauntily.

Eli made a strangled sound and jogged up ahead.

Laurent redirected his snarl at me, a flash of something clouding his eyes.

My amusement died and I reached for him. "Emmett didn't mean—"

The wolf stiffened and swung his head toward the office towers. Then he bolted off, almost knocking Emmett and Eli over as he passed them.

"What's up with him?" Emmett said.

Eli broke into a run, his gun drawn, while I sent Delilah

up ahead to scout while I followed as quickly as I could on wobbly legs. Damn it! I *was* the Scarecrow.

My animated shadow ended up between Eli and Laurent as the wolf veered sharply into the darkness along the side of the road on the outskirts of the city.

Delilah kept pace, but before my brain could process what my shadow was seeing, my palm tingled under the weight of the scythe in her hand.

Adrenaline kicked in, giving me the second necessary to brave the darkness and plunge in after them.

"Wait for me." Emmett was so close behind that he almost knocked into me.

The darkness formed only a foot-deep barrier, and once inside, moonlight clearly illuminated a desolate forest. The dark area between the bridge and the houses had been a blank terrain. I crunched over some pine needles. If those were places they conserved magic, why create these woods?

By the time Emmett and I caught up to the group, Delilah had decapitated one of the vamps and Laurent had dispatched the other, the wolf already racing for Eli, who moved warily from tree to tree.

Eli caught my sleeve, pointing out drips of blood.

The more I followed the trail—a bloody smear against a low-hanging branch, a long splatter along a pile of dried leaves—the more I worried about whether the injured party still lived.

Giving a soft yip, Laurent snagged Eli's pant leg, pinning him in place. Eli nodded and stayed put while Laurent veered right through a gap in the trees.

Eli beckoned me and Emmett over. "Cloak us," he whispered.

Invisible, the three of us carefully made our way after the wolf.

Up in the distance two eagles were dive-bombing the high

branches of a tree, attempting to get close to... I squinted. A small waving ball of fire?

Laurent rose on his hind legs, scrabbling at the tree trunk and growling. The eagles emitted a series of screeching cries, like they were turning things over to the next shift, and flew off.

A female was huddled up high in the branches. Her lit branch became too short to hold on to and she dropped it down to the forest floor.

Laurent scuffed dirt on it to fully extinguish the flame.

I couldn't see the young woman's expression as we crept closer, but her body language suggested she was barely hanging on. Those birds could have easily knocked her out of the tree, but they hadn't. How come? Were they under orders not to kill her or a directive to prolong her suffering as much as possible?

How had the Sapien even gotten up there? The bottom half of the trunk was branch free and it was too wide to put her arms and legs around to climb it, especially if she was injured.

I eyed the eagle shifters flying away.

Was all of this a trap and we'd been detected?

Stepping out from the cloaking, Eli braced his hand against the trunk and looked up. "Teresa? Is that you?"

I recalled my magic.

"How—how do you know my name?" said a tremulous voice.

"My name is Detective Eli Chu. I was sent to find and rescue you. How badly are you injured?"

"You're really here for me?"

"Teresa, I'm Miri. We most definitely came to help you." Trap or not, there was a hurt kid who needed us.

"My ankle hurts and my shoulder is a mess," Teresa said.

I pulled out the length of rope I'd taken from an

unclaimed backpack at the house. "How are you at tying knots?"

"Uh, okay?"

"We'll take that." I held out my hand. "Eli, I need your rope as well. This isn't long enough."

"You got it." He dug it out of his pack for me.

I let him tie them together, since his knots would be stronger, then handed Emmett one end. "Can you toss this up high enough for Teresa to catch?"

The golem looked up, then nodded. "I think so."

"Do it."

It took a few attempts, but Teresa finally called out that she'd caught it.

There was a tense silence as she gripped the rope between her legs and hissed, but she gamely lowered herself down, using her knees and elbows, since her left upper arm was basically useless.

I didn't even realize my fingers were buried in Laurent's fur until Teresa slipped partway down the rope with a cry and he yelped.

"Sorry," I murmured, unclenching a fistful of fur.

He nudged his head back under my hand. Maybe he desired this connection as much as I did.

That's what I told myself anyway.

Eli caught Teresa and gingerly helped her to the ground, taking her weight as much as he could because of her puffy right ankle.

She cradled her injured left arm to her body, holding fast to Eli's hand with her right one.

The petite young woman, number eight, was dirty, the bloodied sleeve of her lightweight hoodie shredded by eagle talons. Her eyes were haunted, sunk into deep purple circles, but there was a determined set to her chin that gave me hope.

What worried me was how fast she was breathing. Her heart rate must have been off the charts.

Turning so only Laurent could see me, I pressed my fingers to my pulse and pointed upward, my eyebrows raised in question.

He nodded.

Eli pulled out the first aid kit while I rinsed her wounds with water. He kept up a steady, soothing murmur, talking Teresa through every step of his first aid triage, reestablishing eye contact when she retreated into shock, and even coaxing a smile out of her.

I'd seen hints of his field medicine and crisis training in action but never to this extent, when it counted so much. I experienced both a thrill of pride that I'd picked such a good man to initially share my life with and be the father of my child and a wistfulness that he and Laurent couldn't see how alike they were.

After a lot of antibiotic cream and a gauze wrapping for her shoulder (secured with handy-dandy duct tape), along with a tensor bandage on her ankle, which thankfully wasn't sprained, Teresa felt well enough to drink a bit and eat a protein bar, sharing information with us.

Between the abductions and the vampires coming out of the graves, the start of the race was a blur. She barely remembered how she got to the houses, but there'd been an older woman, another player, who'd found the survival packs and was ushering all arrivals inside.

Teresa had left with two men, but when she tweaked her ankle during one of the road shifts, they'd left her behind.

"You dodged a bullet," Emmett blurted with his usual lack of tact. "Or a strangling."

Teresa gasped. "Someone's dead?"

Eli and I glowered at the golem for his insensitivity. Even Laurent growled softly at him. Emmett ducked his head.

Eli placed a hand on the woman's shoulder. "It's okay to

feel grief and it's okay to feel scared. Any emotion or none, just shock and numbness right now, is valid. You've been put in an unthinkable situation. There's no playbook for how you're supposed to feel."

She nodded shakily. "Who died? Omar or Shriyan?"

"We'll have to wait until Laurent shifts so he can answer you," Eli said. "He found them."

Laurent gave a soft yip as if in agreement.

Teresa scrubbed a trembling hand over her face. "Okay." She hadn't seen any other humans since, but she'd figured whoever was left had passed her when she'd gone into the woods. "I hoped that if I couldn't see the monsters, they couldn't see me," she said. "And with my ankle, I was already weakened prey, but I found myself here and had to get away."

I urged her to have more water. "Vamps and shifters have enhanced hearing and scent," I said gently. "Sight doesn't matter."

"Awesome. Anyway, then I got lost in the woods." She laughed bitterly. "This place has ruined my favorite musical."

Oh yeah. She was a theater major. She had only a few years on Sadie, and she was also Chinese Canadian. The girls looked nothing alike but still, I busied myself putting the duct tape in my pack and stifling the urge to bundle her into a hug.

"*Into the Woods?*" Eli said.

I blinked in surprise.

"What?" he said. "Like I haven't heard our kid sing that musical five thousand times?"

We exchanged a wistful look. I prayed Sadie hadn't experienced a panic attack because she was so worried about us. I hated having left her, but looking at Teresa, I didn't regret it. Much.

Teresa mustered up a weak smile. "Yeah. That's the one. There's not much more to tell. I heard a wolf." She glanced at Laurent standing guard. "Not that one though, right?"

"No," Eli said. "He's one of the good guys."

Laurent gave him an amused look and then thumped his tail.

Look at that. There was hope for them yet.

"Even if his choice in sports sucks," Eli added.

The wolf growled.

"You couldn't quit while you were ahead?" I said.

Eli chuckled. "What happened after you heard that other wolf?"

"I climbed the tree," Teresa continued. "That's when the eagles showed up and attacked. I hoped that after the graveyard, there wouldn't be more attacks. It would be puzzles or tests, like getting out of that housing complex." She looked down at her lap. "But I guess not." She shook it off. "I managed to fend them off by lighting a small branch and then you all showed up."

That branch wouldn't have held them off. I was more convinced that the eagle shifters weren't supposed to kill her. Not yet, anyway. I craned my neck up to the treetop. "How did you get up there?"

Teresa traced the path with her finger. She'd grabbed a low-hanging branch two trees over, pulling herself up to a higher branch and balancing to the edge where she grabbed a branch on the next tree. She indicated how high she'd climbed and how she'd swung herself across to the tree we'd found her in.

"Holy shit," Emmett said. "You're like Wonder Woman."

"Not quite, but thanks. Never thought parkour would save my life."

Eli didn't mention it was that skill that landed her here and I didn't either. She'd dealt with enough.

"Uh, not to be rude, but what are you?" Teresa asked Emmett.

"Golem," he replied. "Super rare. I'm like the unicorn of the supernatural world."

"Jesus," Eli muttered.

"Okay?" Teresa's brows scrunched together. "It's Friday, right?" Off our confirmation, her gaze went vacant. "Two days to get to the playground and I don't know how much farther there is to go. We should be off."

"It ends at a playground?" Eli helped her to her feet.

"That's what they said at the starting line." She tested her weight, hissing as she took a couple of tentative steps.

"Here." Emmett gave her his cane. "Use this."

Look at him sharing. My boy was a mensch. I smiled in pride, but quickly lost it because the young woman was still breathing far too shallowly. How long could the human body sustain that level of distress?

My ex picked up Teresa's pack to carry it for her.

She nodded in thanks at them both. "I don't remember hearing about it myself, but a couple of the other players said so back at the houses. They promised the winner immortality, but I just want to make it out alive."

Eli and I exchanged glances. Ian hadn't known about the "prize" until the end.

"Can you survive the Human Race?" The amiable female's voice echoed through the trees.

Fingers crossed that we lasted long enough to find out.

13

WE HID IN AN OFFICE TOWER AT THE EDGE OF THE city while Laurent went ahead to scout since he was the only one who could move safely about in the open.

The building was crudely made, a cookie-cutter steel and black glass tower identical to all the others. There was a working elevator but none of the floors were finished. They were giant open spaces, bare of furniture, and their only distinguishing quality was whether the lights were on.

Emmett stayed with Teresa, while Eli and I went to search the rest of the building. There were no stairs so the hum of the elevator would alert him to anyone incoming.

We were checking the eighteenth floor, but like all the others, it was an open, empty space. While we were the only ones in this building, the dark windows of the neighboring towers were impenetrable.

"They could house an army of vampires and we'd never know," I said.

"I don't think so," Eli said. "This game lasts a week so there has to be off-limits zones where the humans can rest, otherwise none of them would make it out. This Consortium must want a winner because it would be far too easy to just let everyone be slaughtered."

"Inside buildings or houses are out of bounds. That makes sense. The vamps must not be allowed to use compulsion either. Otherwise, they'd have compelled everyone to stand there and be killed." I paused. "That doesn't mean they won't use it on us." I was immune, but the rest of my team wasn't. "Why do you think they're dangling the prize at the start of the game now?" I hit the elevator call button.

"You don't know what it's like to suddenly see magic," Eli said. "Trying to reconcile the impossible with what you're seeing in front of you? The adrenaline, the shock..." He shook his head. "The terror."

I lay my hand on his arm. "I'm sorry. I really tried to make you see magic before Laurent slashed you with his claws."

We stepped inside the car, and I pressed two.

"I'm not saying it to make you feel guilty. My point is that as soon as the perception filter broke, you and Laurent did what you could to defuse the situation and keep me calm." Eli laughed wryly. "As much as you could with the cops beating down the door. But these people were abducted, which is traumatic enough, then they were dumped somewhere unfamiliar and told about a game they're forced to play. It would have sounded crazy, especially the part about immortality."

"I agree. Why do it then?"

"Because the next thing they know there are vampires and shifters after them. At some point, the ones that weren't killed on the spot must have found shelter and food. They had downtime with their thoughts."

"Right, since they're here for a week. Okay, immortality is the carrot to keep going when their reality had been thrown for a loop. Why not promise a huge pile of cash, especially since they stiffed them in the end? Something less outlandish?" I watched the floor numbers descend. "Unless the prize was simply intended as a psychological motivator. What if the point of the game is a sustained terror campaign?"

"It's not just about winning, but having the winner in a specific state of being?" Eli leaned against the elevator wall, his head tipped back. "It makes more sense than anything else right now, though it doesn't help with the why."

His voice was as strained as his neck and shoulders. He'd come home many nights from a crime scene the same way, pushed past the limits of what anyone should have to endure.

"How are you doing?" I said softly.

"I've never been so happy that our daughter has absolutely no athletic ability and is too young to be trained in any other kind of useful survival skill." He rubbed his forehead. "You have no idea how badly I wanted those eagle shifters to get within shooting range."

"Killing is a last resort," I said.

"Because it'll expose us. I know."

"Yes, but not just that. I don't want you to live with something like that on your conscience. I remember the torture you went through the one other time you took a life, and that was in self-defense."

Eli was quiet for a bit. "I'm not sure I'd regret killing anyone working for the game. Does that make me a terrible person?"

"I'm not the right one to ask. Not anymore."

He draped an arm around my shoulder. "I keep questioning whether my foray into magic has made good and evil less black-and-white or more."

"Let me know when you have an answer."

The elevator doors opened and we exited the car.

"Everything quiet here?" I said.

"The wolf's back." Emmett stretched out on the ground with a yawn, using my pack as a pillow. "Went to shift."

I busied myself getting a drink of water, telling myself that my fluttering heart was due to dehydration.

"Good." Eli sat down next to Teresa. "With his intel we'll have a better sense of what to expect out there."

Laurent returned, running his hand through his shaggy chocolate curls, and introduced himself to Teresa. She replied politely enough, but after ascertaining that it was Omar who'd been killed, she shrank closer to Eli, as if Laurent was somehow complicit.

Eli was a great dad, and he'd act as one for Teresa until we got her home to her family, but it hurt to watch Laurent see the young woman's aversion to him just because he was a shifter.

"This downtown core is only about five blocks by five," Laurent said.

Eli looked up from repacking his supplies. "Let me guess. You can't see past it because of fog or darkness or something."

"Actually no. There's a single road out. Flat, empty land on either side. Can't see anything in the distance."

"Why is there so much darkness and empty terrain?" I said.

"Filling in details takes more magic," Laurent said.

"I get that, but the game that Ian played took place in a city. A graveyard, a suburban residential neighborhood, and then a small downtown core. It's a stretch to describe what we've seen so far as a city. I wonder if they changed the layout for some reason?"

"I just hope the playground isn't too far away," Teresa said.

"Did you see anyone or anything else?" Eli unholstered his gun to thoroughly check it over.

"Yes. A cadre of bloodsuckers and shifters patrolling outside of the center towers. There are a bunch of Sapiens holed up inside."

"Sapiens?" Teresa looked to Eli for an explanation.

"Humans without magic, like you and me," Eli said. "We need to hook up with them. Mir?"

I heaved a sigh. "You want me to cloak all of you."

Emmett laughed. "Now you know how I feel."

I toyed with Sadie's amethyst earring. "That's a lot of people. I've never attempted it, especially not when I'm this exhausted."

"You have to," Eli said matter-of-factly. "It's our only way past the bad guys. I'll give you a couple of hours to eat and rest, but then we move out." His expression softened. "If I could take this on, I would, but we're under fire and you're the only one who can get through the trenches."

He was right, and it was part of why I was here at all, but in my fatigue, I wanted to snipe at him. Mom decision: a time-out was in order.

"I need some alone time." I strode to the elevator without waiting for a reply and stabbed the button, grateful that the car was still on this floor.

Laurent slid in right before the door closed.

"Did you hear the alone part?" I hit the top button. "I'm not up to you starting in on me."

"I didn't even see you here. I just came for the elevator ride."

I snorted and crossed my arms like that could protect me from six feet two inches of alpha male. I inhaled his cedar scent, my shoulders slowly unhunching. I could do this. If this section was only five blocks long, I had at most three to get to this other tower. I could hold the cloaking for that long over all of us. Especially if I had a bit of time to recharge.

"We're working on the hypothesis that the immortality prize is a psychological gambit to motivate the players to keep going," I said. "That the game is a terror campaign to produce some kind of result in its players. Any thoughts as to why?"

"Not yet."

When the car opened on the eighteenth floor, I didn't get out.

Laurent didn't say anything, riding back down with me in silence.

I made lists of all the things I'd do when I got home. Hug Sadie. Sleep. Take a hot bath. Hug her again. Eat my weight in cookies. Oh, and steak. Drink the Moscato in my fridge.

"I recognize that look," Laurent said with fond resignation. "You are making a list, oui? What's on it?"

The display showed seven more floors to be alone.

I had to find a loophole in my promise to Zev. I couldn't mention the Ascendant, and I didn't want to lie to Laurent about the artifact at the heart of this tragedy. Not even a lie of omission. Besides, it didn't matter what I called it or whether I claimed to know what Tatiana had been after, the second he mentioned the car crash to his aunt, it would be game over.

The correct thing to do would be to leave Laurent alone until after we could openly discuss everything.

I drank him in: the curls I loved to rake my fingers through, his long dark lashes, the curve of his stubbled jaw, and his strong shoulders and arms. My resolve broke.

Teasingly slow, I rose onto tiptoe, pressing my body against him, my face tilted upward. He had every chance to stop me, but he didn't. Although he held himself stiffly, his eyes were lit up with the green brilliance of the aurora borealis. I swept my lips across his, feeling his small, shuddering sigh.

Laurent skimmed a hand up my side, giving in to our exploratory kiss. It was as soft as the flutter of butterfly wings, but despite its lightness, it had the weight of his full attention behind it. He tasted sweet, this supernova made of stardust candy who was headier than any sugar rush.

I pulled my lips from his, holding on to him by his shirtfront.

"Talk to me," he murmured. He looped a curl behind my ear.

Much as I longed to, I couldn't speak the truth that would change everything. Not until I had a way to do it without breaking my promise.

"It's complicated," I whispered. "Give me time." I turned pleading eyes to his lust-fogged ones.

At my words, they cleared to a razor-sharp gaze, his predatory hunter self instantly in control, and he nodded. "D'accord, but Mitzi? I won't wait long."

By the time the doors were fully open, we stood a sensible distance apart, but this secret was a thick sheet of ice blocking my way back to being the aboveboard friend he deserved.

I treated myself to the chocolate bar stashed in my pack. I'd intended to hold out longer before eating it, but I didn't fall on it like a ravenous animal, which was as good as it got. Plus, I justified carbo loading now for the large magic energy expenditure coming up.

Everyone left me alone, which I appreciated. I didn't sleep, but I managed to quiet my mind with some meditation exercises from the yoga class that Jude and I used to do until I was rested and psyched up.

Even so, when Eli signaled me, I wished for five more minutes.

My stomach in knots, I put on my despised backpack. "Let's do this."

Once we were in the lobby, it took some adjustments to get everyone positioned under the black mesh, hanging on to each other's backs like preschool kids going to the playground.

It was easy enough to avoid the two shifters on patrol, though Teresa gripped the back of my T-shirt so hard, I almost stumbled.

We followed the howls, and we peered around a corner

onto the street where, hopefully, the other humans were holed up.

"Shiiiiiit," Emmett breathed.

What did you call a group of wild beasts and bloodsuckers blockading the entrance with a cacophony of eerie yells, scratching, flapping, hissing, and howling? A shock of supernaturals? A madness of monsters? A doozy of douchebags?

We regarded the congregation with dismay, since they'd notice the front door opening.

Under the mesh, I motioned to the others to creep to the side of the building. Once there, we considered our options. A quick peek showed there weren't any windows along the back, and the glass front door revealed that this tower's interior was identical to the one we'd come from. That meant every floor, including the lobby, was one giant open space.

We couldn't attract attention when we shattered the window. The noise wasn't the problem, the glass was, complicated by the fact that since we couldn't see in through the one-way windows, we couldn't determine where the lights were located. Break the wrong window and we'd be doing so under a spotlight.

I shrugged in question, and Eli rapped on the window that was farthest back with his elbow.

Emmett cracked his knuckles and shoved everyone aside to position himself in front of the glass. He turned to the right. He turned to the left. Took a step closer.

Laurent casually flicked out a claw. "We're waiting."

My magic flickered, revealing our feet. I visualized a giant crochet hook adding length until the black mesh once more swept along the floor.

A bead of sweat slid down my temple.

Emmett stood dead center again, pulled his fist back, and let 'er fly.

I tensed, convinced that the cries would cut out right as the golem struck the glass, just like every time a comment meant for only one person landed in dead silence for all to hear at a party. It had rarely happened to me because I'd been so concerned with blending in that I'd never said anything that could be misconstrued.

Tatiana, surprise, surprise, did it constantly, cackling in glee every time.

While it felt like Emmett took ages, he'd broken and cleared the glass in less than a minute and we carefully scrambled inside the lobby. Our enemies would have heard the glass breaking despite all the noise, but if they didn't see anyone inside and couldn't smell us, hopefully they'd think someone had smashed the glass and run off.

Eli helped Teresa over the threshold. While it wouldn't matter if the bad guys saw her break in, we didn't want them to know she was injured.

I was a puddle of nerves as we crept forward, my eyes darting to find the tiniest hole in the cloak because we were totally exposed on the way to the elevator. Sure, we had a theory that interiors were safe spaces for Sapiens, but even if we were correct, that didn't mean they wouldn't rush the intruders.

The mob out there had sharp eyesight so one pinkie finger sticking out would be as obvious as if we'd set off a flare.

The front half of my magic held strong, but the back half felt like it was crumpling. I ground my teeth together in my efforts to keep my magic intact, but the pressure kept building and building. Any second now, it would get away from me, but unlike an explosive shit, there'd be no relief afterward.

A joyous tear or two slid down my cheek when the elevator doors closed and I dropped the mesh.

Teresa looked at me with wide shining eyes. "What else can you do?"

I flipped my hair off my shoulders. "I have a few more

tricks up my sleeves. Just wait." Ha. Now who was her favorite, Detective Chu?

Eli snorted, knowing exactly what I was thinking.

We found the other Sapiens on the dimly lit sixth floor. Three people provided backup to the woman in her late fifties or early sixties with a no-nonsense expression who barred our way. She was tanned, with pronounced crow's feet, her silver hair scraped back into a short ponytail. A smear of dirt on her gray T-shirt almost covered the number ten she sported. Her elbow was bruised, but she held her switchblade in a confident grip.

"Who are—" The knife fell to the ground, the woman clapping her hand over her mouth with a gasp.

I glanced over, thinking she was overcome by seeing Teresa, but I was wrong.

Laurent stood there wide-eyed, his face drained of all color. "Isla?"

She rushed him, scooping him into a hug and speaking quickly in French.

Eli raised an eyebrow at the two of them and then gave me a look promising we'd discuss this later. He pushed past the reunion to the three others, his notebook and pencil out.

Teresa hobbled behind him, still using Emmett's cane.

Was Isla another family member? Had she been pack? I'd detected a Scottish accent when she spoke English, but that didn't mean she hadn't lived abroad. Would I finally learn more about Laurent's past?

Given how insistently he spoke to her, his dark head bent close to hers, I doubted it.

My desire to make this woman my new best friend warred with a single thought: *What are the odds?*

14

IT HAD TO BE A COINCIDENCE, DIDN'T IT? BECAUSE working out the series of events that had to have happened for Isla to be deliberately placed here to confront Laurent involved a level of mental gymnastics that I couldn't fathom.

"Mir." Eli beckoned me over.

A Black man with a dad bod in an AFC Leopards soccer jersey and some guy with tattoos up his neck and hairy forearms kept to themselves in a far corner.

There were two factions here then: that duo and Laurent's friend leading the other three. Bad blood or just a difference of opinion? Would the two groups first turn on each other before taking out their own or would new alliances be formed before then?

How exciting, I thought wryly. *This place is puzzle heaven.*

Eli introduced Emmett and me to the trio in a clear voice, then said the word "Canada."

I'm not sure if they all understood the word "golem," but they took Emmett in stride.

A brown-skinned woman in cycling shorts and a sweatshirt touched her chest. "Daw. Thai." Player number two, she had powerful thighs and a broad back.

"Daw is a rower." Eli made the motions, so she'd know what he was talking about, and she nodded in confirmation. "She has the same physique as D'Arcy? Remember her from university?"

"Yeah."

The other two were stocky Mateo wearing business casual attire from Costa Rica (number seven), whose arm was in a makeshift sling, and tall pale Felix in a stained button-down shirt from Germany (number four). Neither were athletes. Mateo was an engineer and Felix was a professional chess player, which surprised me.

The Consortium or whomever didn't just choose people for their physical prowess then, but also ones with a high intelligence quotient, able to reason and problem solve better than the average person.

"Mateo was the one who figured out how to escape the shifting streets," Teresa said. "Instead of taking off, he came back to explain it to those of us still picking up our packs at the house."

Mateo smiled. "We are stronger as a team."

"You are," I said. "And now you have us." I raised my voice so the two men in the corner could hear me as well. "We're going to get you out of here alive. All of you. I promise."

A loud crash from outside interrupted any reaction to my vow.

Felix jumped. Daw grabbed the switchblade from inside her bra with a grim look while Mateo stiffened, his good fist up.

All three of them breathed shallowly, their eyes fixated on the elevator, and no one relaxed until it was clear the car wasn't going anywhere.

Eli grabbed the first aid kit out of the pack and set about examining their injuries while the newcomers filled us in.

Mateo spoke in Spanish-accented English, explaining that

player number one, the hairy man in the corner, was Rahm from Israel, and dad bod, number twelve, was Okeyo from Kenya.

He had to pause at this point because Eli had corralled Emmett into helping pop Mateo's dislocated shoulder back into place. Even though I didn't look, the cracking sound and Mateo's cry made my stomach lurch.

Felix took over, saying that the pair kept to themselves. They hadn't caused any problems since they'd joined forces on the way into this section, but they hadn't contributed anything either.

I took notes at top speed.

As forthcoming as the group was, they still huddled close together, barely allowing Eli into their personal space. I kept Emmett and myself farther back.

Eli moved on to Daw, examining the ugly gash on the back of her calf.

"How did you get inside?" I asked since none of the other windows had been broken.

Daw made a hand gesture of an explosion. "Boom."

"Isla had some kind of..." Felix looked to Mateo for the English word.

How would we successfully work together and keep everyone safe if we couldn't communicate? Mateo seemed bilingual, Felix less so. How much did Daw understand? What about the two other men we had yet to speak to? What if we couldn't convey crucial instructions and someone got hurt or killed?

I loosened my grip on the pen and stretched out my cramping hand, ordering myself to take it one problem at a time.

"Little explosive," Mateo said, shaking his head because he hadn't found the right word. "Much light and noise. She works in movies."

"Like a stun grenade," Eli said. He gave Daw an apologetic

smile when the liquid bandage he applied made her hiss from its sting. "I wonder if she has more?"

"A woman who knows her way around a bomb." The golem's eyebrows rose. "Intriguing."

"It drew them away and we got in," Mateo said in approval.

I consulted the notebook. "Including Teresa, we've now accounted for seven of the twelve with three confirmed dead and Shriyan missing." The presumed dead was implied. "Unfortunately, no one knows who the twelfth abductee is, other than it was a Caucasian man."

Eli gave Daw a thumbs-up before examining Felix. "I wish we had names and countries for the deceased and the white guy," Eli said with a bleak shake of his head.

Given how twitchy these three were, I tensed when Mateo asked how we got in, but he accepted Eli's explanation that we'd broken a side window. I didn't want to share the fact of my magic and wished that I'd sworn everyone to secrecy before we'd arrived.

I wasn't worried about my safety, but seeing my magic, or more likely Laurent's, might push these other players over the edge.

My ex proclaimed that Felix was good to go, but gave him an electrolyte pill from the kit.

Isla and Laurent finally joined us, though he trailed behind her in a melancholic fog.

"You've had quite the journey," Isla said. I was right about her being Scottish.

I glanced at Laurent, concerned about his state of mind, but he was caught up in his thoughts.

"Hi." I stuck out my hand to shake. "I'm Miri and this is Emmett and Eli."

"Isla." She had a firm grip.

"How do you know Laurent?" I said, taking the bull by the horns.

"I was married to an old friend of his." Isla didn't offer anything else. She'd either been told not to or was as infuriatingly tight-lipped as the shifter. Also, what did "was married" mean? Divorced? Widowed?

"Henri," Laurent said softly.

My heart dropped into my toes. Not divorced.

"I'm delighted to see you again, lass," Isla said to Teresa. "You cut it close. Anyone not here had two more hours to present themselves then we're off."

I checked my watch. Isla's deadline was Saturday noon Vancouver time.

"How are you getting past the mob?" Teresa said.

Isla rooted around in a pack and triumphantly pulled out a box of Snapz.

"What's that?" Emmett said.

I leaned forward because I didn't know either.

She opened the lid to display a bunch of small paper-wrapped nubs. "Inside the paper is gravel and sand with a tiny explosive. Does feck all in terms of real damage, but they're pure, dead brilliant as noisemakers."

"You just happened to have all this on you?" Eli said. I could have kissed my lovely paranoid baby daddy.

"Aye. I was in London going from our trailer to set with the stun grenade and these darlings to use as practical effects when I was taken."

"You think a bang or two is going to scare them off?" Ah. There was the contemptuous shifter I knew and, well, knew.

"No, but combined with the ropes we'll set on fire, it should buy us a path out the back door. There are less of them there."

"There's a back door?" I poked at the ragged hem on my jeans that I'd snagged climbing in through the broken window. "That would have been good to know."

"There's a parking garage," Mateo said. "We think we'll

have to drive through the gate to get out. No keys of course, but Rahm claims he can hot-wire anything."

The Israeli was a criminal? What a refreshing change from the usual Jewish stereotype. A veritable ambassador showcasing our people's broad potential.

"We rest now," Felix said.

"We're using the seventh floor as our facilities," Isla said. "Should you need them."

Sadly, I did. I returned, in a fresh T-shirt and reeking of hand sanitizer, as squicked out as I was relieved. I was not a camping enthusiast, and peeing on a concrete floor was somehow worse than urinating in nature.

I didn't think I'd be able to sleep around all these strangers, but I passed out within seconds of putting my head on my pack.

As blissful as the respite was, my sleep was light and I was quickly brought back to wakefulness by a squeak near my head.

Rahm picked his way through the sleeping figures over to the elevator, carrying his blue pack.

Laurent's eyes fluttered open sleepily, shut again when the man got into the car, then snapped fully open when the elevator moved. He strode across the floor, watching the numbers.

I joined him.

"He's going down to the parking garage," Laurent said.

"You think he's making a break without us?"

"Merde. We need Isla here to ask if she told him to scout for vehicles."

She wasn't on the floor. Bathroom maybe? Speaking of the woman... "Isla's a Sapien, but she was married to a member of your pack?"

Laurent instantly got that wary look in his eyes, but to my surprise he shook it off. "Yes. Henri. Such a marriage was unusual but not unheard of. He was a carpenter."

I pressed on carefully. "Did he die when you left?"

He hesitated before nodding this time. However, I was positively giddy that he was sharing, finally trusting me with answers.

But I felt totally crappy that I wasn't doing the same.

I ran the heel of my palm across my chest. It was great to learn about his pack, but I wanted to know about Laurent. "Why did you leave?"

He didn't answer me. Sharing time was over.

I'd filled him in pretty thoroughly about almost everything in my life yet he continually refused to answer the smallest thing about himself.

"If you're going to get on my case about things I withhold from you," I snapped, "then lose the attitude when I ask a question once in a blue moon."

"It's not the same," he said.

The elevator had begun its ascent.

"Why not? You're not some international man of mystery with state secrets on the line, Laurent, just another human with a shitty past like a lot of us."

He rubbed his hand over his curls. "What happened to your parents—"

"I'm not talking about my parents, but even then, I told you about their murder instead of giving you the house fire lie I told everyone else. Yet you, *my friend*, haven't shared anything personal. I have to learn it from third parties." The fire inside me was burning me to ash.

"Like the Wise Brothers?" That predatory smile was back, slightly too feral to be civilized.

The elevator stopped on our floor.

I tipped my neck to the side. "If you want to go for the jugular, it's right here. I meant Tatiana and Juliette. If it weren't for them, I wouldn't have learned anything. You didn't even want to share the fact that you had a brother."

Isla exited the car, a crumpled-up shirt and an empty water bottle in her hands. "Laurent doesn't have a brother."

My eyebrows shot into my hairline. Juliette was another honorary family member like Tatiana? Why let me think that her dad, Gabriel, was his actual sibling?

I wasn't about to fight with Laurent in front of Isla, but oh boy, were we coming back to this.

"Did you send Rahm down to the garage to scout cars?" I asked Isla.

"He offered to do it," she said.

"You were always too trusting," Laurent said.

She glanced away before looking back with a wistful smile. "I was, wasn't I?"

Was that a dig about him betraying his pack and walking away? Laurent dropped his gaze and a surge of protectiveness welled up inside me.

Confiding in me wasn't simply about trusting me with his secrets, there was comfort and healing in sharing your sorrow, rather than keeping it bottled up. I knew that all too well.

"Let the past go." Isla patted his cheek in a motherly gesture. "We leave in ten," she said and went to wake the others.

I clamped my lips shut tight against all my questions and crossed my arms.

"Can we finish this discussion once we're out of the game?" Laurent said.

"Depends. Are you actually going to tell me something?"

"I'm not used to sharing," he said.

"So you keep saying, but I don't see you trying to change that. Not when it comes to yourself," I amended. "Yeah, we can table this, but Laurent? I won't wait long."

I should have strutted off in a cloud of self-righteousness, but how could I when I was doing the same thing to him that he was to me? Or was he? My moral high ground was shaky. I was keeping a terrible secret about what my family had done to his family. It wasn't right for me to continue a friendship, never mind be intimate with him, under the false pretense that this history didn't exist.

I sat down against a wall. Did his secret keeping constitute a betrayal? If nothing in his past impacted me or my family in any way, how much right did I have to know about his life before he met me? I wasn't in danger from him; we weren't even dating. Was he simply on a much slower timeline of processing and healing and that's why he couldn't talk about his past?

I'd kept my magic a secret from everyone for almost thirty years instead of allowing them in and letting their love for me help heal the scars of the past. My cousin Goldie, who'd raised me, still didn't know, since I wasn't having this conversation with her long-distance over the phone while she was in Florida, but that needed to be rectified.

Secret keeping and what constituted betrayal was no longer such a black-and-white issue.

Rahm returned, smoking a cigarette. "Found a passenger van. It'll be tight, but we'll fit."

His knuckles were tattooed with Hebrew letters and he wore a thick gold chain. A Jewish bad boy. I bet he was very popular back home with girls wanting to shock their mothers.

He blew out a smoke ring. "The way they're going at the gate, it won't hold long. The garage must not be out of bounds."

Okeyo unearthed a gun from a side holster under his soccer jersey. "No problem."

Everyone except Rahm, Isla, Eli, and Laurent jumped, flinched, yelped, or gasped.

Eli nodded at him. "Finger off the trigger. Pointed away from anything you could unintentionally shoot. You're trained. That your licensed firearm?"

144

"Yes." The Black man's English had a musical lilt. "I'm a politician with a permit to carry. I was at my gun club in Nairobi when I was taken." His eyes dropped to Eli's own weapon. "Hobbyist or professional?"

"Police officer," Eli said. The two men exchanged a mutual respect bro look.

"Where's the van in relation to the elevator down there?" I said.

"Back left corner. Maybe a hundred feet," Rahm said.

"Team up. Those with weapons protect those without. Eli, you cover Teresa and Daw." I gestured what I meant in case Daw hadn't understood, but she nodded. As for our Vancouver player, Teresa wasn't leaving Eli's side. She'd been bonded to him since he treated her wounds. Fair enough, he was her only nonmagic rescuer. Still, Emmett and I had been through the exact same situations as Eli to get to her and it stung. "Okeyo, you've got Mateo and Felix." I motioned for the three men to move together. "Laurent, cover Isla and make some noise."

Laurent shoved his pack at me. "Going to shift." He got in the elevator and closed the doors.

"Shift?" Felix looked around for clarification.

"He's a werewolf," Teresa said. "He's going to do the wolf thing now."

"Oh," the German said faintly. "Right. The wolf thing."

Rahm's eyes narrowed, but when he caught me looking, he guilelessly exhaled a stream of smoke. "I'm good on my own."

"Sure thing." I'd be keeping tabs on him. "Emmett, you're with me."

The elevator opened on a massive white wolf.

Felix and Rahm took steps back, and Teresa tensed. Okeyo's mouth narrowed into a thin line, and his hand curled casually into his belt loops, his firearm within easy reach.

As much as I wanted to scold them for distrusting an ally,

a man who was simply here to help them escape this hell world, I also understood. They'd been chased by people who'd looked just like Laurent, too-intelligent animals with a relentless drive for prey.

We'd have to take it slow.

That being said, herding them into a small elevator with Laurent wasn't exactly easy.

The ride to the parking garage was silent, aside from Emmett's occasional grumbles that he had to carry Laurent's stuff and he wasn't the wolf's mom.

We'd descended to the second floor when once again the female game voice piped up. "Attention intruders. You shall not survive the Human Race," she said pleasantly. Wow. Great coverage. She came through loud and clear no matter where in the game we were. My cell provider could learn a few things from her, though her message lost her points. "Neither will anyone assisting you."

The players turned almost as one to look at us, but before I could find out if we were all still on the same side, the elevator door opened.

The parking garage was dark.

Rahm jerked his chin up. "The lights were knocked out."

On the upside, enough moonlight streamed through the huge hole in the wall so we could see, though there were a lot of shadows. I liked shadows, but not in a hidden space when they couldn't transport me to the KH and all they were good for was hiding monsters.

Case in point, the horde of vamps and shifters streaming through the ripped-off gate and howling for blood.

But hey, I didn't have a lot of time to dwell on it, because that's when I was stabbed in the back.

15

Almost everyone else had scattered, racing for the van, but I blocked Felix, my attacker.

He looked down at the knife on the floor then up at me in puzzlement.

Kicking his weapon out of reach, I lifted my shirt to reveal my high-waisted pants. I'd felt the jab to my kidney, but the blade hadn't penetrated the denim. "Mom jeans for the win, asshole."

Unsexy? Yes. The only clean jeans I'd had? Also yes. Plus, I was kind of hoping these ones would die so I could justify buying a different pair of pants.

Felix bolted.

Emmett thumped the cane that Teresa had returned, a mean smile on his face. "Want me to go after him?"

"No. There was a buddy system and he disregarded it in favor of attempted homicide." I rubbed my bruised kidney and winced. "He's on his own," I said in a harsh voice.

Delilah sprang up from the ground, shadow scythe in hand, and cleaved a vamp's skull in half.

The bloodsucker disintegrated into a pile of ash right

outside the elevator, but there was another one coming in fast.

That gave me an excellent idea.

A single gunshot blast echoed through the garage, and Laurent howled.

Trusting my other team members to take care of themselves, I held still like I was scared.

Closer, that's it. I dug my nails into the side of my thigh, my wide eyes and rapid breathing not entirely an act.

There was a ping of awareness when the bloodsucker broke through into my personal space, her face blurring into focus.

She bared her fangs—

Delilah let loose with the scythe and took out her legs.

The vamp tumbled sideways, still alive.

High on a hot rush of satisfaction, I dragged her into the elevator car, the stumps of her legs trailing smears of blood. "Emmett, close the doors."

He punched the button to the sound of Isla's Snapz exploding in a succession of high, crisp pops.

Meanwhile, Delilah stood next to me holding the scythe over a panting, swearing vampire, who bared her teeth. "Killing me won't change the fact that you're going to die," she hissed in a Boston accent.

"I just want to talk." I said the last word the New England way, squawking out the vowel.

The brunette did not appreciate my superb mimicry and spat a glob of red-tinged saliva at my shoes.

"Guess I'll have a chat with Dagmar about how uncooperative someone from her territory was. Hope she doesn't take out her displeasure on anyone you care about." I widened my eyes theatrically. "Oh, did I not mention I know your boss? Well, wait until you hear that I'm tight with Zev BatKian too."

Define "tight" as caught up in the vamp's spiderweb and it was absolutely true.

"You're lying. No way you know them." The injured bloodsucker sounded unconvinced.

Emmett jerked the silver dragon cane head at me. "She's drinking buddies with Mr. BatKian. He likes sake."

I'd never told Emmett that. Zev must have mentioned it to Tatiana.

I leaned in and brushed a lock of hair off the vamp's forehead. "You want to take the chance that I'm lying? Now, I can kill you right now and we both lose, or you give me answers and I'll not only allow you to regenerate, I'll sing your praises to the master vamps."

More gunfire exploded outside the elevator. Someone was in trouble, maybe Eli. I coiled my fear into a single icy core and reflected that hardness back at the bloodsucker.

Her eyes burned with hate, but she nodded reluctantly.

"How do we get out of here? An emergency exit? A staff-only passageway?"

"There are only two doors for staff." Blood beaded her brow like sweat but her legs were already cauterizing. "Start and finish lines. They won't open until the timer runs out and the game ends. No emergency way out."

"How much longer till the end?"

She turned up her wrist where a digital countdown had been implanted. Fourteen hours left.

I debated whether to spring my most pressing question or keep going with smaller ones to lull her into getting used to answering me. It was a technique lawyers at my old firm had used, and I'd been surprised how effective it was.

"Was the game more of a city before?"

The vamp pulled a bloody hand away from one of her stumpy legs, her body shuddering in a full-body exhale. "Yes."

I steeled my shoulders against any compassion that could weaken me and snapped my fingers. "Why change it?"

"They originally took over an abandoned demon space. A few years ago..." She was starting to slur.

Emmett squatted down and smacked her cheek. "No bye-bye yet."

"Demon wanted it back." She wheezed in a wet breath. "Made parts unstable. Unusable."

Nav was going to lose his shit when he heard this had gone down. Did he know there were vacant demon lots that Ohrists were squatting on, never mind that those demon owners would show up later and screw with the property to get the unwanted tenants out.

"Did they kill the demon?" I said.

She nodded again. Damn. No getting answers that way.

"Who's behind this?" I demanded.

"I don't know," she said sullenly.

Delilah slammed the scythe through the vamp's hand, and the brunette screamed, the tendons in her neck standing out.

"Boooosss," Emmett enthused.

I stood over the vamp in a straddle. "Try again."

"I don't know," she wheezed. "But Jason Maxwell, an Ohrist, runs the gambling end."

Finally, a name.

Crazed laughter from the parking garage sent goosebumps along my skin.

"Hyenas," Emmett said.

Now for the million-dollar question. Please, lawyer technique, live up to your promise.

"You're instructed to keep the players constantly scared," I said. "Why?"

She shrugged stonily, but her eyes had flickered to me when I'd mentioned the constant scaring. Aha. My hypothesis was correct, but I needed an explanation. This elusive piece was the most important part of the puzzle.

The vamp cradled her injured hand, blood seeping onto her shirt. "No clue." Delilah raised the scythe, and the bloodsucker flinched. "I really don't know! Can't you just let me heal in peace?"

It was entirely plausible the Consortium wouldn't share their reasons with their grunts, but she had to have picked up something.

I jerked my chin at Delilah, who straddled the vampire. "Any little detail," I said grimly. "Share it. Now."

Emmett prodded the bloodsucker with his foot. Her eyes were starting to roll back. "Better wrap it up, toots."

She let out a slow, gurgling exhale. "All I know is..." Her final words were so quiet, I almost missed them. "Monsters don't stay in the dark."

I rubbed a finger in my ear, convinced I must have heard her wrong. When Arlo heard I was looking for the Ascendant, he'd told me to leave the monsters in the dark. Now here was this vamp again with monsters and the dark. The choice of words was too similar to be a coincidence.

Was the Ascendant tied to this game?

Had Tatiana stolen the amplifier from this mysterious Consortium or did they have it now? What exactly did the damn thing do?

"Wake up!" I grabbed the vamp and shook her, but she was unconscious, all her energy diverted to regenerating, her legs already lengthening.

The elevator doors opened, and a hyena shifter barreled inside, knocking Emmett to the ground. His cane flew into the wall and the dragon's head chipped, a piece sailing into the air next to a sliver of clay.

The golem had curled into the fetal position, but as hard as his clay skin was, the hyena gouged claw marks along the arm Emmett had thrown over his head.

"Fuuuuuck!" I screamed and ordered Delilah through our psychic link to slam the scythe into the hyena's side.

The animal yipped and ran off, trailing blood, which attracted the attention of another vampire.

Good. Let the two destroy each other.

I grabbed the golem. "You okay?"

His sweatshirt was torn and there were bite marks on his collarbone, but he was otherwise unharmed. "Yeah." He looked at the vamp. "You going to leave her?"

Delilah cleaved the vamp's head off, turning the bloodsucker to ash.

"Nope," I said.

Emmett retrieved his cane. "Dayum."

"If I've learned anything from movies, it's always take the kill shot. Let's move."

Delilah, Emmett, and I sprinted into the gloom and ducked behind the first car. There was no sign of the wolf, nor could I see Eli, but several people had lit their ropes and were swinging them around.

Everyone was screaming, a deafening cacophony of noise punctuated by blasts of Snapz. The scent of rusted iron overwhelmed me, the metallic odor sharp to the point of painful, and my stomach lurched.

We zigzagged from vehicle to vehicle heading for the back left corner, making it about a third of the way when Emmett almost tripped over Felix's ravaged corpse. I spun us around, taking shelter behind a car to process that, when the stench of gas made my eyes water.

I peeked over the hood.

Rahm crouched next to the end of a rope. Its other end had been stuffed into a gas tank, the petrol flowing out of the tank and along the fibers. He pulled out his lighter, and I bit back a scream.

Eli, Teresa, and Daw had taken refuge in that car from a pair of wolf shifters, but my ex had his gun trained on the beasts and didn't see Rahm.

I ran toward them, jolting at a burst of gunfire to my right.

Using a pillar for cover, Okeyo and Mateo faced off against two vampires. Okeyo had his weapon out, but the vampires were only bleeding, not down, and the lead vamp grabbed the gun and tossed it over an undead shoulder like it was nothing.

Mateo called out for help, his voice high and desperate.

This was bad. I cried out for Emmett, but he was wrestling the snarling hyena shifter. The golem jammed his cane between the hyena's jaws, using it to lever the animal off of him.

Rahm lit the rope.

One of the vampires tore into Mateo's neck, blood arcing out.

"Please! I have three children," Okeyo begged his own attacker.

The lead vampire reached for the Black man...

...The lit fuse made its way to the car with my first true love in it.

Praying I wasn't making the worst mistake of my life, I sent Delilah to take care of the rope. There were enough vamps in here that the shadow scythe held firm even when she wasn't fighting the undead.

I sprinted the other way, hopped on the lead vamp's back, ignoring the pain of the blisters rubbed raw in my boots, and hauled him backward off Okeyo.

Emmett cried out as the hyena snapped his cane like it was a crunchy potato chip. The two rolled, fighting, across the floor.

The vamp turned on me. His partner was fighting with a brown wolf shifter over the rights to Mateo's limp and bleeding body.

Okeyo met my eyes and I jerked my chin.

He ran.

My opponent flipped me over his shoulder, my poor spine thudding against the concrete.

While Delilah's vision revealed that my shadow had successfully chopped the rope before the flame got to the gasoline-soaked part, a puddle of the flammable liquid spread out from under the tank.

Rahm crouched by it, lighter out.

My rage was gasoline flowing through my veins.

The vampire kicked my ribs, and I curled into the fetal position with my head covered, peering out through cracks between my fingers.

That assault was the spark that ignited my fury.

Delilah slammed the blade down, severing Rahm's hand.

His blood didn't spurt like a Tarantino film. There was still plenty of it, but I wished for that over-the-top cartoony quality because it would have been easier to live with than Rahm's small frown and blink. That split second where he hung frozen in time before he clutched his forearm and screamed, the lighter skidding off into the shadows.

I didn't even get a second to check if Eli was safe because the vamp lifted his leg to stomp on my ribs. I caught his foot and, channeling a Zev move, bit the vampire's Achilles' tendon. Its hard, ropy feel was disgusting, and I gagged before I could tear it out, so I summoned Delilah to hobble the bastard.

He collapsed and I rose up with a yell of triumph, which was cut short by a woman's scream, followed by two gunshots.

The brown wolf shifter eyed my fallen attacker with a feral gleam, leaving Mateo's body for the second vamp, and bounded in for the kill.

It was too late to help Mateo, but I could still tourniquet Rahm's hand before he bled out and find out what the actual fuck he was doing.

The Israeli man screamed again, this time because another hyena shifter had torn into his intestines.

"Fuuuuck!" I was surrounded by enemies feasting on both fallen humans and their own kind, and I had no idea where most of my team was. The only positive spin I could put on this nightmare was that Rahm's body was doing an admirable job of soaking up the gas.

"Choke on that, asshole!" Emmett roared and staggered to his feet from the other side of a car.

Delilah and I raced to the golem's side.

His hyena attacker gasped and writhed, clawing at his mouth.

Emmett held the broken remnant of his cane. Shards of wood were strewn on the ground, but I didn't see the dragon head until the hyena twisted his head my way, the silver top jammed down his throat.

"I did good, right?" Emmett said, wild-eyed.

"You did great, buddy."

He squinted at me. "You've got a little blood..." He touched his lips, then his eyes rolled back, and he fainted.

An engine's rumble cut through the noise, and Eli leaned out of the open side door of the passenger van pulling up. "Hurry!"

"Help." I grabbed Emmett under the armpits.

The van slowed down enough for Eli to jump out and grab the golem's feet, but we had to run alongside until we were able to get back in.

Daw slammed the door.

Isla gunned it, and we flew out onto the street.

In all the chaos, only a few pursuers came after us, but she shook them off.

Teresa was in the front passenger seat next to Isla. She gave me a wan smile and then faced forward.

Daw sat in the first row next to Okeyo, who had his head

in his hands, leaving Eli squished against the far end of the middle row with Emmett's legs on him.

After checking that the golem was breathing steadily, I maneuvered myself out from under him and moved to the back next to Laurent, still in wolf form, who was hogging most of the back row.

He had a deep scratch down the side of his neck, and his eyes were closed.

"Laurent?" I whispered, scared he was unconscious.

He thumped his tail weakly, then lifted his head just enough to drop it in my lap.

I leaned back against the seat, my legs extended, stroking the bristly fur to get my own heartbeat under control.

We'd lost three people: Mateo, a good man who hadn't deserved his fate, and two others who'd betrayed my team.

Staring out at the darkness with no landmarks to break it up didn't help my headspace. Sighing, I sifted through Laurent's fur, flicking away dirt. Had those two players deserved to die?

Rahm and Felix tried to save their own skins under horrific and unimaginable circumstances. The game dictated that there could only be one person left standing, and my team's desire to save everyone directly contradicted that. Not only that, the game had specifically promised death to anyone assisting Emmett, Eli, Laurent, and me.

I wished with all my heart that the survivors had faith in our ability to do as we promised because they might still be alive. I bit my lower lip.

Who was to say I wouldn't have done the same in their shoes?

My ears rang with the sounds of fangs tearing into flesh, and I stuffed my shaking fists into my armpits, swallowing down the sour taste of bile.

Who was to say I hadn't?

Something had shifted in me back in that garage. I'd

maimed Rahm, making him easy prey, instead of proving I'd come to protect him. I curled my fingers into Laurent's fur, seeking warmth.

Would Rahm have died regardless of my actions? Perhaps, but I'd severely reduced his chances of surviving that bloodbath, and I couldn't claim self-defense. There had been so much chaos and bloodshed that I couldn't stop to think and find a rational way out. I'd existed in the moment as pure violent impulse, desperate to stop Eli from being murdered. Regret was too simple an emotion to feel or not feel. I shivered, my body icy and a vise squeezing my head, the throb pulsing down through my jaw.

Even with the vamps, I'd been savage, driven by a primal brutality. I'd killed them before, but those had been clean kills. I'd tortured that female bloodsucker in the elevator for answers. And the one I'd bitten? I drank some water to scrub my mouth of the sensation of vamp tendon.

What was I becoming? Who was I becoming?

The fault, dear Brutus, is not in our stars, but in ourselves, that we are underlings.

Hiding my magic all those years, that vital part of myself, had diminished me until I was living on the sidelines of my own life. Coupled with the invisibility I felt as a woman in her forties, "underling" didn't begin to cover it. Then I'd reclaimed my magic, feeling more and more powerful and empowered.

Had I gone too far in how I used my powers? Or had I simply adapted to my environment?

I looked around the van at the exhausted and silent group. Was the fact that we sat here together a sign that we had each other's backs or was there a snake hidden among us, coiled up and biding its time to strike? Adapting to its environment?

Under the wolf's body heat, I felt my lids grow heavy.

I reached into my magic coursing through my veins,

weighing my sense of self. I was powerful. I was a survivor. One with some extreme tendencies, admittedly, but I now lived in an extreme world.

Emmett puffed out a loud snore and I relaxed. Thankfully, some things remained blissfully mundane.

16

_____

WE DROVE FOR HOURS THROUGH THE DARKNESS. I slept on and off, woken finally by screams and the van jolting to the left.

"Sorry." Isla corrected our course, breathing heavily. She rubbed her eyes. "A pebble hit the windshield and I thought we were being shot at."

"Jeez," Teresa said. "We're going to need so much therapy when this is over."

Our tension was palpable, our nerves strung tight as a bow's string.

The van sputtered and Isla cursed.

She rolled the vehicle into a rest stop next to a single-story building that managed to evoke both _The Jetsons_ and Communist-era architecture with its futuristic sign reading "Exit" atop a sterile gray workhorse of a building.

"We're out of gas," Isla said.

"How timely," Eli said.

There were no gas pumps.

Laurent had shifted back to human while most of us slept. He rested his cheek against his window, his face too shadowed to read.

"Is this a warehouse?" I said.

Teresa rolled down her window. "I hear music. It's a club."

Emmett sat up, cracking his neck, which sounded like walnut shells breaking. "Did someone say booze?"

"We've regressed another stage on the life cycle," Eli said. "Death, old age, adulthood, and now youth."

Daw's stomach rumbled and she rubbed it.

"I'd kill for a drink," Isla said. "Or a bowl of stale peanuts."

Okeyo didn't look like he'd moved since I'd last seen him, his head buried in his shaking hands.

I looked out the window. "They terrorize you, then give you a time-out. All the better to terrorize you again. It's a mind fuck."

"Mind fuck or not," Isla said crisply, "I, for one, desperately need a normal moment."

"Me too," Teresa said.

"I'd be careful of drinking here," Laurent said. "They might roofie you." Good point.

Okeyo finally turned around. "Why?"

"Every stage has had a psychological component," I said. "You survived death, made it back to the land of the living. How'd you feel when you got to the house and found backpacks with food and supplies?"

"Like I had a shot at getting out of here," Okeyo said.

"Right, but if Mateo hadn't figured out the trick to escaping the shifting streets, you'd have wandered there forever. Disoriented."

"Downtown, you were literally penned in," Eli said. "Towers to signify adult working life. Wondering if that's all there is until you die."

"Once again, there was a way out," I said. "Provided you survived the attacks. Now we're at this club. A place of celebration, cutting loose. Also a place, for women at least, of heightened paranoia. Laurent is right. Drugs in the drinks are the perfect way to mess with us."

"Then there should be another section between here and the playground," Teresa said. "Adolescence."

Isla groaned. "Like I want to relive that. A drink is definitely in order. Besides, it's called Exit. They want us to go this way."

"That's my worry. What do you think?" I asked Eli. He had the most experience and formal training in assessing threats.

"I really don't like that we ran out of gas here," he said. "On the other hand, we're more vulnerable in this van with all the windows than in that building without any." He rubbed his now-stubbled head. Combined with the five-o'clock shadow he'd grown, Detective Chu had a much more menacing air than usual. He studied the club, his jaw tight. "Laurent, can you detect if anyone is in there before we enter?"

"No problem."

"Then if it's clear, we'll stay there until we figure out our next move."

We all headed inside, packs in hand since the van was now unusable.

The night air was cooler here than it had been in the downtown core, but it was also refreshing after the claustrophobic anxiety permeating the ride over.

Laurent beckoned us from the stairs. "We're good."

It was a run-down space with a few rickety tables, scuffed black concrete floors, and grungy walls, and the game designers had tried to distract from the low-rent vibe with a frenzy of strobing lights.

I coughed, waving away the sickly-sweet fog swirling out from machines sitting next to the speakers, and headed for the fully stocked bar. Bland electronica rumbled up through the soles of my feet.

There was no one else here other than the van passengers: no waitstaff, no bouncers, no bartenders.

"Our time-out," Isla said to me. "Just as you predicted."

Emmett slipped behind the bar. "Step right up, ladies and gents."

Daw got there first. "Beer."

I dropped my pack on a stool and leaned over the counter to find Emmett with his head in a bar fridge.

He emerged with a bottle streaked with ice-cold condensation and handed it to Daw.

"Attends," Laurent said. "Let me examine all food and drink and see if I detect anything."

Daw flicked off the cap and held it out.

The shifter carefully sniffed it. "It seems okay, but they might have used an odorless poison." He managed to convey his doubts to Daw.

"We shouldn't drink," I said.

"You said it yourself," Isla replied. "They terrorize us then give us a time-out. Why? No idea. But that seems to be the pattern, even if it's bloody awful. I can't see a point in poisoning us before the game's over." Daw held up her bottle with a questioning look and Isla sighed. "I don't know," she said.

The Thai woman shrugged and took a long swallow of beer. "Very good," she said with a smile.

That broke the others' indecision and they rushed the bar, putting in their own orders.

All except Eli, who did a perimeter check and announced there were no other exits. Foreswearing the booze, he settled himself at a table with some beef jerky and bottled water from his pack.

Laurent pronounced Isla's wine and Okeyo's bourbon free and clear. Teresa opted for a Coke, saying she didn't like alcohol, but Laurent insisted on sniff testing it as well.

Isla had pushed tables up to Eli's. She and Daw were

collecting all the pretzel bowls and depositing them on the group table. Laurent came over briefly to examine them, then headed back to the bar.

I nabbed a stool between Eli and Okeyo and placed my hand on the Black man's shoulder.

"Don't feel guilty for surviving," I said.

"I should have done more." He poured two healthy fingers of bourbon into his glass and guzzled it back.

"There was nothing you could have done." I coughed. The dance floor fog was cloying.

"You managed," he said. "What was that thing? A familiar?"

I scrunched up my face like a little kid admitting to breaking a window with a baseball. "I can animate my shadow."

Okeyo didn't ask any follow-up questions.

I think I was relieved?

Laurent and Emmett joined us. Emmett had a Coke and did not look happy about it.

"It's imperative that we stay sharp until we get to the playground," I said, raising my voice over the music to direct the comment to everyone. "There's a staff exit that unlocks when the game ends. They won't expect us to know that and use it. It'll subvert any last surprises they have up their sleeve." I checked my watch. "We have ten hours left."

I wasn't about to share the name of the Ohrist involved with the gambling side or anything about the Ascendant, but this information was relevant to everyone.

"How do you know this?" Okeyo said, suspicion writ large on his face.

"A vampire told me."

He coughed in surprise, then finished his drink.

Isla shook her head. "Impossible. Laurent is the only one with any chance at taking a vampire on and he was with me."

"You didn't see her magic." Okeyo poured himself another drink.

"You have magic?" Isla set her wineglass down. "You should have mentioned that."

"I knew," Teresa said.

"Didn't you trust the rest of us?" Isla snapped, her eyes flashing.

"Was I supposed to put on a show before naptime?" I said tightly. "While we're asking questions, how did you hot-wire the van?"

"Rahm did it before he died," she said.

"Really? He chose to leave the safety of the van to go back out into that nightmare just to kill Eli, Teresa, and Daw?"

"That doesn't make a lot of sense," Emmett agreed.

"How am I supposed to know why he left? I found the van with the motor running," Isla flicked her hand at me. "Stop deflecting the important questions."

"Lay off," Eli growled. "We've risked our necks to save you. We didn't have to come in here."

"True. You went above and beyond," Isla said sarcastically. "Not many would. Are you truly that altruistic? Or just another mind fuck to give us hope and snatch it away?" She grabbed a bowl of pretzels and her wine and moved to another table.

Teresa toyed with the tab on her soda can, her eyes bouncing between Eli and Isla. Ducking her head, she scrambled off her stool and limped over to Isla's table.

Daw and Okeyo decamped as well, taking more pretzels with them.

"Thanks so much for backing us up," I said to Laurent.

"Nothing I could say would have changed their minds," he said. "I assume the same form as shifters trying to kill them, Emmett is a golem, you have magic, and Eli is clearly aligned with us. Plus, Isla is correct. Who in their right mind would willingly come into this game?"

I planted my hands on my hips. "Excuse me?"

"This place is deadly, and you put yourself into peril for some strangers? It was foolish beyond belief."

"You did the same for us," Eli said. "It's hardly like you and I are friends."

Laurent smiled blandly. "I did it for a sizable paycheck."

"Thanks," I muttered.

Emmett threw his hands up. "What am I, chopped liver?"

"We're getting paid as well," Eli said. "What's the difference?"

Laurent draped an arm over the back of Eli's seat. "Why'd you drag Mitzi into this?"

"She's smart, she's powerful, and she understands the magic community."

I smiled my thanks. Nice to have some appreciation.

"Yes. She is all that." Laurent rested a weighted gaze on me for a second, then shrugged. "Then a paycheck is all it was, and we are all on the same page."

I narrowed my eyes, not buying his act for a second.

He jerked his head at Eli. "As a fellow Sapien, do you want to try and calm them down?"

"Yeah, sure." Eli slid off his stool and headed to the table.

Emmett had snuck off and was halfway to the bar. I didn't have the energy to follow him.

"You still could have said something," I said to Laurent. "Isla is your friend and she has sway over the others."

"Don't read too much into the fact that we know each other." He glanced over at her then sighed. "She won't listen to me."

The other Sapiens allowed Eli to join them, but Isla launched into some diatribe before he could say much.

"Because of Henri or because of something else?" I said.

"I don't know." Laurent shot me a sad smile.

"Maybe you need to have more faith in her."

"Maybe I do." He laughed but it sounded forced. "Seems

constant deadly situations are enough to make me rethink how I look at things." His eyes found mine.

Did he mean us? Hope flared hot and bright in my chest, but before I could say anything else, Emmett wandered back, glugging gin straight from the bottle.

"Emmett!" I shook a finger in threat. If he slid into prophecy mode, he could be stuck there forever or even die. I kept telling Emmett how much I valued him, but it seemed like he needed more affirmation than I could provide to believe in his own worth and take care of himself properly.

Laurent grabbed the bottle away, causing booze to spill over the golem's chin. The intention was sound, I just wished he'd been a bit kinder about the interaction.

"Yeah, yeah," the golem grumbled. "I could go all woo-woo." He slid off the stool and grabbed the bottle.

I raised my eyebrows.

"I'm putting it back, okay?" he huffed and stomped off.

Laurent rolled his eyes, which, fair, but why couldn't he give Emmett a compliment now and then?

Oy vey. I didn't have the energy to deal with fighting with the shifter about yet another person.

I unearthed another protein bar, chewing my way through the cardboardy substance. I'd been impressed with Emmett's behavior so far, but how much longer before he cracked under all this pressure, at which point he'd be a liability, not an asset?

Wait. Tatiana had to know that was a possibility, so why send him? I frowned. The Morph had detected Eli and me under the cloaking, so Emmett's lack of a heartbeat hadn't saved us. That extra leg he used as a blockade had. All of that "expect the worst, plan for the worst" reasoning sounded like a load of bullshit now.

Was he a mole? After all, Tatiana never did anything without clear motivation, and she wasn't being paid for

Emmett's time by Deputy Chief Constable Esposito. What was her angle?

"Where's he going?" Emmett had returned with another can of Coke.

Laurent was headed outside, his pack slung over one shoulder.

"He probably just wants some air. Stop being so suspicious. Tatiana sent him here to help us."

"Where he happened to find a long-lost friend? Stop being so blind, toots. Much as I love Tatiana, she's always playing a second game we have no idea about, and he's no different." Emmett popped the tab on the can and took a long swig before settling in to build a structure using the lone bowl of pretzels.

I rubbed my temples, exhausted by Emmett's accusations, yet unable to fully shake them off either. I tried to catch Eli's attention, wanting him to go speak with the golem, but my ex stared straight ahead with a grim expression, listening to Isla.

She jabbed a finger in the air, punctuating whatever she was saying, and they both stared directly at me, before Eli's gaze darted away, his head bent close to hers.

Emmett's small tower collapsed and he smashed it to dust.

The golem was sowing discord, Eli was blindly trusting a shifty woman, and Laurent was acting cagier than usual.

Was I being blind to their true agendas? Giving them a free pass because of our relationships?

I touched the spot where Felix had stabbed me. A player had attempted to literally bury a knife in my back. Were there more knives in the dark waiting for me, wielded by people I thought I could trust?

Magic tingled my fingertips as I studied the other table.

Why hadn't Eli asked Nav to work this case with him? The Carpe Demon operative was way more experienced than

I was, and his involvement wouldn't have put both of Sadie's parents in harm's way on this dangerous mission.

Unless that's exactly what Eli wanted.

I clenched my fists. He resented me for breaking his perception filter and forcing him to see that magic is real. This was payback.

"Yo! Chu!" I strode across the club, Eli meeting me half-way. "You're not getting rid of me that easily." Shadows swirled around my legs.

My ex unholstered his gun, fanning wisps of fog away. "Sapiens are expendable, aren't we? Isla was right. It's how all of you with magic think. Well, I've got news for you, *babe*, I'm not going easily."

Loud voices came from the players' table, the Sapiens now arguing among themselves.

Emmett arrived at my side. "What's wrong with you guys?" He took two steps toward Eli, his hand held out. "Give me the gun."

The shadows solidified, Delilah standing shoulder to shoulder with me, her fists up.

"You'd like that, wouldn't you?" I shook my head. "You said it yourself. Tatiana always has a second game running. How do I know you're not part of it?"

"Pull your heads out of your asses," Emmett said. "It's drugs."

"I didn't have anything to drink," I snarled. "And how come you aren't affected?"

The golem threw his hands up. "I don't know! Good metabolism?"

"A likely story." Eli motioned for me to get closer to Emmett, training the gun on us both. "Are the two of you secretly in league with each other?" Eli cocked his head. "Or maybe it was all three of you against the pathetic human?"

"Get over yourself with your little pity party act," I said.

"You've tried to take Sadie away from me ever since you found out about my magic, so don't pretend you're helpless."

A table clattered to the ground; glass shattered.

The Sapiens were in their own showdown. Okeyo had his hand on his gun, Daw had her switchblade out, and Isla gripped a jagged broken wine bottle. Teresa held a chair like a shield, the four of them yelling.

The music, the fog, the screaming, it was getting too much. I swayed, woozy.

Two gunshots went off, startling us into silence.

Eli stared in shock at his hands because he no longer had his weapon.

Emmett did, and he'd blown holes through the two fog machines. He blinked, his head jerking back, then chuckled softly and blew on the barrel like it was smoking before spinning it around his finger, at which point he fumbled and almost dropped it. Recovering, he puffed his chest out, swaggering toward us. "If it wasn't the drinks, then there was something in the fog making you all act this way. Everyone outside." When we didn't move, he fired into the ceiling. "Now!"

We trooped outside, too dazed to disobey, but all still arguing.

A loud whistle pierced the air. Laurent came around from the side of the club, glaring like he welcomed the opportunity to blow off steam by committing murder.

"Shut the hell up for five seconds," he barked at us, then did a double take. "Why is the golem armed?"

"I had to shoot the fog machine," Emmett said. "It was making everyone crazy. Too bad you didn't sense it."

Laurent swore.

My paranoia was fading, but as with all nightmares, I couldn't entirely shake the sensation off.

All of us humans exchanged somewhat sheepish apologies.

"Everyone meet out back," Laurent said. "The next section awaits." He headed off.

The players went inside long enough to grab their stuff.

"Can I get the gun back?" Eli said.

"Sure." Emmett handed it over, grip first.

"Gun safety, nice." Eli checked the weapon before chambering it.

The golem shrugged. "I watch a lot of cop shows. Know what's what. I'll go get your packs, o fragile humans. Wait here."

I laughed weakly, holding my hand out for Eli. "That was some shit, huh?"

"I didn't mean anything I said in there." He worried his lower lip between his teeth. "You know that, right?"

"Obviously. And same." I tried not to read into how long it took for him to take my hand and twine his fingers with mine. Still, just like a deep splinter, that last hard shard of paranoia was lodged deep, and I had the unshakable belief that the worst was yet to come.

17

"I KNEW IT!" TERESA BOUNCED ON HER TOES.

Maybe if I stared at the dark high school long enough it would transform into something more pleasant. Like a man-eating tiger.

High school had been a nightmare. I remained infuriatingly flat-chested, retaining a youthful pudge until late in my teen years. That might not have been so bad on its own, but my Vancouver high school had a large Jewish population. In theory, it should have made life for all my people better. But no. These popular kids were the country club Jews and I was not. My activist cousin Goldie would rather have been shot in the head than be a member. It didn't appeal to me either, but it made me a target. I was Jewish, but the wrong kind of Jewish, therefore there had to be something wrong with me.

Long story short, I was delighted to leave all that behind. I didn't expect my teen tormentors to be waiting for me in this game though I didn't entirely rule it out either, but those years had been brutal, just like whatever waited inside for us would be.

Agreeing we'd be safer holing up in there than remaining out in the open for the eight hours left of the game, we stuck together, scouting classrooms for the best place to hide from vamps and shifters.

As it was too dark to summon Delilah, I'd sandwiched myself between Laurent and Eli. There were no lockers, no furniture, no water fountains or artwork, just long, shadowy corridors and eerily deserted classrooms.

Daw called us over.

Floodlights surrounded the primary-colored swings and slides on the playground out back, throwing the final hundred feet between the back of the high school and the end of the game into a dark slab.

"Sports day from Hell," Teresa said.

We turned down yet another desolate corridor, our foot-steps echoing off the walls. Even Laurent was on edge though that might have been because I kept stepping on the backs of his heels.

We ended up in a small gymnasium with a row of windows along the top of the walls and a high-gloss wooden floor.

"What about waiting out the rest of the game here?" Isla said.

Emmett flopped onto the ground. "Sold."

Teresa, Daw, and Okeyo didn't care where they rested. They were tapped out.

Eli and Laurent took positions at opposite doors. The shifter had transitioned into wolf form before joining us here in the gym. Well, that was one way to avoid a conversation with me.

I stayed with my ex, watching him check his ammo and reload his gun. The floor was cold, it hurt my hip to lie on my side, and every tiny shoe squeak and cough boomed through the empty, echoing space.

Sleep proved elusive.

Teresa and Okeyo were conked out. Daw was stretching, which was a good idea. Isla lay on her back, absently rubbing her pec.

The motion reminded me of something, but just as I remembered what it was, Isla left the gym.

I ran after her, cornered her outside, shoved her up against the door, and pressed my palm to her pec.

"I beg your pardon." She pried my hand off her, but I held firm and yanked her shirt collar down.

The incision was smaller than Ian's, but the end result was the same.

"You don't have a tracker." I shook my head. "How did you learn about the implant?"

Her expression pinched tight for a second then she shoved me backward through the gym door and bolted.

The truth hit me like a bucket of cold water.

Isla was working for the game.

It was the only thing that made sense. Ian only learned of his tracker after he won the game, and none of the other players here had shown any awareness of the implants.

Yelling her name, I rattled the gym door, which was suddenly and inexplicably locked.

Everyone came running over from their various corners of the gymnasium.

"She's one of them!" I body-slammed myself against the handle, but the door didn't budge.

Laurent growled at me.

"You have to believe me. She doesn't have the tracker."

"We're being tracked?" Okeyo slapped his body like he could dislodge it.

Eli and Emmett attempted to pry open the doors here inside the gym while Laurent raced to the ones on the opposite side of the room. Luckily, they just had those horizontal bars to push on to open them, but those were locked as well.

The temperature plummeted, my breath coming out in white puffs.

Daw let out a stream of agitated Thai.

Cracks spiderwebbed through the floor, the black painted lines bleeding into the wood. The windows morphed to an impenetrable obsidian.

I couldn't see an inch in front of my face. It was as if all light had been vacuumed right out of the room. "Eli? Laurent?"

My voice echoed off the walls.

Laurent howled.

Teresa cried out.

Eli called my name.

I fumbled through the darkness, my hands outstretched, finding no one.

Fangs ghosted along my neck and I flinched, slamming my cloaking over myself. I kept going, for an hour, a lifetime, feeling smaller and smaller the longer it took to cross this room.

The darkness had legs. It loomed, it menaced, it peered into my soul and claimed it for its own, a dank toxicity making itself at home.

I hit a corner on rubbery legs and slid down the wall, scratching at my skin, desperate to pry out the evil sludge within.

Blurry figures whipped past me, too fast to be human, while the Sapiens called out: for each other, for help, for mercy.

Nothing else touched me, but I couldn't escape the dark. It swelled up inside me, crawling higher until it touched my mind. A perfect moment of madness that held and stretched like an opera singer's note. Crystal clear yet twisted, it strung me tight in its grip, until it snapped.

I spun suspended, blind and deaf, in a vortex. Up, down, time—nothing had meaning anymore. There was just darkness, that place where monsters dwelled.

The evil crooned at me to stop fighting. I was already

made of shadows. Embrace it. I floated, weightless, almost reborn. Yes. Give in.

All I had to do was jump and I'd touch the sky. I'd be like that vast galaxy, terrifying, beautiful, ever-changing. Stars appeared, confirming the rightness of my decision, and I reached for them, but as I did, my arm brushed against something hard in my ear.

The stars glittered, smattering the universe with golden dust.

Damn. This thing in my ear was itchy. I grabbed it to tear it out, and the pointy back part jabbed my finger.

Sadie.

I snapped my eyes open to find myself on the playground and gasped, my hand flying to my mouth.

All of us, intruders and players alike, stood before the finish line comprised of bright yellow letters reading "Did you survive the Human Race?"

Everyone except Emmett and Eli wore crazed smiles. Even the wolf lay on his belly with a glazed look, his tongue lolling out.

"Mir! Thank God!" Eli grabbed me in a hug. "I almost lost myself," he said, "if it wasn't for Sadie's earring…"

Emmett hugged me from behind. "I couldn't get anyone to snap out of it. You guys were lost for hours."

I clasped them back tightly. "Did you have the urge to—"

Daw jumped up, then landed on the ground cackling, her eyes wide open but not taking anything in.

"Jump…" I ran over to the woman and shook her, but she didn't stop laughing.

There was a thud and a grunt.

Eli had knocked Okeyo to the ground, straining to keep him in place. "He was going to jump."

"We have to wake the others up before we lose them to the madness. Emmett, grab Teresa."

With a heavy heart, I left Daw. She was past saving, but Laurent wasn't.

He thrashed, a wildness in his eyes proclaiming that his human side was leaving the building fast.

I grabbed the wolf from behind, wrapping my arms around him, heedless of his agitation. "Don't you dare leave me, asshole. You owe me answers, got it? Plus, what? You're going to let Boo starve? I won't feed her. That poor little kitty will die, and it'll be your fault. Is that what you want?"

I was babbling, but I hadn't fully shaken off the paranoia from the club, never mind this whole experience. As clumsy as my attempt was, I had to keep him from leaving me.

"Incoming!" Emmett hollered.

Vamps and shifters poured out of the high school, an army of violence sent to decimate us at the last minute.

We weren't going to survive the Human Race.

A curious sense of calm settled over me at the almost comical level of opponents gunning for us. I eyed the stars twinkling in the fake night sky. I'd worked through and discarded a lot of thoughts about my mazel, rejecting any notion of destiny.

Free will, baby. I wasn't dying in some bullshit game.

The game makers might want to slaughter my team, but they wanted the Sapiens for something. "Drag everyone over the finish line. Emmett, get Daw."

Okeyo and Teresa woke up once their feet passed the letters, dazed and shaking, but alive.

One problem down. An army of fast-moving others to deal with.

And no staff exit in sight.

I grabbed Teresa and jabbed my shadow scythe against her neck. "Stop or I'll kill her. Eli." I jerked my chin at Okeyo.

My ex picked up what I was putting down and hauled the other man against him, pressing the gun to his side.

The vamps and shifters stopped so suddenly that they

barreled into each other, barely avoiding falling like bowling pins. It was funny, but more importantly, it confirmed that I was right about the Consortium wanting the Sapiens for something, which dampened any amusement.

Emmett wrestled the snarling, biting wolf behind the line, but it hadn't helped Laurent come back from the edge of madness. Maybe I'd been expecting too much.

"Open the staff door," I said. "We're going. All of us."

The vamp in the very front tilted her head like she was receiving communications. Then she smiled. "You can leave, but there's only one way out."

Our opponents stepped back, forming a path to a twisty red slide that was enclosed in a chute.

I eyed it nervously. Obviously, there was a final nasty surprise in store for us, but we had no choice, and I just wanted out.

I dragged Teresa with me through the wall of enemies, resisting the urge to hunch my shoulders protectively around my neck. One show of weakness and they'd descend like ravenous beasts.

The young woman was trembling and begging me not to hurt her. I blocked out her distress because I couldn't clue her in that this was all an act to get us out of here. Her fear had to be real.

The game demanded that terror, and I was nothing if not obliging.

I lugged Teresa over to the slide's ladder.

"Ow!" Emmett shook out his hand.

A ball of fur and rage, white foam flecking off his fangs, barreled toward me. At the last second, the wolf sailed over my head, landing at the top of the slide, his flanks heaving like he was desperate to escape.

His paws scrabbled on the smooth plastic then down he slid into the chute, lost to view.

"Laurent!" Hauling Teresa with me, I dove after him.

The distance was deceiving. On the playground the twisty slide was fairly short, but we traveled for much longer, coming out in an unfamiliar room.

I'd barely gotten to my feet when something blurred past me, and flinching, I manifested my shadow scythe, but I wasn't fast enough.

A dybbuk had flown out of nowhere to inhabit the wolf.

He roared, his body trembling and his eyes wide and mad, scratching and biting himself so furiously that he drew blood.

I cried, "Mut!" The instant the Hebrew letters for "die" appeared on the scythe's blade, I attempted to get close enough to deal with the malevolent spirit but in Laurent's frenzy, couldn't.

"Why is he like that?" Teresa cried. She pressed closer to me, her supposed abductor with a scythe appearing the safer option.

Given Laurent's hatred of dybbuks, this was his worst nightmare.

Before I could answer Teresa, a second pulsing crimson specter with sickly white streaks whooshed past me and bounced off the Sapien. Cursing, I swung my scythe, but the dybbuk veered sideways and slipped away, bouncing off Okeyo, who'd just arrived.

"What's happening?" Eli said, jumping off the slide. Even with his broken perception filter he didn't see dybbuks. Only those with Banim Shovavim magic could.

"Dybbuk."

Eli swore loudly.

Emmett crashed off the slide and Daw landed on top of him, still cackling with that deranged laugh, her eyes vacant.

The dybbuk whipped around, reformed into a narrow triangular wedge with a needle-sharp point, and attacked Daw like a tattoo gun set to warp speed.

Shoving Teresa down, I pushed past Eli to get to the Thai woman.

The dybbuk's point dipped inside her, but it couldn't gain any more of a grip on her than that.

My mouth fell open, my scythe frozen above my head, because it shouldn't have even been able to do that. Daw was a Sapien. If she had any Ohrist blood, even a recessive gene, the dybbuk would have just cruised on in and enthralled her, so she clearly wasn't magic.

Suddenly, the final piece of this sadistic game fell into place for me.

The game demanded terror. It wasn't some psychopathic thrill: it was because the Consortium sought the conditions under which a dybbuk could possess a nonmagic host. That's why the Sapiens were victims of the terror campaign. It was a sick and twisted means to lower their inhibitions and prime them for enthrallment.

The dybbuk dropped another precious half inch into Daw.

I rushed that spirit and cleaved it in half. It leeched of all color and imploded, dead.

Lost as she was, Daw had no idea how close she'd come to being patient zero in a catastrophe of epic proportions.

"Mir!" Eli had his gun trained on Laurent, while Emmett and the others stayed behind my ex. "You've got to get through to him."

The wolf stalked them, forcing them backward, no trace of humanity in those eyes that were as cold, beautiful, and hard as a glacier. He made no sound other than the soft plop of blood from his self-inflicted wounds. Was the dybbuk in charge right now?

A burst of rotting onion smell made my eyes water, and I spun, fearing an even worse complication to our situation, because that putridity was Gehenna's signature perfume.

"I have to deal with this. Shoot him in the leg if he attacks," I told Eli.

"I will." His voice was grim, but his gun hand was steady.

Plugging my nose, I animated Delilah and slid into her

green overlay vision of the world, rapidly scanning the room. There, to the right of the group. A dinner plate–sized circle shimmered as if rippling off hot concrete.

I'd seen this before on the Grouse Grind. It was a tear into Gehenna. That's how these dybbuks had slipped free. There was something important about that beyond the obvious, but it remained frustratingly out of reach.

I scrubbed a hand over my face, barely keeping it together. I couldn't think with all the noise Daw was making, and I couldn't do anything about the tear; only Laurent could, and he was in no condition to hear me out.

"Toots, help," Emmett squeaked.

Laurent had them pinned in a corner.

He and I had barely recovered from the last time I'd cost him his magic. Yes, this would once again be temporary, but he wouldn't forgive me for it a second time.

Brokenhearted, I stepped between the shifter and everyone else. "Laurent..."

Saliva dripping off his fangs, he bristled, making him larger and more lethal looking.

Not making direct eye contact, I raised my scythe and the beast growled. "Eli, you got extra clothes?"

"Yeah."

"Give them to me. Everyone, wait by the door and don't look. Give him privacy."

"Don't worry," Eli said. "I'll make sure."

A bundle of clothes hit me in the back. I reached around for them and sighed at the Canucks T-shirt with the sweat-pants. "Not funny."

"It's all I've got." His voice was strained.

Daw gave an eerie cackle.

Juliette would be my first stop when we got out of here to have the healer check everyone out, but it might be too late for Daw. I prayed it wasn't for Laurent.

There were footsteps and then Eli gave me the go-ahead.

"I'm so sorry," I said.

The wolf pounced, and I slammed my scythe into his shadow as he barreled into me, knocking me sideways.

Muscle roiled under his fur, the wolf's torso contorting like something was punching its way out from the inside. His skin stretched tight enough to force his eyes to bulge from their sockets, and his lips yanked back revealing large pink gums.

His wolf form shifted in four violent crunches: legs, arms, torso, head. White fur fell off him like snowflakes, claws hitting the ground like hail. Naked and shivering, Laurent curled his knees tightly into his chest, his human body so fragile and vulnerable in the wake of that savage transformation.

However, the sound of pain that was wrenched from deep inside his chest was pure animal.

I almost ended up with the freed dybbuk inside me because I was stuck on the look of absolute hurt and betrayal that Laurent shot me before he dropped his head, his shadow gone.

I dispatched the malevolent spirit, coldly watching it implode and vanish, dead, then I kneeled at Laurent's side, my magic recalled. He hadn't fallen unconscious or stopped breathing, but why was he shaking like that? "Laurent? I've got clothes—"

He feebly pushed me away, his teeth chattering. "I've got it," he rasped. He was wound so tight I was scared he would break, despite his strength.

"I had to do it. You know that."

Slowly, he sat up, pulling on the despised hockey shirt without comment.

"Please say something."

His fingers flexed and bunched the hem of the shirt. "Leave me be, Miriam," he said in weary voice like I was one complication too many.

I shook my head, my throat clogged with sorrow and my chest tight with anger. I kept being thrust into these impossible situations with him and he didn't cut me any slack. I was so tired.

Emmett grabbed my elbow as my legs buckled. He glared at Laurent, who was now clothed. "You're an asshole. She should have let you die."

Laurent gave him a tight smile and pushed unsteadily to his feet. "Something we finally agree on."

Saving that jerk from certain death was the opposite of betrayal, even if he lost his magic for good, which he wouldn't. I clenched my fists. He was so cavalier about his death. I'd give anything for five more minutes with my parents. Why couldn't he appreciate the fact that he was still alive?

"Mir, get in here," Eli called insistently from the next room.

I didn't bother checking to see if Laurent followed Emmett and me through the doorway. Nor did I look back at the tear to Gehenna. What was the point? Laurent didn't have the magic to fix it now and neither did I. It went on my mental list of evils to be stopped. Damn, that list was getting long.

Daw had finally gone quiet, curled up on a sofa with her face pressed to the cushions. I was so grateful for her silence that I could have wept.

A low table the size of two conference tables was surrounded by leather couches and club chairs while half-finished drinks and plates of food lay strewn on end tables.

Eli poked at a lipstick-stained cigarette still smoldering in an ashtray.

We'd just missed whoever had been here, but there was no other door visible to follow them. It must have been magically concealed.

My disappointment was muted by the item taking up the entire huge table: a model of the game.

Teresa and Okeyo warily circled it.

The young woman let out a shuddery breath. "Look."

She stood over the graveyard replica where two stationary dots blinked red.

"There's another one here," Eli said, motioning to the part with the homes. "It's the deceased."

We found the final two players who were unaccounted for. One was in the forest where Teresa had been and the other was downtown.

"I cannot..." Okeyo collapsed into a chair, displacing a sheet of paper that had lain there.

I picked it up, reading the detailed profile of player one: Rahm Malka. The sheet listed his age, education, height, weight, rap sheet, and skills. There were also the odds on him winning in comparison to the other players. They were pretty good, so the buy-in to "enter" him was higher than some of the others.

"Good call, Detective Chu."

Eli shoved the paper in his pocket. "I wish I'd been wrong about people choosing Sapiens as avatars," he said quietly. "It's sick." He moved over to Okeyo, crouching down and assuring him that this was almost over. My partner had been a rock through this whole ordeal.

I searched for any other such profiles, even looking under the furniture, because I didn't want Teresa or Okeyo to see theirs, but there didn't appear to be any more printouts. As I straightened up, a glint from under the game table caught my eye.

A paperclip held a couple sheets of small notepad paper together. Eli's name was written on the first one next to the word "Sap." It was followed by "golem—unknown." The second page had Laurent's name next to his shifter status, though no mention of his Banim Shovavim powers.

The final name was mine. "BS" was next to it, underlined twice, like a threat.

Did this handwriting belong to Jason Maxwell, the man who ran the gambling end of this enterprise? Was the Consortium interested in my magic because they'd seen me kill that dybbuk or was something else at play?

I crumpled the papers in my fist, hastily shoving them into my pocket.

"Are we still in the game?" Emmett said.

"No, we're not in a hidden space any longer," Laurent said from the doorway.

"How do you know?" Eli said.

Laurent shrugged. "I can tell."

I gnawed on a fingernail. If we were in the real world, I could get out of here. Maybe even get us *all* out, but that would mean...

Laurent followed my gaze to the shadow cast by one of the couches and flinched.

"I'll be back." I stepped into the Kefitzat Haderech, finding Pyotr asleep on the pile of socks. I gently shook the gargoyle. "Wakey wakey."

His bulging eyes fluttered open and he sat up, yawning. He slid a drooled-on sock off his face and handed it to me.

"Ew. No." I batted the sock away, barely caring how unfazed Pyotr was at my wrecked and grubby appearance. How far I'd come from the woman so desperate to keep up appearances and blend in. I didn't mourn her, though I could do with fifty percent less bloodstains and filth in my life.

"Listen, I've got an emergency." I explained about the game and my theory that Sapiens were being primed to be dybbuk vessels. "Can I bring them through the Kefitzat Haderech without causing offense? They need to get to a healer as soon as possible."

Emmett didn't cause any issues when he came through

here. Maybe for the same reasons that the paranoia and darkness didn't affect him? Lack of a heartbeat?

Laurent was another matter entirely.

Pyotr's mouth hung open, and he shook his head so forcefully, his eyes rattled like marbles. "No."

I put my hands together, pleading. "Please? Isn't there any way you can help?"

He rubbed at the callus on his finger that he'd incurred the last time I caused problems here. Then the gargoyle gave a defeated sigh that racked his entire body.

Hope fluttered in my chest. That meant there was something.

"I will bring you any movie franchise you want," I promised.

"Too much screen time," he said.

I looked wildly around the cave. His fern was totally dead. "A new plant!"

"But reports. In triplicate," he sobbed. "Per person!"

"With a grow light." Waggling my eyebrows, I nudged him with my elbow.

Pyotr pursed his lips. Then he wriggled, first his feet, then his legs, up through his torso and finally his head. He stabbed a finger in the air. "I come to your house!"

"You're allowed to leave?"

He glared at me, his hands planted on his hips. "I have friends. Life."

"I'm delighted to hear that. It's just that you're always here when I show up."

"Yes. You're very lucky to see me that much. I come to your house and you take me to garden store to pick plants. Deal or no deal?"

I scrubbed a hand over my face. How would I disguise him enough to pass muster in public? *Future problems, Miri.* "Deal. I'll take you to a garden store but not until this case is totally wrapped up."

"Is good. Go back through shadow. I will open door to your house for you there. Mitigating circumstances."

I scrunched up my face. "Laurent is with me. The wolf."

"Noooooo." Pyotr buried his head in his hands.

"He doesn't have Ohrist magic. Just Banim Shovavim."

"That's whole other batch of triplicate!"

"Garden store! You'll love it!" I patted his shoulder and jumped back through the shadow into the room. "Everyone huddle up. Uh, Emmett?"

"Yeah, I got her." He carefully scooped Daw up.

"We're going home." I clapped my hands together, yet no door appeared. Had Pyotr kiboshed my plea in the face of all that triplicate?

Teresa and Okeyo slumped in defeat, but Laurent sighed, his eyes briefly closed.

I frowned, my lips pressing in a thin line as I caught the tremble of Laurent's hands before he clasped them behind his back. He was scared to go back into the KH.

An open door appeared in the middle of the room leading directly into my living room, and my smile stretched wide.

Sadie's tense little face popped into view.

I ran inside and scooped her into my arms. She practically melted against me.

Eli kept his cop persona up long enough to usher everyone except Laurent into my house because the shifter hesitated. My ex shook his head, then joined the rest of us, swinging Sadie up off her feet.

Jude slung her arm around my waist, her head resting against mine. "Bad?"

I didn't know if she was talking about the game or Laurent, who took a deep breath, his shoulders stiff, then shot forward just before the door disappeared, but the answer was the same. "Unimaginably so."

I had to get everyone healed and back to their families, track down this Jason Maxwell who ran the gambling end,

186

find out why Isla betrayed us, stop the game, visit Zev, and exchange some hard truths with Laurent, whether he wanted to or not.

For now, all that mattered was that I was alive, and I was home with my family. Everything else could wait until tomorrow.

18

LAURENT WAS THE FIRST TO DEPART.

I walked him to the door, trying not to stare at where his shadow should have been. "Do you want to wait for Juliette?"

Eli had phoned Deputy Chief Constable Esposito to update him, who in turn was corralling Tatiana and Juliette.

"I can't take that much concern right now," he said.

"Your Ohrist magic will return. This isn't like last time."

He gave me a wry smile. "My head knows that, but after everything that happened in the game? I'm not..." Laurent tapped his temple. "I'm jumbled."

Me too. "Do you want to talk about it?"

"I'm not sure I'm up to it yet." He took the first step and paused. "But thank you for saving me. I mean that."

I caught his arm as he turned to leave, certain that if he departed on that note, I'd never see him again. "Laurent."

He waited expectantly.

"I— Will you call me when your magic returns? Please?"

"Yes." He pressed his lips together, then blurted out, "What did you see in the gym?"

"See?" I was thrown off by the abrupt change of topic.

"Nothing. It was darkness to the end of time. Why? Did you have visions?"

His brow furrowed, his eyes growing distant. "Yes," he said softly. He paused and licked his lips nervously.

I rolled onto the balls of my feet, positive he was about to tell me what they were, but shaking his head, he took a step back.

"I'll call you," he said.

Crestfallen, I nodded, my hands clasped tightly behind my back.

He brushed a lock of hair that had escaped my ponytail away from my face. "I promise." With that he headed down my front walk.

I watched him until he turned the corner and was lost to view. I was about to shut my door when I had the strongest sensation I was being watched. Peering in both directions on my quiet street, I found nothing to cause alarm, though the hairs on the back of my neck stood up. Since I was safe behind my wards, I forced the maelstrom of emotions in my chest down and returned to the living room, determined for my daughter's sake not to look as messed up as I felt.

In a flurry of concern, Jude had done what all Jewish mothers do best: feed people. She'd ordered enough pizza and pasta to feed a small army, hovering around the Sapiens and making sure they ate something.

Daw still wasn't responding, and she certainly wasn't eating, but she'd been made as comfortable as possible, and she hadn't started laughing again. I wasn't sure that was actually better.

Teresa seemed to be bouncing back after her ordeal. On the surface at least. She chatted with Sadie about the theater program she was in and ate a couple slices of pizza, while Okeyo remained quiet, pushing his pasta around his plate before managing a couple of bites.

He asked to use my phone to call his family in Kenya, and I gave him my cell, directing him upstairs for privacy.

Tatiana showed up soon after with Juliette.

Eli and I were whisked off to be examined, and our bruises and minor injuries were healed. The psychological scars would take time, but we had a good Ohrist therapist we were already seeing.

When Okeyo returned, he was more animated than before. Talking to his wife and kids had helped immensely, though he had no idea what to tell them.

"Tell them you were kidnapped for political reasons," I said.

He nodded sadly. "It might be the easiest lie to swallow since it's not uncommon in my country. I just wish I had someone I could talk to."

"Ask Tatiana and Juliette." I nodded toward the women. "Between the two of them, they'll be able to track down a therapist with magic in Kenya who will believe you."

"Thank you."

My boss instructed Eli and me to show up in the morning. She and Esposito had a meeting to determine which steps to take next.

Juliette took me aside to say she'd look in on her uncle. I smiled, grateful he had her in his corner.

Since Emmett was going back to Tatiana's, he carried Daw out to my boss's gold behemoth of a car and got her settled in the front seat.

Eli and I said goodbye to Teresa and Okeyo. The young woman hugged Eli and me tightly. He told her to call him anytime and that he could recommend a therapist who was excellent at helping Sapiens process the existence of magic.

Okeyo, more formal, shook our hands, though his gratitude was just as heartfelt.

"We're here for you too," I said. "Anytime." We'd given both Teresa and him our contact information.

He gave us a shaky smile. "No disrespect, but I hope to never see either of you again."

Eli nodded. "Totally understandable." They shook hands one last time and then we watched Tatiana drive off, wincing as the car lurched and stopped its way to the main road.

I grimaced. Jeez, Tatiana, hadn't these people suffered enough?

"Then there were two," I murmured.

"Yeah, but a pretty kick-ass two," Eli said. "I can't believe we actually rescued Teresa..." His breath was a foggy exhale in the cool night. Something flickered over his features, then he shook his head. "It's not over, is it?"

"No. I'll fill you in on the bigger picture, but what happened to you back in the gym?"

Eli had much the same experience that I did. Darkness, terror, general evil encouraging him to jump. I understood why Emmett wasn't affected, but why was Laurent the outlier with visions? While I hadn't asked Teresa or Okeyo, not wanting them to have to relive it, if neither Eli nor I had had visions, then why Laurent? Was it due to his Ohrist magic?

Who could I even ask?

Back inside, Sadie proclaimed that she didn't want to know any details. We were home and that was good enough for her, but she also didn't want to do our *Buffy* rewatch tonight. I couldn't fault her for that. She took her lucky earrings back, kissed us good-night, and went up to bed. Tomorrow she'd go to Eli's place for the week.

Jude, however, stayed late listening to the entire story.

We'd broken out a bottle of Merlot at the start of the tale and were well into our second bottle by the time I posed my hypothesis of why the game existed.

"It's about dybbuks," I said.

Jude groaned. "Can just one thing in this dang world not be about dybbuks?"

"Between what Ian told us and what Eli and I experienced, I think this Consortium has been running the game as an experiment for decades, adjusting the parameters as needed," I said. "Dybbuks only possess Ohrist hosts and can't even do that unless their inhibitions have been lowered."

Eli slammed the bottle on the table without topping up his glass as intended. "That's why there were all the mind games and a whole terror campaign? Those fucks are trying to turn Sapiens into hosts?"

"Yeah. Strip away the perception filter so they see magic, then find the right conditions to do the Sapien version of lowered inhibitions. The winner is both primed for dybbuk takeover and strong enough to withstand possession."

"I wonder if dybbuks are drawn to Ohrists because our magic makes us strong enough hosts in addition to giving them powers once they're in control of the body," Jude said. "Otherwise, wouldn't it be better to possess any human, even a Sapien if possible, then go back to being tortured in Gehenna?"

"You'd think." I ran a finger around the rim of my glass, my stomach tight. "They almost managed with Daw. Part of a dybbuk slipped inside her but couldn't go any further."

Eli swore under his breath. "But it made it that far because she'd been driven insane."

"Walk me through the gory details," Jude said. Her expression grew grimmer and grimmer as Eli and I took turns narrating the events. "After all that, the game ends at a playground, the Sapiens sliding into a veritable rebirth in their new, improved form. The transformative journey is complete." Jude held up her glass. "Evil bastards."

"Well, they're hoping to complete it," I said. "Through physical and psychological terror, the Consortium is stripping the Sapiens down to a newborn state, but thankfully, they haven't pulled a full phoenix yet."

"If dybbuks had access to most of the world's population,

the chaos would be unimaginable," Eli said. "We'd self-destruct."

"Maybe that's the point?" I took a sip, letting the fruity wine smooth away some of my jagged edges. "Get rid of the weak and undesirable while rich and powerful Ohrists hide away until the dust settles?"

"How do you know it's Ohrists?" Eli said. "Could be vamps or demons."

"Doubtful. Whoever set this game up went to a lot of effort. Vamps are allowed to turn Sapiens, and the new vamps are reliant on their sires. Why bother with unpredictable dybbuks? As for demons, they can do a ton of damage without exerting a fraction of that energy required for the game logistics. Plus, there's the whole betting angle. From what we saw in the final room, this was a private party for high rollers."

"Blood Alley runs games like that," Jude said. "But yeah, vampires have their own territories and don't need to be secretive."

Eli shook the last of the wine into his glass. "From what Nav's told me, demons don't care about accumulating cash like humans do."

Jude's eyebrows rose up. "Who's Nav?"

Eli shot her a flat look. "Like Mir hasn't filled you in."

She laughed. "Yeah, totally. Plus, I've met Daya." Jude patted his arm when he groaned. "Yes, sugar. Be very afraid."

"Trust me, I will." Eli turned to me. "We've got a Consortium of magic humans. Ohrists and Banim Shovavim?"

I shrugged. "I wouldn't rule out my kind being part of it." Or did they want one of my kind to join them? Me, specifically?

"How do you find them and stop them?" Jude said.

"We might not be able to," Eli said. He held up a hand at my protest. "First, there may not be a 'we.' I was put on this case to find Teresa. It's highly unlikely that Esposito will sanction me to continue investigating a magic Consortium. On the books, I was helping out with a missing person case. There is absolutely no way to justify this when most of the department doesn't know about magic."

"Shit." I hadn't thought about that, but Eli was right. "It'll get turned over to the Lonestars. This is enough to prove that someone is violating the prime directive."

I was perfectly fine with that. Let it be someone else's problem. I'd fill Ryann in on everything and then her people could run with it.

"Well," Eli said, "I hope they throw all their resources at finding them because the people in that Consortium are monsters."

I jostled my wineglass, sloshing alcohol onto my hand.

Jude grabbed a napkin to mop up the spill. "You good?"

"Yeah," I lied. "Just tired."

And terrified. The connection between the Ascendant, Arlo's admonishment, and what the vamp in the game had said had just dropped into my brain.

The dybbuks were the monsters that Arlo warned me should stay in the dark. The same ones that the vamp said don't stay when I'd asked why the Consortium was doing this. That alone was horrific, but it wasn't my new deduction.

One meaning of "ascendant" was dominant power or importance. Arlo intended to fly with the angels, but he hadn't meant it literally. He wanted to be in their league, and how had he done it? He'd shown the angels "the cracks in the seams"—a portal to Gehenna.

What was the tear in the room where the dybbuk had enthralled Laurent if not a crack in the seam between our reality and another very dangerous one that I was all too familiar with?

The Ascendant opened a door or doors to Gehenna to let out dybbuks. And Zev BatKian wanted it.

19

I none too gently encouraged Eli and Jude to leave. The second they were gone, I scoured myself in hot water, threw on some clothes, and after telling Sadie I'd be back soon, tore out of the house, Blood Alley bound.

Except I'd barely made it to my car before I was picked up and slammed against the hood so hard that for a moment, two moons wavered overhead like I was on an alien planet.

"Did you seek to distract me with a wild goose chase?" Zev's fangs descended, his face pressed close to mine.

Delilah was behind him with my scythe against his neck in the blink of an eye.

"Get off me," I snarled through the grip he had on my throat.

Time teetered on a knife's edge for a single spun-out moment, then he roughly released me.

I sat up, massaging my skull while Delilah stepped back, though she hung on to the weapon. At least I wasn't bleeding. "I'm going to find the Ascendant before you, and when I do, I'll destroy it. You'll never free the dybbuks."

Zev's mouth fell open, and he stared at me, gobsmacked. Under other circumstances, it would have been comical, but he recovered quickly enough, menace vibrating through the tight line of his body. "Enough of your games, Ms. Feldman. I've run out of patience with your stalling."

"And I've run out of patience with your lies." I crossed my arms, absolutely done with anyone or anything treating humans as a means to an end. "I saw your expression when I mentioned the monsters in the dark at our last meeting. You understood what Arlo Garcia meant by the cracks in the seams, didn't you? That the Ascendant opens a door to Gehenna to release dybbuks."

"Why would I give a damn about dybbuks?" he said indignantly.

"Chaos. Terror." Even as I said it, it didn't feel right.

Vamps were bloodthirsty. Literally. However, they fed and most of the time left humans alive. Hell, look at the Blood Alley shenanigans and existence of donors. There were enough people happy to provide a taste or two without having to resort to murder, and Zev didn't let the undead run around killing people for fun.

"Then why would you care about Gehenna?" I said. "Give me one reason to believe you that this isn't about hurting humans or I'll make sure you become the most hunted being out there."

He raked a cold, assessing glance over me. "Do you truly believe you could escape in order to carry out your threat?"

"Delilah got the jump on you once tonight. I'll take my chances."

He straightened his suit jacket with a sharp snap on the lapels. Moonlight winked off his sleeve, and he was missing a cufflink. This master vampire who literally destroyed a statue for having a tiny flaw was publicly imperfect.

I couldn't wrap my head around anything horrible enough for Zev to show a chink in his heavily fortified armor or allow him to be caught off guard by my shadow. Why was he becoming so unraveled?

"Look," I said. "You know I can keep a secret. If this isn't some nefarious plot against humanity, then tell me. Let me help, because despite your accusation, I've done nothing but try to find the amplifier for you as quickly as possible." I notched my chin up. "Trust me or kill me."

Bold words, sure, but his constant threats were tiresome. Besides, I'd come through for him on more than one occasion, and I'd never betrayed him. To the vampire's very slim credit, my past behavior would count for a lot.

Zev clenched his fists, a muscle ticking in his jaw. He rocked forward then back as if the struggle with this decision was physical. "I need…" Exhaling, he shook his head. "I need a word with the estrie who sired me." His eyes burned with the fervor of a man bent on vengeance.

Estries hadn't been seen in a few hundred years. Did he plan to kill her? That didn't make sense, but he didn't require her to make new vamps either.

"The estries are in Gehenna? How do you know?" I said.

"They aren't in the demon realm or here on earth. I've long suspected they were in Gehenna, but until now had no way to verify that." He crossed his arms and sighed as if I was testing his patience.

"I swear I didn't send you on any wild goose chase," I said, stopping in front of the vampire. "Can we move this conversation to the porch? The chairs are more comfortable than this hood."

I let him go first. There was standing up for myself and then there was turning my back on a dangerous vampire.

Zev sat stiffly in the cushioned Adirondack chair, arms on the rests like he was riding a foreign beast.

"The quote you provided me with?" he said. "'The fault, dear Brutus, is not in our stars, but in ourselves, that we are underlings.'" He worried at his upper lip with even white teeth before a small sigh escaped him. "It refers to the Woods Bank."

197

I wanted to tip my head back against the chair and soak in the night sky, letting the fresh air soothe me, body and soul. Instead, I angled my chair to keep the vampire in my direct line of sight. "I've never heard of it, but a bank is a great place to stash things."

"It's not a traditional bank. Woods is the last name of an Ohrist family. Hundreds of years ago, the matriarch turned a copse of trees on their land into safety deposit boxes, so to speak. Each trunk is a magically hollowed space large enough for a person and whatever goods they wish to store." How wild and wonderful. "The business was passed down through successive generations with the trees offered to a select clientele." His phone chimed, and he pulled it from his jacket pocket and scanned the screen almost apprehensively before putting it away.

His anxiety was rubbing off on me. I wanted the vampire who was fully in control back, not whatever this was.

"What about the quote?" I said.

"A quirk of the founder who loved Shakespeare. One only accesses their services if they've been invited by a current member and then thoroughly vetted. The quotes allow the Woodses to track who invited a person, in case of trouble."

"Why didn't you think of this place before you hired me?" It wasn't like him to overlook such an obvious possibility.

"I did." He shot me a look dripping with disdain. "I was assured by the head of the Woods family that they had no such item in their possession."

"They lied to you?" I rubbed my hand across my neck, wondering how bad their death would be.

"No. He wouldn't dare." He drummed his fingers on the armrest, sounding almost distracted. "I'd called in a rather large favor I'd been owed. Otherwise, they would never disclose what they guarded."

"Ah. That's why you think I sent you on a wild goose chase. That truly was Arlo's answer to where I'd find the

Ascendant. He might have lied, but I'm not sure he was capable of it. Not in the state he was in." I fell into a pensive silence. "This other case with the Consortium also has a connection to the Ascendant, which I only just discovered. In fact, I was coming to tell you about it when you so rudely choked me."

"You believe that the Consortium has it?"

"That or Tatiana stole it from them. I have the name of someone in their organization. Let me follow up tomorrow and I'll report back immediately with any findings."

Zev threw his head back looking up at the night sky. What had this estrie done to him? I would have paid a small fortune to know what was going through his head to make him look so defeated. "Very well," he finally said. "But I cannot impress upon you strongly enough that time is of the essence."

"Understood." I paused. "Uh, do I have your word that you don't want the Ascendant to harm humans?"

He tilted his head to expose his neck. "Trust me or kill me."

An interesting dare if we both didn't know I'd never take him up on it. I still needed his protection from whomever had restarted the hunt for the Ascendant.

"Touché."

I was so zonked, I could barely keep my eyes open long enough to strip off my clothes, my lids half shut before I hit the mattress.

Sadie's quick goodbye before she left for school Monday vaguely registered, but I didn't achieve full consciousness until midmorning. Yawning, I stretched out my limbs. My department store sheets had never felt so decadent and luxurious.

Once I was fortified with so much lovely caffeine that my leg was jittering and a completely fattening double chocolate chip muffin that I wolfed down with zero regrets, I wrote out my to-do list: Jason Maxwell, Tatiana, Ryann, and Ian.

I tapped my pen against the notepad. Tatiana wanted to meet today, but it would be best if I found Jason Maxwell before being ordered to turn the case over to the Lonestars, which I fully expected to happen.

Plus, there was one other thing bothering me. My hypothesis about the Ascendant being tied to cracks and seams and dybbuks getting free had one big flaw with it. Arlo never got the magic amplifier, so how did he show the angels what it could do? I could be wrong about its powers, but it fit together so well.

I sent Tatiana a text asking to chase down a lead before meeting with her. I framed it as wanting to have as much information as possible in case the Lonestars took over, but I also needed answers about the Ascendant for Zev.

No, not just for the vampire. Had my parents known what they were stealing? Ninety-nine percent of me believed that they hadn't. That they would never have agreed to get involved with such a dangerous artifact unless it was to destroy it.

What about that one percent?

I stared blankly at the table. They'd raised me to be polite and kind to others, and the one time I'd shoplifted some candy on a dare, they'd been furious because stealing was wrong, especially from a small business owner in our community. I'd forgotten all about that until now.

Did they live by a Robin Hood mentality of stealing from the rich or was all of it a ruse?

Tatiana's responding text saying that we could meet tomorrow shook me out of my stupor.

Time to get cracking.

My attempt to meet with Arlo for a second time was a

bust. I was very careful not to mention his name, and yet I found myself blown out of the KH and into my living room. Message received.

If I couldn't get answers from the source, I'd get them another way.

I logged into all the databases at my disposal compiling data on everyone called Jason Maxwell. Next, I compared all details to social media profiles to confirm employment or other personal details that would knock them off my list.

Hours later, I'd narrowed it down to four candidates. My stomach was growling, my eyes were dry, and my neck and lower back were killing me thanks to my shitty posture. I made myself toast with melted cheese as a late lunch/early dinner with a side of baby carrots and potato chips for dessert. After what I'd gone through, I deserved a factory's worth of the salty carb-laden delights.

With a full belly, I hit the KH to chase down all four Jason Maxwells. I struck the one in Melbourne off because he was in the hospital recovering from open heart surgery. The second, in Oklahoma, was promising until I engaged him in conversation, pretending to be a passerby admiring his garden, and was subjected to a forty-five minute lecture on roses. He not only bred them, he competed internationally with his flowers and had named his two tiny dogs after different breeds of the flower: Mr. Lincoln and Lady Banks.

By the time I extricated myself from his enthusiastic monologue, I never wanted to see another rose again, which sucked for the gorgeous bush in my yard.

That left two more Jasons to check out. Hmm, go to London or Majorca? They were equally likely home bases for a man working for a shady Consortium, but I went to England on a hunch that the gamblers would attract less attention coming and going in a large city. I had no idea where the gambling room was located, but London certainly had its share of private clubs to easily cater to an exclusive Ohrist membership.

The British Jason Maxwell was obviously wealthy, given his large Georgian townhome in the chic Kensington district of London, and the fact that his door was opened by a freaking butler.

I didn't have a card to present or a convenient excuse. I just waltzed in, cloaked, to poke around.

When the butler didn't find anyone at the door, he stopped by a study to inform the slender, bespectacled man behind the desk in fancy-ass pajamas that it must have been children playing a prank and ask if Mr. Maxwell wished for a snack before retiring for the night.

Maxwell declined the offer, and the butler departed, closing the door behind him.

I dropped my cloaking, but the man didn't even flinch.

He closed his laptop, studying me with the palest, coldest blue eyes I'd ever seen.

We had our winner.

I turned the lock. "Hands in the air where I can see them and face the window." If he was an Ohrist, he required a line of sight to use his magic on me, and most also had a telltale flick of their hands.

He held them up but that was as far as he obliged. "Or what?" He had an annoying nasal quality to his plummy voice. "You hardly look like much of a threat."

"Well, I survived your game and the Consortium seems interested in my Banim Shovavim magic." I dropped into an uncomfortable wingback chair upholstered in a scratchy plaid. "I found your notes. What an honor to get two underlines."

He opened his mouth, but I held up a hand.

"Speak with your back to me." I made a production of letting my shadows swirl up my body.

He turned his chair around before they'd hit my shoulders. "Don't get too excited. The underlines were mine. There aren't many of you around, and I was surprised."

Uh-huh. I cocked an ear for the sound of anyone approaching. I didn't hear footsteps, but my other questions were more urgent.

"Tell me about the Ascendant." I peeked under the blotter for any hidden papers because his desk was empty save for the computer, a notepad, and a silver pen, but there was nothing there.

"You found—" Those words tumbled out of him then he cleared his throat. "You found out about its existence?"

Ha. The Consortium didn't have it.

That was good in terms of their experiments, but bad in terms of finding it. I examined the books on his shelves, letting him stew, while I formulated my follow-up questions. His tastes ran to military fiction and statistics with nary a tome on mythology or magic or anything indicating he was involved in the dybbuk-creation side of things.

"Tell me if I'm correct." I tugged on a sconce and then a decorative finial in hopes of a secret passageway or hidey-hole. Nothing. "The Ascendant opens a way to Gehenna."

"Can I put my arms down?" he said.

"No. Am I right?" I checked for a safe behind the framed old map on yellowed parchment that was the sole piece hanging on the wall, but there wasn't one.

"You're correct."

A zing of excitement shot through me, but as pleased as I was to have unlocked the Ascendant's power, it didn't explain how Arlo Garcia had gotten hold of the amplifier to use *before* Tatiana gave it to him.

I rubbed my temples. "When did the Consortium last have the magic amplifier?"

"How would I know? I'm not privy to such things."

Oh yeah? I narrowed my eyes. *Then why do you sound so smug?*

I knocked his chair around to face me, and Delilah leapt

on him, straddling the man with her arm wedged against his throat. He clawed at her, his pajama sleeve falling to his elbow, but my shadow was stronger than he was, and I made sure to stay out of his line of sight.

He flushed redder and redder, making sputtering noises in his attempts to breathe.

I ordered Delilah to let up on him. "If you want to continue breathing, then answer me, Jase."

His eyes flashed in hate. "We haven't had it in almost thirty years."

"Was it taken by Arlo Garcia?"

"We suspect so, yes."

Arlo wasn't part of the Consortium because if he had been, it wouldn't have taken Tatiana three years to find the Ascendant. What was I missing?

"Sir?" Some manservant rapped politely on the door.

"Play it cool," I murmured.

"I'm busy at the moment," Jason called out.

The person went away, but my time here was limited.

"Why aren't dybbuks constantly flooding out?" Dybbuks were getting into that room where Laurent had been inhabited, so after the Consortium had originally torn through to Gehenna, that door had stayed open for years.

"I have no idea," Jason said evenly. His eyes darted to my shadow.

Delilah still sat on him, walking her fingers up the side of his neck like a total creeper. His being in pajamas didn't help that image. Honestly, I couldn't say how much of that was me and how much of it was her own initiative, but his shudder was deeply satisfying.

"I truly don't know," Jason reiterated. "It's been this way from the beginning, and the dybbuks that do come out are called back at sunset on Saturday just like all others since they never find a host."

They didn't know that Laurent had been enthralled. Thank you, universe, for that stroke of good luck.

I frowned. Either the tear or the Ascendant was too weak or unstable for more than a dybbuk or two at a time to get through or the Consortium hadn't used it properly. I picked up the silver pen and uncapped it. Calligraphy nib. Fancy.

"Final question. Does the quote 'The fault, dear Brutus, is not in our stars, but in ourselves, that we are underlings' mean anything to you?"

I was grasping at straws, but perhaps the Consortium had a different take on it than Zev.

"The fault in our stars quote is a password."

"I know about the Woods Bank," I said. "Any other meaning? Where is the Ascendant now?"

"I don't know." Jason spat the words at me, right as his fingers twitched.

I jammed the calligraphy pen into the back of his hand, aborting his magic use. I didn't know what type of power he possessed, nor did I want to find out.

He screamed, clutching his bleeding hand.

"Sir!" The manservant pounded on the door.

"One chance to change your answer." I wiggled the pen and he hissed. "It hurts more coming out. Anything?"

"I've got the key!" the butler cried.

"The Consortium will find you and kill you," Jason spat.

"They can take a number."

The knob rattled.

Shutting Delilah down, I jumped into the KH. I'd made another enemy, but I'd gotten a concrete lead. I examined Jason's blood on my hands clinically, almost distantly. I could live with my actions today. Maybe one day at a time was all I could hope for.

20

THE ELDERLY ARTIST GREETED ME ON TUESDAY morning, flinging the door open in a cloud of rose perfume, the gold bracelets on her chiffon sleeve quivering in indignation. "What have you done?"

Was she mad about Jason Maxwell? Had she faced retaliation of some sort due to my actions? Or worse, was this about the Ascendant? I twisted my hands around, my head bowed in anticipation of a magic thrashing. "I—well—look, things were very difficult and—"

Tatiana flung a hand at me. "Cookies," she seethed. "I am not paying her to have a tea party."

I blinked. "Say what?"

"Marjorie. She was so happy to see that golem of yours—"

"I don't legally own him, nor did I create him so—"

"That she showed up this morning with cookies for him. They're having tea in my garden. Three years that girl's been with me, and how many times have I gotten cookies?" Her raspy New Yorker accent grew heavier.

"I'm going to go with zero." I blotted my brow, relieved this wasn't about me, and slipped past her into the foyer to kick off my sandals. "You also abuse her on a regular basis."

"Pshaw. It's character building." She slid her oversize glasses up her nose. "Good God, Miriam. Why did you raid a flour sack factory? Am I not paying you enough to buy real clothing?"

My ankle-length sundress and yellow cardigan were perfectly nice. "You're not paying me enough to build my character."

"Don't be such a snowflake." She seated herself on one of the sofas in her living room like a queen.

The windows were thrown open to the sun, the row of plants, some flowering, some with broad, waxy leaves, lending a hothouse-level humidity and rich, earthy scent to the otherwise elegant room. Tatiana had switched out the painting in the position of pride over the mantel from the one of Jackie Onassis from the Dollhouse Collection to a vibrant abstract with geometric shapes heavy with bold golds and oranges.

I tilted my head. "It's a face."

"A self-portrait."

"I only see crow's feet when I look in the mirror." I sat down.

Tatiana gave a throaty chuckle. "Then you're not looking hard enough for who you really are."

"Have you spoken with Deputy Chief Constable Esposito?"

"Yes. Ohrists trying to turn Sapiens into hosts. This is bad business." She toyed with a bracelet. "Thank you for helping Laurent."

"Of course. Did you speak to him today?"

"No. He's holed up and not answering. Emmett told me." Tatiana rearranged two decorative cushions, eventually settling them back into their original places.

I tapped my fist against my thigh. I was doing my best to wait for him to call first but it was hard.

"What was the lead you went after, bubeleh?"

"The man running the gambling side of things."

She raised an eyebrow. "And?"

You stole their door opener to the bad place.

But I couldn't say that. Not to Tatiana, possibly ever, and certainly not when I didn't know how much she knew about the Ascendant and what it really did.

She'd spent three years searching for it, so it was fair to assume that she'd learned of its nature. What had she thought about handing it over to Arlo, her client? Would she really be willing to do anything for the money? Would she be one of those Ohrists who'd just hole up and wait it out while humans fell victim to dybbuks?

Any guilt over not sharing my parents' role in her car crash eased. My black-and-white views about secrets and betrayal no longer felt as solid in the face of her dooming humanity by being part of Arlo's power-mad scheme to "fly with the angels."

I'd made allowances for every instance where Tatiana prioritized a paycheck over ethics, but this was too far. My search for the Ascendant had become as much about absolving Tatiana—and my parents—as the artifact itself.

I shrugged in answer to my boss's question. "Maxwell confirmed their evil agenda, refused to answer any other questions, and then threatened me when I encouraged him to be more forthcoming."

Tatiana's lips quirked at my light way of describing the encounter. "A dead end?"

"Only metaphorically. What do you take me for? On a more serious note, though, I'm guessing we're turning this case over to the Lonestars?"

"Obviously," she said. I was pleased and a bit surprised that she didn't argue about losing the case, given there was no love lost between Tatiana and the magic cops. "There wouldn't be anyone to pay us."

I snorted.

"I'm going up to my studio for a bit. Ryann is coming over in a couple hours." Tatiana stood up. "Once we've officially handed it over, we'll return to my memoirs."

"Good job finding Teresa Wong and surviving that game," I said to her retreating back. "I'm so impressed with your work, Miriam."

"Sounds like someone needs their participation trophy," she trilled back.

"Yeah, well, people give me cookies." I smiled at her faint humph.

With time to kill, I checked in with Zev. After our last encounter, I felt like we'd moved past texting to actual phone calls. A more personal connection. Nice thought. I was sent to a voice mail without any greeting attached and left the message that I'd spoken to the Consortium guy and to let me know when we should meet.

The head vamp texted me a few minutes later to come to Blood Alley immediately. There was no helpful emoji to denote tone. I replied with a thumbs-up in case he was unfamiliar with the concept of these pictograms and their incredible usefulness.

His reply was swift. *Never send me one of those again.*

I made my way there, humming the disco classic "Born to Be Alive," with the sun on my face and the wind in my hair. I even snagged a parking spot close to the gates, but my optimism about this meeting was short-lived.

Rodrigo met me inside, once again wearing the silly-looking chauffeur's cap trimmed in gold braid.

I scrunched up my face. "Are you covering a bald spot? I totally support you doing whatever makes you feel like your best self, but have you considered branching out? A fedora? Maybe a smart derby? You'd look very fetching in one."

"Mr. BatKian has been called away unexpectedly. Your meeting is canceled."

Zev wanted this meeting as soon as possible, so why bail?

Uneasy, I surreptitiously backed up toward the exit. "Everything okay?"

"Yes." Given how weary Zev had been lately, I doubted that. "He'll reschedule as soon as possible," Rodrigo added.

"As long as you're here, maybe you can help me. Did Celeste take up residence at Damien's old place? I need to speak to Ian."

"I'm not at liberty to say where Mr. BatKian's grand-daughter resides," Rodrigo said, looming over me. "Don't go looking for her."

I pushed him out of my personal space, but he went precisely nowhere. "You're blotting out the sun. Step back."

He didn't budge an inch.

"I'm not looking to start trouble," I said. "I'd like to compare my findings with Ian's experience. I need two minutes with the man, that's it."

Rodrigo thought about it, then nodded. "Wait here."

"Thank you, my fine fellow." I tipped an imaginary cap at him.

A muscle in his jaw ticked, then he pivoted sharply and stalked off.

Look at me, bringing joy and delight to this person's day.

My upbeat mood lasted the first ten minutes I was kept waiting. I buoyed myself up for another fifteen with multiple games of *Tetris*, but after that I was bored and annoyed. If this was payback for my cracks about his dumb hat, well, all right, I guess he'd gotten me.

Just as I was about to leave, Rodrigo arrived with Ian. The Undertaker took my "I need two minutes" as fact and set a damn timer on his phone.

Ian had regained his color and was much steadier than the last time I'd seen him. He was still quiet, but calm, only hesi-tating a second when I said I had a few more questions for him.

"Did you go into a high school gym in the game?" I said.

"Yes, near the beginning."

I rubbed my chin. "Where did the game end?"

"A cemetery."

They'd flipped the game in the past five years since Ian had played.

"What happened when you got there?"

Ian clenched and unclenched his fists. "There were open graves everywhere. The three of us still alive..." He swallowed.

Rodrigo placed a steadying hand on the man's shoulder.

Ian took a deep breath. "Vamps arrived. We were told to pick a grave."

I gasped.

"Fumiko and Lukas fought back. They..." He dropped his gaze to the ground, scuffing his foot against the concrete. "I was a coward and I jumped in a grave."

"You saved yourself," I said gently but firmly. "There's no shame in that. You shouldn't feel guilty."

"I thought I was dead anyway because they threw dirt over me."

I closed my eyes against the horror of it. "How did you get out?"

"I begged them to stop, then one of the vamps said that I'd won and I could live. Not just a normal lifespan but forever. All I had to do was choose it."

The timer went off.

"We're done," Rodrigo said.

Ian slumped in relief.

"Just one more—"

Rodrigo led Ian off with a "don't even think about following" glower.

Whatever, dude. I had other places to be.

I drove back to Tatiana's home for our meeting with Ryann, unable to get Ian's experience out of my head. Being buried alive trumped the darkness I'd experienced for worst nightmare ever.

Even thinking about it while sitting in my locked sedan in broad daylight made my skin crawl. The thunk of the shovel, the feel of the dirt raining down on my face, everything growing smaller and more enclosed.

I rolled my window down, taking huge gulps of air.

Ian was only offered hope in the form of immortality at the end, whereas my players had it dangled over them from the start.

And as scary as that darkness inside me had been, it wasn't the pure terror of Ian's experience. Both versions of the game involved violently stripping away the perception filter and a terror campaign. Given how broken Ian ended up, did the game designers decide they'd gone too far with him?

I drummed my fingers on the wheel, waiting for a light to change. The experiment as designed with Ian's group hadn't worked, so they'd changed it. This information might not help Ryann find this Consortium, but it couldn't hurt. I prayed the Lonestars took these fuckers down hard.

When I got to Tatiana's, Emmett answered the door in a chic silk dressing gown and ascot.

"How are the Sapiens?" I said.

"Teresa and Okeyo are fine. She went back to her family, and he's at the airport waiting for his flight to Kenya. Juliette brought Daw to another healer she knows for extra help."

To my surprise, when Emmett led me into the kitchen, Ryann and Tatiana were sharing an open tin of homemade cookies. My employer had crumbs on her dress.

"Have fun," the golem said and left.

I waved bye to him over my shoulder. "This is cozy."

"Ryann brought a little something to thank me for our good work on the missing person case," Tatiana said smugly.

Our? Tatiana hadn't done much beyond find us a way into

the game, but I let it lie, because the room smelled of ginger-bread, and I craved one of those babies.

I sat down at the table with them and reached for one, only to have Tatiana slap my hand away.

"These are mine."

"I'm glad you're enjoying the gift," Ryann said. "They're not much, but hopefully it expresses my gratitude for your helping get those poor people out safely." She bit into her cookie. "Mmm. This batch turned out well."

Tatiana brushed crumbs off her lap and selected another cookie. "Bullshit," she said pleasantly. "This isn't a gift. It's a bribe because the Lonestars aren't allowed to touch the Consortium so you're buttering me up hoping I'll do the rest of your righteous dirty work."

Ryann choked, coughing.

Tatiana sighed. "The cookies were a good touch, but your fake smile needs some work, because oy vey."

I thumped Ryann on the back. Say what about the Consortium?

The Lonestar's eyes widened even more cartoonishly than normal. "How did you know that? Did you speak to someone?"

Tatiana helped herself to another cookie. "You think I've got rocks for brains? We hand you proof that some secret organization is violating your precious prime directive in a big way and then you show up with cookies? Someone high up kiboshed your investigation."

"Whoa." Ryann bowed, her hands in namaste formation. "But the cookies really were a gift."

Tatiana huffed a sigh. "Stop making puppy dog eyes, Miriam. It's pathetic. Take one already."

"If you insist," I said cheerfully. "Were you given a reason that you had to stop?"

Ryann shook her head. "I was told to allocate my resources to local matters."

"You think Lonestars are involved?" I bit into the ginger-bread, savoring its spicy kick.

Ryann's shoulders drooped. "You always think the worst of us."

"It's not like she doesn't have reason." Tatiana flapped a hand. "One of yours covered up her parents' murders."

My lovely cookie turned to sawdust, forcing me to muscle down the lump. Tatiana was defending me over my parents of all things. I felt like shit on the bottom of Satan's shoe.

"In this case, she's wrong." Ryann tapped the six-pointed gold star tattoo on her wrist. "There was never an official decree to stay away from the game before. My Lonestar predecessors didn't think we had to bother. To me, this signals new pressure on my organization from the Consortium."

As expected, the cop wrung every last detail out of me, though I was completely forthcoming except about the Ascendant. I even told her that I'd spoken to Jason Maxwell to confirm what the Consortium was up to. Needless to say, she wasn't too happy about that.

"As one of the few people capable of killing dybbuks," I said, "I had a right to know if I'd correctly surmised their agenda. Your permission wasn't required."

"Tatiana is growing on you." Ryann didn't sound like she thought that was a good thing, but my boss didn't apologize her way through life.

The elderly woman smirked.

"Anything else?" Ryann said.

I debated whether to mention Ian, but he didn't know anything about the Consortium and wasn't relevant to the Lonestars. "That's it. Are you going to let the Consortium get away with this?"

"My hands are tied." She sent me a pointed look.

"Oh, come on. If they're that powerful," I said, "I can't take them down." I didn't expect them to retaliate for hurting Jason because he struck me as the type of man who wouldn't want his bosses to know I'd gotten the better of him, but any direct approach on them was a different matter.

"Are you paying us?" Tatiana said.

"Really?" I crossed my arms. "Every single case you've had a bad feeling about, but this one you're fine with?"

"I'm not if it's pro bono. Well?" Tatiana got up and opened a kitchen drawer.

Ryann looked down at the tablecloth, absently tracing an infinity symbol on the fabric, until she caught herself and dropped her hand. "I have a slush fund I could redirect without anyone being the wiser."

My boss returned with a pen and a pad of paper. "Write the amount down."

I spread my hands wide, gaping at them. "I can't believe you two are discussing this. The Consortium stopped the magic cops from going after them directly."

"Which is why you're perfect for it." Ryann nodded enthusiastically, while writing a number down. "They won't expect you."

"I infiltrated their game. I'm on their radar."

Tatiana snatched up the paper. "This will do."

"Just kill me yourself," I said. "It'll be faster."

"Leave the theatrics to Sadie," Tatiana said. "She's better at them. You're not going after the Consortium."

"We had a deal," Ryann said.

"Be real," Tatiana said. "Even if you found and arrested every single member, with their power they wouldn't even merit a slap on the wrist."

"They're violating the prime directive," Ryann insisted.

I swung my head to Tatiana because this was getting good. What had she agreed to take money for?

My boss made a raspberry sound. "That doesn't matter and you know it. Now, if you want to stop your directive from being further violated, there's only one way to go about it. Miriam?"

I blinked stupidly at her for a moment, my brain racing. Then I slammed the table. "The only way to win is to destroy the game!"

Tatiana pointedly rubbed at the spot on her table that I'd hit. "What did I say about theatrics?"

"Sorry."

"But you're right," she said.

Good, because now that the idea had been planted, I had to be the one to see it through and be certain that no one else would ever suffer through that horror.

"What's to stop them from creating a new game somewhere else?" Ryann said.

They didn't have the Ascendant to create an opening to Gehenna, that's what.

"They took over an abandoned demon space for this one," I said. "It was enormous. I doubt there's many of those up for grabs or that Ohrists could create something that large."

"She's right," Tatiana said. "Before you showed up, I got through to Laurent, who apprised me of the scale of their game." Wait, what? He willingly spoke with his aunt in his current headspace? Okay. That was good. I guess. "It's much larger than Blood Alley, larger even than the Park, which is one of the bigger hidden spaces in the world."

I hadn't known that.

Ryann scratched a hand through her buzz cut, her brow furrowed. "The Park exists because it uses the real Stanley Park as a foundation. Given the game world's size and detail, it couldn't have been created from scratch." She nodded. "We can rule out a re-creation."

Having secured Ryann's agreement about destroying the space, as well as her fee, Tatiana wrapped up the meeting.

I lingered after the Lonestar's departure, wanting a

moment alone with my boss. "Will you be paying Laurent to help with this like you did with sending him in?"

"I didn't pay him squat," Tatiana said. "He was very determined to go in after you." Grinning, she nudged me.

I'll just bet he was, but not for the reasons she thought. His lie about being paid, his pointed comments when we were in the game? He'd intended to confront me about the Ascendant. I rubbed my arms. That bastard.

Laurent had made me feel horrible about keeping mum when he'd known the entire time. Plus, he'd continued to keep his own secrets—even something as small as not correcting my impression that Gabriel was his brother.

I curled my hands into fists, my cheeks flushed. However, there was a silver lining to this. By figuring things out on his own, Laurent had found a loophole. We could have this out without me breaking my promise to Zev.

Tatiana replaced the lid on the cookie tin. "Do you have a plan?"

For destroying the game? Yup. For Laurent? Most definitely.

21

I DIDN'T CONFRONT LAURENT RIGHT AWAY BECAUSE it was too easy to be emotional when I was angry. I wanted my feelings to cool and harden into a brilliant diamond.

After a turbulent sleep, I armored up on Wednesday for my first visit of the day: a demon. I wore a red pencil skirt, a red silky blouse, and red heels, with my hair pulled tightly back into a sleek ponytail and a slash of red across my lips. I'd worn all the pieces separately while employed by the law firm but had never had the guts to go for such a bold, monochrome look.

Hello, brand-new day.

I'd given myself one last, admiring glance when, speak of the devil, Laurent texted me, asking me to come over and talk. I didn't answer, not ready to deal with him yet.

I drove to the curio shop on the edge of Gastown that had been run by a demon called Chester until he'd been murdered by a Banim Shovavim. The business had been a neutral drop-off and meeting spot for demons, and as it was still in business, I figured the new proprietor wouldn't be human either.

After parking down the block, I approached the red shop door with a confident stride. Above it was an oval-shaped cream sign edged in a black filigree design, with the word "curios" in script. In its center was painted a rosy-cheeked maiden whose white nightgown slipped off one chubby pale shoulder, her dark hair tumbling out of her updo.

As I reached for the door, the letters "ity killed the cat" floated next to "curios," and the maiden was replaced by glowing red eyes and an evil smile.

"You don't find signs like that anymore," a woman behind me said.

Was she Sapien? Ohrist? Demon? "No, you don't. Especially the…" I waved my hand around. Which sign did she see?

"She's like something out of a Frederic Leighton painting." A smile creased the woman's plump face. "Absolutely lovely."

"Right." Oh good. She saw only the regular sign, not the devilish smile. The Sapien and I entered the store, and I groaned.

The person behind the counter was not a demon, though I'd have a better chance of getting my soul back from Satan than assistance from Clea, the second-in-command of Carpe Demon.

The operative shot me a glare as severe as her dyed-black bob.

I browsed through the treasure trove of goods, waiting for the other customer to clear out and composing an argument that would sway Clea to my side. Why was she here anyway? Had Carpe Demon taken charge of the shop?

Not much had changed since the last time I'd been here. The store still reeked of patchouli. To me, dybbuks didn't have any particular scent, but that's what they smelled like to Laurent, and I wondered if it was an innate odor to demons as well? Strips of vintage wrapping paper covered the walls and delicate paper parasols jetted down from the ceiling like stalactites. Objects from old clocks to baby doll heads to china figurines, candelabras, and empty glass bottles crowded the shelves, while the walls were adorned with faded vintage photographs and even the occasional goat skull.

To the left of the glass counter with the old-fashioned cash register was a narrow staircase. Mounted along the wall was a dragon with a cocky look on its face as if daring you to enter its lair.

I tamped down a smile. It was similar to Clea in that respect.

My goth adversary wrapped up the bronze lion medallion that the Sapien had purchased in brown paper and waved her off with a smile, which, if you squinted, might almost be called friendly. She cracked open a new roll of quarters and dumped them into the drawer in the register. "What do you want?"

I approached the counter, my heels ticking a rapid beat, channeling the badassery of my red outfit. "I'm looking for information."

She cracked her gum and slammed the drawer shut. "Try the tourism office at Waterfront Station."

"Well, it's not your affable customer service that landed you here. Why would anyone—" I bounced on my toes. "Is this a punishment? What did you do?"

"The previous owner and I had a disagreement." Clea stabbed an X-Acto knife into the top flap of a small box on the counter. "I'm filling in until we've vetted a replacement. Come back next week when I'm gone."

"Look," I said, exasperated. "Much as you think I'm some mercenary, unlike your noble self, Sapiens are being kidnapped and forced through a nightmarish competition as an experiment to turn them into dybbuk hosts."

"Are demons involved?" She unwrapped a series of tiny demon masks carved out of wood, each one more hideous than the last.

"Not as far as we can tell, but they're using an old demon

space to run this game." I wrinkled my face at the collection, but she nodded in satisfaction.

"Then it's the Lonestars' problem."

"It should be their problem," I said, "but they've been ordered otherwise."

"*You're* going to fix it?" She laughed.

The diamond-hard rage inside me glittered, urging me on. I slammed my hand on the counter, making Clea flinch.

"Yeah, I am, and you're going to help, since Ohrists have been running this game for decades under your noses in a reclaimed demon space."

"Just because someone is squatting in a former demon space doesn't make it our problem."

I jabbed a finger at her. "Get over your bullheaded issues with me and tell me what I need to completely obliterate the place."

Clea tapped the X-Acto knife against the counter a couple times, sizing me up.

I held her gaze.

"How big is the space?" she said sullenly.

I tamped down my smirk of victory. "Huge. Larger than the Park."

"That won't be easy to destroy." Her eyes narrowed. "How about a trade?"

"For what?" I didn't trust her for an instant.

She reached under the counter and retrieved a wooden box about three inches high, which was overlaid with brass carved into ornate deco designs. "Open this puzzle box. None of us have had any luck. We can't use brute strength or magic on it because of what we fear is inside." Yikes. That didn't sound dangerous or anything. "Figure it out and I'll burn a favor I'm owed to get what you need."

"Why do you think I'll be able to crack it?"

"You love puzzles, don't you?" She picked up a black

marker, wrote a price on a sticker, and placed it on one of the masks.

"Yeah, but jigsaw puzzles, *Tetris*... Hang on. How do you know that?"

"Eli mentioned it to Nav and me at lunch."

My hackles rose. "You had lunch with Eli?" Why didn't he mention that to me? If it was just Nav, okay, but he was fraternizing with someone that he knew didn't like me.

Clea shot me an odd look. "Yeah. Will you do it or not?"

I took the box. "When I bring this back, open, you hand over the means to destroy that space."

"I said I would."

Tucking the puzzle box under my arm, I strode back out to my car. Once inside, I phoned Eli.

"Yo, Mir. What's up?" There was a familiar loud clang on his end of the phone and he sounded a bit breathless. I'd caught him at the gym.

"I just saw your buddy Clea," I said. "Heard you talked about me."

"Come on, it's not like that."

"Why didn't you tell me? You know she hates me."

There was silence. "Sorry. Having some water. Look, Nav and I arranged to have lunch yesterday, and Clea guilted him into bringing her. I didn't tell you because it would upset you and it wasn't a big deal."

No, it wasn't. I fiddled with the puzzle box in my lap, wondering why that had pushed such a button for me. Would I have cared if I wasn't already feeling guilty about keeping my own secrets? Eli's wasn't even anything hush-hush, it was lunch, but given how close we were, I'd automatically expected him to tell me even the smallest thing involving me, and the fact that he hadn't stung.

"I overreacted," I said and let him get on with his day.

I put the box in my purse and checked my phone for any

texts or calls from Zev, but as he still hadn't made contact, I fit the key in the ignition.

Had Laurent expected me to broach the subject of the Ascendant and Tatiana's crash and that's why he didn't mention it? I'd been so focused on not hurting him and not forcing him to choose between his aunt and me that I'd forgotten how few people he let inside his walls. If I was touchy about perceived betrayals, they were a hot button for Laurent.

That diamond-bright anger inside me shattered into dust, my shoulders slumping. After wiping my palms off on my skirt, I started the engine and drove over to Hotel Terminus.

Sadly, my dismay amped up when it came into view. My first impression of the hotel was that Laurent left the dirt- and rust-streaked exterior as is to keep people away, also using its appearance to make people underestimate him, because how could someone formidable live here?

Now I had my doubts. This run-down hotel was so like its owner it hurt. A disaster on the outside and a shining beautiful jewel inside. Had Laurent left the exterior like this because he believed it was hopeless? Boarded up and falling apart?

Was he honestly unable to see the strong foundation and good bones? Its worth was so obvious to anyone who bothered to look. The wrought-iron railings were made with a precise and timeless craftsmanship, requiring only some rust remover, while the black chevron pattern that ran horizontally between each of the three stories added an affable charm to the sleek, sharp edges.

Laurent put all his time and energy and love into restoring the interior, then fiercely guarded who he let see it. Except, I'd seen glimpses of the exterior that matched the passion that burned inside him. The man he'd been before something had happened to distort the reflection of who he now saw in the mirror.

Boo scampered past me as I walked toward the side entrance, slipping through the ajar door. The gray kitten was no longer the tiny ball of fluff I'd first met. Larger and sleeker, she was a rambunctious teenager, and like her human counterparts, she was testing her boundaries, pouncing on a sneaker and batting it between her claws.

Piano music floated on the breeze, a dreamy classical piece that I recognized as Chopin's Fantaisie-Impromptu in C-sharp Minor.

I rapped on the door and called out his name, but he didn't answer. Even if he was in the back, he'd be able to hear and smell me with his… I dropped my hand. He didn't have his shifter magic back yet. I debated whether to stay or go, but my desire to finally clear the air between us won out. I walked into the foyer and stopped at the sight of him at the piano, shirtless, his back muscles flexing as he poured his soul into the music.

Closing my eyes, I let the rapid notes flow over me like water. Shivers skated over my body at the chords crashing down like the pounding of waves, the melody easing to a gentle swell, his touch light and dreamy.

My breath caught on a lingering note, then the tempo picked up, and I opened my eyes. Laurent swayed, hunched over the keys, the music growing and growing to a crescendo that spun back out like sugar for the final notes, dusting the room with the same gold as the afternoon light.

My eyes were damp when he finished, my throat thick.

He danced his fingers over a couple of keys. "I haven't played for anyone in a long time."

"A shame."

He spun around on the bench, his eyes flaring hot and bright as he drank me in. "I'm glad you came."

"Uh, good. Can I sit down?" At his nod, I slid off my heels and crossed the checkerboard parquet to his huge sofa near the fireplace.

He remained where he was, scooping a wriggling Boo into his lap.

I pointed at his regenerated shadow. "Your magic's back?"

"I believe so." He held up a hand. "I only tested my claws."

"Hopefully all is well." Weighing my next words carefully, positive Zev would sense if I broke my promise, I moved aside his shirt that was tossed carelessly over the back of the sofa, resisting the urge to press it to my nose. "Tell me what you know."

Laurent scratched Boo's ear. "You have to be more specific."

"I can't." I smoothed out my skirt. "I promised Zev."

"Ah. That." He bowed his head, his attention on the cat, but when she bit his finger and jumped off, Laurent gave me a wry smile. "Guess that's my cue."

I bunched my fists into my skirt material. "Yes."

He frowned, looking off, as if slotting his words into the correct order. "The day you ran out of Tatiana's with that ridiculous excuse about shoes, I couldn't understand why you were so flustered, so insistent on knowing when my aunt's car accident had happened." He shook his head. "Only that you freaked out when you heard 'Mack the Knife.'"

"Did you piece together the whole story?" I raised stricken eyes to him, torn between relief and regret. How would this change things between us?

Laurent joined me on the sofa. "It was a guess at first. Tatiana's favorite song plus your interest in her accident, specifically the timeline that fit your parents' murders. They were part of this somehow."

He reached for his shirt and shrugged into it, doing up the buttons with strong, elegant fingers. It should have looked silly paired with the loose board shorts he wore, but Laurent could throw anything on and make a person look twice in admiration. It was his combination of utter indifference and incredible grace.

"That got me wondering about your uncle's letter and our visit to Poe and the Casino," he said. "This Ascendant is at the heart of Tatiana's car crash, isn't it?"

I hugged a pillow to my chest. "Did you ask her?"

Laurent's eyes softened. "No. I haven't said a word to my aunt. I asked Emmett if you'd mentioned the letter to him. That's when he told me about the prophecy." He paused. "What does the Ascendant do?"

"It opens a door to Gehenna," I said. "Like the one we found on the Grouse Grind."

"Merde! That's how the Consortium had dybbuks." He rubbed his chin, his expression softening from angry to thoughtful. "If there was more than one amplifier there wouldn't be the same urgency to find it, so the tear on the mountain must have either been a natural weak spot or a residual effect of the Ascendant's existence."

Boo raced in, carrying a tiny toy mouse that she dropped at Laurent's feet. He absently picked it up and chucked it across the hotel for her to chase.

"Now BatKian has you looking for the amplifier," he said.

"Yes, and before you ask, I only figured out what the amplifier did at the end of the game."

"BatKian doesn't care about dybbuks," he said.

"Yeah, well, dybbuks aren't the only thing in Gehenna that we have to worry about."

Laurent's brow furrowed. "What else would he... There are estries there?"

Part of me loved how I could tell Laurent something and he immediately got it and made the next leap. Plus, it felt good to give him some information about Gehenna for a change.

"That's what Zev thinks. And no, I don't believe him about wanting to speak with his sire. Well, not entirely.

There's more to it than he's admitting, but the more I learn, the better my chances of preventing the Ascendant from causing further damage."

"Damage like my aunt's car crash that your parents caused." He didn't shift, didn't growl, and yet hearing him say those words aloud made me feel more exposed and vulnerable than if he'd had his canines at my throat.

Part of me hated how I could tell Laurent something and he made the next leap.

I nodded, unable to meet his eyes.

"How much time went by between you learning about your parents and your promise to Zev?" he said.

"A couple of days."

"In which you avoided me," he said neutrally.

Laurent only took that tone of voice when he was pissed. Even if I appreciated where his reaction came from on a psychological level, I crossed my arms, my jaw clenched.

"I didn't play you or manipulate my way into your lives," I said. "I was in shock when I figured it out, and I wasn't ready to tell Tatiana and potentially lose her." I rested my cheek against the cushion, the fight draining out of me. "Lose either of you. But I didn't appreciate you playing this passive-aggressive game of implying you knew something while we were dealing with the Human Race. If you had something to say, you should have just said it."

"You're right and I'm sorry." Laurent drew his knees into his chest, his bare feet resting on the sofa. "This wasn't why I texted you. It wasn't because *you* owed *me* answers."

22

———

"WHAT I'M GOING TO TELL YOU ISN'T AN EXCUSE, but it is why I reacted badly to you not being upfront with me." Laurent sighed. "Where do I start?" He pressed his lips into a firm line with a sharp nod like he'd decided something. "Gabriel, Juliette's father, is my brother-in-law."

I frowned. "You have a sister?"

He shook his head.

"A brother married to his sister?"

He shook his head again.

The penny dropped and my eyes bugged out. "*You're* married?!"

"I was." He fidgeted, his eyes darting around the room, looking at anything except me.

Knowing him as I did, I had a horrible suspicion about what had happened, but I wanted to hear the story from him. "Tell me about her."

His expression grew distant, his face imbued with a vulnerability he rarely showed, then he lit up with a soft smile. "Delphine was an annoying brat. She used to come visit her great-aunt every summer in Paris and I'd be stuck playing with her."

"Tatiana?" I guessed.

He nodded. Good thing he wasn't really related to Tatiana. "It was the cliché story that one day in our teens she showed up and I saw how beautiful she was."

"You got together then?"

He chuckled. "No. I was a horrible teenager. Gangly, acne, angry. She rightfully wanted nothing to do with me."

I smiled, but my heart was breaking. Not because he'd been in love or married. We all had pasts and my ex remained one of the most important people in my life. No, it was the wistfulness in Laurent's voice and my terrible certainty where this was headed.

"We fell in love during university. Tatiana and Grandmère were delighted. Apparently, they'd been planning our wedding for years." His lips twisted wryly, but his hand drifted down to his heart.

It stayed there a moment before he caught it, making a fist, which he dropped to his side.

"Was she a shifter as well?" I said.

"No. Delphine made things bloom." His eyes met mine, and I hugged the pillow more tightly. Oh, Laurent. He took a deep breath. "After our wedding, she came with me when I challenged the alpha and won pack leader status. We were happy there." His voice had become brusque, like he had to recite the facts stripped of all emotion to get through it.

I was well acquainted with that tactic.

"It was the largest European pack so things would get hectic, but about seven years ago, there was a dangerous conflict between a Croatian and Portuguese pack that sucked up all my time. Delphine hadn't been sleeping well, but she didn't want to add to my worries, so she didn't say anything." He spread his hands wide.

"She became enthralled," I said softly.

"Oui." His words came out huskily and he cleared his throat. "I suspected something was wrong and I kept asking her, but she said it was nothing. I only found out when—" He ran his thumb over his left ring finger.

"You don't have to tell me." I traced the play of sunlight over the line of his strong calves and his tanned olive skin. The rays lengthened, dancing up the deep red walls while I waited for him to say something, even change the topic, but when he just sat there, hunched into himself, I stood up.

His head snapped up and he stared at me with bleak eyes, his hand held out. "Don't leave. I need to say this out loud."

I sat back down, remembering another husband's need to share a memory with me and how heartbreaking Zev's tale of his wife's death had been. I didn't want to know anything beyond Delphine's eventual possession, but I couldn't leave Laurent if he'd never spoken about this with anyone. And knowing him, that was a real possibility, his emotions festering inside him.

My eyes damp, I blinked rapidly and took his hand, cupping my other hand over his almost desperate hold.

"I woke up one morning," he said. "It was raining and Delphine adored the rain. She said that everyone always chose the sun but that was easy. Rain added richness, quenched the earth's thirst. When I didn't find her inside, I went out to the garden, expecting she'd be soaked, wearing some ridiculous grin because she never took proper care in the rain." His leg bounced, his breath coming faster.

I stroked his hand.

"She lay under her favorite red oak tree. Her dress was twisted around her like a wet rag, and her hair spread out like vines, but she had the most peaceful look on her face. She'd" —his voice cracked—"stopped her own heart with her magic before she could become fully possessed."

"Before she could hurt anyone she loved," I said softly.

"She'd done that already," he said.

I leaned over to him. "Laurent, you can't blame her for dying. Or for not telling you she was enthralled when you

230

had no way to save her at that point. You didn't have Banim Shovavim magic then."

"You don't understand." He withdrew his hand, and I folded mine together, feeling the loss of his touch. "I don't mean me." He bit his lip. "Delphine was pregnant."

Rarely have I been stunned into silence. I stared at the ground with my elbows resting on my thighs. My mind was a jumble of thoughts.

Some dam had broken inside Laurent, and he didn't stop speaking. They'd found out after her death that Delphine was two months pregnant. The pack healer said Delphine had come to him to confirm it a month ago, but she was waiting until she was three months to tell her husband because they'd had trouble conceiving.

No wonder he treated secrets like betrayals, even ones like my parents', which didn't directly affect him. It all reminded him of the hurt that he'd suffered years back, hurt that he couldn't bear to see others go through.

"I'm so sorry." The words were so inadequate, but he nodded in understanding.

"This wasn't why I asked you here either." He muttered under his breath in annoyed French. "I told you I was jumbled after the game. That I'd seen visions." He paused. "I saw Delphine."

I exhaled a soft curse.

"She was under the oak tree, asking me to join her. All I had to do was take her hand."

I whistled, shaking my head. Eli and I had experienced random darkness, still evil and terrifying but hardly tailored to our inner demons. It was curious, Emmett's combination of Ohrist magic, which animated him, and the Banim Shovavim necromancy magic for his divinations allowed him to skip the insane train the rest of us had been forced onto in the gym, yet Laurent's combination of those powers meant things hit him harder and more personally. "I'm sorry you had to relive that."

"When you saved me from the dybbuk, I still hadn't shaken off her voice. I thought I'd forgotten the sound of it," he added quietly. "I wasn't sure what was real. Or what I longed to be real."

This entire visit had gotten a lot heavier than I'd expected. I was used to Laurent deflecting and hiding, not brutal honesty and vulnerability.

"Now?" I said.

"I can't stop thinking about the game."

"You're not alone."

"It was just so fucking pointless what they were doing to Sapiens. Then Isla of all people being there?" He shook his head. "After I left the pack, her husband was killed in the ensuing power struggle. She told me that when we first spoke and even then, it never occurred to me that she'd betray us." He laughed bitterly. "Me. The most suspicious person ever and I didn't see that one coming. It hit me hard."

"That's understandable."

"Not for the reason you think." He took my hand, gazing into my eyes. "I believed in someone who didn't deserve my faith and lied to someone who did."

I looked down at our joined hands. "What do you mean?"

"You burst into my life and pushed and pushed and infuriated me. Honestly, you were quite the bully."

"Please." I fanned myself. "You're making me dizzy with praise."

He booped the end of my nose. "You are very sarcastic and still I am happier around you than I've been in a long time. I don't just want to be your friend, and if it's too little too late, then I'll pretend to understand, but I'm hoping you'll give me a chance. Let me take you out."

"On a date?" I said stupidly.

"Yes, Mitzi. Would you please go on a date with me?"

It was emotional whiplash. Everything I'd yearned to hear him say and yet here it was, under the worst possible circumstances. "You're in shock from the visions and Isla," I said. "You were forced to relive an unimaginable grief and I totally get grasping at something to feel alive, to understand what's real, but I can't be that for you."

"That's not why—" He raked a hand through his hair. "I wanted you to know. How I felt about you."

"I don't believe you, not when you made it clear that dating me was the last thing you desired."

"You're wrong," he said quietly. "It was everything I desired. And that scared the shit out of me because I'd excelled at making sure I never felt too deeply about anyone again."

I clenched my fists because he was making my point for me. He did care about so many people. He always had, and the fact that he didn't see that even now meant he wasn't ready for this. But damn, did I wish otherwise. "I'm honored you felt you could tell me about Delphine, but—"

Laurent jumped to his feet, muttering under his breath, and marched off.

"Hey. Where are you going?"

He stomped around in the kitchen before returning with his phone, which he stuffed into my hand.

It was open to a text exchange between him and Nav from last night.

Laurent: *I've been very stupid about Miriam.*

Nav: *You think? Have you finally grown a pair?*

Laurent: *Have you returned Eli's hockey shirt for me or is it still under your pillow?*

Nav: *reverse peace sign emoji*

I handed him back the phone. "Is this supposed to prove something?"

He tapped the screen. "Oui. That I texted you because I was planning to ask you out."

233

"Nope. Nowhere does it say that."

Laurent reread the message. "It is clearly there."

Men. Where had I left my shoes? "I still don't think you should ask me now."

"Why not?"

"This isn't the right time." It reminded me of how I'd told Eli that I loved him first. His response? "Thank you," followed by an awkward kiss on my cheek when I longed for an enthusiastic affirmation to cue the explosion of hearts and dancing woodland creatures.

If Laurent meant to date me, I wanted that to be first and foremost in his head, not stemming out of a memory of his deceased family. That didn't sound great when I replayed it, but it was what it was.

"Then when is the right time?" He followed me to the foyer. "It happened years ago."

At the thought of putting my heels back on, my feet throbbed in protest, and I did so with a wince. "You need to grieve them properly, and I need to be done this business with Zev."

"What are you talking about?" he said, exasperated. "I mourned them."

"If that were true, you'd have moved on with your life. Gone back to your pack, I don't know. You wouldn't have become obsessed with killing dybbuks at great pain to yourself. You're like a monk with a hair shirt and whip." I held up a hand. "I'm not saying you have to stop, because you're doing a good thing, but you said it yourself again and again. Your priority is killing dybbuks. When your priority is living, then you can ask me."

He leveled me with a long look, then gave one of his infuriating French shrugs. "Alors, I rescind the question."

"You're an ass."

"I will ask again at a more suitable time. Act surprised and delighted."

I chuckled despite myself.

"Meantime, if you need my help finding the Ascendant, call me. I don't give a damn about the promise. If BatKian gets mad that you roped me in, he can deal with me."

Under his shirt, I gently traced the scar that the vampire had given him.

Laurent caught my hand. "This is different."

I really had to get to the bottom of that dynamic between Zev and my boss.

"Yeah, it'll be worse if you interfere with something he wants," I said. "He's trusting me, to a degree, and he has knowledge we don't. I'll find the Ascendant faster and be able to destroy it faster if I keep my enemy close. Sadly, you can't be part of this because he can compel you." I grabbed my purse, confused about its weight until the puzzle box clacked against my phone. Exhausted, I rubbed my eyes.

Laurent's lips twisted wryly, and he appeared to be weighing out his next words. "I'm motivated differently now. There's a lot to be said for motivation in the face of compulsion."

"Uh-huh," I said doubtfully. "What are you going to do about Isla? You want me to come with you to find her?"

"I have no desire to find her."

I did a double take. "What? She turned on us. She made us believe she was on our side. How do you not want her to pay for that?" Isla should have been the one to lose her sanity, not Daw.

His expression grew pensive. "Maybe it's different because I remember the person she used to be. A good person. Or maybe it's because I've grown so much and am so self-aware." I snorted, and he gave me a mock-stern scowl. "I don't want revenge." He sighed. "I'm tired of revenge. I want to live for the right reasons, not keep trying to die for the wrong ones."

He meant that. A kernel of hope lodged in my chest, and I lay my hand on his cheek. "I'll call if I need help."

He pressed a chaste kiss to my knuckles then shut the door behind me.

I wanted to live for the right reasons too. My parents could have left me a detailed confession and it wouldn't change anything. They'd still be gone. They still hadn't prioritized our family, or me, over the job that had gotten them killed.

I tilted my head to the clear blue sky. I had my family, my friends, my weirdo supernaturals, and Laurent, who'd surprised me in many ways today.

Okay. I'd get the Ascendant, tell Tatiana everything, and then once and for all, put my past behind me.

I was differently motivated now too.

23

Zev finally deigned to be present for our meeting at Blood Alley.

I zipped down there, singing along to some disco classics on the radio, intent on striking those final items off my to-do list and moving forward with my life.

I'd just parked in Gastown and locked the sedan up when I knocked into a woman in sunglasses. A burning sensation streaked through my body and I gasped, as frozen in place as when I'd been stung multiple times by a wasp.

"Are you okay?" the woman asked, the picture of concern. She hovered around me, giving the only other pedestrian a wave to communicate that she had this.

As soon as they disappeared around a corner, her demeanor changed. "Listen up," she said in a hard voice.

Since I couldn't speak and was stuck there, bent double, it was easy to obey.

"You shouldn't have messed with the game."

I'd underestimated the Consortium's ability to find me this fast, fighting now to call up my magic. Sadly, there was merely an echo of it, like it was buried under ice. Still present but with an inaccessible heart.

Help. I sucked in a breath but couldn't get enough air into my lungs. Zev. He'd been the last person I called.

"What do you want?" I wheezed, my voice barely above a whisper, while I fumbled one-handed to hit the redial button without her noticing. Even if it went to voice mail, hopefully Zev would hear enough to come and help me.

"The Consortium wishes to meet you," the woman said.

"I'm free next week."

She gripped my shoulder, and I went from hunchback impression to surfboard, my body stiffening out. I swear my eyes bugged out of my head like in those old cartoons.

"You're free now." She motioned at a black car with tinted windows pulling up to the curb.

My mouth went dry, my heart thundering in my ears. Never go to a secondary location. My love of crime shows had taught me that much. I'd have screamed, but there was no one on the street with us. Where were all the damn tourists when you needed them?

My heels slid against the pavement as she dragged me closer to the vehicle.

The door opened and a man in a suit, also with sunglasses and a Bluetooth device in one ear, got out of the driver's side and opened the back door.

The interior of the car swam with that same darkness that had been in the gym.

I grabbed on to the top of the door with clammy hands, fighting as hard as I could to remain on the sidewalk, but my limbs were weak.

The man grabbed my arm. His hand tensed, then fell away, as did the woman's grip, leaving me to collapse against the car door, my body slamming it shut.

Zev stood there holding a large black umbrella. I could have kissed his perfectly polished shoes. "Come along," he said simply.

The directive tugged mildly at my brain, but it wasn't

intended for me. With their sunglasses on, it was hard to tell whether the man or the woman was more shocked to find themselves following docilely behind him.

The woman whipped off her glasses, glaring so hard at Zev's back her face was contorted.

I laughed. "Your freezing magic doesn't work on him."

Zev stopped at my words, turning to raise an eyebrow at me. "Did you presume otherwise?"

"Nope," I said hastily. "Just enjoying the moment."

We all traipsed into Blood Alley behind the vamp. Once we were safely ensconced behind the gates and I guess under some kind of sun protection, Zev closed the umbrella and handed it to me without looking to see if I'd take it. Or, you know, asking me to hold it.

Nice way to waltz through life.

"Now, who do you work for and why were you harassing Ms. Feldman?" he said.

The pair opened and closed their mouths, their throats working. They were trying to obey but all that was coming out were strained, garbled moans.

"They work for the Consortium running the Human Race," I said.

Zev crossed his arms, his foot tapping. "Your employers' names. Now."

Their jaws starting flapping at crazy speeds, their eyes rolled back into their heads, and their bodies convulsed.

"I think they have a counter spell on them that's keeping them from speaking," I said.

"Yes, thank you for that very elementary observation."

I totally would have made a snarky face except Zev muttered he didn't have time for this and snapped both their necks in a blink.

My swallowed gasp became a cough that I fought to get under control.

The vampire snapped his fingers at a passing Ohrist

employee. "Clean this up," he said. "As for you, Ms. Feldman. Let's talk."

Moments later, I sat down at the bar in the small private sake club while Zev perused bottles. He was impeccably turned out, nary a wrinkle to be found, but he seemed... I frowned, trying to pinpoint it. Threadbare. Like one good crack would shatter him as easily as the delicately wrought sake cups he set out.

I licked my lips. I'd developed a taste for the drink since he drank only the finest brands. However, it was not to be.

He poured only for himself before setting the bottle next to him.

Subtle, dude.

"Can we add this Consortium to the list of people you'll protect me from?" I said.

The vampire sipped the sake, making a humming sound of pleasure.

My smile may have grown a tad sharp because his lips quirked up.

"I suppose we must, though you do have a knack for making yourself unpopular. I'll discreetly spread the word about you being under my protection. Did your visit yield anything useful?"

"Two things. First, either the Ascendant is weaker than people believe it to be or the Consortium didn't know how to use it properly."

Zev stroked his goatee. "I wasn't aware its use had specific requirements." He poured me a drink. Score! "What was the second thing?"

"The Consortium were definitely the last ones to have it before Tatiana stole it from them on behalf of her client Arlo Garcia." I savored a taste of the bold, earthy alcohol. How it paid to be on Zev BatKian's good side. "When pressed about the Shakespeare quote, my quarry tied it again to the Woods Bank. I know you asked them, but I doubt that Arlo lied. Is

240

there any way the owners of the Woods Bank might not know they have the Ascendant?"

He drummed his fingers on the counter, then ceased. "The Ascendant isn't really there." He smiled meanly. "However, someone wants us to believe that it is. They'll have a silent snitch alarm on the contents and come running." Off my confused look, he added, "A snitch alarm notifies the owner that someone is interested in their item, allowing them to learn that party's identity. However, the reverse is also true. You will go and set off the alarm."

He rattled off the location of the trees outside a village in France.

A physical location, not a hidden space.

"Isn't everyone using the Woods Bank going to be paranoid?" I said. "Doesn't every client alarm the contents wanting to know who's after their stuff? Also, how does anyone come running to France?"

"Part of the family magic allows the renter of a particular tree to access it day or night," Zev said. He didn't elaborate further. "As for the alarms, most items won't have one. They trust the Woodses' magic to keep people out of the trees since there hasn't been a break-in in three hundred years. Also, snitch alarms are magic. Place one on another magic item and it wreaks havoc. The tree in question will have a nonmagic item inside it."

"I can't tell what's magic and what isn't."

"Fortunately, I know of a device that can."

"That's useful, but the trees have magic on them too."

"Which is why you'll need to use the Kefitzat Haderech to get inside each tree and check the contents individually using this device. I advise you stay cloaked the entire time."

I planted my hands on my hips. "Are you kidding me? There could be dozens of trees there. Hundreds even. For that plan to work, I'd have to go through and check every single one."

"Exactly so." He won our stare down. "Shake any item without magic to set off the snitch alarm. Take photos of whomever shows up and bring them to me immediately. I'll narrow it down from there."

The door opened and I flinched, not up to seeing his friend Yoshi, since our last visit had ended with that ancient vamp feeding off me, but it was Rodrigo, who whispered something in Zev's ear.

He was sending me off alone to search, which meant there'd be no way for him to know when I found the Ascendant. Could I hide it in the KH and say that Smoky had destroyed it? I couldn't hand it over until I was clear on what Zev planned to use it for. Beyond that, I didn't want him to create rifts to anywhere that monsters lived.

Zev frowned and stood up abruptly, pulling out his phone. "We're done. It will take me some time to procure this item, so I expect you to be ready to go at a moment's notice."

I made puppy dog eyes at the rest of my delicious sake, but Rodrigo was already marching me to the door. "Sure thing," I said.

There was a slight downtick in Zev's mouth, all his attention now on his screen. I'd been forgotten.

Eli and Sadie invited me to go out for a family dinner, so I changed into something less formal. My red skirt and shirt were wrinkled, and there was no way I was wearing anything other than sandals. Besides, we were just walking down Main Street to our favorite sushi place.

I looped my arms through theirs, feeling lighter than I had in a long time. Saying that I'd appreciate every day after surviving that game was a nice thought, but realistically, gripes and petty complaints would filter back in.

Right now, however, I was just going to enjoy life to the fullest.

Laurent and I had had a major breakthrough, this job of Zev's would soon be over, leaving me free to tell Tatiana about my parents, and once I got the puzzle box open, I'd destroy the Human Race. The game, I mentally amended, not wanting to tempt fate.

The restaurant owners called out ohayou in greeting when we entered. As both Eli and I had been eating here for years, they motioned for us to grab a table.

My mood grew even better when Eli told me Juliette had given him and Deputy Chief Constable Esposito an update that physically Teresa and Okeyo were fine, and although healing would take time, they were strong mentally as well.

I thanked our server for the green tea and menus. We tended to rotate through the same favorite dishes, but I'd decided to try something new today.

Eli and Sadie placed their orders, and I chose the seared tuna belly as it was one of the few things I hadn't tasted on the menu.

"What about Daw?" Sadie said, breaking her chopsticks apart.

I nodded, wondering the same thing.

"Juliette is hopeful that in time Daw will recover. A healer from Bangkok is flying over to take her home and continue her treatment." Eli poured soya sauce into the small dish.

"Good," Sadie said. "That's over then."

Eli shot me a look. Ah. He knew it wasn't quite over yet. Not for me.

"Guess what?" my daughter said.

"What?" I snagged the bottle of soya sauce.

"Nessa and I had our first self-defense training session with Dad." She flexed her biceps and winced. "He's a hard-ass."

Eli cracked his knuckles. "By the time I'm finished with the girls, no one will dare mess with them."

"How sweet," I said. "We'll have to coordinate with Laurent about more specific training so Sadie can protect herself from Ohrists."

The server brought out the first few dishes.

Eli dumped wasabi into his soya sauce and stabbed at it with a chopstick to dissolve it. "Speaking of the guy, where's my hockey shirt? I bet he burned it."

I stuffed a piece of sushi in my mouth, chewing so I wouldn't laugh, and shrugged.

Dinner was a lighthearted affair, and we stuffed ourselves so full that we took the scenic route home, wandering through the neighborhood to help us digest.

We'd cut through a nearby park, Sadie angling for cupcakes, when the wind picked up.

I wrapped my cardigan tighter around myself.

Eli laughed. "A bit late for crow o'clock."

While Sadie sang the *Twilight Zone* intro, I looked up at the sky expecting to see thousands of crows winging their way from downtown Vancouver to Burnaby like they did every night and froze.

It wasn't crow o'clock. It was ravenpocalypse.

Hundreds of them landed on the branches of the trees here in the park, jammed wing to wing, their cold, black eyes trained on us.

"This is too Hitchcock." Eli focused on his feet, holding a hand in front of our daughter's face. "Sades, look away."

I barely heard him over the pounding of my heart, gripping their arms with sweaty hands. "Count of three," I whispered, "I cloak and we run home to the wards. One. Two."

A raven larger than the others landed on the grass, shaking out their feathers.

Poe. I felt it in my bones.

Slamming my mesh over us, I shoved Eli and Sadie to get

them moving, but we barely made it past the dog park fence when the ground shook, knocking the three of us to the dirt.

Before I could restore the cloaking, we were pinned down by an invisible force. I lay on my side, able to move my arms and head, but not get up. My leg was bent at an awkward angle. It wasn't broken, but my knee throbbed painfully.

Eli was on his knees, Sadie on her butt.

She pressed a shaking hand to her heart, her breathing fast and shallow.

I shivered, the sight of my girl having a panic attack while I was unable to protect her making me want to jump out of my skin. I struggled to get up, but I was helpless. "Sades, honey. Breathe deeply. In and out. You can do it."

Two shadows fell over us, the people's faces coming into view: Jason Maxwell and Isla.

An icy spark of fear deep in my belly exploded into shards, freezing my blood and zapping all the strength from my muscles. I blinked rapidly as if I could will these two somewhere far from my family—like the depths of the earth.

Eli got a ferocious look on his face, reaching for the weapon he hadn't brought to dinner. "Daw trusted you," he said. "How could you?"

"For immortality." Isla beamed at Jason. "I told you I could find Miriam."

"Haven't you done enough?" I said. "Leave my daughter alone. It's me you want."

"Personally, I don't give a damn about you," she said, though she averted her gaze from Sadie. "I'm just doing what I was ordered."

"Poe," I pleaded.

The raven did nothing to help, nor did any of the other birds. Was Jason or Isla the new player Poe had warned me of? Was that why they were here? They tricked me into bringing this player into being during a game of blackjack and now just sat there impassively? I'd have strangled the feathery asshole if I could.

Jason flexed his hands, one of which was wrapped up from where I'd stabbed him, but only sparks came out. Nothing magic happened. He shook them out while I pressed on.

"Jason's lying to you," I said. "Even if Sapiens can host dybbuks, they'll die, leaving the dybbuk in control of your body. Just like with Ohrists."

"No." Isla fixated on me with gleaming eyes. "The point is to find a way to let us remain in control. Then everyone who's ever caused us pain and preyed on us will be at our mercy."

"You're a fool," I said. "It's not possible."

"Enough talking." Jason flicked his fingers, and the breath left my lungs, my body slowly compressing like the trash compacter that almost killed Luke, Han, Leia, and Chewie. Except substitute my organs for the *Star Wars* characters. He shot more magic, grinning at my wheezing bagpipe impression. "Finally. My powers have been on the fritz thanks to your antics. Anyway, my employers have granted you one chance to live. Did you find the Ascendant?"

Blood leaked out of my eyes and nose. My head was about to split like a ripe melon.

"She can't answer you if you kill her," Eli snarled.

"True." Jason let up the pressure long enough for me to answer the question. When I shook my head, clawing at my throat for air, he sighed. "Sadly, they expected too much, as I told them. But at least it affords me the pleasure of killing you."

Eli stiffened, scrabbling at his throat.

My vision narrowed down to two pinpricks of light. Sadie remained in the throes of her panic attack, and I couldn't leave her here alone at Jason's mercy. I fought as hard as I could to stay conscious and do something, anything, but I couldn't access my magic. Our impending deaths were a pit I couldn't scale.

I seized up, my lungs burning.

A loud whooshing sound deafened me, and then everything grew still and white. I was convinced I'd died until I realized that I was holding my breath. Jason's magic had lost some of its power, and I gulped down air, though I was still stuck in place.

Despite my initial assumption, the brightness wasn't death, it was Sadie's shadow looming over us, made of dazzling white light. All except for the pitch-black eyes, which mirrored Sadie's, even the whites of her eyes now obsidian.

I gasped. No. Not that. Not magic. What even was this? My stomach dropped into my toes. "Sadie!"

She didn't hear me.

Eli's mouth had fallen open, his upper lip curled back and his eyebrows in a deep V.

My daughter held up her hand, the shadow mimicking her.

Isla ran full charge toward my daughter, but when she hit the shadow's palm, it was as though she'd run into a brick wall. A shriek pierced the night, and Isla slammed backward into the dirt.

Jason spun, eyes wide, and drew back a hand as if he was going to fling a ball of magic.

Sadie's shadow elongated its arm in a tentacle of hard light and touched his shoulder.

Jason's body bucked, swirling magic drawn from him like taffy and sucked into the shadow.

"Oh my God," Eli whispered.

Jason's hold on me fell away, and I pushed shakily to my feet. "Shut it down, honey."

The man screamed, his face red and the tendons in his

neck straining as his power poured out of him and into Sadie's shadow.

When I couldn't physically move her, I sent Delilah to block Jason from her shadow. I didn't give a damn about him, but Sadie glowed so brightly that I had to avert my eyes. I was terrified she'd overload from magic absorption.

The white light dimmed.

Jason's legs buckled, and he crumpled to his knees.

"Tell me where that gambling room is." Unable to understand his slurred answer, I shook him. "Speak clearly and enunciate."

He spat out an address in London, then with a roar, he tore free of my grip and lunged for my child.

I grabbed his fingers and snapped them backward.

Jason yowled in pain, sparks of magic crackling off him to fall uselessly to the ground.

Sadie was pale, her dark head bent close to Eli's as her dad spoke soothingly to her, but her shadow and eyes were normal.

My heartbeat pounded in my ears. I yearned to let Delilah tear Jason to pieces, and while I wouldn't traumatize Sadie with the sight, I let the full force of my hatred and savagery fuel the dark stare I gave Jason.

He flinched.

I leaned over him, like I was imparting a secret of great worth. "I saved your magic for a special reason."

With a single shove, I cast Jason into a shadow, flinging him into the Kefitzat Haderech. Hopefully the smoke monster would kill the Ohrist like he'd sworn to do to Laurent.

Isla, pale and trembling, got to her feet. "I'm sorry!" she cried and ran off.

It would have been so easy to stop her. I shook my head. Isla was consumed by hate and grief in the wake of losing her husband and what had befallen her pack and her family.

Living with that barb in her soul was a far worse fate than anything I could inflict on her.

I let her go.

Chest heaving, I faced my family. "Are you both okay?"

Eli, shell-shocked, didn't answer, but Sadie bounded into my arms, hugging me.

A tremor ran through her body. "Mom? I don't feel so good." Her eyes rolled back into her head, and she fainted.

Eli, his face hard, marched over to me and, taking our daughter from my arms, walked away.

Poe cawed in satisfaction, and I rounded on them. In all the chaos, I'd forgotten about the birds.

"Was Sadie the new player? Answer me!" Delilah grabbed the shifter by the neck.

Poe's rapid heartbeat pulsed through my connection with my shadow, and for one wild moment, I longed to snuff it out.

The raven cawed, more subdued, and nodded.

"Come near me or my family ever again and I'll end you."

Delilah released them.

Poe burst into flight, the other ravens following them into the sky like an inky feather dusted across the sunset, leaving me to wonder if I'd destroyed my child's life.

24

"YOU SAID SHE DIDN'T HAVE MAGIC," ELI SAID tightly, pacing the kitchen.

I'd phoned Juliette in a panic, asking her to come check Sadie out, and the two were currently in the living room. I was listening to Eli with only one ear since he'd been on the same accusatory rant since the healer had arrived.

I stirred sugar into my tea, took a sip, and gagged, forgetting that I'd already added sweetener. Had I caused Sadie to gain magic, or had she had it all this time, repressed until her moment of intense panic that her parents were about to die? And what exactly were her powers? Because what I'd seen didn't make sense.

"Once again." I took a deep, calming breath, holding on to my mug for strength. "We need to hear what Juliette has to say."

"You keep saying that," he hissed, "but you clearly know more than you're telling me."

"I have guesses, same as you." I slammed my mug onto the table. "Was your being fine with magic all an act? Or is it only okay for me to be a freak so long as Sadie is human?"

Juliette cleared her throat, and I swung my gaze to the stylish young woman hovering in the doorway refastening her dark ponytail.

"How is she?" I said.

"Physically fine, but she's confused. I am too." She spoke with a heavier French accent than Laurent did.

"Why?" Eli hurried for the living room, but Juliette blocked him.

"The most important thing is that we all remain calm right now," she said. "Sadie wants us to discuss this together, and I agree."

"We can do that," I said, glaring at Eli.

"I'll stay calm," he muttered and pushed past Juliette.

Sadie sat up on the sofa with her favorite knit blanket thrown over her. Her eyes were clear, and her body was relaxed.

Relieved, I slumped into the chair next to her. "How do you feel?"

"Tired, mostly. Who were those people?"

Her dad took the seat at the other end of the sofa, repositioning her feet to be in his lap, with his hands draped protectively over her legs.

Juliette sat in the other armchair.

"They're connected to the game that your dad and I infiltrated," I said. "The woman was one of the kidnapped Sapiens and that man was an Ohrist involved with the Consortium behind it."

"Will he be back?" Eli said.

"No." No one asked me for clarification.

"May we discuss Sadie's magic now?" Juliette said. "Everyone understands that Ohrists are born with their magic, yes?" The question was mostly for Eli, who nodded.

I reached over to grab the pillow behind Sadie's back that was sliding out from behind her.

"Bien," the healer said. "Ordinarily, Sadie's magic would have shown up when she was born."

The pillow fell to the ground, reality seeming to swing around before righting itself. I stared at my daughter, who gave me a small smile and a shrug.

"You mean her Banim Shovavim magic would have shown up at puberty," Eli said. "I'm not Ohrist and neither is her mother."

"Ohrist magic has a slippery quality to it, like silk," Juliette said. "Where Banim Shovavim magic is rougher. I know this from healing both Miriam and Frances Rothstein." Frances had been the Banim Shovavim who'd placed the death curse on Tatiana. "If Miriam had even a trace of Ohrist magic, say with a recessive gene, the texture of her magic would feel different." She held up a hand to stave off Eli's next question. "My uncle has both, and I've worked on him before."

"Ohrist magic for the win." Sadie held up a fist.

"Hold up. You're saying I'm the source of her magic?" Eli managed to frown, blink, gape, and do a double take all at once. "Impossible."

Let's be honest. Had we not been discussing my child, I'd have jumped up, yelling "Ohrist magic! Booyah!" while moonwalking just to annoy the fuck out of Eli. Plus, I was delighted my daughter and I both had powers.

I studied her carefully, looking for any of her tells that she was hiding her feelings, but she had a small proud smile, and her eyes were lit up. I squeezed her hand. She'd face challenges ahead that she hadn't expected, but she was one stubborn kid. If she wanted this, she'd make it work for her. I ignored the voice in my head whispering about players and gameboards.

Eli pointed at me. "Explain this."

"You're being a dick." I crossed my arms. "That explanation enough?"

Sadie kicked her dad. "Stop trying to blame Mom. I'm magic because of you, Dad. Suck it up." She scowled at him with a stubborn set to her jaw.

"It does beg the question," I said, "of why wasn't Sadie born with magic?"

"Juliette thinks it's because your Banim Shovavim magic blocked it from coming out," Sadie said. "It short-circuited and it took this long to be set right."

"Not quite," Juliette clarified. "Sadie doesn't have your magic or a recessive Banim Shovavim gene, but the very fact of an Ohrist baby getting nutrients from a mother with a different type of magic caused this confusion."

Eli sat with his head buried in his hands. He'd checked out.

I wasn't a total monster. Obviously, I felt sorry for him. A bit. Through my smugness. Not only had Sadie inherited magic from his side of the family, it meant he had a recessive gene but no ability, and I couldn't tell which fact upset him more.

However, right now, I had a more urgent question.

"Are you sure she was born with it?" I said hesitantly. "Could it be something that recently occurred?"

The young women stared at me with curious expressions while Eli raised his head up.

"Meaning?" he said.

"I have to tell you something, but I swear I had no idea this was what it meant." Twisting my hands in my lap, I laid out the entire story of raven shifters bringing things into existence, the game of blackjack I'd played with Poe, the raven drawing blood from my finger, and the announcement of a new player.

I finished to shocked silence.

"That's why all the birds were there?" Sadie said. "To watch? Pervy."

"I knew it!" Eli crowed. "Chus don't have magic."

Our daughter flinched, hugging her knees to her chest.

"They do because Sadie was born with her magic," Juliette said. "Miriam didn't cause it to spring up out of nowhere."

"You're positive?" At her nod, I sighed, silencing the voice of doom in my head.

All Poe had said when the raven bit my finger was that I was surrounded by magicians and now there was one more. An unexpected one. I'd played their words over enough times to easily recall them now. I was the one who assumed it was some villain coming after me because of my parents. Never had I been so happy to be wrong.

"How can you be sure?" Eli gave a dismissive wave. "It's magic. It's not science."

The healer stiffened and sat up very straight. "I have trained and studied magic for years." She spoke with the same haughty authority that I'd heard in her uncle many times. "The only thing Miriam's confession does is clarify things. Without that card game, Sadie's magic would have remained buried forever, instead it untangled the blockage and released it."

He bowed his head. "Maybe that would have been better."

"Excuse me?" Sadie's eyebrows shot up and I shot daggers at my ex.

Juliette murmured an excuse about water and fled into the kitchen.

My daughter threw up her hands. "What part of this do you not get, Dad? If Mom hadn't played that game and I hadn't gotten my magic, you'd both be dead. And who knows what would have happened to me?" Her chest rose and fell raggedly, but it wasn't anxiety. Not from the red flush on her cheeks.

"Be that as it may," Eli said, "it changes everything."

"Why?" I snapped. "Because Sapiens are better? Purer? Do you look down on Nav or is all right for others to be sullied so long as your precious bloodline is pristine?"

"Magic was real," Eli said to me in a low, hard voice. "But you never mentioned it. Not when we were dating, not when we were having a child together, not even when you accepted it back into your life. Yet the second you decided I needed to know, you got angry that I didn't immediately accept it. That I dared to need some fucking time to deal with the shock."

I rubbed the back of my neck, his words landing like barbs.

Shaking his head, he moved over to the window. "My baby has powers. Not from you. From me. Has my mother been magic all these years and not told me? Was my dad? If they were, why wasn't I let in on it? But again, I'm not allowed a single second to process that? I'm just automatically the bad guy?"

My fury ebbed away.

Sadie looked at her father and then to me with a pleading look. I didn't know how to fix this, but for her sake I'd try.

"Eli—"

He held a hand up, and I lapsed into silence.

Juliette returned a moment later, remaining in the doorway as if taking the temperature of the room before sitting back down.

My hand flew to my mouth, and I chortled, holding my belly because the laughter had an edge to it that hurt, but I couldn't stop. The universe was so fucked up. I'd been worried about whatever I'd brought into existence with that stupid card game, but if I hadn't played, Eli and I wouldn't be alive. Sadie might not be either. The Wise Brothers, the Human Race, I'd assumed that every game in the supernatural world had dire consequences.

I wiped tears of mirth from my eyes, my chuckles subsiding, and took Sadie's hand. "My badass baby, you saved us."

She flipped her hair off her shoulder. "Damn straight I did. Like mother like daughter." She sniffed. "Some people should be grateful for that."

"I'm allowed to be scared for you, Sades," Eli said quietly. "Your mom is an adult, and she knew about magic her entire life. You've had a lot dumped on you in a very short time with this on top of it. You can't tell Nessa or Caleb. You'll have to carry this secret with you, unable to share it with people you love. Ask your mother how hard that is."

"It's really hard," I admitted. "Mostly because I had no one to talk to. Yes, I'd known about magic, but I'd only had it for a year before I lost my parents and went to live with Goldie. When I reclaimed it, there was no one for me to ask, and I was the only Banim Shovavim in an Ohrist community. It's not the same for Sadie. She has me, and Juliette."

Juliette smiled. "Of course she does."

"And Jude, and Nav, and Laurent," I said.

"Plus Tovah," Sadie piped up. "Ava and Romi's niece. She's an Ohrist and she's my age. We've been texting. Oh, and I have Uncle Emmett." Her eyes sparkled.

Eli slapped a hand to his forehead, almost as distraught over hearing Sadie call the golem her uncle as he was over her having magic. "Give me time."

"Look on the bright side, Eli," I said. "It's your daughter who got the active Ohrist gene in your family and not your sister. You know she would have tormented you with it. How fun would that have been?"

He glared at me. "Is that supposed to make me feel better?"

"Yeah."

Reluctantly, he shrugged. "Okay. Yes. True."

"You always said you'd love me the same if I was queer or trans," Sadie said.

"I would," Eli said.

She shrugged. "Then why is this different?"

I tilted my head at him, awaiting his answer.

Eli braced his elbows on his thighs, his hands folded in

front of his face. "Look, I love you more than anything. That hasn't and will never change. Whatever anger or grief I'm feeling right now has nothing to do with you having magic. I swear." He sighed. "A few months ago, my biggest fear for you was boys. Or girls. Mostly boys though because I know how those horndogs think. Maybe your chemistry grade."

"Hey," Sadie protested. "A C+ is totally respectable."

Eli gave her a flat stare. "Suddenly, I lived in a world with magic, and I had to worry about vamps getting to you. Now, it's not vamps. It's dybbuks. It's Lonestars. It's magic battles that I can't help you with at all." He took her hands. "You aren't supposed to save me, my girl. That's supposed to be my job."

That was kind of sweet.

Sadie didn't think so because she snorted. "Are you serious? Geez, Dad, welcome to the twenty-first century. You can unlock my chastity belt, and did you know I'm not legally property either? I can vote and everything."

Juliette unsuccessfully stifled a laugh. I didn't even bother trying.

Eli sat back, his arms crossed. "All right, child. I get it."

Sadie wasn't done. "I'm not the Lieutenant Uhura of Team Feldman-Chu. I'm Kira Nerys. Got it?"

Eli shot me a triumphant look. "She's Kira, not Buffy."

There it was. His real fear, that he was losing Sadie to magic. A world that I was part of in a way that he could never be. He wasn't mad at me, he just craved reassurance that Sadie was still his baby girl, and if he got it from her being *Star Trek* crew instead of the Slayer, that was perfectly okay.

"Yes, she is," I agreed. "And thrilled that I am that all this is out in the open, it doesn't explain how Sadie animated her shadow. That's a Banim Shovavim power, but hers was made of light, which is pure Ohrist."

"That's the confusing part," Juliette said. "I will have to

dig deeper into how this is possible. Again, it might go back to your pregnancy."

"Sades," I said, "do you know what you did with that man's magic? Did you absorb it or did you null it?"

She scrunched up her face. "Both? I'm not more powerful, and I didn't take on his powers, just kind of sucked them out and killed them. I didn't even think about what I did. It was pure instinct, and it shocked the shit out of me."

"Language," Eli chided.

"Dad, I eat magic. I can swear." She flexed her fingers and slowly released a deep breath. "I've been thinking about it, but I have no idea if there's anything else I can do."

"You need to train with Nav," Eli said. "He has light magic."

"She should train with my uncle as well," Juliette said. "He's the only one with both types of powers. Sadie has a cross signal with your Banim Shovavim magic, even though it's not genetic."

My daughter groaned. "Does that mean more running?"

"It means whatever they tell you," Eli said. "Right, Mir?"

I smiled, glad he wasn't shutting Laurent out as a resource. Or me. "Right."

Juliette told Sadie to call her if anything about her magic didn't feel right or she had any questions.

After Eli and Sadie thanked her, I walked Juliette to the door, adding my profuse gratitude, while she artfully threw a large scarf around her neck and shoulders.

"Sadie will be okay," she assured me. "It's a bit of a puzzle, but I hear you like those." She grinned.

I blushed. Laurent had been speaking about me to her? I stepped onto the front stoop with her, some kids across the street groaning as a basketball bounced off a backboard in their driveway.

"Laurent told me about Delphine," I said. "About all of it.

I'm sorry. It must have been awful losing your aunt that way."

Juliette pulled car keys out of her small leather bag. "It was. She was wonderful, but life must go on, yes? We owe it to the dead to live as fully as we can to honor them. My parents impressed that on me after we lost her."

"It's a lovely sentiment and not true as often as it should be." Here I was, forty-two years old, only feeling like I was accomplishing that for the first time since I was a kid.

She slung her purse strap over her shoulder. "Some of us need more help than others."

"If you don't mind me asking, your father and Laurent. Are they estranged because he left the pack?"

"No. My uncle finds it easier to believe that everyone is mad at him and run away than see anyone else's grief. Tatiana had hoped to break him of that, but she's the same way."

"What do you mean?"

"She blames herself for Delphine's death. Tatiana isn't close to most of her family, but she adored her niece. She believes that if she'd been less focused on her career and been around more, that Delphine would have turned to her." Juliette shook her head. "She wouldn't have. That wasn't Delphine's way. My mother was her best friend and even she didn't know that Delphine wasn't sleeping well, never mind about the pregnancy." She gave a wry smile. "That's the problem with people who heal or grow things. We tend to everything except ourselves."

"I hope you break that pattern."

"I'm trying. It's part of why I came here, regardless of what my uncle believes. Plus, I missed him." A wistful look crossed her face. "Missed who he used to be. But I am seeing glimpses of that man again." She leaned in and kissed both my cheeks, then ran lightly down the stairs to her car.

I'd witnessed such depraved behavior since I'd reclaimed my magic, and the Human Race had been some of the worst.

Right now though, the sky was bright, and my chest fizzed with giddy lightness. Maybe we'd needed to experience that evil to bring out the best in ourselves.

I snorted. The adults kept fumbling along taking baby steps out of our negative patterns, while my daughter had shown how to handle a curveball with confidence and resiliency. Be more like Sadie. I smiled. I could do that.

25

DESPITE EVERYONE IN MY LIFE TELLING ME HOW great I was at puzzles, I spent all day working on this stupid puzzle box and getting precisely nowhere. I was tempted to smash it with a hammer, but if the thing inside was as dangerous as Clea believed it to be, I didn't want to unleash it in my living room. Especially not on my precious sofa. That said, I did everything short of hitting it with my scythe, though I did use the weapon to try to bore a hole through the box. Nada.

I didn't fare any better using Delilah and her green vision either, which sucked because I'd had high hopes for it revealing some divot that would unlock the whole thing, but it was smooth and sealed tight with nary a hinge.

I'd resorted to lying on my back on my living room rug, holding it above my head and squinting at it with first one eye open and then the other while downing copious amounts of peanut M&Ms to amplify my alertness, and thus my cognitive abilities.

The ground thudded.

Delilah jumped in front of me, her fists up, facing a very put out gargoyle.

He blinked at his surroundings then turned in a slow circle, wide-eyed.

I sat up. "Pyotr?"

The gargoyle picked up the blanket thrown over the back of my sofa and rubbed it against his cheek with a rumbling sigh.

"How—no, *why* are you here?" I snapped my fingers twice.

Pyotr dropped the blanket and pushed past Delilah while flipping me off. "Why you hate me? Triplicate!"

Oh, okay, he wasn't giving me the bird. That was just him showing off his callus, which had grown to the size of a large pebble.

"We had a deal," I said. "You let Laurent in and deal with the reports in triplicate and I'd take you to the garden store. I haven't forgotten. I just haven't wrapped the case up yet."

"Not that! Other reports." He narrowed his eyes at me. "Other *unexpected* reports."

I scrunched up my face. "What other… Oooh. The man I sent into the KH?"

He glared at me. "No Ohrists in Kefitzat Haderech. You know this."

"Yeah, that's kind of why I sent him."

Pyotr made a strangled noise.

"I didn't think you'd have to fill out reports." I paused. In hindsight, this should have been obvious, but I wasn't exactly thinking about bureaucratic procedure at the time. "What did Smoky do to him?" Okay, there was a bit more anticipatory glee in that question than I'd intended.

Pyotr planted his broad stone hands on his lanky hips. "I'm not telling."

I nodded in satisfaction. "That bad, huh?"

"No. You're that bad. I file complaint." He whipped a rolled-up paper from the back pocket of his brown pants and shook it at me. "Deal with golem from now on when you come."

"I'm very sad to hear that." I put on my best distressed face. Honestly, if he went through with this complaint and banned me from his presence, I'd be incredibly upset. This wacky gargoyle had wormed his way into my heart.

"Good." He jutted his chin up. "Now I leave and you never see me again."

"Oh. Maybe... No. You wouldn't want that."

He peered suspiciously at me, his hands on his hips. "What?"

"I bought brownies the other day from a fabulous bakery." Zev had yet to contact me to tell me that he'd gotten the magic-detecting artifact, so I'd run a few essential errands while I waited. And yes, brownies counted. Shrugging, I shut Delilah down. "But you don't want to spend more time with me to try one. I get it."

Pyotr took a step toward a shadow that would take him back to the KH, then he crossed his arms. "I will eat your brownie now and then never see you again."

"That's big of you," I said somberly.

Fighting a smile, I led him into the kitchen and poured us glasses of milk.

Pyotr took one sip and spit it out. "Poison!" He clutched his throat.

Scared I'd induced some weird chemical reaction between his type of stone and lactose, I grabbed my phone to call... who? But then he stuck his tongue out, his eyes bulging, and I shook my head. Overkill, buddy. "Are you allergic to milk?" I asked in the same voice I'd use on a toddler.

"Yes." He nodded vigorously. "Cure is make chocolate." Yup. Just as I'd figured.

I grabbed some sweetened cocoa powder and stirred it into his drink. "How do you know about chocolate milk?"

"Malorie gave me." Off my blank stare, he added, "My other friend."

"Spending a lot of time with her, are you?"

"Yes. Malorie is bestie."

Obviously, I wasn't jealous. Any woman who had a gargoyle for a best friend didn't have much of a life.

Pyotr made a sad face. "Fern is dead, but soon I will have new plant friend."

"That's too bad. What did you do with it?"

"Ate it." He shook his head, his brows furrowed like I was missing a basic concept of plant death, and poked the box that I'd left on the table. "What this?"

"A puzzle box. It might have a demon artifact inside so be gentle with it." I set the brownies on the table.

At the sight of the treats, Pyotr lost all interest in the puzzle box. He picked up a brownie, gingerly licked it, and a curious look came over his face. He nibbled a corner and a tiny moan escaped him, then he stuffed the entire thing in his mouth, chewing with a look of bliss. His eyes rolled back, making the sound of marbles jingling.

"What are the rules around you leaving the KH?" I said. "Do you live there?"

"You think I am Gollum living in cave with My Precious?"

"How do you know *Lord of the Rings*?" I narrowed my eyes. I'd never shown it to him.

"Malorie gave me book. Says books better than movies."

"That's usually true." So, she had one redeeming feature. Big deal. She was still probably an oddball. "How nice of her." I pulled the bakery box closer and selected a brownie.

"I live in Moscow," he said, returning to my earlier question. He reached for another brownie, hesitating at the last second, his eyes flicking to mine.

I sighed. Those puppy dog eyes of his would be the death of me. "Go ahead."

He crammed that one in his mouth as well.

"Is there a large gargoyle community there?"

"Family. Always feels like too much." He sprayed crumbs everywhere.

"Chew with your mouth closed. And take bites." As a responsible adult, it was my duty to model good eating habits, so I bit into my snack, making sure to chew thoroughly and swallow before asking my next question. "Were you working today? Are you allowed out during work?"

Pyotr modeled my behavior. "I'm on break before filing complaint." He rattled the paper at me again, but there was considerably less heat in his action.

"I'll miss you, but I had to get rid of that man, and sending him there was the fastest way. He was a bad person."

Pyotr licked chocolate off his face. "How bad?"

"He was going to kill me and my family, and he was part of a group attempting to turn Sapiens into dybbuk hosts." Had Jason lived he would have continued to facilitate Ohrists profiting off the human suffering in the game.

Pyotr gasped then banged his fist on the table. "Then I'm glad boss tore his head off."

I choked on my brownie. Once I'd stopped coughing, I forced myself to visualize the grisly image. I could justify my actions because of the life or death situation, but I refused to deceive myself. I'd known—no, I'd counted on Jason meeting a violent end.

Jason Maxwell wasn't like the players in the game, desperate to survive. He was human garbage profiting off misery and suffering.

I could live with my culpability in his death. "I'm glad he's gone."

Pyotr casually draped his stone fingers over the bakery box, pulling it closer. "I take this as payment for wounds." He jabbed his hugely callused finger at me again. "Malorie never cause triplicate."

A muscle ticked in my jaw, but I took the hit. "Then it only seems fair to have the brownies. And I'm so sorry."

The gargoyle screwed up his face like I was trying to trick him, then he ripped up his complaint paper. "I changed my mind. You must face me. Every time. With brownies."

I swept the pieces into my hand and walked over to the garbage can to dump them in. "Yeah, that's not going to happen. Too many treats aren't good for you, and I care about your health."

His fat lips pulled off quite the pout. "I will ask Malorie for brownies." His chair scraped across the floor as he stood up. "You stay here with stupid stinky vampire puzzle." He stomped out of the room.

"Wait! Pyotr. You can smell vamps?" I grabbed the puzzle box and ran into the living room, but he was already gone.

I'd assumed that Giulia was a gargoyle anomaly in terms of her powerful scent ability because she was a cat, but what if that's how Pyotr found vampires who snuck into the KH to cause trouble? I tried one last time to open the puzzle box and failed. That's it. BatKian could put aside whatever urgent business he was on and spare me five minutes for an update and to open this thing.

Sadly, Zev ignored my texts about the box in favor of sending Rodrigo to menace me on my stoop.

The Undertaker handed me a small V made of an aromatic wood. "Touch any item with it. If it vibrates, there's magic."

"Care to be more precise? Touch it how? A good touch?" I dropped my voice. "A bad touch?"

"Put the prongs against the item. You want to get off on it, that's your business. Sanitize it after, that's all I'm asking."

"I was thinking 'bad' in the villain sense. Jeez, Rodrigo, pent-up, are we?"

He clenched his jaw, eyeing me like he was fitting me for a body bag. One he'd personally tailor.

I smiled brightly. "I'll thoroughly check every item in the Woods Bank with it. Did Mr. BatKian say anything about the puzzle box?"

"Yeah. You can give it to me."

I dropped it in his meaty palm. Relief! Finally, I could stop worrying about this and let Zev solve a problem for me for a change. "When can I get it back? Opened."

Rodrigo closed his fist over it. "The moment you hand him the Ascendant. Fail and he'll destroy this." He clomped off.

"Wait! No. That's not fair." If I didn't bring Clea the opened box, she wouldn't give me a way to destroy the reclaimed demon space and end the game once and for all.

My pleas fell on deaf ears.

The only piece of luck I had today was that the KH didn't have a problem with me bringing the magic detecting device, an Ohrist artifact, through. I checked before I brought it in.

According to Pyotr, it was only people with that magic that upset Smoky. Maybe that was why Emmett was safe. Without a heartbeat, the KH didn't register him as different from say a fork or a chair with Ohrist magic on it. He was a thing, not a sentient being to them.

Yawning madly, and wishing for a triple espresso, I stepped inside the first hollowed-out trunk. A painting of a man sprouting white bushy eyebrow was hung on the rough bark and illuminated by a warm overhead bulb. I'd been in there all of three seconds when a fat branch shot out, snagged the edge of my cloaking, and tore through it as the branch impaled itself into the opposite wall.

I dove for the door back to the KH, rolling through it as branches crisscrossed the space and, like lasers in a museum, protected the client's painting.

There were shouts from outside the tree. I slammed my door closed as the one to the forest in France opened. While I heard muffled voices, I couldn't make out their words, but their tone said it all. Be on the lookout for an intruder.

I waited a good long time before peering back inside the tree, but the branches had retracted, and any guards had left.

I twirled my hand up, Delilah rising like a tornado, ready for action.

She leapt across the inside to land on the trunk, stuck to it like a gecko by her hands and feet. Magic pulsed up from the wood through her feet and into my own, but she didn't set off the security system.

Let her test the items then. I'd stay where I was.

She placed the V-shaped wood against the canvas and a mild electric shock snapped through me. *I wouldn't call that a vibration, Rodrigo.*

Since the item was magic, Delilah rocketed back into the KH and off we went for another sock. Each new tree I inspected required a new door from the KH and thus a new sock. Pyotr was kind enough to let me leave them with him until I left for good this visit.

The next hour was almost as tedious as it was painful. One or two mild shocks might not have mattered, but Delilah tested dozens of items. My shadow was unaffected, but my hair stood on end, my heartbeat jumped around like it was in a mosh pit, and my hands had mild burns on them making me feel hot, cold, and light-headed.

Pyotr didn't have anything to treat them, though he impressed upon me that garden stores carried lovely aloe vera plants.

I sat down on the small pile of socks I'd accrued to rest. "What is the point of a scorpion with hands?" I shuddered, my words slurring from pain. "It rapped on the glass of its tank."

I'd found only two nonmagic items so far: a bottle of wine that didn't have a snitch alarm on it, and a taxidermied horse that did. I doubted the elderly man who showed up to check on his possession, speaking to the dead horse in soothing tones about how his ex-wife would never get her hands on his baby, also had the Ascendant, but I took his photo as Zev had requested.

I stumbled to my feet, woozy.

"You don't look good," Pyotr said. "Stop now."

"Can't. Three more." I took the sock he handed me and blotted sweat from my chest and armpits.

"You desecrate sock," he said.

I wagged a finger at him. Maybe three. It was hard to tell. "The sock is mine to do with as I please."

Delilah stalked ahead of me through the gloomy path to our next door, her solid form flickering.

My entire body was tense from the strain of keeping her whole, but I had to keep her animated until the final tree was examined. I sang "I Will Survive" in my head like it was a magic chant, refusing to think of the consequences if I didn't find the Ascendant.

I needn't have worried, because the second to last tree contained an old-fashioned black phone sitting atop a small table adorned with mother-of-pearl. I perked up, my gut saying this was it, and sure enough when Delilah, now hanging from the ceiling, pressed the detector against it, nothing happened. I slumped in the doorway, partially out of relief, and partially because I was running out of energy to stand up.

On my order, Delilah shook the phone to activate any snitch alarm. I dismissed her, peering through the cracked-open KH door, my cloaking on and my camera at the ready.

The old-fashioned phone rang. And rang. And rang. Its trills grew more and more insistent.

My fingers twitched, wanting to answer it, but the threat of tree impalement was stronger, and I stayed where I was until the ringing stopped.

The moonlight from outside illuminated the person who stepped in.

She was small, thin of form, but old. Her movements were all very deliberate, though quite canny—despite her white hair and bony fingers, she was quick under her shawl, and her eyes bore a glint of fire as she scanned the tree.

Eyes I knew all too well. Eyes I had laughed with.

Tatiana.

My phone hit the ground, and my cloaking fell away. In my flinch, my elbow whacked the door, which swung wide open to reveal me.

Emotions flitted over Tatiana's face too fast to decipher, and she clutched the chunky beads on her necklace.

I put a hand to my head, unable to think through the hurt and rage brewing inside me. All this time I'd agonized over keeping her in the dark, worried myself sick over any betrayal, and she had the magic amplifier? No, she couldn't.

"It's a trick, right?" I twirled a finger around the tree. "You set all this up trying to find out who has the Ascendant?"

"The what?" Her annoyed look was pure "don't talk nonsense," yet the hand at her throat trembled.

A buzzing filled my ears, and I swatted the air as if to bat away a mosquito, but it was the sound of truth dawning. Not with a ringing clarity or a trumpeting peal, but flies landing on the cesspit of my broken beliefs.

"You've had it all this time." I let out a half sob, half laugh. "Was everything a con to cover your tracks? The car accident, the stolen amplifier, having to rebuild your reputation?"

She did a double take, barely more substantial than wrinkles and the weight of her years. "How do you know about that?"

Oh. I grabbed the door frame for balance. I didn't want to be right. "You killed my parents, didn't you? Noah and Adele Blum. That's how they got the jump on you. The shark. The great macher. You hired them to cause the accident and steal the Ascendant. Then you had someone get it back and kill them."

Tatiana had gone still, her eyes wide. "Your p-parents?"

"No more lies!" Shadows exploded from me.

Delilah slammed Tatiana against the inside of the tree. My boss, my mentor, my *friend's* trembling sensed through my shadow's hold was delicious.

One snap and I'd have revenge.

Seething, I moved to her side, forcing her to look me in the eyes, hating that even now her pain was mine. I poured steel into my voice. "How many years had you been watching me? Waiting to play me, to use me?"

Tatiana inhaled sharply, her eyes flashing. "You dare speak to me of cons, you snake?"

She blew my shadow off her, turning Delilah into tattered wisps.

Before I could once more access my magic, a tree root funneled up from the earth and snagged my leg, lifting me off the ground. Shadows swam over my skin, but the root wound around up my body, squeezing like a hungry python.

"Shut down your magic," Tatiana ordered.

Any more pressure and I'd black out, so I did as she asked, the shadows churning inside me.

"You wormed your way into my life. Into my trust." Spittle flew from her lips, a crazed light in her eyes. "I wish that I'd killed your parents. That I'd known of their involvement and made them suffer as I did."

She spoke the truth. About my parents at least, though she had the Ascendant. I felt it in my gut. How had she gotten hold of it if she didn't get it from my parents?

"Did you know what Arlo intended to use it for?" I croaked out the words. If Arlo wanted to fly with the angels he wouldn't have just cared about the dybbuks. He'd have wanted to prove he could call forth anything in Gehenna.

"Dybbuks can only possess Ohrists with lowered inhibitions," she said. That was all she knew about then. "It's easy enough to keep ourselves safe, and those that don't, deserve what they get."

"Did..." I swallowed to get moisture into my mouth, wanting to hurt Tatiana, yet my stomach twisted at playing this card. "Did Delphine?"

The elderly women flinched like I'd hit her. "Don't you dare speak her name."

The root stuffed itself into my mouth like a gag.

Tatiana's expression softened, and she tsked. "Poor Sadie," she crooned. "Never to know what happened to her mother."

I made garbled begging noises.

The root slammed me against the wall and compressed my cracked rib cage, knocking the air from my lungs.

A slice peeled off the main part of the root, weaving in front of me like a cobra. Tatiana's cold smile given form.

Then the cobra struck, impaling me in my gut.

I felt a heavy pressure and wetness, but the pain didn't register. I was high on adrenaline and the urgency to break free. "Don't hurt my daughter."

My words were unintelligible, but the pleading in my eyes was clear because Tatiana patted my cheek.

"Don't worry, bubeleh. I'll take good care of her."

With that, she walked away into the night, leaving me bleeding out.

26

I WAS SWIMMING. I SHOOK MY HANDS FREE OF droplets but they stayed wet. Almost sticky. No, I didn't like this water. It was too cold. I tried to get out, but I couldn't find the shore.

Hadn't I just been in a forest? Why did I smell fresh cut wood?

Someone called my name, and I followed the voice, but a snake popped up, its forked tongue hissing. I swam as fast as I could, because the shadows would save me, but I became tangled up in writhing snake bodies like kelp, dragging me down to the bottom.

I fought and fought, but they were so heavy that I gave up. I giggled because one of them seemed to be wearing a brown plaid shirt, but the water claimed me, and I went under.

Finally, I woke up, lying on the stone slab covered in socks, with Pyotr standing over me, twisting his hands.

"Stabbed with tree," he said. "Not good."

I lifted my bloodstained shirt. My gut was fully healed without even a scar, but my heart felt like it had been stitched to the outside of my chest and scoured with sandpaper.

"How did you find me?" I considered staying where I was,

half-buried, letting socks land on my head, but I sat up, dislodging the pile onto the cave ground.

"Shadow came."

"Delilah?" The gargoyle nodded. Had I sent her out like a flare? "Did you heal me?"

"No."

I pressed him but he wouldn't elaborate, and I got the impression he was scared to say more. Regardless, I wasn't about to question my luck.

"How long was I unconscious?"

"Three hours."

Good. Sadie and Eli wouldn't have to know what had happened.

I gasped. *I'll take good care of her, bubeleh.* Sadie. I jumped up, frantic. "I need to go home. Now."

Pyotr searched my face, but made the narrow green door appear. He handed me a bag of socks. "Here. From before." He narrowed his eyes, then added one more.

I ran out of there, not stopping until I startled the shit out of Eli by stepping into his living room and calling his name.

He bolted up from the sofa, where he'd fallen asleep like he often did in front of the television that now showed some old sitcom rerun. His brain, however, hadn't caught up to being fully awake, and he blinked at me blearily a few times until my blood-covered shirt registered. He jumped to his feet, his T-shirt bunched above his boxer shorts. "Who's dead?"

"No one." Pushing past him, I sprinted up the stairs, needing to see Sadie.

She was out cold, twisted almost horizontally on the mattress, the covers wrinkled up around her. Asleep and safe.

I rested my head against the door.

Eli tugged on my hand. "What happened to you?"

Putting my finger to my lips, I went downstairs and sat on his sofa. "It was a misunderstanding. I'm fine."

274

"Yeah," he said sarcastically. "You totally look it. What the fuck?"

"It doesn't matter." I pushed through my fatigue to figure out what day it was. Friday. "Keep her home from school today and this weekend. Don't let anyone, and I mean anyone, in to see her."

"Is this about her magic? About yours?"

"No. It's…" I pushed my fingers into my hair. If I told Eli what Tatiana had done to me and how she'd threatened our daughter, he'd go after her. Even if he didn't, he'd never forgive her.

I didn't blame him. Were I in his shoes, I wouldn't either, but he didn't understand how our shared history had done a number on both my boss and me. Despite months of working together, of me saving her life, and her giving me opportunities to be a stronger more confident woman, in that moment at the tree, we'd both assumed the worst of each other.

She'd almost killed me and still, all I wanted was to figure out how we'd been put into these positions and by whom. I could let her murder attempt go, but there wasn't any walking away from the mystery of our past until I'd solved it.

I wasn't going to steal the Ascendant from her, and I wasn't going to rat her out to Zev.

Where did that leave me?

I had to buy time with the vampire.

"Please, just promise you'll keep Sades home behind the wards. You too. Call in sick."

"Miriam." His plaintive tone stopped me in my tracks.

How quickly I resorted to keeping secrets. I bunched the hem of my shirt in my hands.

How terrifying to trust people, though.

"Tatiana found out about my parents. She has the magic artifact that they went after her for, and which Zev hired me to find for him. I need time to straighten everything out, but I will. I want the past over with once and for all, Eli, because it's been slowly killing me all these years." I swallowed. "I want to live for the right reasons. Will you help me?"

He searched my face for a long time before nodding. "You're not alone. Remember that."

"I will, but it's too dangerous for you to get involved."

"Oh, not me. I meant the kid. Between magic and her hormones? Yikes." He threw me a thumbs-up. "Go kick butt, Feldman."

I kissed his cheek and hurried back to my place, my brain whirring for the best excuse to give Zev, but I'd barely gotten inside when one of the shadows in my living room moved.

I screamed, bashing my shin on my sofa.

Zev sat forward, a streetlight casting his features as the purest marble. The puzzle box sat unopened on the coffee table before him. "Tell me you have good news, Ms. Feldman."

I'd stood a chance, a slim one mind you, had I sent a text to Zev to buy time until I'd spoken to Tatiana. In person was quite another matter.

"I—" I swallowed thickly.

His eyes were feverish and tendons stuck out on his stiff neck. He didn't even glance at my blood-soaked shirt. "Where is the Ascendant?" His words were rushed and totally unlike his usual clipped pronunciation.

"It's complicated. I need another day."

"There is no more time." There was the barest quiver in his unfailingly polite tone. Then he slammed his fist onto my wooden coffee table, shattering it.

I fell to my knees, sweat beading on my forehead. He'd pulverized the puzzle box. I pushed my fear—that he'd exposed us to something demonic and all hopes of destroying the game—down in the face of his presence.

My time had run out.

I could warn Emmett that Tatiana had to close her wards

against Zev before he could get to her, but if I didn't tell him the truth, he'd kill me. "Tatiana has it."

Zev's eyebrow twitched. "Tanechka?" The whisper of her name was barely more than an incredulous puff of breath. For the briefest instant his face lit up with what I could only describe as salvation. "Excellent work."

"Please don't hurt her."

"As if I could," he said softly. He stood up. "We're going to pay a social call." He motioned for me to leave my phone. "Come along."

Eli's curtain twitched when Zev led me outside, but I shook my head and the curtain fell back into place.

A familiar black limo idled partway down the block. Rodrigo opened the back door and I got in, followed by Zev, who sat across from me.

The ride was smooth as silk, the interior was all posh leather seats, inset speakers, and an entire bar, and I'd have climbed out the moonroof had I been able.

The terse silence choked me as I pointlessly tried to scrape blood off my shirt. Would Tatiana try to end me again? Who would Zev protect if it came down to me or her? I'd led him to the Ascendant, but she was his Tanechka. Whatever that entailed.

I was practically crawling out of my skin by the time we pulled up to her house. I hid behind Zev when he knocked on her door, but I was the first thing Tatiana's eyes darted to when she opened it.

"I thought you'd be easier to kill," she said. "How disappointing."

So much for hiding. I stepped up next to the vampire.

"Tanechka," Zev chided her gently.

She crossed her arms. "Don't 'Tanechka' me. Why are you here?"

Emmett thundered down the stairs, stopping when he saw me. His eyes widened at my blood- and filth-covered self, and my body sagged. "You're alive." His relief was unmistakable.

"Hey, buddy. Yup. Alive and...yeah."

"May we come in?" Zev said.

"No." She shut the door.

I braced for the vampire to push past her, since he already had permission so this question was merely for etiquette's sake, but he stood there.

"Remember," Zev said mildly, "I let him live."

Tatiana stilled, the door open a crack. "Don't you dare do this now."

Emmett and I exchanged confused glances, but despite my danger, I was kind of excited. Was I finally going to get the goods on them?

"I am asking you for five minutes when I gave you so much more," the vampire said. He tugged on his suit jacket, his fingers gripping the hem for a moment too long. "Please."

He'd said please? Oh fuck. None of us were getting out of here alive.

Tatiana reluctantly nodded, allowed us entrance, and turned on the small lamps in her living room.

I sat next to Emmett, wanting a friend during my last moments, while Zev took the chair closest to Tatiana.

"Give me the Ascendant," he said. Wow. Didn't expect him to just jump to the heart of things.

Tatiana narrowed her eyes at me. "You went running to him that I had it. Why?"

Zev cut me off. "I hired Ms. Feldman to find it for me."

"You're fired," she told me in a hard voice. "Go back to your law library and your stultifying life until you cement into a pillar of beige."

I slumped back against the cushions, smothering a flinch. My eyes were gritty from this very long day, and that was without the mostly dead part. "I swear I didn't know you had it."

"You knew about your parents though."

"Only since you got back from Moscow. There was a—" I cut myself off, not wanting to implicate Emmett with the prophecy. "A letter from my uncle Jake. Combined with what I learned from James Learsdon, the man who set Davide Forino up, I put things together."

"You should have told me immediately," she snapped.

I bowed my head. "You're right. I should have."

"Now you come here trying to take it from me. Just like your parents did. Mazel tov, kid. You've got that Blum killer instinct."

I flinched at the word "killer."

"Give me the Ascendant," Zev said.

"You couldn't use it even if I did," Tatiana muttered.

"Why not?" He raised an eyebrow.

She didn't answer.

"I don't have time for this," he snarled. He leaned forward and looked into her eyes. "Give. Me. The Ascendant."

Tatiana struggled against his compulsion, her eyes wide with shock and hurt. She stood up and grabbed on to the top of the sofa but couldn't defy him. Tearing free, she dragged herself toward the stairs.

Quivering, Emmett grabbed my hand.

I squeezed back just as hard. "Why is your..." I paused, keeping the estrie secret. "Need so urgent?"

The vampire ignored me, tapping his foot impatiently until Tatiana returned with a blue velvet pouch, which she placed in his outstretched hand.

"You swore to never compel me. I'll never forgive you," Tatiana spat.

"You think that," he said, "but you will. I forgave you, after all. What do I need to use it?"

Tatiana answered through gritted teeth, "A Banim Shovavim."

I jumped to my feet. "Is that why you hired me?" Emmett

pulled me down, but I shook him off, too furious to do more than pace. "I should have known it wasn't about protecting me in exchange for working for you or doing your memoirs or professing that I'd liven things up. You wanted me for one reason and one reason only." I was furious that I had to blink away the dampness in my eyes.

Tatiana bit down on her bottom lip, then she gave an uncaring shrug. "You were just so exploitable."

Zev laughed. "You and I were always more alike than you'd admit, Tanechka."

I stopped, frowning. How had the vamp exploited me? He'd hired me because I was a Banim Shovavim? Sure. Cloaking and traveling the KH would be advantageous when the Ascendant could have been anywhere, but if he'd already known I had to be the one to use it for him, he wouldn't have asked Tatiana what to do. So how were the two of them alike?

Tatiana threw me a mean little smile. She'd figured it out.

Zev had offered me protection because the hunt for the Ascendant had begun again. I frowned. He'd claimed that whoever was searching for the magic amplifier didn't know about my magic yet, but I'd accepted the job because someone had killed my parents and McMurtry. The thing is, I'd been at the Lonestar's death and I'd been left alone.

The killer had to know who I was, so they must not have believed I was a threat. Still, even if they weren't the ones hunting for the Ascendant now, whoever was had to be deadly.

Had Zev lied about protecting me? I shook my head. He wouldn't outright lie when he'd given me his word on that. *Exploitable.* There was an element of gullibility I was missing here.

My brows shot up. James Learsdon had never said there was anyone else hunting for the Ascendant. Only Zev had. And like a fool, I'd believed him.

"Learsdon was the only person ever after the Ascendant,

wasn't he?" I said. "You let all my assumptions and fears based on the past do your work for you."

Zev inclined his head in acknowledgment. "I always said you were clever. Incredibly easy to manipulate when it comes to the safety of you and your family, but you get there in the end."

"Our deal is void," I said through clenched teeth. Anger lashed across my skin, my shadow magic whispering to me to set it free.

Sparing me the barest impatient glance, Zev pulled a silver orb out of the velvet bag.

The magic amplifier was no bigger than my fist, and other than looking like a space egg, it was unassuming to the point of bland.

"Tell Ms. Feldman how to activate this, Tanechka, and we'll be on our way."

"I told you, we're done," I said.

The vampire swatted me aside like I was a mosquito, not making contact, just getting me out of the way. "Get on with it. I'm running out of time." The thread of desperation laced through his menacing tone settled under my skin like a splinter.

Time for what? How could any conversation with the estrie who sired him be that urgent?

"She has to use her Banim Shovavim vision to open it in a hidden space," Tatiana said tightly. "Then you call forth whatever you want to let loose."

Images of Arlo's fate washed over me, and I shook my head violently. "I can't use it. I'll be damned to eternal torture in the KH."

Zev replaced the orb in the pouch. "Ms. Feldman was under the impression that the Ascendant was either too weak to effectively work or that the Consortium hadn't used it properly." He raised his eyebrows at Tatiana.

I gripped the arm of the sofa. "Did neither of you hear me? I won't do this!"

Tatiana's lips were clamped shut, but the answer burst out of her despite her best efforts otherwise. "The BS that opened it for the Consortium was half-Sapien."

I flinched at the use of the slur against my kind.

"And?" Zev said.

"The Consortium didn't know that until after I'd stolen it from them." The words were dragged out of her. "The user's half-Sapien ancestry diluted the Ascendant's ability to perform properly."

"Wonderful. That was all I needed, thank you." Zev stood up and held out a hand to me. "Come. We have an old friend of mine whom it's time to pay our respects to."

"Forget it," I said. "I won't risk damnation for that."

Zev blurred away, his hand closing around Tatiana's throat. "What about for this?"

The noise of distress she made shattered me, but I kept my gaze steady. "You're bluffing. You can't hurt her. You said it yourself."

He tightened his hold, blood welling up under the press of his nails. The skin on her neck was papery thin. "How far do you want to test me?"

Tatiana clawed at her throat, whimpering.

I despised him. Despised them both. But I despised myself most for still caring. Still, I wasn't going to pay the price for the vampire's desires. "I'm not prioritizing anyone's life over mine."

"Not even Sadie's?" Zev met my gaze calmly like he was inquiring about the weather, his hand still wrapped around Tatiana's throat. "Need I remind you of my open invitation into your home?"

His misbuttoned shirt and red-rimmed, sleepless eyes were a warning sign that any other promises he'd ever made would be forfeit if I didn't acquiesce.

"You win," I said bitterly.

There was no triumph in Zev's gaze. He released Tatiana, studying his hands before clasping them behind his back. "Anything else I should know?"

"Isn't that enough?" Tatiana said bitterly.

"You'd better hope it is." With that, he stalked toward the front door, my arm gripped in his hand.

The scent of Tatiana's perfume grew stronger. "I won't hurt Sadie," she said from behind once Rodrigo, Zev, and I were outside. "But I never want to see you again." She shut her door, the dead bolt sliding into place with a *ka-thunk*.

I wasn't sure which of us she spoke to, and it hardly mattered since I wouldn't be back.

Zev's nails dug into my biceps, but he didn't stop walking. He shoved me into the back of the limo and we drove to Blood Alley.

"At least give me a phone to say goodbye to everyone." My eyes had welled with tears from sorrow, yes, but also because I was furious.

Zev didn't answer me, staring out the window and drumming his fingers on his bouncing leg.

I scrubbed a hand over my face. "Will you at least tell everyone what happened to me?"

"I'm sure Tatiana will let them know." *You bastard.*

My chest tight, I stared out the window gathering every good memory of my loved ones close to sustain me, but they were fuzzy and distant like an underdeveloped photograph.

Rodrigo didn't park outside the gates. He drove into a parking garage a few blocks away, went down a level, and through a hidden space entrance, coming out in another garage in the vamp's territory.

A short elevator ride solved the mystery of where we were: underneath the club, Rome. It made sense that there'd be a way for them to get supplies in and out without garnering attention, but this new fact didn't mean much in the face of my impending doom.

My positive thinking that maybe the angels wouldn't notice one little estrie being coaxed out of hiding was squelched under the fear that estries hadn't been seen in hundreds of years and I had no faith in this cockamamie device to bring a specific one back, even if I was a full Banim Shovavim.

Rodrigo left us when Zev dragged me to the level with the dungeon, but we didn't go into the cell I'd previously been locked up in. He pressed his hand to a spot on the stone wall and a panel slid away, revealing a narrow, windowless prison lined in iron.

The light from the corridor reached only partway inside.

Hovering on the outside of the threshold, Zev tossed me the egg-shaped orb.

I shivered, hunching my shoulders against the damp cold that wormed into the marrow of my bones.

Laurent used his claws to tear through reality to Gehenna, and the only other rifts to that dimension appeared as shimmering round circles. How would a smooth silver orb that didn't even have any heft to it do the trick?

I manifested Delilah, viewing the seamless egg through her green vision, but it didn't reveal anything. I sniffed it; I licked it. I tossed it on the floor, but it was so light that it merely bounced.

"Open it and call my sire," Zev hissed.

"I'm trying." Taking a steadying breath, I closed my own eyes, allowing only the green vision to remain. Slowly I turned the orb in my hand, and my breath caught at the tiny depression near the wider bottom. I pressed my thumbnail against it, and the amplifier flipped open into two perfect halves.

I half expected a lighter to pop out, but the insides were just as smooth as its polished case. I flicked a finger against the orb, speaking at it like a cell on speakerphone. "Hello? Kian?"

Nothing.

"Kian, sire of Zev!" I brought out my most commanding voice, with no trace of my default Canadian politeness. This was a from-the-gut issuance, defying anyone to disobey. "Come forth and join us."

Deafening silence.

I looked at the vamp. "Is this thing work—"

All sound was sucked from the cell and shadows exploded from the orb, plunging the prison into darkness.

The orb grew heavier and warmer in my palm, pulsing in time to the trumpeting of my heart.

Suddenly, with a noise like Velcro tearing, a horizontal crack of light appeared like a crooked smile, and a wash of whispering voices cascaded over me.

My eyes watered against the stench of rotting onions.

The voices grew louder—from whispers to murmurs, still indistinct yet a lulling croon, encouraging me to own the power.

Shadows crackled between the orb and my palm like a feather's kiss. My lips parted, dark twists dancing over my skin and the warmth spreading through my body.

All could be mine for the taking.

The orb pulsed more insistently, yet there was no trace of the estrie.

Out in the corridor, Zev gave a guttural cry wrenched from his very depths. He was a creature of darkness caught by the stark light as he howled at the loss of all hope.

Darkness and light.

An aborted game of cards.

My smile dimmed, and I scratched at the shadows on my skin.

Would this moment have come no matter what?

I held the silver artifact up.

Did the sunshine I'd seen in Poe's game of memory represent my well-being and not the fate of the world like I'd assumed? What path would assure its life-affirming blaze?

"Bring Kian forth!" Zev roared.

Should I accede to Zev's wishes and avoid the wrath he'd unleash at being denied his agenda? Remain silent?

Or was it already too late to save myself?

I tossed the orb into the air and caught it, snapping it shut. It fit in my palm like it belonged there, my fingers curling protectively over it.

Decision made.

27

Shuddering, I pitched the Ascendant into the crack as hard as I could, draping myself in the revulsion I felt for opening this gateway.

Arlo had kept the amplifier for his own purposes, but I wanted nothing to do with it. If Senoi, Sansenoi, and Sammaneglof could be convinced of that, perhaps they'd spare me.

The murmuring voices cut out with a shocking abruptness, but Zev screamed, a furious wail that spiked into the top of my head.

Any fear of the vampire's retaliation fell to a distant second as the crack opened wider, like a mouth with jagged teeth, and a rank wind blew back my hair. Something was watching me. Weighing me.

I backed up with quick, jerky steps, my breath coming in short, shallow pants.

"I don't want to fly with the angels!" My heartbeat in my ears practically drowned out all other sound. "I want this to end!"

There was a high-pitched scream from very far away. It

drew closer and closer, growing so loud that clapping my hands over my ears didn't dim it one bit.

The light stuttered, and a black ball flew toward me.

I barely jumped out of the way before it hit the wall and unfurled into a limp figure on the ground.

The crack didn't disappear.

"Close!" Goosebumps skittered over my skin from that unseen presence, but the rift remained. I leaned into my words, throwing all my power behind them. "I COMMAND YOU TO CLOSE."

Unbelievably, it did.

I crept toward the estrie. She was barely more than rags and bone, her face covered by long, stringy hair, but her chest rose and fell faintly.

"Is she alive?" Zev said.

"Yes," I said hoarsely.

He ran a weary hand over his face. "You destroyed the Ascendant."

Dybbuks couldn't use it on the Gehenna side because they were nothing more than malevolent spirits. Also, they were too busy being tortured. Any other beings there weren't imprisoned so wouldn't need the amplifier either. Gehenna was the safest place for the orb to be.

"We had no deal to the contrary." I notched my chin up. "This concludes our business, yes?"

Zev glanced from the estrie to me and then nodded.

A rush of adrenaline hit me hard, and I went in search of Rodrigo on rubbery legs, finding him standing guard at the top of the stairs. "I'd like to go home now."

My magic was tapped out so badly that even once I left Blood Alley, I had no juice to access the KH. I just wanted a ride in a warm car.

Rodrigo motioned me to go ahead. "Nothing's stopping you."

"I have no purse, no phone, no money." I waved a hand

over my bloody shirt. "And I look like a serial killer. How am I supposed to get there?"

The sooner I did, the sooner I could drink myself into a numb stupor. There had been so much to deal with, from Tatiana to my kid having magic, being a target of not one but three angry magical entities, and now me turning down phenomenal cosmic power. I needed a break. I didn't want to feel these huge emotions anymore.

I didn't want to feel anything.

Rodrigo smiled, the first one he'd ever given me that reached his eyes. "Walk."

Hoping his limo crashed into a fiery wreck the next time he drove it, I left the club, alone in the dark.

My new career had burned to the ground, a woman I admired had played me and been played in return, and for all my feelings of empowerment, I'd been nothing more than a pawn.

Shivering, I left Blood Alley.

A dandelion sprouted up through a broken section of sidewalk. Its stem was bent, and it was missing a couple of petals, but despite being trod on, it fought to survive.

Stupid weed. I ground it underfoot and continued on my way.

My walk was made longer than usual because I stuck to side streets due to my bloody shirt, so I didn't make it to my place until dawn. I knocked softly on Eli's door to let him know that Sadie could go to school and there was no need to worry her with the details. Everything had been sorted.

My lip trembled when I said that.

Eli opened his mouth, but I shook my head. Kindness would be my undoing right now.

I stumbled into my house, not craving a drink anymore. It

had only been a means to an end of blotting everything out, and since I was blurry with exhaustion, I stepped over the wreckage of my coffee table, collapsed on my sofa, pulled the blanket over me, and passed out.

I slept well into the afternoon, but all those hours of rest did nothing against the fatigue sunk deep into my bones. Even a long, hot shower and copious amounts of coffee didn't help, and I wondered if I'd ever feel refreshed again. If I'd ever be free of my past, able to bound out of bed each morning to take on a new day with enthusiasm.

Putting on talk radio so I wasn't alone with my thoughts, I methodically checked all pockets before dumping the laundry in the wash.

Part of me insisted that even if I didn't work for Tatiana, the game still had to be shut down. I jammed some towels into the washer. I wouldn't do it for her, I'd do it for all those poor Sapiens who'd lost their lives and to prevent anyone else from experiencing that nightmare.

Another part of me knew how futile it was to bother: a drop in an ocean of cruelty. Even if I shut it down and thwarted the Consortium, so what? There'd be another Consortium, another way that Ohrists took advantage of Sapiens. Or Banim Shovavim. Or each other.

I dumped detergent in and started the washing machine. Let saving the world be someone else's problem. Satisfied with my decision, I even did some home renovations. The laundry hamper that I'd turned upside down worked great as a new coffee table and hid the pile of detritus underneath it.

That crack to Gehenna rose up in my memory like a smile, and I gripped the top of my sofa before thoroughly stuffing that vision inside a locked box deep in my soul.

The good news was that I didn't have time to dwell on the fate of the world, my parents, or anyone's well-being. Nope. I was too busy being entertained and informed by daytime television while eating low-fat, only slightly stale pretzels.

Between real-life baby daddy drama, tips to refresh my fall wardrobe, and exciting uses for quinoa, the hours passed quickly by.

Honestly, it was the vacation I hadn't known I needed.

It was also the vacation that was rudely interrupted that night by multiple calls from Emmett. I ignored them, since I was, you know, on vacation, and they eventually stopped. I didn't even feel guilty, because he was either calling about the dybbuk enthrallment hotline or Tatiana. If it was the first, tough titty. Ohrists knew the dangers of lowered inhibitions during the Danger Zone. Not my problem.

If it was the second? Not. My. Problem.

The sofa was so comfortable that I slept there that night as well. Zev was damn lucky that he hadn't damaged it with his little tantrum. Why go all the way upstairs, get changed, and get into a cold bed, when I'd warmed these cushions up quite nicely, the glow of the television screen was cozy, and all my delicious snacks were mere steps away?

I tipped the last of the dry cereal into my mouth. Probably should get milk at some point.

Nobody phoned on Saturday morning, which was great, because I'd settled in to watch a fascinating documentary on fungus. I had not known that they were classified as plants as recently as the 1960s, and I was a sucker for a good fact.

Plus, this replacement coffee table was a great height to rest my feet on. I might just keep the hamper here permanently. Rattan went with everything, right?

When someone knocked loudly on my door, I turned up the volume, but even once I'd hit maximum levels, the British narrator now screaming about a fungi that created zombie ants, I was unable to drown out my visitor.

Dragging my blanket like a bedraggled cape, I flung my front door open. "I'm. On. Vacation." I shut the door on Laurent.

He braced his hand against it before it closed and leaned

in. Dark stubble dusted his tight jaw, his curls were rumpled, and he smelled so good. A cedar anchor. Except he belonged to my real life, which I wasn't dealing with at the moment. "The golem showed up at my place last night," he said. "With a suitcase."

"Not my problem." Such a handy phrase with a wide spectrum of applications.

"Tatiana has been on a tear," he said.

I shuddered at his word choice, slamming the brakes on another vision of that ghastly crack.

Laurent narrowed his eyes. "Care to comment?"

"Nope." I struggled to push him back. "If I miss the rest of the zombie ants, I'm going to be very put out."

"Zombie...?" He shook his head. "She made Marjorie cry. Raymond quit. Still nothing to say?"

I stilled. Poor Marjorie. And Raymond, wow. Way to show backbone. I shut down my emotions even though my feelings box bulged dangerously. "Talk to your aunt," I said. "I don't work for her anymore."

"Oh, I know that too. Emmett told me everything. What's wrong with you?"

"*Me?!*" I flapped my cape like it would infuse me with lasers to smite the French jerk.

My neighbor across the street glanced over in alarm, her grocery bags spilling out of her hatchback.

I smiled and waved, before pulling Laurent inside and shutting the door. "Why am I to blame?" I hissed.

His brow creased. "Who said anything about blame? Where's your to-do list? Your plans A through L?" He raked a thorough gaze from my frazzled bedhead, along my wrinkled sweats with a coffee stain, and down to the fleece-lined knit socks with pompoms. "You aren't the type to lick your wounds. You're a fighter. Come on, Mitzi." He smiled gently. "How do we make this right?"

I pulled my blanket cape closed, annoyed at him for seeing

me that way. Didn't he understand that the harder I tried, the more I was let down?

"I'm on vacation," I mumbled and burst into tears.

"Ah, ma chér." Laurent bundled me into his arms. "I think you've learned all there is about zombie ants."

That did it. I cried on him until I was worn out, wrung out, and thoroughly wilted.

Then I came up with a plan.

Laurent rounded up Emmett and Tatiana.

I'd cleaned up my house, banished the laundry hamper back to its proper place in the bathroom, and was currently spying through the curtains waiting for their arrival. I wore the most "take charge" of the various outfits I'd tried on, rehearsed my speech multiple times, and practiced my stern mom face in the mirror until it was perfectly terrifying.

Then Tatiana arrived, dragged up my front walk by Laurent and Emmett, who each had her by an elbow, and all my preparations flew out the window. The woman with an indubitable sense of fashion, even in sleepwear, was wearing the rattiest pair of pajamas I'd ever seen. They were so faded that any one color would be embarrassed to claim it as its own. She wore no makeup, no jewelry; the only "Tatiana" thing about her was her red oversize glasses.

I stifled a sigh of relief that she'd been able to cross my wards, meaning she hadn't come here to hurt me, and allowed myself a single delicious moment of pettiness.

"You look like shit." I stood in my doorway with my arms crossed. I'd ironed my red skirt and paired it with another red blouse from my law firm days. We fighters had an image to protect, after all.

"My mistake," Tatiana sneered. "I thought the dress code was abductee casual."

"Hmph," I sniffed, mostly so I didn't laugh.

When Emmett passed me, I touched his arm to hold him back while Laurent took his aunt into my kitchen. "Are you all right?"

He scowled. "She made Marjorie cry. She's never gone that far before."

"She'll apologize."

"You'll fix this, right?"

"I'll try, buddy."

We took our seats at the table. I was sandwiched between Laurent and Emmett and across from the elderly artist.

Attempting to get things back on track, I launched into my very fine speech. "'The enemy of my enemy is my friend' is an ancient proverb that suggests—"

"It's *Star Trek*," Emmett said.

"What?" I said.

He nodded. "Yeah. Captain Kirk said it in the reboot. I saw the movie the other day."

"He said it," I said with exaggerated patience, "because it's an ancient proverb."

"Proverb, schmoverb," Tatiana said. "You don't even put out food? What is this? Starvation torture?" She thrust out her hands, her thumbs extended. "Just put the screws to me already."

Laurent stared at the floor, his shoulders silently shaking. Oh good. He was going to be as useful as Eli was whenever Sadie got snippy in a fight.

"Fine." I kicked Laurent's leg, making his shoulders shake harder. "My parents tried to kill you, and you hired me with a hidden agenda." My voice warbled, and Laurent placed his hand on my thigh. "Zev screwed us both over. That sum things up to your satisfaction?"

"It's a start," she said, fanning herself. "I'm a little faint because of my fast metabolism and lack of food in defiance of the Geneva Convention on the treatment of prisoners of war."

Guffawing loudly, Laurent had to leave the room to compose himself.

"Jesus." I stomped around my kitchen and returned with a block of cheddar and an unopened box of crackers on a stack of small plates. I threw a steak knife down next to everything. "Happy?"

Emmett frowned. "The plating leaves something to be desired."

"Many, many things." Shaking her head, Tatiana tore into the crackers.

Her stupid nephew howled with laughter from the hallway.

"If everyone could stick to the topic," I said icily. I snapped my fingers at Laurent. "That means you too, Chuckles."

He slunk back in and took his seat.

"Did you steal the Ascendant from Arlo?" I said.

"Mitzi," Laurent admonished. "She was attacked on the way to deliver it."

"No, she wasn't, because Arlo used it. It's what got him damned in the KH." If I was correct, then Tatiana was culpable for the crash. It didn't absolve my parents, but if she hadn't stolen it back from her client, no one would have gone after her.

Too bad that didn't make me feel any better.

"I didn't steal it," Tatiana said. "Arlo called me in a panic a few days after I'd given it to him asking me to hide it." She sliced off some cheese. "He handed the amplifier over, and the crash happened on my way home. By the time I was recovered enough to understand what had happened to me, Arlo had disappeared."

"I spoke to him. He's being tortured—" My voice cracked, and I cleared my throat. "In the Kefitzat Haderech."

"Where's the Ascendant?" Tatiana said. "I want it back."

"I destroyed it." I dusted off my hands. "Done and done."

Tatiana stabbed the cheese with the knife like she was murdering a poor whale with a harpoon.

I smiled meanly, one eyebrow raised in challenge, but she didn't call me out. "We have to find out why Zev needed the estrie who sired him," I said, "and undo whatever he's wrought by making me free that demon."

"It worked then?" Laurent said.

"Yeah. Anyone got a problem with that?"

"I'm on board with anything that screws him over," Tatiana said.

Emmett banged his fist on the table. "That's your plan? More revenge? You two suck. I thought you were going to work things out." He pointed at Tatiana. "So you would stop being such a bitch. And you?" My turn for a finger jab. "Didn't turn into a zombie again."

"It was a documentary with zombie ants," I said through clenched teeth and glared at Laurent.

"My English not so good," he said in a thick French accent.

Tatiana chortled and helped herself to more food.

I turned flashing eyes on my former boss. "I'm not going to sit here and be mocked by Ms. False Pretenses."

Tatiana made a snarky face at me, much like a petulant five-year-old.

I dug my nails into my palms to keep from smacking her, but Laurent stroked my back, and little by little, I relaxed. "We also have to find whoever hired my parents, and for that I require your assistance, Tatiana."

"You think I didn't already look for whomever was behind the car crash that destroyed my life?" Her voice was clogged with emotion. She took a breath before speaking more briskly. "For a long time, my world was pain and surgery and more pain in recovery, but it gave me time to think and understand that it hadn't been an accident. Not when the Ascendant was stolen." She toyed with the knife. "I devoted myself to tracking down possible players until I'd narrowed down the thief. Then I paid a visit."

Under the table, I grabbed Laurent's thigh. "You said you didn't kill my parents."

"I didn't. The first I heard about their involvement was when you brought them up at Woods Bank. No, the Ohrist I found must have hired them. He had an iron-clad alibi for the time of the accident, but after further discussion, he admitted to being behind the crash. I thought his alibi had lied, not that he'd subcontracted to two people I'd never heard of."

"It was genius," Laurent said.

I raised my eyebrows at him.

"I mean it was terrible, but using two unknowns to get at Tatiana? She'd have sussed out any serious contenders, but your parents' movements wouldn't have been on her radar. Powerful people tend to only expect those who are equally powerful to come at them."

"Like how Ohrists forget that a Sapien with a gun can kill them?" I said.

Laurent pointed at me. "Exactly."

"Wait." Emmett held up a hand like a kid in class asking a question. "So, this Arlo character hired you to find the Ascendant. You did, but then he gave it back and it was stolen from you. After that, you stole the Ascendant back from the Ohrist before you killed him?"

"He's dead?" I gave a pained exhale. "I could have questioned him about my parents."

"He was older than me. He wouldn't have been alive now anyway," Tatiana said.

"What was his name?"

"Calvin Jones."

I crossed my arms. "Did he suffer?"

Tatiana smiled broadly—like Bruce the shark from *Finding Nemo* when he's once again had a taste of blood.

Jones used my parents and was on the top of my suspect list as the person who'd murdered them to tie up any loose ends. I didn't care about justice; I wanted retribution. As I couldn't be the one to deliver it, Tatiana torturing him would have to suffice.

Laurent tapped my arm. "If Jones had the Ascendant, he probably ordered the crash, but I doubt he killed your parents."

"Why?"

"Because someone killed McMurtry the same way."

"You're right." I thought it over. "If it wasn't Jones then that person is still alive. Or at the very least, they're intimately connected to this case. I can still find them and unearth the truth." Glad as I was about that, it didn't entirely ease my anger at my former boss. "You killed Jones, then I came along and you had your gullible Banim Shovavim."

"Don't flatter yourself," Tatiana said. "You weren't my first."

"That makes it so much better," I said snarkily.

"Her first Banim Shovavim hire." Laurent wagged a finger at his aunt. "Stop being deliberately obtuse."

"Your English has drastically improved," I noted. "What a quick study you are."

He grinned, then turned to his aunt. "I told Miriam about Delphine."

Tatiana snapped her cracker in half, the cheese falling onto the plate. "Juliette didn't say something? My mistake."

"Who's Delphine?" Emmett said.

"My great-niece," Tatiana said in a firm voice.

"My wife." Laurent smiled wistfully.

I placed my hand on the small of his back.

Emmett and Tatiana had identical wide-eyed blinks but for very different reasons.

Laurent touched his ring finger. "She died. She was enthralled and two months pregnant. I didn't know until afterward."

"That's awful." Emmett studied his folded hands, his tone subdued. "I'm sorry."

"Thank you," Laurent said.

Tatiana and I exchanged surprised glances at that emotionally honest interchange, then we both stiffened and looked away.

"I mention it now," Laurent said, "because if I can be honest, you can too."

Tatiana glared at her nephew. "I liked you better when you were stoic and angry." She threw up her hands. "I didn't hire you, Miriam, because you were Banim Shovavim," she said testily. "Not entirely. All those other reasons were still true. You were the first Banim Shovavim who seemed capable of earning my trust enough to confide in about the Ascendant."

"Aww," Emmett said. "That's sweet."

I rounded on him. "No, it's not." Glaring at Tatiana, I ticked items off on my fingers. "I extricated us from a murder charge. I saved you from a death curse. I proved myself again and again. What the hell else were you waiting for?"

"I would have asked soon." She popped a cube of cheddar in her mouth, making a big point of chewing and being unable to speak further.

Everyone in this room sucked. Her most of all. She hadn't uttered a single word of remorse for her murder attempt.

"What were *you* going to do with the amplifier, ma chère tante?" Laurent said.

"I don't know." When we all stared at her incredulously, she rolled her eyes. "At first, I wanted vengeance. After Delphine, well." She shrugged. "When I spoke to Calvin Jones, he let it slip that he was planning to sell it to someone else, but he died before I could find out who." She sounded annoyed that her torture had prematurely ended her interrogation.

I sat forward. "Could that person still be alive? They might be the one that killed McMurtry."

"Doubtful," she said. "I always wondered why Jones had waited that long before lining up a buyer. If he was worried about Arlo's disappearance, that was more reason to get rid of the Ascendant right away."

"His competitor had vanished and then his subcontractors were dead." Laurent spread his hands. "I'd have laid low with the artifact too."

"In which case, Jones didn't kill Mom and Dad, and the buyer wasn't a part of this." I gave a cruel smile. I might still get my vengeance.

"Your parents, your problem," Tatiana said. "I have no issue with their killer."

I tensed.

Laurent placed a hand on my thigh. "The amplifier involves both of you so we will all work together to get to the bottom of every last mystery concerning it. No more secrets. Yes?"

It took a while to get past all the resentment floating around but eventually we all agreed.

"I'll drive Emmett and Tatiana home," Laurent said.

"I never said I'm living with her again," Emmett protested.

"Then I'll drop you and your suitcase off on the corner of your choice," Laurent said. "I packed it and put it in my trunk."

"You're as mean as she is," the golem grumbled.

Tatiana and Laurent made identical snarky faces.

"Apologize to Marjorie," I said.

"Destroy the Human Race," Tatiana retorted.

"The game," I specified, "not the—"

"Yes, Miriam." The artist waved off my addendum. "We know."

"Regardless." I tossed my hair off my shoulder. "I don't work for you anymore. Destroy it yourself. I'll get you the means to do so."

Tatiana's nostrils flared. "I can no longer cavort about engaging in such high-risk activities. So despite the fact that you look a good thirty years older than me, due to your refusal to hydrate, it's on you to finish the job."

"Laugh and you're a dead man," I muttered to Laurent.

He clamped his lips together.

I crossed my legs and draped an arm along the back of my chair, coolly regarding my ex-boss. "You'll have to pay my freelance rate. It's very expensive." I could finish this one job for the homicidal maniac. For the good of humanity.

"I'll pay your current monthly salary, and as someone in my employ, you'll treat me with the respect I deserve."

"Respect? You impaled me with a tree and threatened my daughter's life. You're lucky I simply want to move on from my entire experience of working for you." Otherwise, I would so sue her ass. I knew plenty of good lawyers and statistically one of them had to be an Ohrist.

Laurent growled, his fingers morphing to claws. "You didn't mention that's what she'd done," he said to Emmett.

"I didn't know that part. Duuuude." The golem shook his head at Tatiana.

"It was one tiny root." Still, she tugged on her collar, avoiding his gaze. "I concede that the attempted homicide was too far."

"Too far?" I gave an incredulous laugh. "It's a miracle I survived."

Tatiana crossed her arms. "I came back for you. Happy?"

"What?"

She waved a hand at Laurent and Emmett. "The grief

these two would have given me if I'd let you die. You were gone from the tree, so I left."

I put my hand to my heart. "I'm so touched. For all you knew, they'd taken away my mangled corpse. Out of sight, out of mind, huh?"

Tatiana slammed her palm against the table. "Let me remind you that you attacked first. Remember?"

Oh yeah. I twisted my old engagement ring around my finger. "Then I will concede that is a fair point."

"Very generous," Laurent murmured with a straight face.

Emmett shook his head. "You women are whack."

"Also, the gargoyle assured me you were fine," Tatiana said.

"Pyotr?" I frowned. "You spoke to him?"

"Yes. It was nice to speak Russian again."

I snorted. So glad she had a pleasant après-murder visit.

"As for Sadie," Tatiana continued, "I wouldn't ever hurt her. I swear on my love for Delphine."

Laurent didn't tense up at her name. In fact, he gave his aunt a fond smile, which she returned. "Je t'aime, Tatiana."

Her mouth fell open, then she blinked rapidly, turning away so we didn't see her dab at her eyes. "Je t'aime, Laurent."

Holy shit. I gaped at the two of them. Was Laurent truly ready to move on with his life?

He nudged me. "Mitzi?"

"Huh?" I fit my old engagement ring back on my finger because I'd twisted it right off.

"Do you believe Tatiana about Sadie?"

"Oh. Yes, okay. I believe her."

"Are we in agreement on your continuing employment?" Tatiana held out her hand.

I didn't want to type up a new résumé and look for another corporate gig and explain why I'd left the law firm. I thinned my lips. Perhaps because it was more fun doing this. And I might have missed the ornery old coot.

There was just one thing to iron out. No, two.

"Tell me the deal between you and Zev. Who did he let live?" Had he meant Laurent?

"You don't get all my secrets, Miriam. In or out?"

"I want to be an equal partner with you," I said. "No more minion status."

Tatiana laughed. "Get over yourself."

"Wait." Emmett's hand shot up. "I want that too."

"Traitor," she sniffed.

"Emmett too," I said. "That's the condition. Cassin, Feldman, and Associates."

Emmett stomped his foot. "What the hell? You're treating me like the *Gilligan's Island* theme song where the Professor and Mary Ann got lumped together as 'the rest.'"

"I have seniority and you don't have a last name," I said. "Well?"

Tatiana glared at me. She lifted a chair and slammed it down. "This isn't a union shop. I run a dictatorship."

My shoulders slumped, but before I could retort, she jabbed a finger at me.

"I was very happy with my high-handed ways, but you had to come in and screw everything up." She took off her glasses and rubbed the lenses with a napkin, not meeting my eyes. "You hurt me."

"I know," I said softly. "You hurt me too."

She put her glasses back on. "Cassin and Associates doesn't sound so bad."

"Sucker!" Emmett fired finger guns at me. "You're 'the rest' too."

I could live with that. "We'll have more say in things?"

"You already bulldoze your opinion into every aspect of the business. What's left?"

Laurent snickered, and while I didn't smack him, my look promised retribution later.

"Emmett and I aren't Ohrists like you, and I didn't grow up accepted by the magic community. I want you to remember that we have important and valid viewpoints."

The golem puffed out his chest. "Yeah, what she said."

"Fine." Tatiana held up a hand. "But it's still my reputation on the line. Maybe, at some point, in the very far future you might make partner. Like when I'm dead."

I held up a finger. "We also want business cards."

Tatiana's eyes narrowed. "Plain card stock and I'm not paying for a fancy logo."

I crushed her in a hug because she'd hate it. "Mazel tov! You've got yourself an associate."

"Two of them." Emmett wrapped his arms around both of us, squeezing just as tightly.

My partner held herself stiffly, a shudder running through her before she pushed me off. "Very well. Blow up that game, Miriam, then you can go play spy. Emmett, home."

Emmett and Tatiana headed for Laurent's truck, but I held the shifter back.

"Thank you for your support," I said. "It meant a lot. Except for the part where you were completely useless."

He chuckled. "You want help destroying the game?"

"Nah."

"Call me after?"

"Yes."

His smile widened. "À bientôt." With that he jumped down the stairs and hurried after Tatiana and Emmett.

As for me? I had a game to destroy. I was an associate, after all.

28

After changing into something more suitable for breaking, entering, and kicking butt, I returned to the curio shop just before closing.

Given Clea's look of surprise, she hadn't expected me back this soon. Or at all. "Failed already?" She sounded almost cheerful, dusting off chachkas with an old-fashioned feather duster.

She'd hung the masks she'd unpacked during my last visit on one wall, their empty eyes tracking me.

Shuddering, I turned my back on them. "Zev BatKian destroyed the puzzle box."

"I'm devastated that our business dealings are concluded," she drawled. "Bye now."

I leaned over the counter. "Clea, there are two things you want more than anything."

"Yeah?" She narrowed her eyes. "What's the first?"

"To keep humanity safe. If you don't help me, people will die, and the ones who live will wish otherwise. You didn't see what the game did to them. I wouldn't inflict that suffering on my worst enemy."

She gnawed on the inside of her cheek. "What's the second?"

I hit her with my brightest smile. "To keep me out of your life. If you don't help me, I'll show up every day to have lunch with you. With magazines where we take quizzes to improve our sex lives and bond over nail polish colors."

"I'll be back at HQ tomorrow. You'll never get across to the rock a second time."

"You willing to bet on that?"

Her scowl grew darker and I took a step back, but she didn't pound me to smithereens with her superstrength. "Jeez," she bitched. "You even take the fun out of messing with you."

"I beg your pardon?"

She toyed with one of her facial studs. "The puzzle box wasn't a demon artifact, okay?"

"A gargoyle said it smelled of vamp."

"It belonged to Celeste, but she couldn't open it either, so she gave it to me." Clea shrugged. "I was curious how to open it."

I picked up a pointy hatpin from a small jar. "Everything about burning a favor was a lie? You don't have a way for me to destroy the demon space?"

"No. That part was true. I don't screw around where demons are concerned." She pulled two small, corked vials out of the cash register drawer and held them up to the light.

"Pink glitter?" I spun the hatpin. "I'm not making a scrapbook."

"Much as I would love to hand this over and let you learn all its delightful properties on your own," Clea said, "Nav would stick me with extra store duty if you didn't come back in one piece." She slid the vials across the counter. "Two rules. First, don't swallow any."

I rolled my eyes.

"Roll away, but swallow even one sparkly molecule of this

and watch the fun ensue," she said balefully. "Second, pour the glitter out in a single pile."

I shook the vials. "Are you sure this is enough? It's a very large space. Bigger than the Park, remember?"

"The glitter is demonic. Don't apply human logic to it."

"Can I safely transport it through the Kefitzat Haderech?"

"Yes, because the pink stuff is inert until you add the vinegar in the other vial, but add it immediately to the open glitter to activate it."

"Like epoxy. Got it. Will I need to clean anything up?"

She barked a rusty laugh. "No. It's self-cleaning. Do not stick around once you've poured it. Trust the glitter to do its job."

Setting the hatpin down, I scooped up the vials. "If you're scamming me, I'm going to come visit you every day. And make up badges to wear out. The Ladies Who Lunch. The Lunch Ladies. The Lunchable Babes."

She pressed her lips into a thin line. I recognized that look.

"Are you counting to ten?" I laughed. "Do I make your head throb?"

"Get out of the store before I throw you out," she said. That monotone of hers was starting to grow on me.

After a quick stop back home for some gear, I stepped through the shadows, tugging free in the Kefitzat Haderech to the sound of a girl reading from one of the *Lord of the Rings* books with a light Jamaican accent.

The Black girl was in her early teens, wearing a pleated skirt and a gray sweater vest with a school crest over top of a white short-sleeved shirt.

Pyotr was engrossed in her story, and I was able to watch them for a minute, unnoticed. The gargoyle quietly repeated certain words after she'd read them, like "hyacinth" and "gorse."

She reached the end of the chapter and placed a bookmark

between the pages.

"One more," Pyotr whined.

"Not today." She rubbed his head. If he'd had hair, she'd be ruffling it. "I have to study. Oh. Hi."

Pyotr jumped up, hopping from foot to foot. "Now my friends meet. Malorie, Miriam."

I'd been jealous of a kid. No. Her age didn't matter. I'd been jealous, and that wasn't right. This sweet, kind gargoyle deserved every friend he had. I smiled. "Nice to meet you."

Malorie looked about as interested in meeting an "old person" as I would have been at her age but shook my hand politely enough before grabbing a canvas messenger bag and slinging it over her shoulder. "Mi a leff, inna di morrows."

"Inna di morrows," Pyotr said.

"Nice meeting you," she said to me, and left through the narrow green door.

I helped myself to a sock, wanting to ask if Malorie had solved the riddle and saved herself from ever being damned here in the KH, but I also didn't want to know if she hadn't.

"I'll be back shortly," I said.

I ran along the dimly lit path, eager to finish this job.

Right before I entered the gambling room, I cloaked myself in case of cameras. Nothing could tie me to the devastation to come.

Other than having been cleaned up, the room hadn't changed since my last visit. The tabletop model of the game didn't have any blinking lights on it so they must have removed the bodies. I hoped they'd given them a decent burial even though the families would never be allowed to properly mourn them, their disappearances forever a question mark.

There was nothing else to search, no books, no cabinets, no shelves.

I still didn't find a door leading to another part of whatever building this was, but since I needed access only to the game, I stepped into near darkness back in the room with the slide, which I had to climb to get into the game itself.

I'd worn a pair of old runners with sticky soles for this very reason, and even so it took me longer than it should have before I emerged out of the chute and climbed down the ladder onto the playground.

The house lights were on instead of the huge light towers. No one else was present but that didn't mean they weren't here in the game. They wouldn't survive once I activated the glitter, but they'd chosen to work for the Consortium. They had blood on their hands.

Vamps preying on Sapiens, I could understand. It's what they did. It's what they were *allowed* to do, and I wouldn't mourn any vampires who died when I destroyed the game.

But the Ohrist shifters? Maybe the Consortium had put a gun to their heads, threatening them if they didn't comply, but I doubted it. There were enough bloodthirsty and sadistic people out there to find shifters willing to kill fellow humans. Perhaps these shifters were just as much a product of conditioning as the vampires. After all, they constantly had it reinforced that Ohrists were superior to Sapiens.

Ohrist or vamp, employee or Consortium member, every single being was betraying their fellow (or formerly fellow in the case of vamps) humans. Be it for money, a sadistic thrill, or the determination of those at the top to carry out their experiment, all of them had to be stopped.

The madness of this game had to end.

Still hidden by my mesh, I slipped on an N95 mask, leftover from the time Eli helped me strip and sand my fireplace mantel. I carefully unscrewed the vial cap and poured the glitter in a pile on the ground, then added the vinegar and waited for a reaction.

A pink furry arm bulging with muscles sprouted from the twinkly sludge like a freaky plant grown on steroids. Its hand burst out and grabbed my foot.

The arm was joined by a second one and then a fuzzy torso. I'd have laughed at its adorableness were I not now hanging upside down, held by my ankle.

While cloaked.

My magic swirled down my arm into a scythe, but I shut it down because I needed this demon alive. I madly toed off my runner, freeing my foot and landing awkwardly on my shoulder.

The demon's eyes blinked open from the center of its fur. Had the wind not been knocked out of me, I'd have laughed because it reminded me of Gossamer, the monster from the Bugs Bunny cartoons.

I scrambled to my feet, hurried up the ladder, and popped myself into the chute, my fingers curled around the top so I could watch.

The monster grew and grew, expanding out and up until its fur brushed the top of the dome, its eyes tiny pinpricks of white. It cracked its jaw from side to side, then let out a sulfurous belch that shook the slide.

I hung there, hidden, my eyes watering from the stench, but wildly curious to see what it did next.

The demon's lower jaw dropped, hitting the ground.

I looked into its gaping maw and shivered. My brain kept trying to see something, a shadow, a glimpse of a lighter patch, but there was nothing. Not darkness, not some cosmic void, simply an absence of all things.

The swings disappeared, followed by the light towers and the grass. Not eaten, not sucked inside the demon, just gone as he pointed his mouth their way.

Something wet dripped inside my skull and the wooden platform attached to the slide disappeared, causing the chute to tumble down.

I pushed off as hard as I could, the plastic tube vanishing behind me. Sweating in terror gave me an extra boost of speed, and I made it out alive. I shot into the room that the dybbuk had attacked us in on my ass, breathing heavily, and clutching my invisibility mesh around me like a security blanket.

Clea had given me a demonic devourer. What a product!

If I'd stayed a second longer, would I have ceased to exist in one fell swoop or would my innards have dissolved into mush? I touched a hand to my head, feeling woozy, but not like my brain was melting anymore.

I was too shaky to stand up, but I wasn't safe here. The devourer wouldn't get me out in the real world, but a member of the Consortium could enter at any moment, and I didn't have it in me to remain cloaked much longer. I used a chair to push to my feet.

Was that what Clea meant by it being self-cleaning? The demon would devour itself at the end the same way it devoured the rest of this demon space leaving no trace of anything?

Motion from the tabletop model caught my eye. The playground, the high school, and the nightclub were all gone. A fog rolled over the model toward the downtown core, leaving nothing but the bare table underneath in its wake.

I shuffled closer, careful not to touch it, yet watching in fascination.

It took less than a minute for the entire model to be devoured. All that was left were the yellow letters of the starting line reading "Can you survive the Human Race?"

Like a taunt.

The fog whipped into a whirlpool, funneling tighter and faster and then winked out.

An alarm blared and heavy footsteps thundered over my head.

I dove under the table, the shadows rippling outward like a warm, shallow pond, and then falling off me like droplets when I landed in the KH. Uncaring of the rough cave floor, I rolled onto my back and laughed. Ever since I'd kept my parents' involvement in Tatiana's car accident from her I'd felt off, like I was keeping track of a litany of lies and who knew what truth.

This victory on the heels of all those secrets coming out—the good, the bad, and the ugly—filled me with a lightness. I swear I could float.

"What's funny?" Pyotr stood above me with his hands on his hips.

"Vacations are boring." I stood up.

"You're weird."

"I've heard that before." Grabbing a sock, I waltzed out the narrow green door, but I didn't go home. I'd had my pity party, been a zombie, and now I'd returned from the dead.

I stepped into Laurent's living room. "Hi. Hope it's okay that I just dropped by."

"Hey." He put aside the book he'd been reading and came over to me. "It's done already?"

"Yup. I'm very efficient." Rising onto tiptoe, I tilted my face to his. "Ask me again."

His brow furrowed, and it took him a hot minute to figure out what I meant, but when he did, his smile eclipsed the sun. "Miriam Mitzi Feldman, will you go on a date with me?"

"Yes, Laurent Huff 'n' Puff Amar. I'd love to."

He swung me into his arms. "We're going to have sex now. That's not the date."

"What kind of woman do you take me for? We do this in the correct order or not at all."

His mouth fell open, and he hurriedly set me on my feet, sputtering that he didn't mean to insult me, by which point I was openly laughing. His nostrils flared. "I am no longer in the mood."

I grinned. "Yeah you are."

"Yeah. I am." With that he threw me over his shoulder and loped into his bedroom.

29

He lay me down on his bed, and lightly stroked his fingers through my hair, while I snuggled closer, taking in the flecks of amber in his green eyes and the tiny lashes on the end of one lid that had gotten crossed.

He skipped his fingers along the back of my skull and cupped it while dragging his lips along my jaw. His light kisses to the corner of my mouth slowed, lingering.

There was a different current between us, a solid foundation allowing for an almost lazy anticipation. None of this was going to disappear; it was only the beginning.

Twining my fingers with his, I rolled onto my back with Laurent half on top of me, savoring the warmth from the press of his body and the certainty of his kisses that tasted like mint.

We kept our hands laced together, falling deeper and deeper into our embrace.

I bit his bottom lip and swiped my tongue over it to lave the sting. His moan rumbled through my chest and my breath hitched.

Laurent gazed at me with hazy eyes, his breathing as ragged as my own, and slid his hands free to run his fingers along my hips. "I need..." His mouth claimed mine, our tongues tangling.

I wound my fingers into his hair and wrapped one leg over his, arching against the hard press of his cock. My nipples tightened into stiff peaks, and I rubbed them against his chest, hissing at the friction.

He pushed my shirt up, gently pinching one nipple. Groaning, I arched underneath him, his hands tightening on my rib cage. His mouth worked lower, trailing kisses down my neck, and sucking on the hollow above my collarbone.

Dizzy, I pulled off my shirt, pitching it into the corner, then fell back to the cool softness of the mattress as his lips worked their way lower, branding me. He sucked a lace-covered tit into his mouth, his lashes falling half shut and a dreamy sigh escaping those beautiful lips.

I pushed his shirt up, forcing him to stop and strip, his pecs flexing and his shoulders bunching.

Laurent popped the clasp on my bra, dragging one strap then the other down my arms, and we drank each other in, memorizing every dip and divot.

"I must taste you again." He framed my face in his hands and claimed my mouth.

I was light-headed under the force of his attention, getting drunk on his kisses and the sensation of his bare skin on mine. But I desired all of him. I fumbled at the buttons of his jeans.

He kicked them free, making short work of my own pants before dipping his thumb into my cleft to rub against my clit.

Gasping, I clutched his shoulders.

He tore his wet, swollen lips from mine to shoot me the wickedest grin I'd ever seen.

I shivered and reached for his cock, but he batted my hand away like a cat.

"Non," he said arrogantly. "Not yet."

He pressed a kiss to my stomach then slid down the bed,

nudging my legs wider. In one swift motion, he licked into me, and I bunched the top blanket in my fists, squirming and giving breathy moans. "Oui," he said, chuckling against my inner thigh. "More of that."

One finger slid inside me, and my eyes rolled back in my head. Holding one hip to help me ride his fingers, he flicked his tongue over my clit, slow and teasing at first, then faster, both of us lost to this.

My entire body tightened, and I bit down on my lower lip, coming as I called his name.

"Good?" he said.

"Very." I took a ragged breath. "Now may I have your cock in me?"

"Since you asked nicely." Quickly he put on a condom, then kneeled at the end of the bed and stroked himself twice. "I want you."

I licked my lips. "I'm right here."

He gave me a shy smile. "Yeah, you are, aren't you?"

Moonlight glinted off reddish highlights in his hair, and he drank me in like I was a piece of music that he needed to play to soothe an essential part of himself.

My skin tingled, and I caressed his cheek, needing to ensure there wasn't a single wrong note between us. "Laurent?" He raised an eyebrow at my question. "Thanks for asking me."

His eyes flared hot and bright then he tackled me, his kiss rough and possessive as he thrust inside me. He pinned my hands over my head with one of his, using the other on my clit as he fucked me.

I wrapped my legs around his back, wanting him deeper.

"Mitzi?"

Now it was my turn to look at him in question.

He pressed his hand against his heart. "Thank you for saying yes."

"Fuck." I shuddered, a second orgasm tearing through me

right before he convulsed with a groan and collapsed next to me. "You better take me on a hell of a date to top that," I said.

"Now you're giving me performance anxiety." He got up and went into the bathroom to dispose of the condom.

"Yeah. That ego of yours is so fragile."

"Good." He dropped back down beside me. "You understand that I must be handled with great care. Will you stay the night?"

I mean, my own bed was cold and so far away. "That would be nice."

He settled us both under the covers, wrapping me in his arms, and kissed the top of my head. "Bonne nuit."

"Sweet dreams."

I hadn't shared a bed with anyone in quite some time, and I wasn't sure how I'd negotiate space and temperature. Laurent followed me like a heat-seeking missile all night, crowded against me, and threw off heat like a furnace. I, in turn, spent the night sticking my feet in and out of the blankets and stuffing them against his legs when I got too cold. The first time I did that, he woke up enough to mutter something under his breath in annoyed French, then hauled me against him, spooning me.

It was kind of great and got even better when he woke me with a latte in bed the next morning.

I took the mug from him and slapped his butt. "Thanks, cabana boy."

"You don't even name me? I'm the Red Shirt of your sexual servicing?"

"You're such a nerd." I kissed him.

"Better," he said when we came up for air.

After he fed me fat, fluffy blueberry pancakes with proper Canadian maple syrup, I headed over to Blood Alley even though it wasn't yet noon. Either the vamps or the human minions might have intel on why Zev had brought the estrie here.

I spent most of my time inside the club at the top of the property, eavesdropping on employees. I skulked around for a few hours without learning anything, but as I was leaving Rome, I smelled smoke. Still cloaked, I headed around back.

A solid fence had been erected around a small area with a single locked gate. It was too high to see over but smoke and ash rose from the crackling fire I heard beyond it.

A sign on the gate read "Keep Out!"

Extremely curious, I summoned Delilah. She jumped to the top of the fence, crouching silently, and I gasped.

Rodrigo, wearing thick gardening gloves and a face mask, pitched a vamp's corpse into the flames. The desiccated body reminded me of a mouse I'd found inside my garage wall once, just a pruney husk. Another vampire corpse lay at his feet but was soon added to the fire with the first one.

Other than their shriveled state, the bodies looked uninjured. What had killed them and why burn them under secretive conditions?

Rodrigo waited until the flames were thoroughly extinguished, then raked over the ashes, and poured several bottles of bleach over top.

Bleach. Why would you need bleach for dead vampires? I'd killed plenty and I'd never—

I stopped. Zev had not been himself for the last couple weeks.

Bleach. The acrid scent cut into my nostrils. For a vampire contagion?

Admittedly my vampire siring knowledge was *Buffy*-based, but could a single estrie provide enough transfusions to stop an undead pandemic?

It didn't surprise me that the master vamp had kept all this a secret because if I was right, this was a massive vulnerability that he wouldn't want becoming public knowledge. He was no different from Laurent or Tatiana in that regard.

I recalled Delilah.

Zev wasn't that different from me. None of them were. We are all too proud and scared to show any chink in our armor.

I remained lost in thought as I headed through the unkempt lawn teeming with statues outside Rome that I'd dubbed Gargoyle Gardens. It was creepy being all alone out here even in daylight, and I doubled down on my thoughts as a distraction.

James Learsdon was dead because this ancient vampire called Dagmar believed he'd given her a phony elixir. But I hadn't ever asked myself what that elixir did or why it was so important to someone who had eternal life. Not until now. What if it wasn't just Zev's vamps that were suffering? Dagmar's cadre of vamps were in New England, so how widespread was this disease or whatever it was?

I hit the top of the lane as a vampire hobbled toward me, his body stooped and twisted. Silver was threaded through his dark hair, and his face was gaunt.

It was Yoshi, looking decades older than he had when I last saw him. His lithe frame was dangerously thin and wasted, but he didn't appear to see through my cloaking.

He grasped the doorknob, his shoulders sagging, and rested his head against the door like even that tiny movement had sapped his energy. Beating a fist against the wood, he threw his head back to the heavens with a snarl.

I swallowed, my mouth dry.

Taking a deep breath, he opened the door and slipped inside.

I ran back through the gargoyle statues and inside the club, flying down the stairs to the basement and along the corridor, hoping Zev was awake. My magic had fallen away by the time I rapped repeatedly on his office door.

He opened it with a scowl. "You were making enough ruckus to be heard two floors away."

"Was it all because of Yoshi?" I voiced the question as softly and respectfully as I could.

Still, Zev hauled me inside his office none too gently and shut the door. "I'd be careful what you say next, Ms. Feldman."

"Your search for the Ascendant was for the same reason Dagmar went after James and the elixir, isn't it?" I said gently. "The last time I saw Yo—your friend in the sake bar, he didn't look so good." My eyebrows shot up. "Was that why he asked to drink from me?"

"Too clever by half, aren't you?" Zev's eyes glinted, his words a lethal purr.

"Did my blood help?"

He blinked at me, then physically drew back, his face a perfect blank mask. "Only temporarily," he finally said.

"Did the estrie cure him? Did she give him a transfusion or something?"

"It required far less of her blood than that, but yes, he's recovered."

At a steep cost. Would Yoshi regain his full health? Looking at Zev's expression, I decided not to ask. Yoshi had violated my memories when he'd fed off me, but I didn't want him dead.

Necessarily.

Nor did I regret my part in his survival. Better that I'd helped than Zev go rampaging in thrall to his emotions because he'd lost his best friend.

I shivered at the very idea. It was so easy to dismiss Zev as cold and unfeeling, capable only of deep anger due to the circumstances of him being turned. When he'd betrayed Tatiana, I'd believed that even that relationship, the one human person he was attached to, meant nothing.

How wrong I'd been. Zev had taken no glee in compelling

her. He'd sacrificed that relationship, one that may have lasted decades, for the one I suspected had lasted hundreds of years with his best friend.

"Don't ascribe some human sentimentality to me," Zev said. "Yoshi is a strong ally, even now. It was in my interests to keep him alive." Off my blink of surprise, he rolled his eyes. "You wear your thoughts on your face."

"I wasn't thinking that at all. Just wondering if he was older than you. Is he even of your line?

"He is much older and no." He paused. "The one who sired him was killed long ago."

I sank into a new miasma of thoughts.

Zev's lips quirked. "I feel your mind whirring, Ms. Feldman. Do share."

"If you've got the only estrie seen in hundreds of years and she can cure anyone who gets this disease, then in theory, you've become the most powerful vampire in existence."

"It's not theory," he said.

"You can control her? Isn't it the other way around if she sired you?"

"Do I seem like the type to go into this unprepared?"

I guess being sired didn't come with any type of maternal bond since he had her locked up in the dungeon—at least I hoped he did—but even if he could control her, that wasn't exactly good news.

"You get to choose which of your kind lives or dies. Dies for good, I mean." I whistled.

"Am I supposed to give you a pat on the head and send you out this door alive now?"

"Absolutely," I said.

"Why is that?"

"The enemy of my enemy is my friend."

"Ancient proverbs," he scoffed.

"*Star Trek.* Good reboot. Okay, not so much friend as

client. Luckily, I work for a magic fixer, Cassin and Associates." Tatiana needed to get on those business cards pronto. "We do excellent work and I have a feeling that you're going to need our services in the future. When you're at the top, there's only one direction to go."

On his gloriously gobsmacked expression, I headed out. I had one last promise to keep.

"This is never going to work." I poked one of the bushy eyebrows that Sadie had glued onto Pyotr.

My daughter slapped my hand away. "Stop it. You'll make it crooked."

The gargoyle admired his new look in the mirror. Along with the eyebrows, he sported a heavy beard, matching dark blond wig, and any exposed skin was slathered in concealer. "Is dashing!"

"Are you sure the neon sign was okay with this and you didn't sneak out?" The gargoyle was always in the KH no matter when I showed up, but this was his second visit to my home. Not only that, we were taking him out in public.

I must have been mad to listen to Sadie's idea that we bring Pyotr to the garden center in disguise. If the KH didn't enact any retribution, I'd be busted for violating the prime directive and thrown on Deadman's Island.

"Yes. Is fine," Pyotr said impatiently. "I am employee. Get time off."

I shook my head, eyeing him critically. "I don't know."

Sadie placed a hand on my shoulder. "Stop freaking out. People see what they want to. They'll think Pyotr is just some weirdo human suffering from a sucky skin condition. Okay, come on," she said to him. "We need to get the rest of your disguise on."

A baseball cap, baggy coat, and gloves awaited him downstairs.

"Exciting." Pyotr grinned at me before bounding after my child. I'd been informed earlier that Sadie was now tied with Malorie for his favorite friend. Hopefully, I'd beat whatever plant he acquired today and remain in the top three.

"Remember to keep your wings invisible!" I massaged my temples. We'd be fine. Behave normally and others would do the same.

"Are we getting this show on the road or what?" Emmett poked his head in the bathroom. He wore a black nylon track-suit with his own baseball cap, and concealer covered his red clay skin. Sadie had mentioned our outing to the golem, who'd insisted on being part of it.

There was a sharp clap from the foyer followed by Sadie bellowing, "Five minutes to go time, people!"

Emmett thudded down the stairs.

I gave my reflection a mostly confident thumbs-up and followed.

My now-magic child was laughing and wrestling with her uncle golem for a pair of heart-shaped sunglasses while her new gargoyle friend adjusted his cap to fit his stone head with the seriousness of a hostage negotiator.

Life had certainly taken a one-eighty in the last few months. I smiled. I hoped it stayed this way.

"Ready?" Sadie said.

"You bet."

Thank you for reading THE SHADE OF THINGS!

Things heat up in BENT OUT OF SHADE (Magic After Midlife, #6).

Miriam Feldman's road to happiness is littered with potholes.

322

Between her search for a vampire's missing fiancée and getting answers about a creepy amulet tied to her parents' murders, Miri is making enemies across the whole supernatural spectrum. Fun! Meanwhile, her daughter is acting out, and teen attitude is sooo delightful when you throw magic into the mix.

Then there's that business with the Leviathan, but she's embracing positivity—even when it involves a sea monster. Her ascent up the ladder as a magic fixer is on track, and she's got a first date with a certain sexy French wolf shifter to look forward to.

It's pedal to the metal as she outruns and outplay deadly opponents set on revenge.

Bent out of Shade is the penultimate book in the Magic after Midlife series. It features a later in life romance, a mystery with heart-stopping twists and turns, and a magical midlife adventure.

Get it now!

Every time a reader leaves a review, an author gets ... a glass of wine. (You thought I was going to say "wings," didn't you? We're authors, not angels, but *you'll* get heavenly karma for your good deed.) Please leave yours on your favorite book site. It makes a huge difference in discoverability to rate and review, especially the first book in a series.

Turn the page for an excerpt from *Bent Out of Shade*...

EXCERPT FROM BENT OUT OF SHADE

Bouncing on her toes, Sadie swung around to her dad with a gleam in her eyes. "Can I?"

Eli rubbed a hand over the back of his neck, though Nav looked as confused as I was.

My shoulders crept up and I turned slowly and menacingly to Eli, who'd once again fallen prey to Sadie's puppy dog eyes. "Can she what?"

"I might have promised her a feel-better treat if she couldn't null its magic." He tossed his shades onto the couch.

"What kind of—" I put two and two together and groaned. "Not Phoebe."

My kid had whipped the mini flamethrower out from the back of her loose shirt with a flourish.

"Our duplex is not insured for inside use of that weapon." I'd checked.

"It's on the lowest setting, Mother." With a dramatic sigh, Sadie uncapped it, her finger on the trigger.

"Don't 'Mother' me, child. Not committing arson is a perfectly reasonable request."

"Dad promised."

I ground my teeth together hard enough to take off a layer of enamel. Oh goody. Now I was somehow Bad Cop for telling our daughter not to incinerate her father's home. "A little support here?"

"Sadie," Eli said, "your mom is right."

I leaned back into the couch and crossed my arms smugly. "Thank you."

"You have to use it on the patio."

I face-palmed.

"Yay! Come on, Nav! Let's flambé this puppy." Sadie flung open the sliding door and bounded into the yard.

"By all means," Nav grumbled, poking the crab-demon with the light staff. "Allow me, a respected and formidable demon hunter, to do all the grunt work while you sit there, Your Majesty, and bask in the glow of your child's love."

Eli blew him an air kiss, and Nav whacked the demon in response.

Stunned from all its up close and personal time with the light staff, the demon wove precariously as if drunk.

"You are so making it up to me later," Nav said.

"Gross!" I yanked my feet onto the sofa before the demon crashed into them.

At Nav's prodding, it slid across the plastic, but he prevented it from bashing into the dining room table and spewing venomous pus. Or was that poisonous? Whatever. Dead was dead.

"'Gross' says the woman sleeping with my best friend." Nav pushed his sunglasses into his hair. "None of us are overjoyed at the incestuousness of this situation."

"Not you and Eli, dummy. The demon. Its pus bubbles were vibrating." I threw a hand over my face. "Look out!"

The demon spun like a tornado, knocking Nav's feet out from under him, then scampered nimbly outside.

I jumped up to run after it, but Nav was already halfway

out the sliding door, staff held aloft like a spear. Remarkable reflexes, that man.

Eli lifted a corner of the sofa to release the tarp. "Thank God that's over."

What an adorable optimist.

BECOME A WILDE ONE

If you enjoyed this book and want to be first in the know about bonus content, reveals, and exclusive giveaways, become a Wilde One by joining my newsletter: http://www.deborahwilde.com/subscribe

You'll immediately receive short stories set in my different worlds and available only to my newsletter subscribers. There are mild spoilers so they're best enjoyed in the recommended reading order.

If you just want to know about my new releases, please follow me on:

Amazon: https://www.amazon.com/Deborah-Wilde/e/B01MSA01NW

or

BookBub: https://www.bookbub.com/authors/deborah-wilde

ACKNOWLEDGMENTS

Thank you to my author friends who keep me sane, my readers who make me laugh, my family who puts up with me spacing out and talking to myself, and my wonderful editor for always pushing me to become a better writer.

ABOUT THE AUTHOR

A global wanderer, former screenwriter, and total cynic with a broken edit button, Deborah (pronounced deb-O-rah) writes funny urban fantasy and paranormal women's fiction.

Her stories feature sassy women who kick butt, strong female friendships, and swoony, sexy romance. She's all about the happily ever after, with a huge dose of hilarity along the way.

Deborah lives in Vancouver with her husband, daughter, and asshole cat, Abra.

"Magic, sparks, and snark! Go Wilde."

www.deborahwilde.com

Made in United States
Troutdale, OR
10/24/2024

24114671R00206